RAPE OF THE FAIR COUNTRY

I thought of my river, the Afon-Lwydd, that my father had fished in youth, with rod and line for the leaping salmon under the drooping alders. The alders, he said, that fringed the banks ten deep, planted by the wind of the mountains. But no salmon leap in the river now, for it is black with furnace washings and slag, and the great silver fish have been beaten back to the sea or gasped out their lives on sands of coal. No alders stand now for thy have been chopped as fuel for the cold blast. Even the mountains are shells, groaning in their hollows of emptiness, trembling to the arrows of the pit-props in their sides, bellowing down the old workings that collapse in unseen dust five hundred feet below.

Plundered is my country, violated, **raped.**

List of books by Alexander Cordell:

RAPE OF THE FAIR COUNTRY
THE HOSTS OF REBECCA
SONG OF THE EARTH

THE FIRE PEOPLE
THIS SWEET AND BITTER EARTH
LAND OF MY FATHERS

RACE OF THE TIGERS
IF YOU BELIEVE THE SOLDIERS
A THOUGHT OF HONOUR
THE BRIGHT CANTONESE
THE SINEWS OF LOVE
THE DREAM AND THE DESTINY
TO SLAY THE DREAMER
ROGUE'S MARCH
PEERLESS JIM
TUNNEL TIGERS
THIS PROUD AND SAVAGE LAND
REQUIEM FOR A PATRIOT
MOLL
TALES FROM TIGER BAY
BELOVED EXILE
THE DREAMS OF FAIR WOMEN
LAND OF HEART'S DESIRE
SEND HER VICTORIOUS

For Children
THE WHITE COCKADE
WITCH'S SABBATH
THE HEALING BLADE
THE TRAITOR WITHIN
SEA URCHIN

Rape of the
Fair Country

Alexander Cordell

Blorenge Books

First published in Great Britain 1959
by
Victor Gollancz Limited

This edition published
by
Blorenge Books by arrangement with
the literary executors

Blorenge Cottage, Church Lane, Llanfoist
Abergavenny, Monmouthshire NP7 9NG
Tel: 01873 856114

>>>>>>>><<<<<<<<

Printed by Mid Wales Litho Ltd.,
Units 12/13, Pontyfelin Ind. Est.,
New Inn, Pontypool, Torfaen NP4 ODG
Tel: 01495 750033

ISBN 1 872730 15 9

To my wife

'Pay ransom to the owner
And fill the bag to the brim
Who is the owner?
The slave is owner,
And ever was,
Pay him.'

EMERSON

CHAPTER ONE

1826

THAT JUNE stands clear in my mind.

For apart from it being the month Mrs Pantrych went into the heather with Iolo Milk and had her second in January, it was the time my sister Morfydd stopped going steady with Dafydd Phillips and put him on the gin.

Very strange, all this, for never a drop passed Dafydd's lips before he set eyes on Morfydd, and with poor Mr Pantrych dead eight months everybody knew Iolo was the father, for not a child in his family had run its full time.

A terrible girl for the men was Morfydd, especially in summer when there was a bit of life in them, and if ever a man was dangled on a string it was Dafydd. Fresh from Bangor, he was, following the iron up to the Eastern Valley, and mad for my sister the moment she bowed back at him. Terrible to see somebody get it so bad; wandering around town hoping for a glimpse of her, not knowing if he was in Brecon or Bangor. Off his food, too, so his mam said; making up poetry and going to Chapel to pray for her soul, while Morfydd, like as not, was up on the mountain with her new boy from Nanty, deep in the corn or down in the heather, fretful because it was Mothering Sunday.

It was a good summer that year. The days passed in rich splendour, with the corn so thick and tall around Bwlch-y-drain farm that the tenants could not open their gate for carts. The nightingales sang loud and clear in the moonlight, something that had not happened since the industry came to town, and every morning I climbed to the crest of Turnpike and looked over the golden valley of the Usk to watch the mountain change from brown to green as the sun got going.

From the day I was four years old my father took me up to The Top on his morning shifts at the Garndyrus furnaces; on

7

his back at first, but later we walked hand in hand. But he would leave me on the crest of Turnpike because of the swearing men. And I can see him now, waving as he walked round the Tumble. Home to Mam, then, and in later years to school; sitting by windows hoping for a furnace flash, every inch of me up in the heat and glare of the iron. First out at the school bell, race to Mam for tea, and away up to The Top with me. There I would wait for him until darkness; lying on my back listening to the drop-hammers of the Garndyrus forge or watching the kingfishers sweeping their colours over the brooks.

There is no green on the mountain after dark. Sulphur is in the wind then, and the sky is red with furnace glare all over the ridges from Nantyglo to Risca, and when the night shift comes on the world catches alight. From the valley comes the singing of the Irish and the screaming of the babies they have nineteen to the dozen. The lights of the Garndyrus Inn go on, the workers crowd in for beer, and an hour later hell is let loose with their fighting. But not my father, who could hold his beer with any man on the mountains. He preferred to come home to a decent supper and listen to my mother's gossip; of how Mrs Pantrych ought to be ashamed of herself for going big in the stomach unwedded, or grumbling about the prices in the Tommy Shop, and if ever a man wanted transporting it was Iolo Milk, for if he was not the father of Gwennie Lewis's first as well as Mrs Pantrych's second she was very much mistaken.

"Hisht, Elianor," said my father. "Not in front of the children, please. There is enough wickedness for them to pick up in Town without hearing it at home."

Sit chewing, with your elbows on the table and listen to grown-ups. Very pleasant is the scandal when you are seven years old. Watch Morfydd's dark, lazy smile, Dada's frown, Mam's little red hands cutting bread or sweeping the big black kettle from the hob. Hear the spit of water from the spout, the dying sigh of scalded tea in the pot. Bustle, bustle goes Mam, her mouth a little red button, well up on her dignity.

8

"No good blinding yourself to facts, Hywel," she says. "That Iolo Milk is a bad one, and never again will he enter this house while I have growing daughters. Three times today he has looked through the window and knocked once on the door."

"A scandal, pestering a decent household," says Dada.

And there sits Morfydd with a face of innocence, eyes to tempt a saint, but she winks at me over the brim of her cup.

Terrible to have a loose sister.

"Speak to him, Hywel," whispers Mam. "Something will have to be done or I cannot face the pastor at Chapel next Sunday."

"Aye," sighs Dada. "Where is Edwina?"

"Down at the Company Shop, but back this minute."

"There is a girl to give an example," he says, and glances sideways at Morfydd. "Strong for her Chapel is Edwina, a daughter to be trusted, with no men trailing her like rams. So let me say something that is on my mind, eh, Morfydd? Iolo Milk do not pester this house for nothing, so any girl of mine seen with him on the mountain leaves home quick, and Iolo Milk goes six feet down without a service. Do you understand, girl?"

"Yes, Dada," says Morfydd.

"Then do you mind me."

This takes the smile from her face, which is a pity, for Morfydd is beautiful, especially when smiling. But a clean-thinking man was my father and determined in his manner. The way he caught my mother was determined, too. It was at the Cyfarthfa Horse Show that he bowed to her and her sister, and when the fair was over he invited them home in his trap. Not a word passed between the three of them on the ride, Mam said, and when they reached her father's manse Dada handed them both down, bowed and was off. She thought it was the end of him and went to her room and wept for hours. But a week later he was back outside her gate. Straight up to the front door he went and asked for her father. Ten months later Mam had been signed for, sealed, and had delivered her first in our two-bedroomed house in town.

"Good God," says Mam. "Here is Iolo Milk now. Speak to him, Hywel."

"Aye," says Dada.

"But no violence, mind."

"Just man to man, girl. Do not bother yourself."

Very smart is Iolo, with his black hair plastered down and in his new coat and trews, with the carnation he wears in his buttonhole especially for ladykilling. Bang, bang on the door. There he stands, six feet two of him, cap in hand, white teeth shining.

"Good evening, Mr Mortymer," said he.

"Good evening, Iolo," said Dada. "Very fancy you look in that new suit. Up with the chest to show it off, man—in with the stomach by here," and he tapped it. "Aye, very smart you look. Courting, is it?"

"No violence, remember," breathed Mam.

"God forbid," said Dada. "Is it Morfydd you are come for, Iolo?"

"Please God," whispered Iolo, "and with your permission, of course."

"For a little stroll up the mountain, is it?"

"Just a stroll, Mr Mortymer. No harm in a bit of a stroll, you understand, with a maiden as respectable as your Morfydd, not like some I could mention."

"Back before dark, is it, Iolo?" asked Dada.

"Aye, indeed, and the lighter the better, see, when a decent girl is involved. Back in half an hour, if you like, Mr Mortymer, if that suits you better."

"It do not," said Dada. "Head on one side, if you please, for I have been puddling all week and I cannot see in this light. Bend a bit, too, for you have grown inches since I saw you last. And smile, man, do not look unhappy."

And Iolo, the fool, held his chin up, beaming.

One hit and he was out, flat out in the yard, with his hands crossed on his chest and ready for burial.

Good God.

"And me a deacon," said Dada while the women screamed.

"This house is open to Christians, Chapel or Church of England, but pagans and fornicators stay without."

It is good to be sleeping with your sister, with your feet where her knees begin. We always kissed Mam goodnight in the kitchen, but my father came in later with the lamp. And I can see Morfydd now, hear her sighing after her fourteen-hour shift down the Garn pulling trams—reaching up for Dada's kiss. Then, when he shut the door we would settle together in the belly of the bed. With the house gone quiet she would whisper:

"Iestyn, you asleep?"

Lie quiet and see her rise in the blankets, careful of the squeaks, for ours was a bed you would not sell to the devil for courtship. One eye open, watch her slip out. Up goes her flannel nightdress and she is there in buttoned boots; on with her dress, a comb through her hair, and away through the window she goes like a witch on a broomstick.

God in heaven, you think, one day that girl will be as full as Mrs Pantrych. For you have heard Mam say this in the kitchen. Scramble out of bed and run to the window. She is climbing the mountain stained silver, her hands searching for a hold, her long black hair streaming out behind her. Shiver, and listen. An owl hoots from a thousand feet up. Morfydd hoots back. Iolo Milk is up by there, lying on the tumps, smiling at the stars; responsible for the next generation of furnace workers if he has his way, says Mam.

And there is Dada in the room next door, snoring his way up the path to heaven, while Morfydd, his beloved and eldest, goes hand in hand with Iolo Milk to the gates of hell.

CHAPTER TWO

ON MY eighth birthday my father put my name on the books of the ironmaster and took me to work at the Garndyrus furnaces. It was either the furnaces or the Abergavenny Hiring Fair, and I chose the furnaces, for some of the farmers were devils with the stick. Starting work at eight years old was late to begin a career, for some of the children in town began work at seven, or earlier. Take Sara Roberts—she was about my age but she had been chipping the rock from the iron vein since she was five, and Ieun Mathers lost one foot under a tram at five and the other when he was six. Still, there was no comparison between my family and the likes of these. The Roberts sat a long way behind us in Chapel for their father was a plain limestone digger, work that could be done by the foreigners, and he took home a bare three pounds a six weeks. My father, on the other hand, was a forge expert lent to Garndyrus by Mr Crawshay Bailey of Nantyglo, and was paid twice as much. So the fourpence a week Sara took home made a deal of difference.

Grand to be pulling on your trews of a winter's morning with the frost making you hop. Dada and I were due on shift at first light, so I hopped quietly, for fear of waking Morfydd. She scrubbed at the manager's house in Nantyglo until ten and then went down the Coity Pits getting coal and seeing to the children in charge of the doors. They thought a lot of Morfydd in Nanty, I heard, for she had quick fingers with bleeding when the children were caught in the trams, and she could deliver a baby underground as well as any doctor. She lay in the bed now, her face white and her hair flung black over the pillow. Downstairs Dada was hitting the tub, making the noises of a man being drowned, next door Mam was snoring. The moon was putting his fingers round the room as I pulled my shirt tail between my legs. With my boots in my hand I got to the door.

"Iestyn."

I turned. Morfydd was sitting up.

"Up The Top, boy?"

"Aye," I said, dying to be gone, for I could hear my mother stirring in the bed next door and if she came down there would be talk of my first day at work and what has he got in his eating bag and has he washed and combed his hair properly.

"Wait, you," said Morfydd.

"To hell. I am late already."

"Come over by here," she said.

Sighing, I went round the bed and her hand went under my shirt.

"Where is the vest?"

"Dada does not wear one. It holds the sweat."

"On with the vest I knitted you last week or you do not leave the house alive," she said. "Too young you are to be going up The Top. What time is it?"

"Six o'clock," I replied.

"Six o'clock and a child goes to work. A plague on the whole bloody system. . . ."

"Swear and I tell Dada," I said.

"Tell and be damned," said she, climbing out to the boards. "You at work first light while the brats of ironmasters eat at eight before riding."

Her face was dark with anger as she reached for the long drawers and pulled them up her legs. Up with her nightdress, a lift to her breasts to give them a start for the day, on with the ragged dress now, pulling in her waist with her leather tram-towing belt, and she whispered to herself, her eyes large and bright with growing anger. "See now, if there is trouble on these mountains then I am having a hand in it, for there is not a man in town with the belly to shout." She hit me across the ear. "Go then. Be like a sheep. Go to work years too early and draw starvation pay, but come back here weak in the chest and you sleep under the bed with the china, is it?"

"To hell with the bed, I will sleep with Edwina," I said, and I went through the door and down to the kitchen like a rabbit.

My father was kneeling by the grate blowing flames into the fire. Edwina was asleep under the table, her naked arm lying across the boards like an accident. The kettle was in tears on the hob and bacon sizzling in the pan. Dada did not turn as I entered.

"Trouble with Morfydd, boy?"

"Aye. Because I am going up The Top."

He sighed. "Take no heed, I expected it. The Scotch Cattle will be enrolling Morfydd before she is much older." Smiling, he gripped my arm. "Not much there in the way of muscle, but the furnaces will put it there, and quick. Away and wash now."

Lovely it is to plunge your body into frosty water when rime is lipping the tub, to know the shock of lost breath and fight to get it back. Trickles of freeze run down your blue chest and soak the waist-towel; splash and thresh about and take great breaths of the white mountain mist. Down into the lungs it goes, making the blood run in hot agony; rub, rub with the towel and sing for courage. No hair on the chest or belly like Dada but it will come after a month of Garndyrus where grown men die in the heat and frost, says Morfydd. Cross the legs for the towel is soaked and letting it down to the privates.

"*Bore da' chwi!*" shouts Twm-y-Beddau, the coal-trimmer from next door. Naked as a baby he is and his children throwing buckets at him.

"Good morning!" I shout back, shivering.

"Up The Top today, Iestyn?"

"Aye, aye!"

"Good lad. Dead you will be before you get there, whatever!"

Up with the dry towel and pull it like a saw across the back. Shout, dance, sing, and heat comes from the agony of the morning. On with the shirt, pull the flap between the legs and go like Risca for the door before the fingers of frost have you back. Change your mind and race down the garden. Fling open the door and Morfydd is sitting on the seat.

"Good God," said she, "is nothing here private?"

"Quick, you, or I will do it in my trews."

"Do it and to hell," said she, "I was here first. Hie, back here this minute!"

Her hand went for the vest. "Right," she said.

Off with her, on with me. I watched her go to Dada by the kitchen door.

"Dada," she said, "Iestyn will not wear the vest I knitted special and it is cold enough for furs."

There is a bitch for you.

"Vest on," called Dada, "and buttoned at the top, please, and be so good as to shut that door."

Two sheets of *The Record*, read one, use the other, and away.

Morfydd felt me for the vest when I got in, but I had no time to be angry for my lips were wet with the smell of bacon in the pan.

There is good to be a pig and give such joy. No smell like you in every corner of the house; up in bed with Mam, opening Edwina's eyes, tickling the end of Twm-y-Beddau's nose —out of the window and straight up the mountain to the heaven all pigs go with nothing on their conscience. Edwina put her face from under the table, blinking.

"Good to see you," said Dada. "And remember that you are supposed to be cooking the breakfast. Outside with you and wash your hands and sharp to table, please."

There was never any strictness in my father when he spoke to Edwina. She crawled out on all fours and smoothed back her long white hair from her face, smiling.

My second sister, Edwina, was nearly thirteen then.

To make a picture of her would need the hand and eye of a London artist. She was beautiful, but the serenity in her face, pale and proud, was something more than beauty. Her eyes were the palest I have ever seen, slanted so high at the outer corners that they turned the gaze of strangers. Mystery, deep and pure lay in Edwina, and when she was in school no other child would sit with her for fear of the *tylwyth teg*, the supremely fair and terrible ones who lived at Elgam Farm.

She touched my hand as she passed the table and I drew it

back as if scalded. The hurt lay in her eyes, but I could not help it. All the people in town treated her the same, and little wonder. Rub shoulders with a *tylwyth teg* on a Sunday and the coal face might have you on Monday. Look one in the eyes, and watch for your toes in a tram, and more than one God-fearing man has had molten iron over his hands for calling goodnight to footsteps he believed to be human.

A white girl, Tomos Traherne, our preacher, called her once, which is only another name for wickedness.

Edwina's eyes were big at me as she went out to wash, and she smiled so gently that I knew she had something under her apron that would come out at breakfast. But I did not worry for I was into the bacon now and packing bread in after it, thinking of the trams running the finished iron down the mountain to the canal at Llanfoist and through the arched bridges to Newport.

But she had her say at table. Morfydd was cutting bread, Dada sipping his tea. I knew something was coming by the rise and fall of her pointed breasts and the quickness of her fingers.

"Yes, girl?" asked my father, not looking at her.

Edwina swallowed hard, shivering. God knows why she was scared to death for he never laid a finger on any of us.

"True, is it, that Iestyn starts work today?" she said.

"Aye. And what of it?" he asked his tea.

She screwed her hands. "The English preacher do say he is going up years before time."

My father blew steam from his tea. "Does he now?"

"Aye. And I heard him tell the owner straight that it is terrible to see the little ones on The Top in winter and that heaven has no place for the father who sends them there."

It was out. Sweat sprang to her forehead and she closed her eyes and wiped it into her hair.

"Excuse me," I said, getting down. "I will start going."

"Wait, Iestyn." Rising, my father went to the fire and lit his pipe. "Let us be clear, Edwina. Is it the English preacher saying this or my daughter?"

"Little matter," said Morfydd with a sniff. "Everybody in

town is thinking it." She washed that down with tea. "Including me."

"Good," replied Dada. "Now let it be said without English preachers and owners."

No nerves in Morfydd. She smiled dangerously, her dark, rebellious eyes lifting slowly. "*Diawl!* Too young he is, and you know it. We are not like the Hughes or the Griffiths—a penny a week less and they starve." She cocked her thumb at me. "You send a baby to work in iron in a house that is already taking thirty shillings a week. It is not Christian."

Dad blew out smoke. "Take my shift at the forge today. Dressed in trews you might run the house better, I doubt."

"Easy to say, but no answer," said Morfydd, and pushed her chair back and stamped to the fire.

"O, please, do not quarrel," begged Edwina, gripping herself.

"Shut the snivelling. It do gain nothing," whispered Morfydd. "I say a bitch on every man who sends a child under ten to work with fire. God help us, the owners will be snatching them from their cradles soon, and that is not the only injustice. Half the town is in debt to the Company Shop and the other half starving. The place is in rags at the height of winter. Over the Coity in Nanty we work like horses and here we live like pigs, and when Hill says grunt we grunt. . . ."

"It is written," said Dada. "As poor we must labour."

"Aye, labour, and sweat by the bucketful. Right, you! Does Tomos Traherne tell you what else is written? Suffer little children and such is the Kingdom—that is written, too, he says. But Sara Roberts chips the ore when she is not as high as His knee. Little Cristin Williams is buried with cold and Enid Griffiths gets the iron over her legs at nine!"

"As poor we are born to suffering," said Dada quietly.

"Whisht!" cried Morfydd. "Suffering all right and called early for the Kingdom, by order of the masters and the preachers who take their money, eh? Listen! The God of Traherne is a pagan Christ. Sick to death I am of the bowing and scraping and tired enough to sleep for a month, and if Iestyn goes to Garndyrus he goes without my permission."

"This has been a long time coming out," said Dada.

"But not soon enough," breathed Morfydd, her eyes on fire. "If there is not a man with the belly to lead us we can soon find another out of town. Mr Williams comes from London to speak to us and there is not a soul at his meeting . . ."

"Wait. What do you know of Williams?"

"That he stands for fair wages and decent hours like the workers are fighting for in London."

"You have been to his meetings, then?"

"Yes, and not ashamed of it."

"Nobody says you should be, but you will keep his talk out of the house or find another place to live, for I will not have it used as a political platform. Save your speeches for the mountain, and do not blame me if the Baileys run you out of Nanty, for they are dead against lawyers."

"The Baileys have more friends than they think," whispered Morfydd.

"O, Morfydd!" breathed Edwina, her hands clasped.

"Yes," said my father. "For I am a worker and a good worker knows his place, and perhaps you will tell me what we would do without the Hills and Baileys, who have put their every penny into these mountains and are entitled to something back, even at the cost of sweated labour."

"And perhaps you will tell me what they would do without us," shouted Morfydd. "The masters of these towns are bleeding us to death, and if Williams had his way he would kick the backside of every ironmaster from here to England."

"Easy in front of the children, please," said Dada.

"Labour indeed! Crawling through the galleries where the masters would not rear their pigs, and them sitting in the middle of their Company Parks paying wages in kind and their prices in the Tommy Shops higher every month!"

"Finish now," said Dada.

"God help me, I am not started," said Morfydd. She swung to me. "Away to Mam and say goodbye, Iestyn, and remember that it was your father who sent you to work years before your time for pigs of ironmasters who have money to burn."

"Enough!" roared Dada, and hit the table with his fist in a

sudden fury that sent me from the table and scrambling up the stairs.

My mother was sitting up in bed as if awaiting me.

"Trouble downstairs, is it?" she asked.

"Yes," I replied. "About the ironmasters as usual, but finished now. I am going to Garndyrus this morning unless Dada changes his mind."

"He will not change it. That Morfydd will get us hung with her speeches and shouting."

"Chipping the ore first," I said, "and then on the trams with the Howells boys to learn spragging. Away now, is it?"

My mother nodded as if not seeing me, and the lovely smile went from her face. I will always remember my mother as I saw her then, for beautiful she looked with her long, brown hair over her shoulders. A noble face she had, with the stamp of the manse on it. You could see she was not born at a tub. Pick, pick went her fingers on the blankets, always a sign of trouble with her. I was half way through the door when she called me back.

"Iestyn, bad times are coming, Dada says, and money will be shorter. Another little one is with me. Clothes will be needed, extra milk and food. That is why you are going up early to Garndyrus."

Swollen in the waist she had been these last few weeks and sickness with her in the morning, which I had heard was a bad sign. A terrible business it was when these babies came, with Wicked Gwennie Lewis in a bother with deacons and Mrs Pantrych the scandal of the neighbourhood. And when Dathyl Jenkins caught her first the sidesmen pulled her out of the front row at Chapel and chased her up the mountain with Bibles and sticks. Morfydd lived in dread of having one, for I had often heard her praying about it. And here was Mam smiling and nodding about it as brazen as the foreign women.

"Good God," I said.

Often I had seen the Irish women in town, big in the hips and stomach, setting out for Abergavenny market with their baskets. Mrs O'Reilly for one. There is a size for you is that Mrs O'Reilly. Down North Street she goes like a ship in full sail, with the wind under her skirts and her bonnet streamers fluttering, rosy face glowing, smiling one way and bowing another, not giving a damn for her trouble, though every soul in town knew it was Barney Kerrigan, Nantyglo. Then Dathyl Jenkins, the daughter of Big Rhys, I saw once in the Company Shop. Happy as sin and as pretty as a picture looked Dathyl that morning—lifting her stomach sideways to get it through the crowd and pushing the people about with it inside and chattering like a magpie. Mervyn Jones Counter had something to say, as usual:

"There is healthy you look, Dathyl Jenkins. Three of a kind you are having, is it?"

"Two for Crawshay Bailey and one for Will Blaenavon, I am thinking," said Dathyl. "Marrying, we are, next Sunday at Brynmawr, so Will says, thank God."

"No chance for Chapel, then?" asked skinny Mrs Gwallter with her nose up.

"Dead I will be before I enter Chapel," said Dathyl, putting her stomach on the counter. "Brynmawr to make it respectable, says Will, and to hell with Tomos Traherne and the deacons."

"A loaf of bread," said Mrs Gwallter, "and two penn'orth of accidents, please. A terrible thing it is, Mervyn Jones, when a woman does not know the father."

"Worse when she does," replied Dathyl, giggling as Mervyn cut the meat. "All bone and muscle is Will, but I would not give your Mr Gwallter bed room," which put the other women into fits.

But Dathyl did not marry at Brynmawr or any other place, for Will was absent at the altar. Sorry in my heart I was at the time, for all the town was talking, saying it was this one and that one, and Owen Howells had a finger in the pie unless Morfydd was mistaken, although Big Rhys, Dathyl's father, laid poor Will out for burial in the Abergavenny Fountain and his three farmer friends beside him.

And now Mama.

"Well," said she now. "What is it thinking?"

"Sorry I am," I said. "Will there be trouble for you?"

Her eyes went big, and she began to laugh, making the bed shake. She put out her arms and held me tight, laughing in tears, as women do.

"O, Iestyn," she said. "So small you are to be working for me while I lie here like a lazy old lump. Listen, boy. The tales they tell you in town are nothing to do with your mam, for I am respectable."

"Good," I said. "Now I am from here."

But she caught my hands. "Take care on the mountain, boy. Keep clear of the trams and away from the horses, and try to stay out of the wind, eh?"

I kissed her and was down into the kitchen before she could wink. Morfydd, her face still flushed with anger, was waiting with a scarf she had knitted for herself.

"Round here, you," she said, tying me up and tucking in the ends. "Freeze if you must but do it in style." She gathered my things from the table. "Eating-bag, tea-bottle, vest back on, hair combed, scarf. Right now, away!" She pushed me through the door. "No fighting with the men and keep off the women."

"I will pray for you," whispered Edwina.

"Aye," said Morfydd. "Very warm he will be after prayers. Move your backside, boy. Dada is waiting and scared to death of being late."

She tried to kiss me but I pushed her away and ran into the dark street. My father had already left the Square, and I could hear his iron-tipped boots ringing on the cobbles. Gasping, I joined him with a quick upward glance, knowing he was frowning.

"Only one way to go to work, Iestyn—early. Please remember it."

"Yes, Dada."

"Which shows respect for the man who pays you—Mr Crawshay Bailey of Nantyglo, who has been kind enough to take you on his books and lend you to Garndyrus."

"Very kind," I said.

We clanked on past Staffordshire Row. The moon was bright and full and shivering with frost and the stars over the mountain looked cold enough to faint from the sky. My father said:

"You are going to work before your time because of a new baby coming, do you understand?"

"Aye. Mam has told me now just."

"A bit of a surprise for you, eh?"

"I heard the people talking but did not believe them," I replied.

The little shuttered windows leaned over us. Chinks of light shone from slits in curtains, yawns came on the wind.

"Iestyn," said my father. "Some things you must know when starting work. Tonight, when we get home, the new baby may be with Mam. Do you know how it will come?"

My face went hot despite the cold, and I was thankful for darkness.

"Aye," I said. "Out of the stomach, and with pain."

"Well done. And do you know how the baby was put into Mam?"

We took the middle of the road now for Mrs Tossach was pouring slops from her window.

"Yes," I answered, wishing myself to the devil. "It was put by the seed." A funny time to talk of such things on a first day at work, I thought.

"Well informed, you are," said he. "Who told you this?"

"Mr Tomos Traherne, preacher, and Moesen Jenkins, the son of Big Rhys."

"There is a mine of information. And does Moesen Jenkins know who put the seed into Mam?"

"Aye," I said. "Iolo Milk."

"Good God," he said, and whistled long and clear at the moon. "Did he explain when it happened?"

"Yes," I said. "On the outing to Abergavenny you were on day shift and Iolo Milk partnered Mam and they went up the mountain together. . . ." I stopped, suddenly fearful of his anger, and gripped my hands in my pockets, swallowing dry in the mouth.

"Continue," said Dada. "Do not spare me."

"And the seed from the heather went under her skirt and into her, because it was spring."

This had a terrible effect upon him. He went double and pulled out his handkerchief and put it around his face and made strange sounds.

"Is it sad with you?" I asked.

"Upon my soul!" he answered, and blew his nose like a trumpet. "It is a pity to spoil your innocence. You have many things to learn, Iestyn, and in good time I will tell you them. Meanwhile do not talk of Iolo Milk and your mother in the same breath, and give me the name of any man who does. But one thing I will tell you now, Iestyn, for you are going to work with men. A child comes from a woman with enough pain to kill a man, and from that part of her body that is sacred to God, for He sent His Son that way. Are you listening?"

"Yes."

"So you will close your ears to rough talk about a woman's body, and scorn men and boys who speak of it with foul jokes. For if you heed the things men say on the mountain you will be telling the secrets of your mother, and I will disown you for it, and so will God. Do you understand me, Iestyn?"

"Yes," I replied, hot as fire.

"Swear if you like up there. A bloody or two is good for a boy, but not at home or in front of women, or I will have you for it."

"Yes," I replied.

"Fight if you like, but not for sport, and then only with boys bigger, or I will start fighting. Girls are working up at Garndyrus so do not wet before them or drop your trews before them like some men do, but treat them as your sisters."

"Yes, Dada," I said, knowing that he was very firm on this point.

"Nobody to see, my son," he said then, taking my hand. "Two men together go easier up a mountain."

The town was beginning to wake. The houses were bright in moonlight, their little square windows white with frost. A baby was crying in the house of Evans the Death, and I thought of him lying upon his back, his beard staining the blanket—dreaming of corpses, no doubt; of little Mrs Timble who would not put her knees down, said Morfydd, and Butcher Harris who burst. Next door Marged Davies was getting dressed without bothering to pull the curtains, and pretty she looked standing by the candle, waving her arms into her bodice, trembling her pear-shaped breasts. Enid Donkey was standing in the shadows of Shop Row, getting into her nosebag, Mervyn Jones Counter was scratching in his books in the window of the Company Shop. Everybody was getting up now; pots clanging for breakfast, smoke curling from chimneys. Little Willie Gwallter was shouting for his turn on the seat, crossing his legs on the pavement. Wicked Gwennie Lewis was feeding her baby on the bed. Dogs were barking, cats being booted, babies being scolded for wetting the beds. And poor Dafydd Phillips lies stiff in his straw, longing for Morfydd no doubt, for his mam is shouting her head off for him to get up for shift. On we went to Turnpike. The clamour of the town died. On to the mountain along the icy road that led to Garndyrus.

CHAPTER THREE

A FINE looking lad was Moesen Jenkins, son of Big Rhys, tall and straight for his ten years, with a handsome face and dark lashes to his eyes. He looked up as if expecting me as Idris Foreman led me into the cave near the Garndyrus Inn, and rose, leaning against the rock wall with his hands in the tops of his trews. Eight other children were working there, chipping the rock from the iron vein, going faster when they saw Idris, who paused, his eyes on Moesen.

"New boy, Iestyn Mortymer," he said. "Come to work like the rest of us, and no fighting, mind."

"Fighting? *Diawl!* This one is a friend of mine," said Mo, his eyes glinting. "How are you?"

"How are you?" I said, wondering if it was best to hit him flat and have it over and done with.

"Pleased I am to hear it," said Idris with a hitch at his little fat stomach. "Responsible to the Agent is anyone found fighting, to say nothing of the toe of my boot into two backsides. Start here, young Mortymer. Sara Roberts has two hammers as usual and she will lend you one."

I knew Sara. She was about seven years old and lived in the Tumble houses with her mother, father and little twin brothers. She was dressed in rags, not clothes, and the holes in her mam's black stockings showed her knees and ankles caked with dirt, but pretty, she was, with her dark hair hanging either side of her face. Her eyes were big as she smiled up at me and threw me the hammer. Most of the other children were from the Tumble, too, but some from the Bridge Houses that the ironmasters had walled up for homes; arches where the trams rumbled overhead and the smoke-pipe went through the sleepers above. Ceinwen Hughes, for example. She had lived in one since the day she was born six years ago. Now she sat beside Sara, trying to lift her hammer, for until she could lift it she drew no pay. Her mother had taken the molten iron over her shoulders and had been lying in straw since spring, so Mr Hughes got Ceinwen signed on because there was nobody at home to take care of her. She had seen this winter through so far, but according to Morfydd she was weak in the chest and would not see another.

Sitting down beside her I got busy chipping.

"First day at work, eh?" said Moesen, thick in the throat, for we passed each other in the street like hackled dogs since our fathers had fought near Cae White months back.

"Aye," I replied, "or you would have seen me up by here before."

"You will have your belly full before you are finished."

Sara said, "Do not mind him, Iestyn. It is not so bad with Idris Foreman in charge, although the last one was a bastard with the stick," and she pulled down the neck of her dress and showed me the bright red weal over her shoulders. "But Moesen's father had him coming out of the Drum and Monkey and put him flat and kicked him over to Pwlldu where the colliers saw to him proper."

"Which will happen to more than one I could mention," added Mo, glowering at me.

The trams were going past the entrance, bringing limestone from the Tumble quarries and furnace slag to the Garndyrus tips and the foreign women on the ropes were grunting a song as they pulled them up the pitch. No ribbons in their hair, these women, but their plaits held down by string; sweating like animals and cursing for colliers, with the muscles of their backs bunched and shining with sweat and their breasts as flat as a man's through too much tram-towing underground.

Hundreds of strangers had come to Garndyrus since the Works opened under Hopkins and Hill. Sara's father was one. He had walked from Aberdovey with Sara strapped to his back and the twin boys in his arms while his wife carried the bag, but he was respectable, every inch. The foreigners were different. The masters imported them in hundreds, bringing some from Ireland as walking ballast to live like pigs in the little fenced compounds of the valleys.

The sun was rising now and Idris came in to turn out the lamps. I was shivering to have the bones from me, and many of the younger children were in tears. The wind was whistling into the cave, bringing slag dust from the furnace trams, my breath was misting in the frost and my fingers in agony.

And Moesen Jenkins was after me from the start.

"Iestyn Mortymer," said he, showing me his hammer. "You are a pig and your dada is a pig, and a little tap with this hammer would stir your brains if you had any."

The other children turned up their faces at this, but I just went on chipping, so he said:

"Any trouble from you, Iestyn Mortymer, and I will have you in lumps and dangling from hooks."

"Aye?" I said.

"Aye," said he, "for pigs do hang from ceilings and so will you."

"No trouble from me," I replied. "I want my wages for a new baby coming, and sent home the pair of us if we are found fighting."

"Frightened, he is."

"Shut it and quick," said Sara, her blue face going up. "No fighting in here with the little ones about." She smiled at me and I saw her teeth missing in the front. "Can you fight, Iestyn Mortymer?"

"Aye," I replied, "and no need for hammers."

Moesen made a rude noise with his mouth.

Sweating, me. My heart hitting away under my vest.

"Hisht, Mo!" whispered Sara. "He will have you for it if you do not shut it."

"And quick," I said. "Foreman or no bloody foreman."

Mo sighed at the ceiling. "Twt twt," he said in pain. "There is going to be a bother soon, for I do not stand much from kids," and he got up, unbuttoned his trews—and did it against the wall like the men, watching me over his shoulder.

"Away with that," shouted Sara, "or I will have it flat with this hammer. Shame on you, Moesen Jenkins, for piddling in front of the children, and I will report it to Idris Foreman."

"That is what I think of his dada," said Moesen, putting it

away, "and I will do it again as soon as I can over the whole family, for they are a disgrace to a decent community, says my mam."

Too much. The sight of him sitting there in his dirt brought me upright. The furnaces were in blast now, belching as the puddlers tapped them, and the cave was swirling with smoke and steam. Bright flashes lit the shadows as I took off my coat. I tried to remember all the things my father had taught me—bend forward, left hand out, right fist high; keep the hands loose until the strike, hit on the twist with the shoulders, not the arm. A stone in the way now. I kicked it clear, circling Moesen who was sitting cross-legged.

"Up," I said.

Moesen climbed up slowly, his eyes lazy, his white teeth shining. He was two years older than me and inches taller. Ceinwen began to cry and Sara snatched her clear, and the other children dropped their hammers and ran deeper into the cave.

No fool was Moesen, for he came from a family of mountain fighters. Once I had watched him fight in the street. He had the brute strength of his father in him, but not the science of my father who had taught me the value of the long, straight English left that knocks a hooker off balance and leaves him open for the following right. On tiptoe now, I waited for Mo to rush. The knuckles of my left hand were tingling. Nothing like a hit on the nose to make a man angry and a boy cry, says Dada.

Science, me. But not a patch on Sara. She was between us when she saw we meant business, holding us apart with her little fists bunched.

"Right, you," she said. "No kicking on the ground, no thumbing in the eyes, no butting with the head or scratching. A fair fight or not at all, boys," then one of her hands went right, the other left, and the furnace-grit she was holding sprayed into our faces, blinding us.

"And anyone who tries at me gets the hammer," said she, and sat down and went on with her chipping.

Well.

Moesen and I clapped our hands to our eyes and hopped like country dancers, and the tears streamed from us while we called her all the bitches in creation.

"Water in the tin down by here," said Sara, "and any fighting in this cave will be done by me in future."

Groping, we knelt together, splashing the water into our eyes and cursing.

"There is a bloody hag for you," gasped Mo at length. "But I will have you up on the mountain, Iestyn Mortymer, or die doing it."

"Seven o'clock up by Balance Pond," said I, "and I will flatten your nose for you."

At midday the iron bar was beaten for dinner.

Down with the hammers and away we all went, Sara leading, to the furnaces glowing red. The workers were streaming in along the tram roads; mule drovers, limestone carriers and ore tippers, and all gathered around the furnaces, their hands outstretched to the heat.

My father did not go to the furnaces. I found him sitting alone on a tram with his eating-bag open and his tea-bottle steaming. Good it was to see him there, and I noticed many of the younger women giggling and nudging each other for glances at him, smoothing back their hair and putting years on themselves, but my father had eyes only for me.

"Well," said he. "How is the first day going?"

"Fine," I said, climbing up beside him. "Working with Sara Roberts and Mo Jenkins chipping the vein for Number Two Furnace, and a bit of it in by here." I touched my eyes.

He looked hard at me. "Is it cold with you, boy?"

"Enough to freeze you solid, but no matter. There are many younger than me."

He bit deep into his loaf and chewed, looking at nothing. Then, "No trouble with little Mo Jenkins, remember."

I could not lie to him. "No fighting after tonight, Dada." I went at my eating-bag.

"For God's sake," said he. "You do not waste much

time," and he drank, wiping his mouth with his sleeve. "When is it?"

"At seven o'clock, up by the Balance."

He groaned. "Hell and fury, we will be getting a name for pugilism. Come and get warm, then, or you will be nicking some muscles," and he shouldered his way through the crowd and pulling me after him to the hearth of the furnace.

"Back, there!" shouted a ladle-man, and the crowd spread to a wide circle to watch the liquid iron coming out.

Great is the ingenuity of man that he digs rock from a mountain and boils it into iron.

The firebox door swung back and there was a blaze of white heat as the flames curled up in smokeless red and gold. The people shielded their eyes from the glare as the plug was knocked out. I saw the lip of the moving iron, sheet-white at first, reluctant as it struck the misted air. Steam rolled as it took its first wet breath from the mountain; a hiss, a sigh, and it was down, down, a writhing globule of red life flashing at the plug. Black it turned, the white water in pursuit of the impure in the sand-mould; popping, cracking, its fingers diverting into flaring streams. Flame gathered along the moulds and a shining bed expired into a mist of purple, growing rigid in shape and colour to live for a thousand years. The furnace roared, the sand-mould hissed. The plug was sealed. The firebox belched relief.

It was dark in the cave by four o'clock and Idris Foreman came in and gave the stick to an Irish boy who was not working. After he had gone Ceinwen Hughes fell asleep against the wall, but we did not wake her, and Brookie Smith, a gipsy boy, stole what was left in my eating-bag—Brookie Smith, the bastard son of an Abergavenny trader, who two months later starved to death on Christmas morning. The hours dragged by in fear and shivering, with some English gentry peeping into the cave at the little Welsh workers. My hands were blistered and there was blood on my hammer when Idris Foreman hit the bar at half past six.

"Up a dando!" cried Sara, and was away with us after her.

But at the cave entrance I remembered Ceinwen, and went back. She was still asleep against the wall, her legs blue to the thighs and her breathing a whisper.

"Come, you!" shouted Moesen from the entrance. "No hiding and running for home, Mortymer."

"Ceinie is asleep in here," I called. "Does she stay and freeze to death?"

It was then that I saw the good in him. "Eh, dear!" he whispered, peering. "Wetted herself, too, poor thing, and she is soaked. There is a pity. Warm her by the furnace, Iestyn Mortymer, and I will run to the forge for her dada."

It was evil-black outside, with sleet coming down and the wind doing his tonic-solfa around the damped-down furnaces. Number Two was still glowing bright as I carried Ceinwen from the cave and laid her at its base. I was rubbing her legs for warmth when Idris Foreman came back and laid his stick above the ringing-bar.

"What is happening here?" he asked, peering.

"Ceinie fell asleep, sir," I said, "and frozen to an icicle, and Mo Jenkins has run to fetch her father."

Idris sighed and sat down on the slag beside me. "He is wasting his time, then. Doing extra time is Mr Hughes for losing a day with his dying wife. Wonderful men are our employers, but if I had my way I would burn the tails from every ironmaster between here and Cyfarthfa." He lifted Ceinwen and took her closer to the fire. "Whee!" he said, "cold is this baby. Terrible that children are allowed into this hell in winter."

"No choice for Mr Hughes, sir," I said, growing confident, "with his wife caught by the iron and nobody at home to take care of Ceinwen."

"Aye," replied Idris thoughtfully. "No hope for any of us, I am thinking." He rocked the child against him. "Unless we are saved by a Union half the workers of the iron towns will be six feet down and none of them working."

"My father does not care for a Union," I said. "Loyalty to the masters is what counts, he says."

Idris looked at me sharp. "Aye? And if your father says

jump into the firebox of this furnace, young Mortymer, would you do it?"

I did not reply, and he smiled at me. I saw his big teeth broken and yellow and his little eyes gleaming from the sagging folds of his blistered face. Clearing his throat he spat past me.

"Young you are yet, Mortymer, and not enough brain grown to put your heart right. But when you are warm in your bed tonight give a thought to the mother of this child and ask the Christ if it is right that she should be burned to the lungs and lie in straw while her baby freezes in a tunnel."

I played with slag, uncertain, giving quick glances at his face.

"Speak up, boy," he said. "Straighten out your tongue, for we may need you to free this God-forsaken country."

"What is a Union?" I asked.

"God help me! Do not say it has not been explained to you?"

"Plenty of trouble in our house about it, but no explanations," I said.

Idris looked at the sky for words, then said carefully, "If a man were to thrash this child with only you near to stop him, then you would ask my help to put him down, and that would be a Union. But first we would talk with him, to save fighting."

"My father speaks of Scotch Cattle," I said. "What are they?"

"If I refused to help you save this child and you were to drag me from my bed and flog me and burn my furniture because I would not help, then you would be like Scotch Cattle."

"They are wicked, then," I asked, fearful for Morfydd.

"Dung, and the spoilers of our cause. For a Union is built upon comradeship and is formed for negotiation, not violence. But mark me! Since the owners reject negotiation, violence will come. Blood will be spilled on these mountains before they are finished."

Footsteps hammered the grass and Moesen ran up.

"Mr Hughes says to hold Ceinwen by the furnace until eight o'clock, sir," he gasped, "and he will see you square for it in the inn next pay day."

"Right," said Idris, "but not for payment, so back with you and tell him to take his time."

"We are in a hurry," said Mo. "But he promises to come by eight o'clock."

"What hurry? Women before twelve years old, is it?"

"To fight, sir," I said. "Up by the Balance at seven."

"*Dammo di!*" said Idris. "But it is legal enough to tear each other to pieces in private time, so go. And if you fight like your father, Mortymer, I will be happy to carve Mo a coffin, big as he is."

We left him rocking Ceinwen on the slag. He began to sing as we climbed the tram road to Turnpike and his voice was bass and pure in the blustering wind.

Fighting by the Balance Pond was the custom, and everything there being convenient for bruising: near home in case a man had to be carried; a gallows head with an oil lamp on it so you could see who you were hitting; and three feet of mud for the loser.

I was shivering as I ran to my father who was waiting there, but not with the cold.

"Sink him quick, boy, for the love of God," said he, "for I am damned perished."

Big Rhys Jenkins and some of his criminals from the Drum and Monkey bar were there, huddled against the sleet. Moesen was stripping off his coat.

Off with Morfydd's muffler, away with my coat, shirt off, start on the vest.

"Vest on," said Dada.

Tighten the belt to hold up the trews, for there would be hell to pay rent to if they dropped while fighting. Ready, I turned. Moesen was stripped to the waist, looking as big as a man, his brown body shining under the flickering lamp.

"Ten minutes, is it?" asked Big Rhys, very polite.

"Five," said my father. "Two years and six inches, what more do you want?"

"Five, then," replied Rhys. "Quite enough time to bury the Mortymers," and he pushed Mo forward. "Into it, the pair of you."

"Hammer the nose," whispered my father, holding me under the flaps of his coat. "A fine straight nose, that, for the English left, and a bend in it will help his looks."

Helped by the toe of his boot I stepped out to meet Moesen.

The mountain grass was wet against my back with the first blow of the fight. I stared at the faint stars, shook my head and climbed up. Mo came in like a tram, fists flailing, but I stepped away and he went past, fighting himself, to wheel and come in swinging.

"Left," called my father, but Mo had already taken it in the mouth and I felt the glorious pain in my knuckles as his head snapped back. My head was clearing now and I stood on tiptoe shooting lefts through his swings while he stayed, flat-footed and grunting.

"Nail him!" yelled Rhys, and Mo leaped in, his fists thumping against my body. We stood shoulder to shoulder, hitting at everything and mostly missing, and then Mo lowered his head and charged.

"Uppercut," said my father, and I dropped my right and hooked it up into Mo's face. He staggered, and I swung the same hand at him and caught him flush in the mouth. Blood spouted down his chin and as his jaw dropped in pain I steadied my hands and hit him left and right in the body before knocking him flat with a swing to the face. Turning, I walked to my father's knee.

"Heaven help us," said my father. "Are we staying here all night?"

I looked at Moesen. He was crawling to his father on all fours, wondering if he was in Garndyrus or China. As he dragged himself up Big Rhys called "Time", and he staggered and turned, jumping after me like a mad thing, but I had a left in his eye before he could blink and another on his nose when he did. His face was dancing before me in the swinging light of the lamp, sleet flying across it, and I saw his eyes, suddenly bright and alive and the blood streaming over his bared, white teeth. The wind buffetted us as we circled, looking for openings. I tried a long right, but he ducked it and hit me about the body with vicious little punches that drove me against Big Rhys. Rhys held Mo off with one hand and pushed me clear with the other, and for thanks I hit his boy twice with my left before he could settle himself for his rush.

"Again," said my father, and I did so, knocking poor Mo sideways.

A terrible thing is this English straight left. The tap-tap of it is maddening to a grown man, let alone a boy who cannot keep his temper. Moesen was crying with rage and pain, and he came in upright, hooking to have my head off.

"Now," called my father, and I stood my ground and let fly at Mo's chin with every ounce of my strength. He took the blow full on the point and dropped flat upon his face and lay there, sobbing and clutching the grass. Rubbing my knuckles I turned and walked back to my father.

He called to Rhys, "Mr Jenkins, I say finish this. He is bleeding like a little pig and he has the courage of a lion."

"To hell with you, Mortymer. He has another minute to go, and he will last it!"

"There is a swine of a father," whispered Dada. "You will handle it, then. Take this boy as you would Edwina. Waste the minute by keeping him off. Hit him down again and you will have me to fight after. Do you hear me?"

Moesen staggered from his father's knee and wandered towards me, but he suddenly gathered his strength and rushed, hitting me solidly for the second time. The gallows light swung across the sky and I tasted the sweet salt of my own blood. In he came again, crying aloud, but I danced away. The light was gleaming on the little bunched muscles of his body and in desperation I drove at them to check his next rush, but the blow never reached him. Instead, I saw the swing of his boot, and bent. The boot took me in the side, pumping out my breath in one long gasp. And the next kick caught me in the mouth.

Very pleasant to be floating in a dream and to wake in your

father's arms. The wind was rocking us and crying in dark places. It was warm and comforting under his coat. I looked around. The light of the gallows was directly above me. Big Rhys, Mo and the Drum and Monkey men had gone.

"Very handy you are with fists," said my father. "But you will rarely fight with gentlemen. Next time I will teach you how to miss their boots."

"Christ," I said. "There is a tooth missing," and felt my mouth.

"Two," said he. "I have another in my pocket, and please do not take the Lord's name in vain. Up on your feet now; do not make a meal of it."

I looked at him as he brushed water from his eyes. "Up a dando!" said he. "We will go to our graves sitting by here. All right for you, mind, for you have been kept warm fighting. And your fight, remember, not mine, for Mam plays hell with pugilists. You will make the excuses for being late at supper."

"That will be worse than boots," I said.

A strange thing happened then. My father kissed me.

"I am freezing solid," said he. "Look, I am streaming from the eyes." And he wandered about, kicking at stones and cursing while I pulled my clothes over my aching body.

A first day at work to remember, this one. A bleeding nose, a tooth in one hand, another in Dada's pocket, and a boot in the belly.

There's a mess to take home to Mam, and all for twopence.

CHAPTER FOUR

IT IS strange that memory will fade on some things and hang like hooks on to others.

Jethro, for instance, was different from the rest of us, and I will always remember the hell of that first twelve months when he took my place as baby in the house. There was no sense in his behaviour; bawling all night if he was in any bed but my mother's, and half the day out of temper. Every doll in the place was pulled to ribbons, not a plate left unsmashed within his reach and rivers of blood would have flown had he got his hands on a hammer. Nothing was sacred. Mam had him on the breast all that year and when he could not get at her he was fishing down the front of Edwina and Morfydd.

But in the eyes of my parents Jethro could do no wrong.

"The devil himself," hissed Morfydd, "but with the tail in front. Now do you listen to that palaver!" And she thumped over in our bed and hit the pillow and pulled the blankets up round her ears.

I could hear Mam walking the boards next door with Jethro screaming on her shoulder and my father and me due up on furnace shift at six o'clock.

"Listen," said Morfydd.

"Hisht, my little one, my precious," said Mam. "Wind it is, Hywel. Wind in my precious baby."

"Then up with it, woman," said Dada, groaning.

"Hitting him for holes now, mind."

"Then feed him, girl. I expect he is empty."

Mam sighed. "Empty? *Diawl!* Tight as a ball he is, for he has been at me hours."

"Wind it is, then," said Dada. "A little drop more will clear it."

"If I have it," said Mam.

The old bed grumbles as Mam climbs back in, with Jethro still screaming to wake our dead grandmother.

"There, there," whispered Dada. "A fine man he is going to be, Elianor. A fighter for his rights, eh? All this good food you give him. Hand him here, girl. Now! On this one, my son. No, Elianor, the other, there is none in that old thing, girl. Hisht, Jethro, Mama says the other. On you, my pretty little fighter."

Silence. Mam sighs like the well of life going dry, and Morfydd rises in the bed.

"The damned little glutton," she said. "A bull calf it is, not a baby," and she hit the pillow and buried her face in it.

The bitter winter went by without a nudge of the elbow in our house, but some were not so fortunate. Sara Roberts lost one of her brothers with cold and Ceinwen Hughes died with the chest, and a blessing that, said Morfydd, for Mr Hughes had enough to do to care for his crippled wife. Mrs Pantrych had another, making three, and Gwennie Lewis had her second on her father's birthday and went to live in the disused ironworks in town for scandal.

I remember, too, the cold of the early morning tubs, with the wind coming down the Coity tearing at my trews; the frosty walks home from Garndyrus with my father; the dreary quiet of Hush Silence Street and the little square windows loaded with ice; the lights coming from the Drum and Monkey where the men were putting away the beer and quarrelling about Unions. The wind whistled to take years from your life when you returned with bread and meat from the Shop. But the coldest man in town that year was Dafydd Phillips.

Went mad for Morfydd did Dafydd that winter. Terrible to see him mooning around hoping for a glimpse of her with his blue nose sticking over the top of his muffler and coughing to have ribs up. Here he comes again. Peep through the curtains, wait for his knock, go like Risca to the front door. Open it.

"Morfydd says she is out, Dafydd Phillips."

And over my shoulder he can see Morfydd spitting on the iron and going at my father's Sunday shirt.

"Morfydd!" he calls, sending up steam.

"Shut that door!" she cries from the kitchen. "It is having the legs from me with draught."

"Sorry, Dafydd Phillips." Shut the door in his face, back to the window seat with me, and watch her.

Queer, I thought. Here is a man in trouble, and Morfydd does not raise a hand to him. But if a little one is coming in town, even with a foreign woman, Morfydd reaches for her shawl and goes to help, cursing for ten. A burn, a furnace scald will bring her. When a coal-trimmer lost his leg in a tram last spring she trimmed the stump with scissors, stopped the bleeding and tied the bandages—in her nightdress, because the man would have no other touch him. Morfydd would go to a dog in need, but Dafydd Phillips could cut his throat on our doorstep and get no more than a blink.

Here he comes again, shivering to lay his bones out.

"Down with that curtain," she said, "or we will have him head first through the window."

"He is dying for you," I replied. "And his mam says he has not eaten solid in years."

"Open that door and you die with him, then," said she, and she spat on the iron and whistled at the steam. "There is mad to expect a girl to go courting in snowdrifts." She sang then, with a voice like an angel.

"Never mind the hymns," I said. "The devil has a place for you."

"And blister in very good company," said she. "Some I know will fry very brown."

Bang, bang. On the back door this time.

"I will go," said she, taking the iron. "Like the rest of them, he will have his chance in the spring."

God knows what she did to him but he went off howling and missed shifts for a week.

The spring is a madness that comes into grown-ups when the sun comes up warm over the mountain. One has only to go a mile from town to see what they get up to. Always in twos, they are, sitting in the heather away from eyes. She is saying no and doing a giggle, and he is trying it on and getting nowhere, although she is hoping he will. Worse still up on the Coity, Mo Jenkins says. Things get busy away from the deacons, for dozens are ferretting about in hedges, and stop-its and pleases are going on all over The Top down to the Puddler's Arms on the road to Abergavenny.

But Dafydd did not have to wait until spring. He had his feet in our house in mid-winter, by special invitation from Dada.

A fair-looking chap was Dafydd Phillips, wide in the chin and brow, and with hair I had always wanted for myself, black and straight and flattened down either side with water. Well set up, too, for somebody half starved, with bull shoulders on him and a nose that had seen trouble in its time, by the look of it. He came through our front door like a man to the gallows, screwing the peak from his cap while his mam, a ferret in widow's weeds, was elbowing his ribs to keep him upright.

"Well!" cried Mam in astonishment, for she was not supposed to know of the visit. "Look you, Hywel, who has come visiting. Mrs Phillips and Dafydd!" And she took the door back on its hinges. "Come you in. Half frozen you look, and no wonder with the weather we are having!" She bustled the pair of them into the kitchen, laughing and chattering, but I knew she was wishing Mrs Phillips to the devil because Mam was Chapel and Upper Palace and Mrs Phillips was Church and Perpetual Fire.

My father rose and gave his fine bow and Dafydd gave it back, his face as red as a turkey's wattle, and Edwina did her new English curtsey with her eyes cast down.

"Edwina," cried my mother, "bring up the chairs to the fire. Iestyn, down with Jethro and fill the kettle sharp. Come close to the fire, Mrs Phillips. We will soon have you warm, *fach*."

"Morfydd is up at the Shop for the groceries," Dada was saying as I got back, "but home this minute, Dafydd, so make yourself comfortable."

Yes, I thought, make the most of it because brooms and hooves will be in here within the hour. Back to my corner I went and got Jethro on my knee again and listened to their chattering. Hypocrites, all of them, saying things to keep the conversation going—Mam raking at the fire and talking nineteen to the dozen over her shoulder, Mrs Phillips laughing and running her finger round the furniture for dust, and my father smiling encouragement at Dafydd who sat white-faced and staring, as still as a man with a stroke.

"Right, is it, that you are working at Nanty now, man?"

"Yes, Mr Mortymer," replied Dafydd, hooking at his collar.

"Phil Benjamin's shift at the Balance?"

Poor at the English was Dafydd, being Bangor born and bred, and his face was agonised. "Aye," said he, understanding.

"They say he is a hard master."

"The harder the better for Dafydd," interrupted his mam. "Industrious, that is the word for him, Mr Mortymer, and ambitious—take my word for it. Finish up well the way he is going. Know you Caradoc Owen, foreman?"

My father nodded, sucking his pipe.

"Great things Mr Owen has in store for Dafydd, mind. Soon he will be taking Benjamin's place, for it is a pit that needs handling and brains, and you are not backward in that respect, eh, man?"

"No," replied Dafydd, looking as brainy as an egg addled.

Dada said, "Caradoc Owen goes hard for a Union, lad. Do you agree with his views?"

"Whee!" said Mrs Phillips, "that is easily answered. No son of mine would join a Union and still live under my roof, Mr Mortymer." Her thin face twisted up. "It is discipline the workers are needing, as Mr Crawshay Bailey says. . . ."

"That is what Bailey says, but what about Dafydd?"

Dafydd straightened and took a breath.

"As strong against a Union as you, Mr Mortymer," said his mother. "I have heard your words about loyalty repeated in town and I agree with them. And it is the same with the Benefit, mind! Nothing but an excuse for drinking."

"Do you agree with Owen's views, Dafydd?" asked Dada.

Dafydd opened his mouth.

"Enough of old Unions and Benefits," said my mother, "for I can hear Morfydd coming and political talk puts the house up the chimney. Iestyn, out to the back and meet her, for fifteen shillings of groceries do take some handling," which was meant to lift Mrs Phillips' eyebrows, and did. She held out her hands for Jethro as he waddled past, but I lifted him and gave him to Dafydd, for there is nobody like Jethro for making friends with a pair of Sunday trews.

"Here with him this instant!" cried Mam in panic. "A soaking boy is this one, and you in that fine new suit."

Morfydd's footsteps were coming nearer as I shut the back door and went to the gate. The stars were like little moons in the darkness, for the night was black with him and freezing, but flashing red and hot over The Top towards Merthyr, and Nantyglo was smouldering crimson on the clouds. In the shadows I waited until the mist of Morfydd's face took shape. Frost was upon her hair and her eyes were dark smudges in the white loveliness of her cheeks.

"Good evening," I said.

"Good God," said she. "Why all the politeness?"

I held the gate open and she came in backwards with the baskets.

"What time is it?" she asked.

"Six o'clock just, and hurry with the food for Mam is waiting to lay supper."

"Then he will be here any moment," she replied. Suddenly she knelt and swept her arms about me, her eyes large and shining. "O, Iestyn," she said, "because I love you best you will be the first to meet my man. Richard Bennet of London I am marrying, and he is coming in a minute to speak to Dada."

Well! There is a situation.

One of them inside asking for the hand and the other coming in with the bride.

"Sad, are you, boy?" she asked, wrinkling her eyes.

"Why should I be?" The spit was suddenly dry in my mouth, but she was not having me as easy as that.

"Because I will be leaving?"

"Go when you like," I said. "I am not worried."

"O, my precious," she whispered, pulling me against her. "Be happy for me. Do not be like that."

A footstep clattered on the frosted road.

She rose swiftly, patting her hair. "Richard! It is Richard!" she said, dreaming. "Ah, but you will love him as I do when you know him. Listen, he is coming!"

I watched her. Her hands were clenched by her sides, her shawl was over her shoulders to show her hair. With the mist of her face turned up, she waited. Beautiful, she looked, with her eyes wide and her parted lips showing the straight white lines of her teeth.

He vaulted the wall as if he owned the place and she ran into his arms. Motionless, they were; as still as black rocks with the stars behind them. Miserably I turned and kicked at a stone, and it rolled with a clatter and hit our shed.

"What was that?" His voice was deep.

"Only Iestyn, my little brother," she whispered back.

He moved to me, his hands on his hips. "Well, well," he said. "The first of the family, eh?"

I looked him over. He was nearly as big as my father. His hair was black with curls and his face square and strong. He stooped, moving easily from the waist, and I sensed the power in him.

"Good evening," he said, and out came his hand. "I have heard a great deal about Iestyn Mortymer."

His words were level and smooth, like most English. There is a horrid way of speaking—every word deep and pure, but without music.

"Richard is shaking hands, Iestyn," said Morfydd in a panic.

Tired of holding it out he leaned against the wall beside me. "Has your sister told you about me, Mr Mortymer?" He was dead serious.

"Aye, now just."

"About us marrying?"

I nodded.

"And what do you think of it?"

43

I searched his face for a smile and found none. "Not much until I have seen you in the light," I said.

This must have been funny to an Englishman, for he brought up a knee and rolled his backside against the wall and bent and brought the laugh deep from his stomach.

"Hush, Richard!" breathed Morfydd. "You will have my father out here!"

This straightened him, his hand to his mouth. Gasping, he said, "My! This is a cool little customer. Are they all like this in your house?"

"My dada is cooler," I said sharp. "And I am not a bloody customer!"

But this only put him into stitches again.

"Iestyn!" snapped Morfydd. "Please do not be rude! Mr Bennet is only trying to be friends."

"Then let him try it on Dada and see where he lands."

"Great Heaven! He's a little spitfire, isn't he? Do they come any bigger?" I heard him say as I rushed past them to the gate.

"Do not mind him, Richard," said Morfydd with hate in her voice. "Only a kid he is, and jealous—do not mind him."

At the gate I fought back the flood of tears that threatened me. I knew I had lost her. No fear of her going to Dafydd, but I knew she would leave me for this one. He would take her away and put her to the tub, and his vests and shirts would be on her line, and there would be no sound of her in our house, no place laid at table. Many men had owned Morfydd, I had heard say, but this one would take her. And then I remembered Dafydd Phillips, and to this day I do not know why I called, "Morfydd!"

Arm in arm with him at the back door, she turned, came back, and stooped. "Finished I am with you, Iestyn! Do you hear me? Finished! Swearing at Mr Bennet!"

"Do not take him in there," I said, looking away.

"*Duw Duw!* Head of the house as well now, is it?"

"Do not go in," I repeated. "Dafydd Phillips is in there, by special invitation from Dada."

"Dafydd Phillips?" The chap had been dead twelve

44

months the way she said it. Then she folded her arms and tapped her foot and made no eyes to speak of. "There is a damned cheek!" she said. "And what has he come for?"

"To ask for a girl in marriage, but no chance this side of heaven with the flies buzzing round her like a jam pot."

"Whee!" She put her hand to her face. "That was nearly a step in the wrong direction."

"Aye," I said. "No good at making speeches, is Dafydd, but by the look of his nose he would stuff this new one up the chimney."

"I do not think so," she replied. "But it was kind of you to warn me, Iestyn." She bent, kissing the air with her lips. "There is friends we are again, boy. I will send Richard away. Will you come in with me, my lovely?"

You can hate people one moment and die for them the next.

I turned my head when she kissed him. But even as she reached for the door he was standing there as if she had taken his legs with her.

"Away!" I said as I passed him. "Not a chance in a hundred, man. There has been a couple of thousand here before you."

This set him off again, double bass. Morfydd waited until he had vaulted the wall before she opened the door. I saw my father's quick frown, Mam's anxious look and the radiance of Dafydd's smile as we entered.

"What have you been doing the pair of you?" asked my father. "Eating the groceries?"

"No," I replied. "That excited she is. She has been curling and combing and making herself tidy for Dafydd Phillips."

After cleaning Dafydd down and swabbing up the pool, Mam took Jethro to bed for punishment, leaving my father to carry on the conversation. Edwina was sitting in her corner reading the Bible, as usual, so I helped Morfydd lay the table.

I was sorry for Dafydd sitting there in soaked misery; hanging on to Morfydd's every word as she cut the bread, but wild horses would not have dragged from him a word of complaint as his mother did all the talking.

"There is pretty you look tonight, Morfydd," she said. "And very handy about the house, too, I am sure."

"But politics will be her downfall," said Dada.

"Love her, Mr Mortymer, there is none of us perfect, and even Dafydd has his faults. Three times to worship every Sunday—Church of England, see, to follow his English father, God rest him. Saw you at Chapel Easter Sunday, Morfydd—remember?"

"Yes, Mrs Phillips, but I have not been there since."

"There's bad! A wife should be humble on her knees before the Lord before she can hope to be obedient to a husband, eh, Mr Mortymer?"

My father smiled. "Obedience and religion are not Morfydd's virtues, I fear, but she is good at public speaking."

"No path to heaven that, though. The soul of woman is black with sin from birth, and only regular Chapel can save it from the everlasting fire."

Dada said, "That is open to argument, Mrs Phillips, for I have known deacons who were criminals and drunkards who were saints. Have you strong views on these things, Dafydd?"

"It is a person's beliefs, sir," said he with deep humility.

"And yours, Morfydd?" asked his mother thinly.

Morfydd was still cutting the bread. She raised her dark eyes, shook her head, and went on cutting.

"Come, Morfydd, you must have views, girl."

"Aye," whispered Morfydd, "but not for airing."

Dafydd shifted his feet, sweating. "Leave it, Mam," he said. "It is not important."

"Come, come," said his mother. "We have a right to know the family we are marrying into."

I looked at my father. His long legs were thrust out. Puffing at his pipe he was staring at the ceiling with his shoulders hunched, a man awaiting an explosion. Morfydd pushed away the bread and put the point of the knife into the board.

"First prove that there is a God by example, Mrs Phillips," she said, "and then I will pray to Him, for there is little enough

46

example given by Chapel botherers, and some wailing in church who would be better lifting elbows in the Drum and Monkey. . . ."

"Steady, Morfydd," said my father, and I saw Dafydd close his eyes in agony.

"And another thing, Mrs Phillips," went on Morfydd. "There are a few things that need putting right with churches and chapels to my mind. So let us all pray the way we like and behave the best we can, and if the God you worship is as good as you say we will all land in the same place. Away, Iestyn. How the hell can we have supper without cups?"

"Well!" said Mrs Phillips, her jaw dropping.

"Aye," said Morfydd. "And knives, too. Are we going to tear it?"

"Things are becoming clear at last," said Mrs Phillips. "Then you do not believe in God, woman?"

"Mam," begged Dafydd, "it do not matter."

"Do it not? Would you marry into a godless house, boy?"

"Mind your words, Mrs Phillips." Morfydd levelled the knife. "There is one behind you into her Bible and another upstairs the most God-fearing woman in town, to say nothing of deacons and pew collectors, so do not be too sharp."

"But you do not believe—answer me!"

Morfydd did not move. Her eyes were narrowed and glittering and her hatred of hypocrites was filling the room. "You will not trap me into rejecting the One I fear, in case He do hear me, Mrs Phillips. The views I hold upon religion are mine but I do not fling them over town three times on Sunday and bury them the rest of the week." She came closer. "If there is a God on these mountains then He must be sleeping. Six years I have worked under the Coity, and there is no sign of Him there. No sign that He looks into pits where children fall under trams or sees a girl of nine caught by liquid iron. God is all right in the sun for the likes of you, Mrs Phillips, for you have never been six inches underground or within a yard of a furnace. And while the masters sing their prayers for higher profits in the place you call God's house, you will never find me with them except for weddings and christenings, and the last christening was Easter Sunday," and she picked up the knife and went at the bread as if she had an ironmaster roped to the table.

Mrs Phillips was already on her feet, tightening her bonnet streamers. "Come, Dafydd, I have heard enough," said she, trembling. "There are enough God-fearing young women in town without seeking out pagans!" On with her gloves now, stretching every finger, fussy little swings of her hips, her mouth a button seeking words she could not find. Then, "And you, Mr Mortymer—you tolerate such views in your house, and you a deacon?"

My father rose. "I have cared for her body until now and my wife has taken her soul to Chapel, Mrs Phillips. Morfydd is eighteen now. Better to let your boy see her in this light; that is why I sat quiet."

"Pleasant to have met you, I am sure," said she. "Say your piece, Dafydd, and show me to the door."

He had been stretched on the rack of words, allowed no questions, no replies. Head and shoulders above the skinny woman before him he looked at Morfydd with the look I have seen in the eyes of a sheep nailed to the board, awaiting the knife. At the door my father gripped his shoulder and turned him.

"Better this way, Dafydd," he said. "If they had agreed on religion it would have come to murder when they got to politics. Do not lose sleep on it, boy."

My mother came down from Jethro a moment after they were gone.

"Away so soon?" she asked, surprised.

"Aye," replied my father. "Congratulations for working it so well, you are sharper than I give you credit for."

"And not even a bite of supper for them?"

"The truth cooled her," whispered Morfydd, staring at the table. "And good riddance. I would not have that for a mother-in-law if it was the last one living."

"Oi, oi!" exclaimed Mam as she sat down to table. "Religion, was it? They come in their droves, Hywel, but we will be searching the mountains for a savage before we wed this one."

"It was cruel, cruel!" whispered Edwina, clutching her Bible, and I saw her eyes bright with brimming tears.

This put a silence on the meal for Edwina never had views on anything.

Nobody was happy that night. Everybody, including Morfydd, I think, had Dafydd in mind.

Later I remembered that it was the meeting of the Benefit Club. I had fourpence in my pocket and another ninepence under the bed saved for Christmas. Nothing like banners and singing to take away bad spirits, the Benefit says.

Away out of this, I thought. Away up the mountain for a walk in the frost and a quart of beer with Mo Jenkins, me.

CHAPTER FIVE

A NEW summer swept over the mountains bright and hot. Dandelions and meadowsweet grew in clusters along the banks of the Afon-Lwydd, where the last speckled trout fought a passage through the pollution of the industries, and the fields were yellow with celandine and buttercups.

Moesen and I, firm friends now, did well that year. Apples had been taken from Coed Eithin Farm in daylight, for Grandfer Trevor Lloyd was as weak in the eyes as a bat in sunlight. Honey had been lifted from Will Tafarn's hives and trout tickled from the Usk under the nose of the bailiff. All these things were sold at cut price for everybody was saving for the annual outing to Newport, and it was only fair that the tight-fisted ones should pay their share towards treating the poor. Little Willie Gwallter, for example; he had a new suit especially for the occasion, bought by Tomos Traherne, the preacher, out of subscriptions, and his father walked him three times round town so nobody would miss seeing him, although you could not see Willie for suit until he raised his cap.

Other important things happened that summer. The masters raised their prices at the Company Shop and dropped wages all round, several more cottages were built in North Street where people were living seventeen to a room, cholera broke out at Risca, and Mr Snell, the English seller of coloured Bibles, began to court Edwina.

A little crow of a man this, thirty if he was a day, with a wig to cover his baldness; a red nose that curved down, a red chin that curved up, with a little hole for a mouth in between, and every inch of his five feet two in the service of his Maker. He was a wandering preacher collecting for the poor, but I had heard my father wonder how much of it the poor received. Most respectable, was Snell, and learned, with fasting on fast days and fish on Fridays and God Save William the Fourth.

"Eggs you will be having with that in bed beside you," said Morfydd. "*Diawl*, Edwina! Get a fat little hen from Shams-y-Coed's and you will make your fortune with poultry. Surely it is a husband you are wanting, not a bantam cock?"

Sitting in my father's fireside chair with my eyes closed I breathed noisily, my ears shivering.

"No body to him, I know," replied Edwina, "but he has goodness and faith. Brainy, too, mind, and a scholar."

"Aye?" answered Morfydd. "I would rather have stupidity if it kept me warm in bed, for brains can be damned freezing things. Not that I can read much myself, but I could not stomach a Lesson for breakfast and supper, and that is what you will have from Snell."

"You are hard on him," came the gentle reply. "It is not every day of the week that a girl is followed by a gentleman out of Eton."

This even opened one of my eyes.

"What is that?" asked Morfydd.

"A place where they learn to read and write and speak languages."

"A school, is it?"

"A school where hundreds of men live together and they won the battle of Waterloo. On the playing-fields, at that."

"Be damned," said Morfydd. "It was fought in France and Grandfer Shams-y-Coed ran the cannon balls down the Blorenge Incline for it. Spinning you a fine old tale is Snell."

"Fought on playing-fields," said Edwina, "so do not believe all they tell you."

"Good God," said Morfydd.

"And very good friends with the Duke of Wellington, too, so kindly give him a little more respect when next you see him."

Which shows what you can learn when you pretend to be sleeping. Very interested in history I was at this time, and pleasant to have this fact straightened out at last, for the English were a mile in front of the Welsh when it came to education.

What with battles and Etons, Edwina was getting in a bad way over Mr Snell. She got up now, sighed and ran her hands over her slim body. A fine figure had Edwina, smaller around the waist in inches than my father was around the neck, but good over the shoulders, and the summer dresses she wore were stretched tightly across the tips of her breasts. Now she stood before the looking glass, smiling and combing and tying coloured ribbons in her hair.

"Educated or not," said Morfydd, "by the time he was plucked he would not make a Christmas dinner. You will sleep with him one day, remember. Eton or not, a husband expects more from a wife than cooking and cleaning."

"Whee, there is terrible!" said Edwina, and she turned and squeezed herself like a tap-room barmaid. "And you not married, either! How do you know what a husband expects?"

"Oi, oi," whispered Morfydd. "It is amazing what some girls know, even if they have not been to an altar, but do not get me on my favourite subject or I will talk all night."

I risked a peep at her. She was lying back in her chair, her eyes half closed, her breast high and full, her expression, brilliant with memories, changing from amazement to pain as she sighed and stretched herself in long, feline grace. She looked as Delilah must have done on the night the roof came down.

"*Whisht!* It is wonderful," she breathed.

"What is wonderful?" asked Edwina sharp.

"Never you mind," said Morfydd, pulling her skirts down. "Yes now, this business of husbands. It is experience you are wanting, Edwina. You cannot go rushing into marriage without a walk or two up the mountain to get the lie of the land, for do not think men like Snell are backward; he may be a rough old lad in a bed. Remember that boy from Gilwern?"

"Lemuel Walters?"

"Aye, Lemuel. He was the same as you. Shy and nervous he was, as jumpy as a grasshopper, but he was a different chap after I had sat him on the mountain for a couple of Sundays running, and now he is a terror."

"And Willie Bargoed. Him too?"

"Do not talk to me about Willie Bargoed!" This sat Morfydd up. "Very innocent looked Willie when I took him up for lessons, but he had the skirt from me in under a minute, and . . ."

I was breathing so hard that I nearly dropped off.

Squinting from under my eyelashes I saw Morfydd's eyes full on my face.

"Asleep, he is," whispered Edwina. "Dead to the world. O, tell me more, Morfydd, for Mr Snell will be having me in the marriage bed any time between now and a year last Sunday."

"Not if Dada has a say in it. *Diawch!* If that thing over there is asleep, then I am twice buried. Both ears flapping from the moment we came in." She caught me by the ankles and heaved me to the floor. "Out of that chair and lay the table quick, and a word to anyone of what you have heard and I will damned fry you!"

"I have as much right to know things as Edwina," I said.

She hit me sideways. "*Duw!* Hark at the innocent! With the company you have been keeping lately you could teach me a thing or two. Who was walking round the Tumble last Sunday with Polly Morgan Drum and Monkey?"

"She is not my girl," I said, hot.

"Pleased I am to hear it, and the moment she is I will be on her doorstep, for this is a respectable house. Keep clear of that one—leave her to Mo Jenkins, for the pair of them come from gutters, and mud always sticks."

"Hush!" warned Edwina. "Mam is coming!"

As I laid the table I thought about Polly Morgan.

Pretty was Polly, thirteen years old, with a figure that turned the eyes of grown men, let alone boys like Mo and me. Her dark hair hung in plaits to her shoulders; she had a fussy little swing to her hips when she walked, a neat little waist, and enough for a grown woman above it, and her lips were high-curved red and half open, as if in the hope of a kiss. Polly had been on my pillow since the night I went to buy whisky for medicine purposes, though Mam drank most of it in tea.

"Good evening, Iestyn Mortymer," said Polly. "There is a stranger," and she leaned her elbows on the bar counter and hunched her shoulders, bringing the shadows deep in her breast.

"Good evening," I said. "Two pennyworth of whisky for medicine purposes, please," and I pushed the bottle towards her.

"Who for?" she asked.

"For my father," I said.

And then she smiled. "Do not come that old tale, boyo. Drink will be the end of you—sinking quarts down at the Benefit, is it? Next you will be sleeping with Wicked Gwennie Lewis, who is not half so wicked as me."

There is forward for a bare thirteen.

"Two penn'orth of whisky," I said. "And a little less old tongue with it, please."

"Phew!" said she. "Independent, eh? But a pretty boy you are, Iestyn Mortymer, so you are forgiven. For some time now I have had my eye on you, so if you fancy ten minutes in a haystack a handful of gravel at my window will always bring me out, never mind the neighbours."

"According to the deacons you are a harlot, Polly Morgan," I said, "and doomed to everlasting fire, so give me the whisky and I will get from here."

"Aye," said she, drawing it and winking over her shoulder. "Fry, I will, so I am making the best of things before I blister. Very disappointing, you are, Iestyn. Many men would pay a sovereign for me, but for you I would be wicked free, and do not look so saintly."

"I am too young for women," I replied, sweating, and reached for the bottle. But she caught my fingers, and the touch of her hand, so smooth and strong, was like a burn.

"Blessed are the fornicators," she whispered, "for the others do not know what they are missing. Nobody would be the wiser, see? Round the Tumble at eight o'clock next Sunday night and grow up two years older?"

"I will not be there," I said shivering.

"If you are not you will be the first to stay away," and she leaned over the bar and kissed my lips.

So Polly Morgan was on my pillow and it took six weeks to get her off.

Clutching the whisky I ran home, cursing her, and that night I went with Edwina to a Reading to cleanse my soul. But the next Sunday I was walking round the Tumble above Garndyrus and came across her lying in a sheltered place with her skirts above her knees and showing her red garters.

"Good evening," said she, sitting up. "For one who is not here you are pretty well on time. Up a dando!" And she kicked up her legs and got to her feet. "Lead the way, Iestyn Mortymer, for there is not enough quiet here for girls as wicked as me."

"You first," I said, every nerve trembling. And away she went along the tram road, swaying at the hips and smiling over her shoulder.

What is it that flashes into a man so that the swish of skirts is music and half an inch of petticoat makes his head spin? Before me were the high-buttoned boots, the skirt, then the waist swelling to shoulders where the black plaits bobbed, and the fragrance of her drifted into my face. There is a fragrance about women that does not come from bottles. My mother smells of lavender from the little bags she stores with her aprons; Morfydd smells of thyme she gathers for the meat, and Edwina of cowslips she puts into her hair. Polly Morgan smelled of heather that Sunday, which is a smell of wildness and freedom; as if she had made her bed in it and bathed herself in mountain springs and pinned wild herbs on her petticoats. The path was lonely and pure with sunlight. Above us reared the mountain with its gorse fanning live in the wind and below us the valley of the Usk lay misted and golden at the foot of Pen-y-fal. On we went until we reached an opening in the rock face. Taking my hand she drew me within it, swung wide her skirt and lay down on the high grass. Quite still she lay, eyes closed, waiting.

"Down by here," she said, patting the grass, eyes still closed, and I obeyed, sitting cross-legged, wondering what to do.

"Well," she said at length. "Unless somebody starts something wicked soon I am off from here to find somebody who will." But still I sat.

"O, Iestyn," she whispered, and rolled towards me, reaching out, her lips pouted for kissing.

And then it happened. The water came down first and then the bucket and we were swamped in rivers that ran down our necks and sent us gasping, soaking us both head to foot. Furious, I struggled to my feet. Mo Jenkins was lying on the rocks above us, grinning.

"Quite still!" he called, and down came a bucket that bowled me over and sent Polly scampering and cursing to tarnish altars.

"And I come next," said Mo, leaping from rock to rock like a deer. "Very kind of you, Iestyn, to get across my girl, so now I will smash your face in, and Polly goes home without trews."

Very fast I went along that tram road, for Mo had long since outstripped me in strength and size, and the last I heard of Polly Morgan was her trews pinned to the signpost of the Drum and Monkey.

"*Polly-Without-Trews?*" whispered Edwina now.

"Aye," said Morfydd in disdain. "Pinned to the Drum and Monkey with *Iestyn Mortymer* chalked underneath, and it took me a ladder to rub it out."

I was hot enough to catch fire, believing the secret firm.

"There is a scandal!" breathed Edwina. "What if Dada finds out?"

"He will find out soon enough if anyone breathes a word of

what he has heard in here," said Morfydd. "Sharp with that table, Iestyn, and do not forget to offer to wash up after."

I was half way through laying the table when my mother, father, Jethro and Tomos Traherne came in.

"No table ready?" asked Mam, her eyebrows up. "No beef cut, no butter? One would think we were in debt at The Shop, and us with a visitor to talk about the outing."

And in he came.

A man and a half was Tomos Traherne; black-bearded and grizzled in the cheeks where years of coal had cut their pattern. He dwarfed my father in size and the town by the ferocity of his faith. Powerful upon a hassock he did good work in the name of the Lord, but on his feet he was the most dangerous man in town, where his thunder boomed over the valleys in pursuit of urchins, harlots and ironmasters. Like the martyrs of old, he had suffered, and wrote religious pamphlets since the night Will Blaenavon parted his hair with a quart bottle and threw him out of the Lamb Row public and his pamphlets after him.

"Sit you down, Tomos," said my mother, and he threw his coat tails before him and eased his great shining backside into the best chair. Perched there, his little black eyes swept the room above his steel-rimmed spectacles.

"Where is Edwina?"

"I am here, sir," said she, stepping into the lamplight.

"Happy art thou in the service of the Lord, child?"

"Happy indeed, sir."

"Right, you! Judges eighteen, verse two. Recite!" Squinting down, he began to fill his clay.

"In those days there was no king . . ." began Edwina.

"Eh? What is this?" He stared at her and smoothed his stomach with great, ponderous hands. "Think, child, think! 'And the children of Dan sent of their family. . . .'"

"'. . . five men of their coasts,'" chanted Edwina, "'men of valour, from Zorah, and from Eshtaol, to spy out the land, and to search it; and they said unto them, Go search the land:

57

who, when they came to mount Ephraim, to the house of Micah, they lodged there.'"

"Good God," said Morfydd.

"Amen," boomed Tomos. "Excellent, excellent!" And he brought out his little black book and put her name down.

"Do not spoil it by examining the other two," said Mam, coming in. "One is a pagan and the other is following her example, from what I hear lately." She looked at me and my heart stopped beating.

"Stay for a bite of supper, Tomos?"

"Just had my supper I have at Mrs Evan's, God bless her."

"But stay for another, for you are welcome," said my father at the door. "We have slices of good roast pork and beef needing a home, Tomos."

But his hand was up and Tomos shook his head. "Everything in moderation, Hywel. As you know, I am not a man of gluttony, which, according to the Book, is one of the sins cardinal."

And him with belly enough for six suppers.

"O, stay!" whispered Edwina from her corner.

"For you, my child, yes," said Tomos, relieved. "Lay another place at table, Mrs Mortymer, and I will do your cooking justice if only to please the children." His little eyes switched to me as I sidled up with his knife and fork.

"Aha! Iestyn!" And I was lifted bodily and put upon his knee. I heard Morfydd's giggle, and hated her, for if there is anything indecent in this world it is one man sitting on the knee of another.

"One question well answered and your name is down for the outing," he said. "Bear ye one another's burdens . . ."

"And so fulfil the law of Christ," I said, scrambling away.

"There is a surprise," said Dada. "We will have a monk in the house before we are finished."

"And Morfydd?" asked Tomos. "What will Morfydd answer?"

"Good on the Ten Commandments, mind," said Edwina warmly.

"Right, then. One of them from you, Morfydd, which is asking little enough considering you are the eldest."

"Thou shalt not commit adultery, Tomos."

"Amen," said Tomos without a blink. "But another would have been more appropriate in a house mothered by such virtue."

"You can have the ten," said she with a sniff, "but I am not bothered if I go on the outing or not. I have plenty to occupy my time."

"So I hear, child. But you will go if only to keep you from wickedness."

"Well," began my father, clapping his hands, "in with the meat, Elianor, for the righteous need feeding as well as the unbelievers, and Tomos looks starved. Will you sing and play for us, girl, while we eat?"

Sweet was my mother's voice that night. The lamplight shimmered on the strings of the harp as they vibrated under her fingers.

Plates pushed away, we listened, for it was not possible to eat when my mother made her music. O, beautiful is the harp and a woman's voice singing with the wind sighing in the eaves and hammering in the chimney! Morfydd was motionless, her eyes lowered. Edwina took Jethro upon her knee. My father was in a holy silence, and Tomos, face turned up, was plucking deep in his beard. And when the song was ended I saw tears in my father's eyes.

"A beautiful song, Elianor," he said deeply. "There is a woman for you, good in cooking, milk and music. Search the mountains for a voice so pure and the world for such goodness."

"Amen," said Tomos, going at his beef.

"O, get on, get on, Hywel!" cried Mam, scarlet now.

"A candidate for the contralto competition, think you?" asked my father. "Charlotte Guest is giving a golden purse next Eisteddfod at Abergavenny, and we could do with the money."

"With you collecting the bass oratorio and Owen Howells winning the tenor, aye, it would be fine to win the contralto purse as well," said Tomos. "Yes, I will have her entered."

"You dare!" said Mam. "My singing is confined to the house. I am not making a public exhibition of myself like Mrs Gwallter and others I could mention."

"Whee!" exclaimed Morfydd. "Flat at the top and sharp at the bottom, and better noises do come from Irish bagpipes."

"The Book is open," said Tomos. "Please do not slander Mrs Gwallter or any other neighbour, Morfydd. Quiet now, all of us, and let me call upon this house of love the blessing of the Almighty God who fashioned it and sustains it in peace and joy. A prayer of thanks to Him, then, each in his own way," said Tomos, "for the brave people of this town, and this house in the Square."

And Morfydd reached out and gripped my hand under the table.

But I washed the dishes just the same and was there with the rag long after the house was quiet.

I was surprised when my father came down into the kitchen and helped me finish them. His eyes were smiling as he said:

"Iestyn, it is a father's duty to talk to his son about women. Earlier today I had decided to ask Tomos to do it for me, but since the Drum and Monkey is involved in this discussion, I think it had better be done by me, for he might be too hard on you. Do you understand?"

Floors swallow people in books. In life they stay solid. I stood before him with the shame flooding to my face and the sweat breaking out in every pore. He put his hand upon my shoulder and gently pushed me into a chair.

"It is not too bad," he said, grinning. "More than one I ran down a tram road before I was your age, but I was careful to make sure it did not get round town. But now to the point— do you remember I raised this subject on your first day at work?"

"Yes, Dada," I said, my eyes down.

"Face me, Iestyn. Do not make it hard. What do you know of these things?"

"Not much," I replied.

"Why did you run Polly Morgan, for instance?"

"To find out," I said, boiling.

"About women? Surely you know much already. Have you never seen Morfydd or Edwina unclothed?"

"Morfydd once, when she was not looking," I said.

"And seen that she has breasts, like Mam, where she will one day feed her children?"

"Yes," I replied.

"And that she is rounder in the hips and a very different shape to us in front?"

"Yes," I said.

"Listen," he said, "I do not intend to do you drawings. You have noticed, for a start, that women have nothing, yet it is from that part of a woman that her children come, do you understand—that you surely know, Iestyn."

"Aye," I said.

"Why run Polly Morgan, then?"

"Because I wanted proof."

"Good," he said. "Now tell me, boy. Is it not true that from the exact spot where a seed is planted in ground the plant comes forth?"

I nodded after some thought.

"Then so it is with a woman," said he. "The woman is the soil and the man is the planter, and the seed springs to life within her and comes forth as a plant—a child."

"Yes," I said.

"Do you remember your Bible—*In The Beginning*. . . ."

"Yes, Dada."

"For in the beginning God created Adam," my father said, "and gave to him a mate whom He called Eve, and He created Eve from a rib He took from the body of Adam that she should be his companion, friend and lover, as your mother is to me."

I asked, "Was it the same with the Lady of Bethlehem, whose husband was Joseph, and who brought forth the Lord?"

"No, Iestyn. That Lady was entered by the Seed of God,

61

not of Joseph—something special, it would need, to make the Son of God, you see?"

"Aye," I answered, becoming interested. "And I would have liked to come that way."

"Why?" he asked, eyes narrowed to the lamp.

"Well, it do seem indecent otherwise. I can understand people like Gwennie Lewis and Mrs Pantrych being shameful, but I hate to think of it with Mam."

This put him on his feet again. "Listen, Iestyn. One day you will know that nothing done by a man and woman married is shameful, if it is done with love. For if our mating is devised by God how can it be indecent? To run a woman for peeps as you ran Polly Morgan is indecent. And to take a woman to bed and divide her body for the seed is a thing commended by God, if done in marriage. But if it is done after drink, say—up on the mountain or round the Tumble with looks over the shoulder, and with a single girl or another man's wife, then it is a disgrace, and God will turn His face from you, and so will I."

"Yes, Dada."

"And the child of such a mating will be damned. Now one more thing before we finish, boy, and then to bed. Is Edwina, who is older than you, as strong?"

"No."

"Right, then. It is to us that God has given the greater strength—to support and uphold women, who are weak. Who, then, made Gwennie Lewis wicked?"

"Men," I said.

He sighed deep. "At last we are learning. And who is making Polly Morgan wicked these days?"

"Mo Jenkins."

He drew himself up. "And how do you stand in the judgment?"

I flicked my eyes to his face and lowered them.

"Good," said he. "Remember, Iestyn, all women are pure until defiled by men of wickedness. So give respect to women, boy, for their bodies belong to the Lord, and are precious to Him as the bodies of Morfydd and Edwina are precious to me. So let us hear no more talk of Polly Morgan Drum and Monkey or hell will come loose in the house."

He got up and ran his fingers through his hair. "A good boy you are for listening, Iestyn. I am going under the table tonight. Away next door to Mam. She is waiting for you."

"To sleep with her?"

"Aye." He sighed. "That is her sole contribution to this conversation."

"Dando!" I said. "Goodnight, Dada."

My mother was waiting with the Cyfarthfa blanket well back.

"Dada told me to come," I whispered, throwing off my clothes.

"Did you understand what he told you?"

"Aye, but I knew most of it before. Over a bit so I can get in."

"No shirt?" said she. "There is indecent. Never mind, it is only your old Mam."

Her arms went about me and she sighed deep in her throat.

CHAPTER SIX

SINCE THE age of six, when I was old enough to go on the annual outing, something always happened to stop me: spots, fevers, threats of the cholera in one shape or another, which made me unpopular with Morfydd who had to stay home to nurse me.

But nothing happened to stop me in the June I was thirteen.

On the great morning everybody gathered at the top of Turnpike and walked down to the inn. The Garndyrus Benefit band was there; furnace-men, colliers, quarrymen and limestone carriers in Sunday suits with their wives and children adorned in best dresses and lace, even if it meant going twice into debt at the Shop. Outside the inn Billy Handy Landlord was rolling out the beer, barrels for the men, bottles for the women and small beer for the children, and Rhys Jenkins and a few other roughs were rolling on their feet before we had moved off.

"Into the trams!" bellowed Tomos Traherne, who had been in charge of annual outings for the past ten years, and I took my family to the road.

"Lead the way, Iestyn," said my father, "for I would rather trust the women to you than those pair of hot-heads the Howells," and my heart nearly burst with pride as I handed my mother and sisters in while my father, Bennet and Snell climbed up in front. Elot, my new tram-mare, was a little delicate with the wind that morning for Mo Jenkins had mixed sulphur with her oats, so I tethered her behind the tram and away we went, spragging down the line, making a rare speed while my father roared encouragement and the women screamed.

"Faster, boy, faster!" shouted Richard.

"O, Hywel!" screamed Mam, "for God's sake stop him!"

"Iestyn, do not be a damned maniac!" shouted Morfydd, clutching at her bonnet, and Edwina used the chance to faint away into Snell's arms. On, on, rumbling and swaying down the Govilon Incline we went like demons until we came to the cable-engine.

"O, heavens!" whispered Mam, patting herself. "There is a madman. In several pieces I am. Hywel, hand me down from this contraption."

Mr Gwallter and Dic Shon Ffyrnig were the cable-men that morning, and they turned our tram and shackled it up and we sailed down the Blorenge bowl, pulling an empty tram up. Down to the Llanfoist Wharf we went, where a gang of broody Irish were waiting by a string of barges, and into them we went as excited as little children. The band came down next, with the beer and food after them, and Will Blaenavon and Rhys and Mo began to load it aboard while the children garlanded the barges and horses with summer flowers. Tomos Traherne climbed on to the prow of our barge and lectured us on how to behave in Newport; urging us to keep away from the gin-shops and beer-houses, which, he said, were the scourge of a decent community, and a special warning to the pugilists about hitting out Redcoats all the time Irishmen were plentiful. Then he read out the addresses of the chapels and churches and begged everybody to attend the singing competition to be held in the public hall, and God help anybody not in a fit state to leave Newport Docks by eight o'clock. Prayers, then, and thanks to the ironmaster who had given a sovereign or two to make all this possible, and Tomos blew on a horn. The horses were whipped up and away down the canal we went with our barge leading.

Wonderful to be moving on water. The silky movement is a drug to the senses when you are lying along the prow of a barge watching the water-lilies and bindweed waving. Soon Pen-y-fal and the Skirrids were well behind us, and the sun, streaming down through the avenue of trees, cast golden patterns on the barges. On, through the drain locks, into the drone of bees and the skimming dragonflies. There is peace for you, lying half asleep after being up since midnight, quivering with the dreams of the happiness to come.

And it came sooner than a soul expected.

"*Diawl!*" whispered my father. "There is an anxious lot!"

"Trouble, by the look of it," said Richard, getting on to his haunches. "Now whose idea was it for the Mortymers to travel in front?"

"Whee!" whispered Morfydd, staring ahead. "Trust Iestyn to mess up anything he organises."

"Spread your stays, Elianor," said Dada. "Trouble is upon us."

"Calm, everybody!" shouted Tomos Traherne from the next barge down. "It is the worthless sent by the devil to provoke us to violence, but we will receive it with dignity. Calm."

"To hell with that," said Richard. "I am receiving no turnips with dignity for I have stopped too many in Covent Garden," and he reached into Mam's basket and brought out a tomato.

"O, Richard, do not provoke them," said Mam while Morfydd was giggling herself double. "Do not provoke them, but do as Tomos says, boy."

Fifty yards ahead the arched bridge was crowded to the footwalks with more Irish than in Dublin, all chattering like monkeys and making rude signs and stacking the parapet with everything man has been able to throw since the creation. Nearer we came, our old horse plodding to a carrot one of them was holding. Louder and louder came the chatter from the bridge and higher went their piles of vegetables, and three little boys were lifted on to the parapet and stood there like sentinels of fate, undoing the buttons of their trews to give us a dousing.

"Good God!" said Morfydd, "here is a cloudburst coming," and she opened her parasol while Mam fought for room under it. Helpless, every one of us, for so grave and determined those little boys stood, holding them up and waiting for the right moment. My father was pressing his sides and rolling with laughter and my tears were blinding me at the sight of Edwina's face and old Snell comforting her.

"Leave them to me!" shouted Snell suddenly, getting on his feet. "There is goodness even in Irish and I am used to handling violence," and he flung his arms wide and appealed to their better natures. But Will Blaenavon was more practical.

"Do not distress yourselves, my little ones," said he, jumping from the prow of the next barge down with his arms full of turnips, "for the committee of the annual outing has provided for all possibilities. Six each, and throw to kill, mind," and he poured them into our laps. "And lend me your knife, Iestyn. I am having those little pinkles on a pin for trout fishing if I die threading them."

"O, Will!" giggled Mam, shaking and streaming tears.

Our barge was rocking with laughter until the Irish let fly, and the first swede dropped took Snell in the chest and bowled him in head first while Edwina screamed and held on to his ankles.

"*Diawch!* There was a shot for you," said Dada. "Iestyn, Richard—up by here with you and let us get organised. Napoleon is finished, but we are still good for others," and we scrambled up beside him in a hail of rotten cabbages and stood over Morfydd's parasol and let go with our turnips. Everybody on the following barges was at battle stations now, and parties had landed ashore bringing armfuls of root crops from poor Grandfer Shams-y-Coed's fields. Hunting horns were shrieking, whistles blowing the alarm and the band had its head well down into its collar, playing *Welsh Heroes* fit to stir Owen Glyndwr from his ashes.

Ten yards from the bridge and the Irish opened fire in earnest, shouting every war cry between Dublin and Belfast, and as we drifted under the bridge the little boys let it go. We took it point blank. Buckets came from that parapet. And there was just time to take a breath before we got it from three more little boys standing on the other side. The Irish were here in strength, crowding the towpath, and with two of them feeding our barge-horse we seemed likely to stay for hours. The Irish confetti rained down, with Irishmen stripping half an acre of field and starting on another. Besides, the law of gravity was a taking a hand, and if the field lasted much longer they seemed sure to sink us.

"A landing-party!" shouted my father. "Follow me every man who can stand!" and he leaped ashore blowing shrill notes with his fingers. Crowds followed him, Richard and I leading. Up the towpath we went, opening our shoulders at anything in sight. The Irish flew up the bridge and we stormed after them with Owen Howells and Griff supporting the charge with the big bass drum and blasts on the trombone. Good parents are the Irish. They packed their brats on the hump and fought like cats, but as we closed the range they wilted and broke. Up the mountain they streamed with the Welsh after them, running hand in hand with little Irish toddlers.

Laughing, triumphant, we came back to the barges. Mam and Morfydd were still sitting under their ragged parasol. Edwina had got Snell from the water and was dabbing at him with a little lace handkerchief. We got the barges lined up again and threw out the vegetables, washed in the canal and whipped up the horses. The sun streamed down, the air was sweet with smells of summer. Out came the beer, the home-baked loaves, cheeses and the women's parsnip wine, and we drank and feasted our way to Newport under the alders, singing and whooping every yard of the way. Good neighbours are the Irish in many respects, I say. There is nothing like a good fight to give a start to the day.

Viking and Dane, Roman and Spaniard have thundered into Newport with sunlight gleaming on spur and mace, for Cardiff is a farming town and never worth its capture. Chained slaves have toiled in the galleys of conquering fleets that came with bloody pennants from the Channel to the North Sea to rape the women and slaughter the men, but the lot bundled together never caused the stir in this fussy little seaport as we mountain ironworkers sailing in by barge for our annual outing. Twenty-two barges, every one decked from prow to stern with ribbons and wild flowers; a brass band letting fly and the banners of the illegal Benefit Clubs waving in the faces of scowling Redcoats. Past moored ships we went; barques from the West Indies with their smells of Eastern spices; alongside white-sailed schooners with prows of sweeping dignity to the tumbledown poverty of the waterfront and the crowded jetties where whole families jostled for position to see us march by. Urchins who had not seen a bath since the midwife danced alongside catching the food we threw; ancient faces peered from little square windows, shouting and laughing, for a town in the clutch of the English is happy at a show of spirit. Groups of Redcoats leaned idly on muskets with watchful, nervous glances at the mad Welsh workers.

There is a place for you, this Newport! London is only half the size, for nobody is fool enough to believe all the English tell you. Great stone buildings dominated by the Westgate, big enough to frighten a countryman to death; broughams, traps, carriages, dog-carts on the streets with fine ladies and gentlemen bowing this way and that and spotted dogs running between the wheels. Dandies by the score, drunkards, men on horseback with a superior air; beautiful girls in hooped dresses walking daintily under frilled parasols, and everybody going about their business with a rush and tear that left me breathless. Richard and Morfydd were first off the barge and were away to visit some of his English friends. Edwina and Snell got into a trap to find the nearest Church of England where he could borrow dry clothes. Mo was ready, his face full of wickedness, and we were off.

Everybody in Wales must have been in Newport that day, for Dock Street was as packed with people as herrings in a barrel. Beggars sat in the gutters and pulled at me for money: men from the French wars, mostly; arms off, legs off, some with their faces shot away. Crippled children sat in the laps of verminous old hags; old men, too tired to die, stooped weakly on sticks. And the streets were filled with vendors and criers, gentry and workers standing shoulder to shoulder. Sailors from the East were there with parrots in cages; mulattos, gipsies and freed slaves from Bristol, as black as watered coal. Bears were being led on chains, carts loaded with merchandise. Fiddles were going, drums being beaten and dogs howling to kicks. The crowd was even thicker in the Fair, the stalls end to end, with people shrieking in foreign tongues, begging us to buy. Wool stalls, flannel stalls from Abergavenny; poultry benches with scraggy necks swinging; stalls where bootmakers were at work, spitting out the nails and hitting them in like lightning. Ostlers were there leading fine Arab stallions splendid with medallions. Here the gentry were buying, their hands heaped with golden sovereigns.

"A penny for anything you like!" cried a voice, and even as I turned Mo tossed her one and she caught it and ran like a hare, shrieking with laughter, without showing an inch of petticoat.

"Damned little bitch," said Mo, blazing.

"Aye, but serve you right," I said. "This is the city and you are caught too easy for my company."

"Come, you," said he. "I will show you things you do not know. Two women in Dock Street who do it with boys half price and I am not paying more than threepence, mind."

"Not me," I said. "I have two shillings to spend and I am taking something back from this fair to remember it, not pox."

"Eight and sixpence!" roared a voice from the crowd, and I shouldered my way through the people to see what was selling.

"Do not go too close or they will have you," said Mo. "I am off after that little bitch to get something for my penny. Hell, I will cross her in daylight."

"Nine shillings," called another.

You can always tell a gentleman by the cut of his coat. This one was tall and lean, with narrow calfskin trews buttoned at the knee and gaiters under, and there was elegance in the spread of his fingers as he helped his fine straight nose to snuff.

"Ten shillings!" This one was beefy, his red face sweating

beer; a farmer by the bulge of his belly and his grin was wide and stained with nicotine.

"Eleven," said the gentleman.

"Eh!" said the farmer. "You have backed the wrong horse this time, my lad, for I am bound to go higher to get what I want for Lancashire. Fifteen shillings, and hand the boy down to me, Mr Poorhouse."

"Fifteen shillings for a boy like this is a scandal!" cried the skinny, mop-headed auctioneer. "With no mother or father to snatch him from your kitchen and half a loaf a day will keep him. Come, twenty!"

"Fifteen," said the north countryman, "and not a penny more." He grinned as the gentleman walked away and slapped his leggings with his whip.

"Dewi Lewis down to Mr Winstanley for fifteen shillings," said the auctioneer, and pushed the boy down the steps. Dressed in the rags of the dock urchins, he stood against the farmer's stomach, his head low, his hair over his face.

"This Lancashire gentleman do beat me," said the auctioneer. "Always gets what he wants."

"Aye, and fifteen shillings to my account, if you please, for I have not stopped buying today."

I watched Pig's eyes as a girl was pushed on to the platform. She was about my age, noble in the face and clean, her ragged dress tight about her waist. Her dark hair she wore over her shoulders like the Irish, her legs and feet were bare.

"Two pounds," said Pig, "and give her here."

The crowd murmured. White-faced women were moving angrily in the crowd. The girl looked down at Dewi Lewis, swept back her hair and joined him by the farmer.

"That will suit me," said Pig. "One for the yard and one for the house," and gripping their shoulders he took them away.

Sickened, I watched the buying. The poor, who had been keeping the poor, sold them. Mothers sold their sons for hire, fathers their daughters, and the orphanage sold its children in droves of ten. Older, I fought my way out of the crowd and came face to face with Mo.

"I got that little bitch," said he, radiant. "I caught her under a cart up by the bull-baiting and tickled her up the drawers before she bit me, look you."

He held up fingers. I turned away.

"What is wrong, man?" he asked, frowning. I jerked my head at the hiring platform.

"Why, that?" He hit me sideways. "You can see that any July at Town Hall Abergavenny—no need to come to Newport."

"What the hell is wrong with you today?" asked Mo.

"Shut your stupid face."

"Come to see the ships, then?"

I slouched through the streets with my hands in my pockets.

"Come and have a grown woman in Dock Street?"

I looked at him, hating the sight of him.

"You are a boot-faced bloody Puritan," said Mo. "Weak in the belly, in tears at the hirings and not enough in your trews for pike-bait."

"I am too young for grown women," I said.

"Right, you. Thirteen, is it? Too young? My grandfather Ben was into his first at eight."

"Aye, and look at him now at eighty."

"Lend me sixpence, then."

"Not if it is for whoring."

"Sixpence more and I can go on the ships."

"Threepence to go on ships—there is the notice."

"Bloody old skinflint."

"But better than a fornicator. So get from here before I drop you, for the sight of you makes me sick."

"Away, me," said Mo. "I will find a man for a friend and go into Dock Street."

"Then go," I said, kicking at a stone.

Disgruntled, unhappy, I went behind the stalls to the entrance of the Westgate Inn, to watch the gentry coming and going. I felt, leaning against the great stone wall, a sudden excitement, a strange presentiment of violence. The square before me was dense with people, a swaying mass with raised fists. The crowd began to chant in Welsh as a trumpet sounded. Hooves clattered on the cobbles. The people, violent with noise and activity, suddenly parted. A troop of fifty Redcoats clattered through them, glorious in pageantry, and marched towards the inn entrance with muskets at the ready. Insults were flung after them in Welsh and English, sticks were raised, but the soldiers marched on steadily with a horseman at their head; men of Brecon Garrison, the thorn in the side of Merthyr and Dowlais. Wheeling to their officer's command, they formed themselves four deep in front of the Westgate, and turning, faced the hostile crowd.

"Trouble in Merthyr again, see?" said a man near me.

"Taking no chances," said another.

"They burned the Court of Requests once and they will burn it again, for Dic Penderyn."

"And blood is running in the gutters. It could be the same here in Newport."

"Aye? It takes men like the Crawshays to bring about a misery like Cyfarthfa, but we would knife their kind in Newport."

"Out of it, you," said a soldier, and gripped me and flung me headlong from the doorway. Tripping, I lost my balance and fell, rolling to the heels of the soldiers with the steps of the inn immediately before me. Hands clenched, I was upon my feet seconds before the gentleman from the hall reached me. He came running, a man of strength by the litheness of his step. He was dressed in black, with buttoned cloth leggings. No dandy, this, for all the lace at his wrists and throat, and his smile was ready and kind as he stood clear while I brushed the dirt from my Sunday suit.

"Are you hurt, lad?"

"No," I said, blazing.

"Good. You were watching the gentry?"

"Aye," I replied. "And no harm in that."

He sighed. "Cats may look at kings, it is said. But the working boy who looks upon gentry without a pull of the forelock can be taken and flung into the gutter, eh?"

I looked at him, turned to go, and swung back.

It was his eyes.

Small and keen they were, set close in his strong face; eyes of steel that flickered over me, beautiful one moment, fierce the next. Shining, they penetrated, and held me.

"Where are you from, lad?" The eyes swept quickly around.

"Garndyrus, sir."

"The annual outing?"

"Aye."

"Then you will know a man named Richard Bennet?"

I nodded, wonderingly.

"You could find him now?"

I nodded, staring.

"Then be so good as to find him quickly and give him this." He brought an envelope from his pocket and put it into my hand.

"Who shall I say, sir?"

He smiled. "There is no need for names, lad." He tossed me a sixpence and I caught it and dropped it into my pocket.

"As sharp as you can," said he, "for it is important."

Turning abruptly, he ran up the steps into the Westgate.

I went to find Richard Bennet but found Dafydd Phillips instead; standing outside a beer-house, full to the back teeth by the look of him, and grinning like a dead sheep. I took a chance.

"I am looking for Morfydd," I said, keeping a safe distance. "Have you seen her?"

"Aye," said he, rocking.

"My father wants her quick," I said. "It is a matter of life and death."

"Like Merthyr," said he, very sober. "The Highlanders went mad there. Women and children were shot down, they say. But like the other agitators Mr Richard Bennet is nowhere to be found when John Frost needs him."

"John Frost," I repeated, going cold.

"Aye. Very distinguished you are becoming carrying messages from the leader. And very foolish of him to send his messages with hundreds watching, thank God for him. Come with me."

"Where are you taking me?" I demanded.

"To Bennet. To hell with Morfydd for once."

Elbowing his way through the crowd he took me back the way I had come, past the Westgate where the people were still jeering at the soldiers guarding the entrance, and turned up Stow Hill. Half way up the hill two fat women were fighting in a circle of cheering men, scratching and tearing at each other, their rags hanging down over their waists and their slack breasts swinging. This delayed us. We turned into a side street. Slum alleys here where mangy dogs nosed garbage bins and skinny children raised their heads from doorsteps. Through the alleys we went with Dafydd not giving a backward look, although I kept my distance in case he was up to tricks. And then he stopped.

"The third door from here," he said. "An hour back I followed the pair of them. Bennet's friends, mind, it is all very respectable, so do not be shy." And then he put his hands over his face and sobbed like a baby. "O, holy God!" he said.

"Dafydd, Dafydd," I replied, sick of him, "go back to your beer and forget her for she is mad about him. You are worth something better than old Morfydd."

This got him into his stride again, blowing and bubbling and bringing me from patience, for beer has several ways out of a man and one is through the eyes, says Dada.

I hit his arm. "Come now, do not be soft. Hang about here with Bennet sober and you will have a hammering. Go down to Dock Street with Mo Jenkins and find yourself a sand-rat and you will feel happier in the morning."

This brought him steady and he stared, disbelieving his ears.

"O God," he said, breathing hard. "From the mouth of a child! Should I debase myself with a hired woman? Seven times seven will you burn, Iestyn!" He caught my arms, pulling me closer. "You wanted Bennet. I brought you to him.

Speak to her, boy. Look, I beg you. Tell her I will work for her, that I will go blind for her. O, great Jesus, do pity me! Listen!" He shook me to make the sense of it. "Bennet will go from here sharp. Tell her I will wait by Stow Corner to take her to the singing. O, Iestyn, tell her?"

"All double dutch to me," I said. "But I will tell her. Now go from here sharp before that door opens and he flattens the pair of us."

Away he went along that alley beating lightning.

Trembling, I went to the door and fisted it. Footsteps sounded. A shadow fell across the glass. A woman, tall and thin and dressed in widow's weeds, opened it. She had the face of a starved ghost, hair to match and hands for gripping tombstones. But behind her was a little polished hall and table with flowers in shining brass. I took off my cap.

"I am looking for Mr Richard Bennet, who is visiting here," I said.

She smiled then, and there was sweetness in her lined old face. "If you are a friend of Mr Bennet then no need for introductions, young man," said she. "Please bring your lady in."

I gripped my cap, frowning, went in and closed the door behind me. The eyes of the old woman were sightless.

"No lady?" she said. "There is a pity. Never mind. Sit you down and examine the comforts of this place. Mr Bennet is entertaining a woman, but he will be down when he is finished with her. A house for courting this, to be sure, but count upon it that only the respectable are made welcome, so if you bring a lady you can be sure of good clean bundling with tea brought up when you ring for it. Shall I give a name?"

"No name," I said huskily. "But if you will please give Mr Bennet this envelope I will go from here," and I pressed it into her hand.

"Stupid I am," said she, chuckling. "But a boy you are, I hear, and too young for courting. First the eyes go and then the ears. Poor old Olwen. Aye, I will give him the letter. Will you see yourself out?"

"And thanks," I said, shivering. "Good day, ma'am."

76

I went to the door and opened it, but impelled by a greater power than decency I slammed it and stood in the hall, watching her high-buttoned boots climbing the stairs. Then, on tiptoe, I followed her until my eyes were level with the landing. Taking a tray from a table she pushed the bedroom door wide and went within. Trembling, I looked into the room beyond her.

I saw a window with sunlight streaming through it on to the crumpled coverlet of a wide bed. Richard Bennet was sitting on the edge of it, dark-handsome in tight satin trews and his white, lace-hemmed shirt open to the waist. He sprang up to take the tray, and then I saw Morfydd.

She was lying on the bed as bare as an egg, singing and smiling and waving around her head the nightdress Mam had missed the day before yesterday, looking as flushed and happy as a bride of ten minutes and twice as healthy.

"Whee!" she cried in ecstasy, "here is the tea!" And she kicked up her legs at old Blind Olwen who thought she was dressed for bundling.

Away, me. Down those stairs on tiptoe like something scalded, through the door and along the street like a hare. Dafydd Phillips was waiting at Stow Corner and flung out his arms to catch me, but I was through him, down the Hill and between the women who were still fighting in ponderous swings, into the shadows of the silk stalls and the seething, jeering mass of the crowd, in search of a haven of decency.

At four o'clock I went to the public hall. I saw my mother and father pacing about, agitated.

"There is a good one," said Mam, hugging me. "Have you seen Edwina? The singing is soon to begin."

"Gone for dry clothes," I said, "but if I know Snell they are on their knees to bishops."

"Morfydd and Richard?" asked my father.

"Visiting friends, I hear—no sign of them."

"O, damn!" said he. "Here is me practising for the last six months and growing horns and not a daughter to hear me sing Handel."

"A scandal," said Mam, patting him. "Your father all ready to lift the bass cup and half the family absent. I will warm the breeches of the pair of them if they are late. In with you, Hywel boy, and sing despite them, and do not go flat on the lower registers."

Along came Owen Howells, the tenor entry from town, and Griff, his twin brother.

"How are you?" cried Mam. "Very confident you are looking, Owen. All ready, is it?"

"Aye," said Owen, "but not at my best, see?" And neither did he look it, for his new jacket was ripped and his nose was across his face, and Griff was not much prettier. Beggars for bathing their back teeth and fighting were the Howells.

"It is his top set, you understand," explained Griff. "An Irishman caught him with a boot and they slip at the best of times."

A good tenor was Owen, but he had never been the same in the upper registers since Will Blaenavon removed four of his front ones over eighteen rounds last summer, and it is one thing to have a plate made by a London dentist but another to sing in public with one made by Dic Shon Ffyrnig, blacksmith.

Yes, tuneful was Owen, but voice for voice he was no match for my father. A fine fierce tone had Dada, with a double bass echo that could be heard in Swansea when he got going; rough and vibrant, he was, with his air going in like church bellows. Bass is the voice for a man; a voice with mud on its boots and a smell of sweat and tobacco about it, and all tenors should be in skirts, especially when they go falsetto, for which they are shot in the Italian opera, Dada says.

Into the hall we went now, Mam leading as usual, and many of the gentry like Prothero and Phillips looked down their noses at the rough ironworkers. Lady Charlotte Guest was up in front, bowing this way and that, she and Sir John being the richest ironmasters in Wales, Owen said—people who could buy up the Baileys with the spare change in their pockets. We took our seats in an unholy quiet and I noticed

Redcoats standing in the corridors. My father leaned over to Owen.

"Plenty of military, eh? Trouble in Merthyr, I hear."

"And Dowlais—that is why Sir John Guest is not here and Lady Charlotte is. Very good at scampering is Charlotte when there is trouble."

"Truck trouble again," whispered Griff. "Rioting in the streets and fighting with the Highlanders. We will give them bloody kilts if they come to Garndyrus."

"Prices up and wages down," said Owen. "It is an Act of Parliament to ban the Shops that is wanted, but half the Members pay our wages and the other half sell the goods. What this country wants is an armed rebellion, for it is people like the Guests who are bleeding us."

"And the Irish by the look of you," said Mam, "so enough of politics or we will finish up in carts to Monmouth."

"But he is right," whispered Idris Foreman, tapping us from the seat behind. "All right for the Guests to give money to music, but they are bleeding us dry. Killed more people they have than ten days of the French wars; emptied more sleeves and tied up more trouser legs than six iron-masters put together. The trouble with Lady Charlotte is that she plays the Christian while Bailey plays the devil, which is more honest."

"Quiet!" whispered Mam, smiling kindly at the big hats coming round and the stares for silence. "A real lady is Charlotte, so not a word against her, please."

"To hell with you," said Idris, very hot. "She buys a house in England for thousands of pounds—somewhere to run to from the cholera in Dowlais—but not a hundred pounds will she spend for a new water supply."

"Remove your chops from my shoulder this minute," said my father. "And do not say to hell with my wife or I will have you in bits. Music it is, not politics, this afternoon, and the soldiers are watching us."

God Save The King, then, done on trumpets and drums with Mam and Dada hauling the Howells twins up on their feet as fast as they sat down, and Idris Foreman making rude signs at the soldiers. Very ashamed I was of my town.

"It is this top set that is worrying me," said Owen.

"Knees back, please," said Morfydd, coming in. "I will sit by Mam."

"There is a wicked girl to be late," said my mother, looking daggers. "Where is Richard?"

"Called away on politics and would not say where he was going, so I am not interested much."

"That is a change," I said. "Sharp enough on other people's business usually."

"You shut it," said Morfydd, flaming. "Richard's business is mine now we are going to marry."

"Thank God," I said. "Not before time."

"Hisht!" breathed Mam, for the big hats were coming round again and a Newport bass was into Handel's test piece and raging the nations together three bars ahead of the harpsichord.

"Where is Edwina?" whispered Dada, his finger up.

"Gone to church, is it?" asked Mam.

"Started for church," I said to her, winking.

"And what do you mean by that?" asked Morfydd, pale.

"Where sisters start for and where they end up are two different things. We are not all so daft as we look, mind."

"Eh! Soon I will brain this damned kid!" said Morfydd.

"Quiet, the lot of you," hissed Dada. "It is bad manners and making it hard for the singer."

"Hard for him?" said Owen in misery. "Worried to death I am."

"What is wrong with you?" asked Morfydd, leaning.

"It is this top set," whispered Owen, rattling it. "I caught an Irishman and they are swines for swinging the boot. As sure as fate it will drop during 'Rest in the Lord' Top C."

"*Duwedd!*" exclaimed Morfydd, and went double, holding her stays.

"Mr Owen Howells of Garndyrus," shouted the adjudicator on the platform, pushing the Newport bass out of it.

"Good God," whispered Owen, white as a sheet.

"'Rest in the Lord', is it?" asked Morfydd, swaying and bubbling.

"Aye," said Griff. "Bring up your knees, girl, away I am quick."

"You stay!" said Morfydd sharp. "Would you desert him in his hour of need?"

"That is what Bennet has done to you," I whispered.

"Carry on, carry on, make a good coffin," said she, scowling. "I will have the skin from your backside when I get you in the house!"

"O, for Heaven's sake!" breathed Mam.

Up to the platform went Owen like a man to a gibbet while everybody clapped in recognition of last year's champion, but Griff had his hands over his face.

"Blood will run in the gutters if that top set drops," said he. "He will have every Irishman with boots from here to Killarney."

A harpist for Owen this time, one with a beard to his waist. The mountains could have toppled then and nobody noticed it as his thick old fingers ran swiftly over the strings. Owen braced himself and took his last breath. Three years running we had taken the tenor cup to Garndyrus. Terrible to lose it through an Irishman's boot.

"Mr Owen Howells has changed his mind because of an indisposition," shouted the adjudicator after a lot of nodding and barging on the platform. "'Comfort Ye My People' he will sing instead," which brought the place down, for anything Handel is popular with the Welsh. So we started again and tidy it sounded, and very apt, said Morfydd.

Brave was Owen. The pure notes flowed out despite his split lips. He did the Comforts all right and was proceeding to New Jerusalem when bedlam was let loose. The doors came open and the mob came in with sticks and boots and hit the military right and left for what was going on in Merthyr. Seats were going up and sticks coming down as my father gathered us and raced for the door, taking time to lift the bass cup as he ran, being still champion. Owen kicked the harpist flat and picked up his cup while Griff tripped the organisers who tried to stop him. Down the corridor we went with the women screaming until we reached the Garndyrus contingent, who had run to save us. With half the elders of the town in pursuit we made for the fair stalls where the crowd was thickest.

Very successful was that day in Newport, with two cups to our credit and not having to sing for them. A much happier day than in poor Merthyr where the Highlanders went mad and shot down the rioters for burning their debt to the Shops.

Listen! Otters are barking along the Usk. The June moon is flashing and the arched bridges step over us all the way from Ponty. Faint is the singing of the night-shift Irish as the homecoming barges drift under the shadows of the mountain. The barge-men are astir, yawning and stretching. Women begin their chattering, tired children their crying. Ropes are coiled for flinging, windlasses turn in shrieks as Llanfoist Wharf comes flaring through the mist. To the hostile stares of the Irish who pelted us, we help our women out and into the trams for the climb back to Garndyrus.

The night was black with him, but the canal flares were alight for the night-shift Irish loading limestone for Hereford Tram Inn. Stripped to the waist, every one of them, despite the frosty June. Good breasts on them, some of these Irish girls, with waists like Edwina's and long, black hair flowing over their shoulders, and enough tricks in them, says Mo Jenkins, to satisfy a good Welshman, though hell was let loose if one of them came full, with Paddy this and Paddy that knocking out the locals with knobkerry sticks, trying to find the father, and more than one lump they raised on Iolo Milk.

"*Phist!*" whispered one, lying in the heather clear of the bank. Very pretty she looked with her hand up, begging, and the other holding her baby for milk, feeding it in Foreman's time and God help her if she was found there.

At the foot of the Incline an empty limestone tram was going back up and I jumped it and lay there watching the stars step over the trees as it climbed. How pure is a cold evening when you are lying in a tram climbing up the face of a mountain! The loveliness of God's earth comes into you, its beauty new in the phantom shapes of trees in moonlight. There is a smell of sweetness from the branches and nightingales are singing above the rumble of the tram, and you begin to compare this beauty with the lives of humans and the messes they get into, for Morfydd was on my mind. And half the mess is caused by this baby business, which, according to what Mo Jenkins lets loose at times, is not very attractive. And even when you have babies there is a bother feeding them, like the Irish girl feeding hers with one hand and begging with the other. Better, I think, to lie in a tram watching the stars go by in the brilliance of summer moonlight.

CHAPTER SEVEN

NEXT SPRING I joined the Benefit Club and went into politics, which were coming more popular that year, and with good reason. Cholera was sweeping the mountains, coming from Dowlais, it was said, because of the water pollution. It got through Merthyr and along The Top, killing hundreds, and picked off a few in our town, and they were felling the trees in Clydach Valley for coffins. The prices in the Tommy Shops were going up monthly because the price of iron in foreign markets was coming down, according to the owners, although what one had to do with the other only St Peter knew, said the pamphlets. Men with big families to feed were fainting at the furnaces and falling under trams and the secret Union was calling for strikes and the workers for armed revolution.

Yes, politics were popular, outright criticism of Church and Throne rampant, and Bennet was at pains to say where his sympathies lay, which did not please my father.

"It would have been more honest had he said he was in politics," said Dada one night.

"Do you splash your business all over town?" asked Morfydd.

"A mention would have been polite," said my mother. "We have enough trouble getting a living as it is without you marrying into a working-class Union, and a London one at that."

"Safe houses make cowards of us," replied Morfydd, set for a fight as usual. "But trouble is coming and we need men like Richard and Frost to lead us."

"There is a trouble-maker," said Mam. "Williams, Partridge, Frost—all tarred with the same brush. They will lead us to transportation before they are finished."

"Mr John Frost is a very fine gentleman," I said sharp.

"Hush, Iestyn," whispered Morfydd.

My father frowned at me. "And what do you know of Frost?"

"Only what I read in *The Merlin*."

"Confine it to that. There is not enough room for two anarchists in this house." He levelled his pipe at Morfydd. "Listen. This town works for one of the best masters on the mountains. If I worked in Merthyr, Dowlais or Nantyglo I would have need of a Union. But under Mr Hill I hold no brief for Benefit Clubs, National Unions or Charters that will never be obtained, for the men who make these organisations are of the same greed as their masters. Those are my views, now away to your torchlight meeting, but do not expect me to fight for you when the military pack you and your friends in carts for Monmouth."

"And what of Jethro and Iestyn? You have seen your generation go from bad to worse under the English. . . ."

"And it would probably be worse under the Welsh all the time we are sitting on iron and coal—as for Jethro, he must manage in his generation as I have managed in mine."

"A selfish, cowardly view," whispered Morfydd. "This house has no manhood, and I would be better out of it."

"Then go!" Suddenly raging, my father rose and flung down his paper. "As soon as you like out of it, for I am sick to death of your politics and slanders. Every day it is the same— Lovett, Frost, Williams. Pigs of ironmasters and starvation wages. Not a single word of loyalty, not one of religion. You would be better on your knees thanking God for what we have given you than whipping the house into a ferment."

Threats to leave from Morfydd. Go, and to hell, from Dada, with Mam sitting behind her spinning-wheel putting in one here and one there, her eyes brimming with tears and saying she had something to do with the pair of them and God knows who is right.

Sick at heart, I left them. Every family was quarrelling then —the old people talking about the good old days and loyalty to the masters and thank God for being hungry. The young people were creeping over the roofs at night to attend the torchlight meetings where men like Bennet, missionaries from the new London Union, hammered into them William Lovett's four demands from Parliament, which were the aims of the Union. The old generation was deaconing in Chapel, bowing to Royalty and keeping the bishops in finery. The new generation was forging pike-heads and moulding iron shot for the little square cannons, and God help the Members of Parliament if the Four Points of the Charter were not granted. A printing press had been dug into a mountain cave and every week a pamphlet circulated denouncing the masters; telling of the prosperity of the iron trade and why wages should be raised and how much Robert Thomas Crawshay had put into his bank since a year last Friday, and the number of singles and twins a wicked old man of commerce was paying for already.

Very informative were those pamphlets, very dangerous, said my father.

And on the barren stretches of coastline from the West Country up to Newport arms were being landed by night.

It was cold for spring that night. A lot of Irishwomen were standing around the Company Shop looking at the food and watching Mervyn Jones hopping about inside and smiling his rhubarb smile, always a sign that he was giving underweight. Next door the Drum and Monkey was packed to the windows with men, and more going in from shift. Billy Handy, landlord of the Garndyrus Inn, was slapping the backs of others going in for their pay.

"Room inside for another," said he with a wicked wink. "But since they are handing out money for work you can make home, for it is something the Mortymers have never been guilty of."

"Had mine," I told him, for still being on the Nantyglo books we were paid out at Garndyrus with Crawshay Bailey's money. "And knit your teeth before you lose them."

A cheeky little face had Billy Handy, I thought. Very pleasant he would look with no teeth. He was to be my first man; I had always fancied him for laying out. Not much taller than me he was inches broader. I hated Billy Handy because he was beer mad. It was said that he had a nice little bit tucked away, too, every penny made out of misery. Get into debt at his inn and he would have the trews from your sister-in-law for selling in Abergavenny market. He was also a pig-sticker, slitting them for money and enjoyment; a man who worked in hot blood through a season of pigs and then beat his breast in Chapel and called down blessings on his innocent soul.

The masters always paid out in the beer-houses. In our town they sometimes paid in silver, but Crawshay Bailey of Nantyglo paid in brass, coins he minted himself, and if a man wanted silver to spend in the open market he paid Bailey six-pence in the pound for the privilege. The Bailey coins could only be used in Bailey's Shops, where the prices of goods were often thirty per cent higher. The secret pamphlets were against payment of wages in the beer-houses, for the beer-houses were owned by the masters, too, and their pay-masters always arrived late so that a man could drink on credit for hours before getting paid, and then be too drunk to count it. There was the time when Big Rhys Jenkins drew what was left of his six weeks' pay at two o'clock in the morning and rolled home drunk with thirty shillings in his pocket. Few of the workers were any good at figures except my father, and he worked out that Rhys must have drunk two hundred quarts that pay night. Had he drunk twenty he would not have been standing, so the rest of the money must have been shared between paymaster, landlord and master.

Above the hoarse shouting and laughter of the men inside I heard dice being rolled and remembered that it was Benefit Club night. Later, there would be a visit from the Garndyrus Benefit and a fight and a smashing of windows, so I put my hands in my pockets and walked on.

Will Tafarn, I saw first. Along the top of North Street he came rolling and singing drunk. Not a hair on his body had Will, for the furnace blow-back that had twisted his mind had stripped him. Belching, he swayed before me.

"Fifteen pints tonight, Iestyn Mortymer. By Heaven! Little Will can still sink it, eh? And a good little hazel stick to have the backside from that woman of mine, is it?" and he lifted the stick, his one eye shining from his white, scalded face.

"She is minding her children, Will," I said. "Not a man but you has touched her."

"She-cat!" he whispered. "The moment my back is turned a tom is between her, so tonight I will bitch her."

Laughing, waving the stick, he was off, for tonight was pay night, and it was a pay night when the molten iron came from the furnace bung like a shaft of fire and took him in the face. And when they doused him with whisky at the Drum and Monkey and carried him home and put him on his bed his wife's brother was in it, visiting from Risca. . . .

So every pay night Martha Tafarn had it black and blue in exchange for the money. I gave her a thought as she watched from her window with her three children locked in the bedroom.

Little Willie Gwallter was out with his mam and I stood aside and knocked up my cap to her.

"Good evening, Mrs Gwallter, good evening, Willie."

"Good evening, Iestyn, *bach*. Seen my husband, have you?" Thin and pale she was and worried about the drinking.

"No, Mrs Gwallter," I lied, for I had just seen Gwallter parting his beard in the Lamb Row Public and pouring in a quart without a swallowing.

"Looking for him, see," she said. "Here is Willie and me without a crust of bread in the house and not a penny to bless us. A pig of a man is Mr Gwallter on pay nights but good otherwise, mind. Never a finger he puts on wife and child, like some I could mention," and she nodded at Will Tafarn who was crawling home, lashing the gutter with his stick. "Aye, a happy family, the three of us." She sighed at the moon and I took the chance to get a penny into Willie's hand. "Only on dirty old pay nights when Mr Gwallter do sink it. *Ach y fi!*"

"Goodbye," I said, raising my cap, and she hurried away

dragging Willie after her, his big, hungry eyes sending thanks over his shoulder.

I walked on. Many of the Irish were coming down from the Tumble, wild in their shouting and singing. Big men, they were, many of them bearded, with their little shrivels of wives and women hanging on their arms and everyone swearing to rise Satan's eyebrows. It was as dark as curtains in Rhyd-y-nos Street, for the women of our town were hard against street lamps, and right, too. It is not every wife who wants the neighbours to count from upstair windows the value of her basket after a visit to the Company Shop, with the shillings and pence in the back pews of Chapel on Sundays.

A little friend I found on the street, shivering to have her teeth out. Hungry days for humans, these, but hungrier still for dogs.

"Oi oi," I said, "has your old mam dried up? Have to eat, *fach*." I gave her bread I had been carrying for days, and if she had eaten that month I doubt it.

"With me?" I asked her, and her little brown tail went round. A glance up the street and I was away heavier, for if a well-covered bitch crossed the path of the Irish on a pay night she was likely to end in a pot at mid-month. Under my coat with her, button it tight, good evenings and good nights right and left to neighbours, for sure as fate if you hate the bloody sight of them you will meet twenty, and away went the pair of us down to the Company Park for a look at the gentry.

When I got to the corner of Queen Street I heard the sound of the Benefit Club procession. In no time it appeared, with Billy Handy striding at its head, the swine, waving the colours on a stick. On either side of him were the torch-bearers, and one was Mo Jenkins.

"Hoi, Iestyn!" yelled he.

"Go to hell," I said.

But this was a fine procession. Owen and Griff Howells were blasting on tenor trombones. Mr Gwallter had the big drum on his stomach, hitting it for holes, and Will Blaenavon was puffing deep with him on the bass horn. Next came the flutes and whistles and Mr Roberts on the ophiclyde and hard behind him Iolo Milk with the serpentine, ending with Evans the Death on Enid Donkey and Phil Benjamin hanging on to her tail. Pretty good it sounded, too, considering most of them could hardly stand. Behind came a crowd like the French Revolution with sticks and staves and banners, making enough commotion to bring out Brecon Garrison. Mo scrambled a path through the crowd and gripped me.

"Come on in, man—do not stand there gaping."

"What is happening?" I asked.

"Hang me for a bastard," said Mo. "This is the Benefit. Round the town twice and then to the Drum and Monkey for a talk to by the Union speakers."

"Finish up in Monmouth, all of you," I said.

"Free beer afterwards, mind!"

"My father will see me and hell will set alight."

"In this crowd? Easier to nip a flea in a wig-sack. Here, take a swig of this to cheer you up for you look miserable to death," and I swigged twice at his gin bottle and the little bitch popped out and sniffed it and sneezed.

"Up with it again," said Mo.

It is amazing how nice raw gin can taste during a procession.

"Will Tafarn is back home beating his wife," I said.

"Aye," said Mo. "I have just heard her howling. Back with that bottle. *Diawl*, there will be a row when your dada smells your breath and thank God I will not be there at the slaughter."

"To hell with my dada," I said.

Wonderful is the feeling of just getting drunk. And there is nothing like marching with comrades, either, for the tramp of boots on a frosty road takes a swing at the senses when the shoulders barging you are the shoulders of town brothers and the band you are marching to is the best in the Eastern Valley. Down Heol-y-nant we went with every window in the place going up and bedsheets and tablecloths waving out.

"Down with your cap, Iestyn," whispered Mo. "Your mam is up at the window."

"Room for her," I said. "Tell her she is welcome."

"Quick!" hissed Big Rhys, and he heaved up his belly and

pulled me under his flaps. "She will have your father out and half the town will be mutilated," and the pair of us walked past my house with Big Rhys bowing this way and that, his thighs hitting me in the behind.

The door of the Drum and Monkey was wide open as we wheeled up by the market place and tramped in. Down went the instruments and straight up to the bar went the band, hammering it for beer. Polly Morgan was too slow by halves and Will Blaenavon lifted her into the crowd for kicking out and began to draw the jugs. Amazing how attractive women look through neat gin. Very severe about Polly Morgan I had been since the night of humiliation, but she would not have stood much chance now. Over our heads she went, upright one moment, head down the next, with her legs bare to the waist and screaming for a pig-sticking. Out she went sharp, for a room of Benefit drinkers is no place for a woman; nor Irish either, come to that, and a pair of Kildare men went after her with Gwallter's boot behind them. Will was serving foaming jugs and Mo got two and was through the legs of the crowd to our corner.

"Down with this, boyo," he whispered. "You are not a paid-up member, see, and it is asking for a ducking."

I had just got my teeth into it when Dic Shon Ffyrnig the Chairman came up with a book and pencil. "A shilling for membership, if you please, or out on your ear and Mo Jenkins with you for introducing a scab."

"He has money to pay, I doubt it," said Billy Handy, "so let the chairman see the colour of it or I will be happy to kick him out."

"A shilling," I said, counting it out. "And do not forget the receipt." A look of wonder on their faces then, for I do not think they had a shilling between them, and if mine went into the Fund for Children it would be a surprise. Often my father had said that more money went up against the wall of Dic Shon Ffyrning's house than ever reached the Benefit Funds. No sight of a receipt, anyway, and next moment Dic Shon was up on a chair patting his belly. A good talker this one, with a plum for a face and a watch-chain over his waistcoat like the chains around Parliament. "Gentlemen, gentlemen," he began. "Wonderful it is to have for each other this great companionship, and very happy is your chairman to welcome you to this glorious anniversary of the Benefit," and he lowered his face and threw out his palms and blessed us. Very holy, it all was.

"And wasting our bloody time, too," roared Owen Howells. "Union men are speaking on the Coity tonight and here we are listening to speeches from tap-room barristers who can do nothing but spout about benefits."

"To hell with the Benefit," bawled Griff the Twin. "I am for a Union."

"And me for a Charter," cried Owen. "A Union first, perhaps, but Lovett's Four Points eventually, and down with the Benefit."

Dic Shon Ffyrnig spat. "From the mouths of sucklings," he cried. "Shut the trap and quick. I, Ffyrnig, have been calling for a Union of workers before the pair of you were on tits, and I organised this Benefit before you knew there was a bloody mountain—so remember it."

"And feathering your nest with the funds," shouted Owen. "To hell with Benefits, I say—a lot of damned subscriptions and nothing coming back."

Most grave was this, apparently. The men went quiet. Terrible to see the look on Ffyrnig's face, for the remark had cut him to the quick. "Am I to understand," he began, "that I am being accused by hints of confiscating public money?"

"Aye," I said without thinking. "A shilling I paid minutes back and still no sign of a receipt," and I was sharp back to my corner with Mo after me.

"The boy is right," said Mr Gwallter. "Take Afel Hughes here. Pounds and pounds he has paid into this Benefit, Ffyrnig, yet his wife is still with the Irish in straw and his Ceinwen girl six feet down, eh, Afel?"

And Mr Hughes nodded, his eyes bright in his gaunt face. Never touched a drop, did Hughes, and very strong for the Benefit.

"But Afel Hughes has not paid six months yet," cried Ffyrnig. "Can I draw money from stone, think you? Upon my soul, gentlemen, I am not a magician to rise sick women from straw and dead children from graves. Fifteen pounds we have in the funds, and how far will that go if the owners put us on the blacklist or discharge labour? How far will it go if we decide on strike action tonight? You have an excellent example of defeat through lack of funds in Merthyr, who could have won her case through the courts had she had the money to pay lawyers."

"She would have needed millions to oppose Crawshay, so talk sense," said Big Rhys. "How do the funds stand, you say?"

"Fifteen pounds," said Ffyrnig.

"There is a queer figure," said Will Blaenavon. "And ten shillings might have saved Ceinie Hughes. Where are the shillings and bloody ha'pennies?"

Bedlam.

Dic Shon Ffyrnig stamped upon his chair. "Order, order, gentlemen. Mr Handy, kindly serve the members with another round, for it is beer we are needing to make us sociable."

"To hell with the beer, it can come later," said Big Rhys, pushing to the front. "Not a good man at figures, I am, but it do strike me that fifteen pounds is a small amount for the members to have saved over six months, and with the greatest of respect, Mr Ffyrnig, I would propose that somebody outside the Benefit and good at sums like Hywel Mortymer should have a look at your accounts."

"Over my dead body," shouted Ffyrnig, blue round the chops. "Mr Billy Handy has signed my accounts and I will not have scum like Mortymer near them, for he is not even a member."

"It is the principle with Hywel Mortymer, not the penny a week," said Big Rhys, "and sorry you will be for mentioning names in public, Ffyrnig, for Mortymer's boy is here and his father will come and squeeze subscriptions from your belly and cut off your privates for roasting."

"Aye," said a voice.

Six men stood at the door. Never have I seen their like for size and ferocity, but never in dreams a man like Dai Probert, their leader. He could have given my father a foot in height and another across the shoulders. He was ragged, one arm bare. The bearskin around his waist dangled to a point at his feet. His face, like Will Tafarn's, was parched by a furnace blow-back; one eye, criss-crossed with scars, was a red socket. In his hand he gripped a cudgel, and around him pressed his supporters, every man armed with iron spikes for leg-breaking. Mo put his elbow into my ribs.

"Scotch Cattle," he whispered. "Under the table with us quick, for now there is going to be trouble. Come to enforce Union membership, see?"

Very cheeky was Big Rhys, his father. With one hand in his belt and the other dangling his drinking-mug, he sauntered towards them.

"Nantyglo, is it?" he asked, innocent.

"Aye." The Bull looked past Big Rhys, adding the strength of the Benefit.

"Then get out," said Rhys. "When we form a Union it will be from this town and no invitations sent to Nanty."

"Before we damned move you, Dai Probert," added Owen Howells in his light fighter's voice.

Probert grinned. "Backward in this town and no mistake," said he. "Talking about Benefit Clubs and a penny a week and living on the blood of the workers in Blackwood." Thrusting Owen and Rhys aside he walked up to Dic Shon Ffyrnig, caught him by the watch-chain and pulled him from the chair. "Too much Benefit membership and too little Union will be the death of a few of you before you are finished." He threw Dic Shon away and he stumbled the length of the room and landed in the arms of Afel Hughes and lay there, staring and trembling. Probert turned to Big Rhys. "And you," he said. "Clever with your mouth, eh? Get out, is it?"

"And quick," said Rhys, "or we will have the six of you in salted hams and hanging from hooks."

Mo whispered, "Listen, you! My father is after him. Watch now, for he has always wanted a Scotch Cattle Bull."

"And bloody got one," I said. "If he puts a finger on this boy he will be slabbed for burial."

"Do you stand for a Union, man?" Probert asked Rhys.

"No," said Rhys, "and I will trim the chops from any man who does, so make a ring and take your guard."

"Is it clean in here?" asked Probert, looking around.

"As clean as a nut, boy. To a finish, is it? I am no man for breathers if I fight for William the Fourth."

"Right, you," said Probert, untying his bearskin. "To the grave, if you like, and when I have done with you I am breaking the legs of every man in here who does not show a Union card."

"First one down gets hobnails," said Rhys, circling, his left hand out. "God help you, Probert, for you have tangled with a professional." His left came out, smashing into the big man's face. The room was silent. There was no sound but the creak of the boards under the feet of the fighters. And then, with a look of terror in his eyes, Big Rhys dropped his fists and stared at the window.

"Good God," he breathed. "The Military!"

Like a top Dai Probert spun, and Rhys was into him with a terrible right-hander that laid open the bone above his single eye. Arms waving, he dropped. The boards shuddered under his twenty solid stones. Rising to his knees, he knelt there, shaking his great head. Blood dripped, splashing.

"Dirty swine," said Probert.

"Aye," said Big Rhys, still circling. "I will be as dirty here as you have been in Blackwood. Up, you big cow, and I will hand you more than you would have from a Carmarthen slaughterer."

"Very handy is my dada with Scotch Cattle Bulls," said Mo.

And as he spoke the door opened and Idris Foreman stood there, half the size of Rhys Jenkins. His eyes took in the scene.

"Dai Probert, eh?" said he. "Up to your tricks here?" His little wrinkled face moved from one to the other. "Big heads and no brains, and no loss to the Union either of you. Away to the counter and drink together and learn sense." He waved his arms in a sudden anger. "All of you back to the bar!"

"There is a pity," whispered Mo. "Bleeding to death he was, and in his shroud in two minutes. Never mind, we will have him after the speeches." He jerked his thumb. "Guests are coming tonight, see?"

"Guests?"

"Your sister!" hissed Mo. "Look you, boy!"

With the bitch held tightly against me I watched Morfydd follow Bennet through the door and into the tap-room. Pale and sad she looked; beautiful in her black, full-skirted dress and her long hair tied with blue ribbons. My father was right, I thought. This was the end of her, for it is one thing to spout fireside politics but another to shout them in public with Redcoats sewing their ears to keyholes and agents of the gentry lying flat under floorboards.

Idris Foreman jumped on to a chair. "Gentlemen and ladies," he began. "Tonight being the feast of the Benefit and a special occasion, I have brought from Nantyglo a guest speaker from the National Union of Working Classes and Others, so give him a fair hearing. For whether you vote for the Benefit Club or the Union one thing is certain—it is time to unite under one flag, so pay heed to suggestions," and down he jumped and up got Bennet ready for fighting. Moans and groans left and right now, for there are enough Englishmen as agents, collectors, schoolmasters and reformers without having to stomach them as friends of the Welsh.

"Go north and see to them up in Lancashire!" shouted Rhys.

"A fair hearing!" roared Idris Foreman, and we all went respectable and quiet, for Idris was big in the Union.

"Gentlemen," began Bennet. "As Idris here has told you, I have been sent by your English brothers to unify working-class labour under a single flag. . . ."

"Ay," said Owen Howells, "a bloody red one and to hell with you for we are not having foreign interference in home affairs."

"A white one," said Bennet. "And when it turns red you will see me sharper out of collective bargaining than any man here. As for home affairs, you have none, nor are you en-

96

titled to any while you sit and whine about exploitation. Are you the only victims? Christ, but I wish you were, for the Union's task would be easy! The exploitation of the workers runs from north, south, east and west to every corner of the country. The evil forged by Throne and Church dominates our towns as well as yours, and while we are making the weapons to fight it you are sitting on your backsides paying pennies into Benefit Clubs."

"This is insulting!" cried Dic Shon Ffyrnig, shocked.

"Shut it!" shouted Idris Foreman. "It is the truth."

"The truth or not," said Big Rhys with a chuckle. "It is sedition and very handy. Let us hear more, Englishman."

"You shall," said Bennet. "The Throne is in hand with the Church and the Church is in hand with the Devil. And while the bishops are gabbling the sanctity of the monarch in the eyes of God the monarch is frittering away fortunes amassed by the starvation of factory children. A pleasant union, this one. Then the monarch blesses the bishops and grants them palaces earned by the rent of prostitution. To make my position doubly clear to you, I say down with the king and off with his head and roast the devils of the Church alive as you once did in old Carmarthen."

"Good God," said Owen Howells.

Very respectful was the Benefit now, as befits a tap-room listening to first-class sedition, for a word outside and Bennet would have stood for hanging, drawing and quartering.

"Yes," said Bennet. "Good God. It is time somebody spoke the truth for it has been whispered around corners far too much in Wales. There is too much spouting in private and too little action in public, which is a shame to a country that gave birth to Owen Glyndwr. There is too much self-pity, too, if nobody minds me saying it—you are not the only ones exploited by my countrymen. Slaves are still being sold in Bristol by men who go on their knees in church. Do you beat your children to save them a flogging by the factory overman? Are your little ones plunged into water to revive them and keep them at the machines? Are they beaten and starved before their mothers? For all this happens in the mills

97

of Lancashire. Do you keep foster-mothers in milk to suckle the babies of the poor because the mothers are too starved to bring forth milk? Do not stare at me. Go down on your knees and be thankful you are Welsh and pay your pennies into drunken Benefit Clubs and to hell with anyone else, eh?"

"Mark your words," said Billy Handy.

"And you your tongue before I come down there and pluck it out," cried Bennet. "For it is the likes of you and Ffyrnig I am roasting. The Welsh Benefit Clubs were founded upon friendship by saints, not men, but they have been murdered by men like you, their funds stolen and their principle of common decency depraved. You take the money and give back nothing. You are the tools of the masters, worse than scum. And yet you have served us. Men like you have proved that the Benefit Club is not only useless but the coward's cure of an ill. Yours is a defence against the filthy conditions, not an attack. The Benefit Clubs are being abandoned throughout the land as useless, the Union is taking their place. And from the Union will spring Lovett's Charter of decency. . . ."

This brought cheers. Many were strong for the Union's new Charter, especially men like Afel Hughes, who were all for cannon and gunpowder under the Houses of Parliament, all Members present.

"No longer will you be driven to the polls to vote for Whig or Tory according to the whim of your masters," shouted Bennet. "Your Union will give you secret ballot, paid Members of your choice, not the lackeys of the aristocracy who make laws to suit the Throne."

The beer was going round now and everybody chattering, always a good sign for a speaker. Bennet had got them going and he knew it. His fist was swinging an inch from their noses. "And next will come adult male suffrage—the right of every man to vote—for why should the policy of the country be formed by a privileged few? These are the aims of the Union —attack, not defence, so away with your Benefit. Wind them up, share what is left of their funds and pay your penny to the Union which stands for the comradeship of men irrespective of creed or colour. Force the masters to new conditions of labour, make them disgorge their profits. Live for your Union—die for it if needs be, and it will be the guardian of your new generations!"

Bedlam now. Typical of the Welsh, this; to hell with him one moment, follow him to the scaffold the next. The door came open and Dic Shon Ffyrnig went through it sharp and Billy Handy was only spared because he was holding Benefit money. Mugs were going up and drinks going down and everybody shouting and fishing out pennies for the new Union. I saw Morfydd's eyes glowing as she took Bennet through the door and Idris Foreman only stayed long enough to issue Union cards. Very happy it all was with Scotch Cattle slapping each other's backs and roars of laughter as jokes went round. And then it happened. Dai Probert's mug went up as Big Rhys cracked him solid with the right. Across the room he staggered, hit the wall and sat down.

"Changed my mind, see," said Rhys. "I am not drinking with Scotch Cattle, and it do seem a pity to let a good fight go by."

Dead silence, and Mo whispered, "Now's our chance, boyo. Here, take this chair leg. Down among their legs and hit their feet from under them."

The men were dividing, the Cattle to the right of the bar, the town men to the left. Nobody shifted then until Afel Hughes took off his glasses—always a sign of trouble. Over in a corner Evans the Death was slipping little bands of iron over his knuckles. And as Will Blaenavon leaped the counter with a barrel-tapper in his fist, the Cattle rushed with Probert leading.

Well.

If the ancient Welsh had fought the Romans as we fought the Blackwood Cattle that night the devils would never have built Caerleon. Men went down like pit-props. Afel Hughes was flat before he got his glasses away, with Mr Roberts on top of him. Big Rhys had got Probert on his knees again and Griff Howells was hitting everyone in sight, while Owen caught a Cattle the prettiest left hook I have ever witnessed,

99

laying him quiet and ready for burial. Dirty Billy Handy had another by the fork of his trews, screwing hard while the devil danced like a Scot and screamed at the ceiling until he was backed through the door and kicked into the gutter. A dirty fighter was Billy Handy, for a man's privates are entitled to respect, especially when fighting. Mo and I were crawling among their legs now, tapping the unconscious ones to make sure and cracking at the shins of the living. I was helping Mr Hughes find his spectacles when I came face to face on all fours with Billy Handy as he was reaching up for another set of trews, so I swung my chair leg and hit him out. Never have I heard such a commotion. Men were slipping on broken glass and the seats of trews were cut to tatters. Big Rhys was giving Dai Probert the hobnails and he was bellowing to deafen—size ten, took Rhys, and every kick was going well in. Will Blaenavon was slumped in a corner, Mr Gwallter was flat on his back with Mr Roberts and two Scotch Cattle under him, and Owen and Griff Howells were into one another because of the shortage. But every enemy was down and out when Polly Morgan threw a stone through the window.

"The Military!" she screamed.

"Excuse me," said Mo, "I am getting from here," and he pushed me aside and kicked his way through the nearest window with me after him followed by the others, for it is amazing how the dead will rise and walk when the Military get among them. There was a crowd of Chapel people outside wagging their heads and slapping their Bibles and I was straight through them, up North Street and down High Street to the safety of the tombstones. There, under cover, I straightened my clothes and brushed myself down, then, hands in pockets and whistling, I made my way home and vaulted the gate at the back.

My father was leaning against the shed, pipe in hand, looking at the moon.

"A little activity in town tonight," said he, very formal.

"Aye," I replied. "Sickening, it is—always the same on Benefit Night."

"Did you see the procession?"

"*Jawch*, no! I have been walking from Abergavenny."

"Then you have not seen the Military in town?"

My face showed wonderment.

"Come then," said he. "I was thinking of a stroll up the Hill. We will watch them looking for the trouble-makers," and he smiled and took my arm and steered me through the gate.

Up North Street we went in the moonlight. There was a crowd of drunken Irish outside the Drum and Monkey and the mounted Redcoats were plunging among them, looking for disturbers. The Chapel people were still outside Staffordshire Row muttering and scolding, and Tomos Traherne was among them.

"Fighting and drinking, as usual," he told my father. "The drunken Benefit plagueing the town on its feast night. But agitators visited and Union cards were issued—to say nothing of sedition and the king's name spoken in defiance." And he bowed deep and grinned at me. "Very happy I am to see you safely with your father and away from such evil. Good night, Iestyn Mortymer."

"Very pleased with you is Mr Traherne, it seems," said my father up by Cae White.

Gapers here; all the neighbours in the kingdom, whistling and chattering like monkeys, and isn't it a scandal and not fit for decent people, with fingers wagging and tongues raised and giving it to everybody from the Mayor of Abergavenny to William the Fourth. I blew my nose to cover my face when I saw Polly Morgan giggling, and when I took my hand down I came face to face with Billy Handy and Dic Shon Ffyrnig. White as a sheet was Billy from the chair leg I had caught him, but he smiled sweet and pure and bowed low to my father.

"Good evening, Mr Mortymer," said he.

"Good evening, Mr Handy."

"A pleasant evening it is indeed, Mr Mortymer, dear me."

"To be sure, Mr Handy," replied my father.

"Too pleasant for neighbours to be mixing with Scotch Cattle Bulls and anarchists and hitting each other out with chair legs," said Dic Shon Ffyrnig, and he lifted the cap from Billy Handy's head and the lump I had raised was as big as a duck's egg and sparkling.

"Solid oak chair legs," said Billy Handy, glum.

"But we will have the bastard, mind," said Dic Shon, "and begging your pardon for the language, deacon."

"And quick," said Billy Handy. "Marked I am now, but in bloody strips he will be when we catch him, and iron bars it will be, not chair legs, eh, Iestyn Mortymer?"

"Indeed," I said.

On we went and turned down High Street.

"A terrible thing to strike a man down with a weapon," said my father, "even a man like Billy Handy. And thankful I am that my son has no need for such treachery, which saves me the bother of flogging it out of him with a mule whip, for if there is a man I cannot stand it is one who hits from behind."

"Aye," I said, sweating.

Crowds of people were huddled outside the school, most of them nodding and bowing to my father most respectfully, and from them came Mr Gwallter, one eye shut tight, blood down his muffler, and stinking of beer to strip varnish from pews.

"Take my hand, Mr Mortymer!" cried he, swaying. "I am one of the Benefit who hit out the Cattle, and proud of it, not skulking. And if my little Willie do grow like your Iestyn, with the courage of a lion and fists to match, then thank God for him!"

"Aye," said my father, handling him gently aside with the smile he always kept for those of poorer intellect. "Home to your wife now, my good man."

"Not like you for drinking, of course," went on Gwallter while I cursed his soul into everlasting hell, "for Iestyn can sink them, and I know you never touch a drop. But for fighting he stands proud with you, man. After the show he put up tonight I would back him against Big Rhys Jenkins."

"Good night, Mr Gwallter," said my father, pushing him aside firmly, and we walked on with my body going colder every step.

"A terrible man for the beer that Mr Gwallter," said my father when we got clear. "He is dazed in the head with drinking and fighting—getting you mixed up with Mo Jenkins, no doubt."

"Aye," I replied, shivering.

"For Mo is strong for the Benefit processions and its feast nights."

"Yes," I said.

"And you were nowhere near the Drum and Monkey but down in Abergavenny, if I remember?"

I closed my eyes, dripping.

Not a word from either of us as we walked on. I gave quick glances at his white shirt. Very sick I felt. It was the first time I had lied to my father, and by the look of him now it would be the last.

"Dada," I said, stopping him, "I have been drinking with Mo Jenkins at the Benefit and round town in the procession and hitting them out with chair legs."

"Well done, my son," said he without a blink. "Never let a Judas betray you, for I would rather lose both hands than hear you repeat a lie. A good boy you are, Iestyn."

There was never a relief greater than mine. "Thank you, Dada," I said.

"But the lie has been told, if not repeated," said he, "and it is demanding punishment. Home now, the pair of us, for a hammering you will not forget this side of Christmas."

Mam was sitting at the fire, going hard at her spinning-wheel when we got in. Edwina, behind the door, was reading the Book. Not so much as a blink from either of them as I came by, and I knew that in this room, not an hour before, I had been tried, convicted and sentenced.

"Into the bedroom," said my father. "Drunkenness and fighting must be stamped out in a decent family before it takes a grip."

"O, Hywel!" sobbed Mama then.

"Silence, woman," said my father. "What would you have me breed—drunkards, rowdies and chair-leg fighters? Out of the house if you cannot stomach it."

A lonely place is the stairs when they lead to the place of punishment, each one creaking like a tumbril. Into the bedroom now. Sit on Morfydd's bed and await the persecutor. Up like lightning as the door comes open. But my mother stands there.

"*Cariad Anwyl!*" said she, choked. "Terrible that our dada is going to lay hands on you, the first of the family."

"Do not upset yourself," I said. "It is me who is having it."

"O my precious," she breathed, "it is the drinking, see— not the silly old Benefit or the fighting, for drinking is the devil incarnate in a house, so have the thrashing just to please me, is it?"

There is a damned woman for sense.

"Downstairs fast," I said, "before he has the pair of us with the same fist."

Downstairs with her, upstairs with Edwina, all her coldness gone, weeping to float ships.

"Iestyn!" she sobbed. "O, Iestyn."

Pitiful are women, one moment stern and cold, the next wet with tears and sympathy. Shivering is in them, a blueness of the face, and trembling hands; loving, yearning, protecting. Weak to bring a man to weakness, and out of patience.

I preferred my father.

Slam went the back door, slam went the kitchen door.

"O, Hywel!" cried my mother, and caught at him.

"Away!" he roared.

Up the stairs now with a giant's tread. The door of the room nearly came from its hinges.

"Out of it," said he, twisting Edwina away.

Slam went the bedroom door to bring down plaster, and he faced me.

"Right, you," he said. "I will give you chair-leg bloody fighting."

Aye. Pretty good reason to remember the night I went into politics.

CHAPTER EIGHT

BEER AND politics have something in common, I found. Men get drunk on both. All that year it was mountain meetings and Unions, Benefit Clubs and secret pamphlets. All over The Top from Hirwaun to Blaenavon the towns were going on fire with the politics; sending their deputations to the ironmasters demanding higher wages and lower Tommy Shop prices. But masters are no respecters of the working-man's rights when the Irish are waiting in their thousands to slave till they drop for a pound of potatoes. The trickle from Ireland widened into a flood that threatened to sink Welsh labour for a generation. But the Welsh and the men of Staffordshire were key men, and they knew it. Soon the tram road men came out, then the forge workers and the rollers. When the puddlers threw down their tools the strike spread like a fire over the mountains. Furnaces were blown out in Risca and Tredegar at the start of winter, mills were broken in Dowlais and tram roads levered up in Nanty. Armed meetings were held in mountain caves and lonely inns. Weapons were being forged with masters' iron in masters' time. The uneasy peace in my town could not last. In the grip of snow, up to their middles in debt to the Company Shop, the men in a body came out on strike.

Sad was my town that winter. The warm red glow was gone from The Top and the moon hung brilliant and cold over the mountains, glinting on the little square windows of the frozen houses, for one in twenty had a fire. The peak of Pen-y-fal and the ridge of the Blorenge were crystal white, guardians of the blackened furnaces of The Top, where the children of the valley Irish, always the first, had begun to die.

But there was food in Heol Garegog, said Tomos Traherne, and the rest of the town starving to death. Food in plenty, thanks to Iolo Milk, for to give the chap credit he always feeds what belongs to him, whether entered in Chapel records or not.

Have a peep through Mrs Pantrych's window for proof. Amazing, said Gwennie Lewis. I cannot believe my eyes, said Mrs Tossach. Tread gently in the snow.

Come nearer.

Here is Mrs Pantrych, beaming, wheezing, large about the stomach with her, busy round her kitchen. In the family way again is Mrs Pantrych; fetching them out as fast as rabbits, says Mrs Gwallter.

"Any day now, Ifor boy," said Mrs Pantrych to her eldest.

"That will be a load off my mind, Selwyn," she croons to her youngest. "The head is well down, girl—waiting for my sign," she tells her Betti.

Six little Pantrychs sitting at the table, backs straight, knives and forks up like Highlanders' bayonets, every one the image of Iolo Milk.

"Hurry, Mama!"

"Hungry as hunters."

"Let us have it now, girl—never mind the basting."

"Good God," said Ivor. "How much longer?"

Bang bang on the cups, roll the plates around, kick him under the table, somebody has her by the hair. Up a dando, boyo! *Phew*, there's a stink! Blodwen is doing it in her trews again—off with them quick, lads, and out of the window for airing.

"Eh dear," whispers Ieun, staring out.

"What the hell has happened now?" asks Mrs Pantrych.

"Blodwen's trews, Mam. I have dropped them on Grandfer Ffyrnig, look you."

"Good grief! Were they wet or full, then?"

"Full," shouts Mrs Shon Ffyrnig from downstairs, hands on hips in the yard. "Who the hell is dropping full trews on Grandfer Ffyrnig?"

"If the old fool dozes in snowdrifts he do deserve to be spilt on, and anyway, the cobbles do belong to the upper storey, and I can show it in writing," says Mrs Pantrych.

"Indeed," sayd Mrs Shon Ffyrnig. "Then these trews stay here on Grandfer's head until he wakes up, and then you will have bloody cobbles."

"Do not mind her, Mam," says Ieun. "Let us get on with the dinner. She is only jealous because we are eating, see?"

Round comes Mrs Pantrych, kneels by the oven, sweating like a puddler and looking twice as healthy.

"Hurry, Mama!"

"Get it on the table, girl."

"I haven't eaten in weeks," says Shoni, "and here I am with chicken. Good old Iolo Milk!"

Open comes the oven, out comes the joint now, brown and sizzling. Six little mouths water as she sharpens the knife. Now for the slicing, good thick portions, tender as a lamb and cutting twice as tasty.

"There is a fine little chicken," says Mrs Pantrych.

"Aye, better than Christmas, Mam. The parson's nose for me, is it?"

"Where is the bloody thing?"

"Language, language," says Mrs Pantrych. "This is not Mrs Ffyrnig's house, mind!"

Munching, crunching, drooling at the mouth, the six little Pantrychs dine. Sweating, sighing, fat Mrs Pantrych watches.

"But no parson's nose," whispers Betti to Gwyn. "There's queer. . . ."

"Aye, girl. Never seen a chicken with a curly tail like this. . . ."

"Eat up, my little ones," Mrs Pantrych beams. "Never mind the tail."

A winter bitch and a spring chicken taste alike on strike. . . .

Will Tafarn has eaten all the honey in his hives, and now he has started on the sugar, for the breadwinner must be fed. Comfortable in his chair Will faces Martha, his wife. His good eye shines at her, the other winks red from the scarred turmoil of his face. The willow stick in his hands is a bow of gold.

"Are the little ones asleep, my precious?" he asks.

"Sound," says Martha. "God be praised."

"Praised indeed," says Will, and raises his burned cheeks—riven by the iron splashes they levered out in six-inch strips. "A good woman, you are, Jezebel," says he, which is not her name but the one by which he calls her. "These are the days of the lost, Jezebel. Yet I, the fruitful labourer, am full while thunder and lightning strikes in the houses of the ungodly. Amen."

Martha raises her face. She is young, perhaps thirty; her hair is white, her beauty gone. "Food, Will," she says. "Not for me, for my children; food for the love of God!"

"Aye, girl. Two sacks of flour are under the boards right by here where I am sitting. Happy, happy is the man who rejoices in such beauty as yours, Jezebel, for in this pit of misery it upholds him to bear all that the Big Man sends, aye!"

"Will!" She is upon her feet now, pleading above him.

"Hisht, girl!"

"Will, they are weeping upstairs, they are weeping!"

"*Hisht*, or you will have the neighbours in. The children will be fed, but all in good time. First you will read to Will?"

And Martha puts her hands over her face.

"Read, my precious?" softly, soothingly, he pleads.

Silence, except for sobbing.

"*Duw Mawr!*" His voice is a scream, the stick is high. "Christ, but you shall read!"

"What verse, Will?"

And he answers, "May the starving die because of their iniquities, and may the Man of the Lower Palace possess them. Judges nineteen, chapter nineteen. Read!"

The Book divides to its worn place, and Martha Tafarn, knowing the words by heart, turns down her face, saying, " 'And it came to pass in those days, when there was no king in Israel, that there was a certain Levite sojourning on the side of Mount Ephraim, who took to himself a concubine out of Bethlehem-judah. And his concubine played the whore against him, and went away from him. . . .' "

"And the name of the Levite, woman?" asks Will through his teeth.

"Mr Will Tafarn of Carmarthen," says Martha.

"And the name of the concubine, woman?"

"Mrs Martha Tafarn, whose name is Jezebel."

Will smiles and lowers the willow stick. "Read," he says.

" '. . . And divided her, together with her bones, into twelve pieces, and sent her into all the coasts of Israel.' "

"And why such a punishment, answer me?" He leans, peering.

"Because she was a whore, because a man made sport with her in her husband's bed, a harlot, even as I, Martha Tafarn, who has brought forth bastard children."

"Amen," says Will. "Off with the dress."

She always gets it worse on strike pay nights, says Mrs Watcyn Evans next door.

And it was a pay night when Will came home on fire.

Up at the top of North Street there is a light in a window.

Wicked Gwennie Lewis is dry of the milk for her third, and she sits on the bed with her first one buried, her third one screaming and her second lying beside her, white as a sheet.

"It is finished," says Gwennie, pressing her breast. "There is a stupid flat old thing that once was the pride of the county —not even a dew drop to wet it," and she takes a breath and tucks it into her bodice. "*Dammo di!* There's a life!" And she bends and kisses the baby. "Sinking my pride for you, boy," she says. "I am off to Mam to see if she has any to spare."

Her door opens, the store-room of the disused ironworks. Light floods the snow. Hugging her sack over her shoulders she bends into the wind on her way down the Hill.

"Good evening, Iestyn Mortymer."

"How are you, Gwennie Lewis?"

"I am off," says Mo, and goes, running.

"What the hell is wrong with him, then? Does he think I have the cholera?" asks Gwennie.

"He is late for his supper, girl."

"Good God," says she. "Are people still eating supper?"

Her face is pinched and pale, the shadows under her eyes deep, the cheekbones proud. "Well, are you, Iestyn Mortymer?"

"Well enough, but getting poorer, like the rest."

"Too poor to spare a penny for me?"

"Aye. Nothing, see—not a farthing—given it all to my mam."

"Mean swine," says she. "And talking of pigs, is Dai Two still living?"

"Only just. They are sticking him tomorrow."

She tosses her head. "*Diawch!* When the town is six feet down and the undertakers dead the Mortymers will still be feeding. Keep your penny and to hell with your pork," and down the Hill she goes to the house of her father. She knocks, crying:

"Mam! Dada!"

But the door does not move, the blind does not turn.

"You are wasting your time there, girl," says a voice. "They are keeping their word never to see you again, so do not lower yourself."

It is Billy Handy come from Garndyrus, smelling of ale, and the prints in the snow behind him are cloven hooves.

"Two children starving," sobs Gwennie. "One short of bread and the other of milk. O, Jesus, pity me, Billy."

"Thank God for me," says he. "Very strange, it is, for I was just walking up to your door."

"With food, Billy?"

His cap comes off and he bows low, squat and black against the snow. "With money, girl, look!" And the silver leaps in his hand.

"Not with you, Billy Handy, not for two-pounds-ten!"

"Not that much money in Nanty, Gwennie. Have a bit of sense, woman. Even Crawshay Bailey is going to a shadow, they tell me. One and sixpence?"

It was a criss-cross baying moonbeam of a night, with the wind wolf-howling around the crooked shadows of the squatting house, a night of witches and besoms and brooms and curses, when Gwennie Lewis bared herself to Billy Handy on the pee-soaked bed of the ruined ironworks, for money, in strike time, to keep her children fed.

Tread softly over the snow of the town on strike, do not disturb their sleeping, six to a bed for warmth. The only people eating are the masters and the parsons, who have never gone hungry yet. But Tomos Traherne, the lay preacher, is doing well on his knees and very powerful with his blessings, and Evans the Death is making his fortune, for the Truck Shop has run out of coffins and shrouds. Hold your breath outside the window of Five Hush Silence Street or Mrs Gwallter will see you. Look down the moonlight into her room. There is no fire, no lamp; frost is shining on their boards. Mr Gwallter, up to his elbows in his trews, face deep in his beard, is getting it, and Tegwen Gwallter is in form.

"Damned loafer, damned pig! A fool I was to give you a second look!"

"Tegwen!"

A long-tongued shrew of a woman she is, with a white, peaked face and a body as a broom, but he loves her.

"Six weeks now! Six weeks, and our Willie has gone to a skeleton, all because of pride . . .!"

"Tegwen, would you break me?" he whines.

"Break you? You fat, pot-bellied swine! They are crying out for puddlers up at Nanty and you sit here idling without a glass of water in the house—flooded your belly with beer when you had it—remember? Throwing it around at the bloody politicians of the Benefit, and where has it landed you?" She leans towards him with hatred in her eyes. "In the gutter where you belong, Gwallter. Do you hear me—in the gutter!"

The old chair creaks as Gwallter rises, and the seat of his great backside, shining with grease, fills the window. Lumbering, he reaches the wall, fingers spread, and leans against it, shoulders shaking. Six feet five, he is; four hundred pounds of iron he can carry on his back. He weeps, whispering, "O, merciful God, save us!"

"Blasphemy now, is it?" she breathes. "*Uffern dân!*"

"Tegwen!"

"Up to Nanty this moment," says she. "And back tonight with money or by God I will go running to Billy Handy and do the same as Gwen Lewis."

The Scotch Cattle were waiting astride the road to Nanty that night, and they strung Gwallter up, stripped off his clothes and flogged him with willow sticks to the bone, and not a sound he made, they say, not a tear he wept.

Cold in our house, too, come to that, with no fire and Morfydd gone to live in Nanty. My father, mother, Edwina, Jethro and me sat around the empty grate on the last night of the strike, and the voice of Tomos Traherne was weak.

" 'Why art thou cast down, O my soul?' he asked, 'and why art thou disquieted within me? Hope thou in God; for I shall yet praise Him for the help of His countenance. In God we boast all the day long, and praise Thy name for ever. Selah. Wherefore hidest Thy face, and forgettest our affliction and our oppression? For our soul is bowed down to the dust; our belly cleaveth unto the earth. Arise for our help, and redeem us for Thy mercies' sake. Amen.' "

Amen.

CHAPTER NINE

AFTER SIX weeks the men got up from their hunkers and their wives and children drove them back to work under the masters' terms, as always. This was the strike that was going to change things, but it did nothing for our house except keep Morfydd from home. After the strike she had left us for a room with a widow woman in Nanty, it was said, but I knew she was living there with Bennet. The end of the strike on masters' terms was a moral victory for my father, of course, but he was dying inside for Morfydd, my mother said. Every night he sat by the window with the curtain pulled back, watching the road; shrugging his shoulders every time her name was mentioned, as if he cared little if he saw her again, but he was a year older with every month she was away. Little else happened that year. Dai Two Pig was reprieved even as Billy Handy was sharpening the knife, for word came that the strikers were breaking. Gwennie Lewis's second passed on to Bethlehem despite the money from Billy Handy, and Sara Roberts lost her other twin brother. By early spring the furnaces at Garndyrus were flaring again and the Irish had their wakes and buried their dead.

Most Sundays, when the women had no jobs for me, I fished the Usk down at Llanelen Village.

Out of bed at first light, me. Crawl from under the table—for Edwina and Jethro slept together in Morfydd's room now—dress in the kitchen and away out of the back door and up the mountain in the cold, spring sunlight.

The hills were April-misted, the old sun red and rosy after his winter sleep. Up to the tram road, down the middle of the Blorenge to Llanfoist Wharf and away down the canal bank where the sheep scamper. Badgers crawled to earth, little lambs did their contortions, Shams-y-Coed's big black bull ran me over the fields regular on those spring mornings when

I poached down at Llanelen. Down to the Old Forge where the blacksmith changes the shoes of the gentry, and full of tales he is: of how his forebears heard the great Howell Harris preach; of another who shoed a horse back to front to save a preacher chased for sedition. But the anvil was quiet, the blacksmith was sleeping as I ran over the bridge and past the board that says *no fishing*. Panting, I lay on the bank of moss with the music of the river flowing over me. Weeds waved, stones shimmered, insects droned. This is the way to fish—with the fingers. I would not give houseroom to rods and deceitful baits. Crawl through the reeds and over the boulders to the big pools where the great trout sleep. Over the last rock. Steady, peep.

Quiet he lies in shade, all two pounds of him shimmering in his fishy world of peace.

Nearer, nearer, quiet as a cobra. Two Pounds waves and leers at the bubbles spinning up in the light-flood, dreaming of fat bugs and flies—spits and rolls his eye at a water beetle . . . dozing and swaying with lazy delight.

Slide over the boulder, in with the hand. Touch mud and send up a smokescreen, for this fish looks clever. Your hand is near him when the water clears and light darts and veers in the depths as the sun comes red and raging over the peaks. Narrow the eyes and reach deeper; bite back the gasp as the river comes flooding over your armpit. Two Pounds flaps his tail six inches from your fingers, shivering with joy at the approaching warmth. For two million years he has been frozen, little wonder that he paddles to meet you. Stretch and push and reach him. Tickle, and watch him grin. There is a daft old fish—old enough to know better. Wriggling like a bride in a feather bed he yawns and spits, rubbing his tail against the palm of your hand. Smooth his belly, stroke him round the privates, tickle him under the gills. Cup your hand and watch him roll into it while everything else with sense is flying for shelter. Count his breathing, open, close, open—act when he yawns and gain an advantage. The river swirls, the foam tumbles, the wind sighs. Two Pounds rolls and eddies, paralysed with pleasure.

Crook the fingers, heave up, throw him wide. Too late he remembers what his old mam told him. Gasping, flapping, he leaps against the green, a silver crescent of sunlight and terror. Getting up I put an end to his capers and stowed him high in a tree away from otters. With a good look round for bailiffs, I whistled downriver to the deeper pools.

The blackthorn was a shower of white blossom here and the chestnut trees and alders grew in profusion along the banks where the deep green moss framed the fumbling rush of the river. High above me, revelling in the growing heat of the sun, a lark nicked and dived, its song crystal clear in the white and blue. Resting now, with my head against the bank, I dozed in the glory of the solitude, watching the heat-flies dancing in early columns at the edge of the river that changed its colour with each fresh rush of the sun. There is a peace that comes into you on the banks of water; peace in the movement of small things that scratch and crawl, in the eternal rush and foaming. And you begin to think of the legions of men who have rested in such a place, weary after battle, sleeping after labour, or stretching out their arms for lovers. The peace is holier, I think, on Sundays, when the bells are ringing in the valley. What a land it is, this Wales! And of all its villages Llanelen is surely the best. The river is milk here, the country is honey, the mountains are crisp brown loaves hot from the baker's oven one moment and green or golden glory the next. Beauty lies here by the singing river where the otters bark and the salmon leap, and I wish to God the English had stayed in England and ripped their own fields and burst their own mountains.

I did not doze for long because a salmon was jumping downriver near the sandy bend, making enough palaver for a man diving. Rising, I pulled aside the branches and watched him. There is a salmon for you—five feet long if he is an inch, and well over a hundred pounds—a hen-salmon, by the look of it—standing on its tail in three feet of water, throwing its white arms about and combing out its long, black hair.

Lovely is a woman naked, bathing in a river.

Visiting the house of Grandfer Shams-y-Coed once I saw a

painting of a woman in water; one of the Greeks, she was, with enough breast and backside on her for three women. I have never understood the old painters, unless their women were different to mine. Once I saw Morfydd dressing for an outing. The old artists would have been hard put to give her a behind like they hang on some of their women, a belly like a drunkard and breasts like a sixteen-stone Irish labourer.

It was the same with this salmon. She could not have been behind the door when things were handed out, for a trimmer figure I have never seen in or out of a set of stays, with long slim legs and as narrow as a boy in the hips and thighs, but plenty in the right places, like Morfydd. I lay among the branches, hot to go on fire, calling myself every swine in creation and breaking my neck for another look. There she was, naked—in the shallows one moment, in the deep the next; splashing about like a mad woman, flinging her hair out and combing it clean, sending the spray misting coloured in sunlight. For minutes I watched her. She dived and swam closer. Nearer, nearer she came. Now, opposite my position on the bank, she stood upright and swept the water from her face, then, with arms held out for balance, she waded in to the shore. With my hands spread to move, I froze. Just beyond my feet, lying on the stones, were clothes. I sank back. Wishing myself to the devil I shut my eyes and listened to the stones turning as she tiptoed to the hiding place. I heard her singing; humming in a minor key between gasps. She was so close now that I could have touched her wet body through the leaves. Her hands were running in sunlight. They paused, then flew to her breasts. She gasped, staring. I stared back. It was so quiet that I heard fish sipping.

"Good morning," I said, sitting up. "There's strange where you came from."

She did not reply. With wild eyes she stooped, snatched up her dress, waved her arms into it and stumbled backwards, her hands pressed to her face.

"I was asleep," I said. "You are lighter on the feet than most, for the slightest sound wakes me. If you have come down to bathe then I will go from here sharp."

She was smaller with the dress on, a ragged dress ripped at the hem and I watched her tying it at the waist with rope. Fear was in her eyes, her face was pale, her fingers fumbling with the knot.

"Do not be afraid," I said. "I have sisters myself and often come down here to bathe with them naked. Look, I will turn my back while you put on the rest of your clothes."

I turned, staring over the meadow and heard her gasping haste behind me. So far she had not spoken a word.

"Where you from?" I asked, not turning, for I was struggling to remember where I had seen her before.

"Newport," said she.

"On your bare feet?"

"Aye. I had shoes when I started but they came to holes at Pontypool and at Llanover they dropped off."

"Newport hirings, is it?" I asked, half turning.

"Yes," said she, calmer, and I remembered. She was the girl the farmer had bought after little Dewi Lewis on the day of the annual outing at Newport Fair.

"And you ran?" I asked, facing her.

She was tying her hair back with faded ribbon and smoothing the wet strands from her face. She was beautiful as an Irish girl, her eyes large and dark, her lips red.

"Aye," she said, her eyes low. "Working like a slave and sleeping in a pig cot, and the farmer tried free with me, so I ran to follow the iron where money is paid for good women."

"For work?" I asked.

"Aye," said she. "What else, for God's sake?"

"Are you hungry?"

"Aye," she said. "Starved, but it is work I am after." She raised her feet. Blood was on them. "I have had berries but too sore in the feet to go much farther."

"Stomach first," I said. "We will see to feet after. Have you a fancy for trout cooked on a spit?"

She was weighing me up for something lunatic. "Plenty here," she replied, "but no way of catching them."

I grinned. "Come with me. Some of the stupid ones climb trees," and I led the way to the upriver pools.

Wonderful to see her face when I threw the trout from the branches, gutted him on a stone with my knife, skewered him and set him over a fire on sticks. Not a word, not a move from her as I rubbed for a flame, but I saw the spit wet upon her lips as I toasted him both sides and laid him flat for eating.

"There," I said. "Now I will disappear while you put him down as best you can," and I gave her the knife.

I might have been something in a grain sack for all the notice she took of me then, for her eyes were on the boulder where Two Pounds lay as brown as any out of a frying pan. And I went from her to a quiet place of bushes and took off my shirt and tore out the arms. When I came back the trout was down without even the head or tail to show which way he went.

"Sit you down," I said. "Now for the feet," and I knelt with the sleeves ready. She was mine now, I felt. Leave her to wander and she would end in an Irish hovel, giving herself to a rich master by day and a poor one at night.

She began to cry then, her eyes flooding and the tears splashing down the sack dress, her fist pressed into her mouth.

"Hell," I said. "Do not start that. Down on your backside with you and let me have the feet, then I will take you up the mountain where my mother will feed you like a dandy."

I bandaged her, and the blood grew in wide stains on Mam's white washing.

"What is your name?" she asked when I had done one.

"Iestyn Mortymer. What is yours?"

"Mari Dirion," she answered.

"There is Welsh in that, but you speak like a north country."

"My father was English and my mother Swansea," said she, "but both are dead. I was on my way south when I starved and went for the Newport hirings."

I nodded, not interested. It was close to chapel time and the river bailiff would be round. Tying the last knot I pulled her up. "Come," I said, helping her up the bank into the meadow.

Up the mountain we went, hand in hand, over the canal, over the top and down into town with the doors coming open and the curtains going back and look what Iestyn Mortymer has got, good God. People on street corners whispered behind their hands but the men knocked their caps and the women dropped a knee at the stranger, all very friendly and polite, and I was proud of my town.

Snell's trap was waiting outside our house. My father was bellowing to Jethro to make haste and Edwina was flouncing about in ribbons and lace when I took Mari Dirion up to the back gate. My mother came through it, her eyes like saucers.

"Good heavens!" said she. "Did you catch this fishing?" which made Mari smile. "A stranger, is it? A friend of yours, Iestyn?"

Not a glance from my mother at the ragged dress, the bandaged feet.

"Her name is Mari Dirion," I explained. "She has run from the Newport hirings, and she is starving."

"O, Mam!" cried Edwina, clutching her Bible. "Church is ringing already and if we wait to take you to Chapel we will be late!"

"Minutes late," said Snell, his feet itching on the road.

"Away with you, then, and give the devil a basting," said Mam, her arms waving. "A child is starving. The God I pray to will last another few hours. Hywel, out to the back with you and knock up another bed. Iestyn, away and tell Tomos Traherne we have a little visitor in need of help from the hirings, and are we within the law to keep her?"

"Aye," I said, and went like a maniac.

"Come, my child," said my father, and led Mari Dirion within.

CHAPTER TEN

TROUBLE WAS coming. It was running in the air, breathed out in tap-rooms, shrieked at the stormy mountain meetings. Merthyr was seething under Crawshay; Risca, Tredegar, Dowlais and Nantyglo were whispering, and my town was little better. The men were taking hours over jobs that could be done in seconds and spent their time in drawing up protests that never reached the masters because of the people in between.

My father had forbidden me to visit Nantyglo now that Morfydd had settled there, for news that she was living in sin with Richard Bennet was quick to get around. Perhaps that was why there was no mention of Morfydd in the house, not even when her birthday came round. Strange are parents to forbid talk of a loved one and lay her place at table; to forbid a visit to her and yet keep flowers in her room.

Morfydd had been gone from home months now. She had stayed with us during the strike, scrubbing at Gilwern to bring home money, but she left the moment it was settled, and best for everybody, too, for she and my father were at each other's throats over politics. The fortnight Mari stayed at home helped to take away the loss of Morfydd, but the house was upside down again on the day Tomos Traherne called to take Mari over to Nantyglo, where he had found work for her with the wife of Solly Widdle Jew, the furniture man.

Living in sin, was Morfydd, it was whispered. No member of a decent family sets foot in Nantyglo, said my father.

Monday afternoon, on with my best trews and jacket, with creases to cut your shins; hair flattened down with water, shoes to shave in, and a buttonhole as big as a bride's bouquet.

In love, me. To hell with rules and regulations.

In love with Mari Dirion of Carmarthen, where her grandfather was born, and to hell with her English relations also.

Trembling, I went from our house that day and climbed the Coity in a riot of early summer flowers, with the heather coming alive and the ferns swinging flat in straight lines to the wind coming over from the Beacons. Larks were singing when I reached the top, and there was a gladness and purity about that Sunday that has stayed with me years. Soft was the wind that day, for he is usually in a terrible way with him up there, bringing up sulphur and cinders from the furnaces at Nantyglo and stripping the trees before their season—hitting them down one way, waiting for them to get up and then hitting them down the other. Like ironmasters, I thought, burning and starving people right and left and paying just enough in wages to guarantee the new generation and treat it just the same.

Tomos Traherne I found on the top of the Coity—of all places for a preacher. On his knees and well down to it, was Tomos, with the sun shining bright on his bald patch and the wind making ringlets in his beard.

"Good afternoon, Tomos," I said. "What are you doing up here?"

"Giving hell to ironmasters," said he, "from the Crawshays of Cyfarthfa to the Guests of Dowlais via the Baileys of Nantyglo and back return journey."

"I will join you in that," I said.

"Eh dear no," he replied, "though I go hot to burn when I see the Hollow of the Scab from the top of the Coity—Nantyglo that was once beautiful being burned out by one English devil after another. No, Iestyn," and he rose to face me and the goodness lay fresh and clear in his lined face. "Just for a walk, I am, and now giving thanks for the glory of the day and the goodness of the Lord to our town."

"Aye," I said. "Thank God we are not Cyfarthfa, with Crawshay starving them and the Redcoats shooting them down, and hangings."

I saw his face in profile then, granite in its strength and purpose. Generations were upon him standing there with his eyes narrowed against the sun and the smoke of Nantyglo flying across the frame of the sky; a second Moses with the

Book in his hands; a giant with the broken tablets of stone at his feet because of the wickedness of the people.

"Will you join me in asking for His justice upon the persecutors?" he asked.

"Aye, if you think it will help," I said.

"Kneel," said he, and we knelt. The wind swept about us, fanning the heather to life and blowing sweetness. "O Lord our God," cried Tomos, very fierce, "do You hearken unto two of Thy children who do call upon Thee for the justice written in the Book of Habakkuk, Thy holy Word. Chapter two, Iestyn, at random; you first, and give it glory."

I let the wind take the pages, and read:

"'Woe to him that buildeth a town with blood, and stablisheth a city by iniquity. . . .'"

"Yea!" cried Tomos, swept away. "'Because he transgresseth, by wine, he is a proud man, neither keepeth at home, who enlargeth his desire as hell, and is as death, and cannot be satisfied, but gathereth unto him all nations, and heapeth unto him all people!'"

"Verse seven!" I said fiercely. "'Shall they not rise up suddenly that shall bite thee, and awake that shall vex thee, and thou shalt be for booties unto them?'"

"'Because thou hast spoiled many nations,'" shouted Tomos, "'all the remnant of the people shall spoil thee; because of men's blood, and for the violence of the land, of the city, and all that dwell therein.'"

We fell to silence. The wind sighed.

"O do Thou hear Thy Word, Lord," whispered Tomos, trembling, "and deliver Thy suffering people from the hands of the greedy and iniquitous, even as Thy Son did deliver the peoples of the earth!"

"Amen," I said, and helped him to his feet and we stood there with the sun hot upon us.

"Look you," said he, deep. "See the scab of Nanty, the blackened hollow that was once my home, Iestyn. The day is coming, mark me, when this town and every other iron town on the mountains will take revenge. Torches will flare, pulpits tremble, the rich flee the land and the crown of England quake before the onslaught of the burned and maimed. What has happened in France can happen here. Men stand so much, no more. Swords will unsheath, muskets fly, blood run. . . ."

"Negotiation is the principle of the Union," I said sharp.

"Aye?" and he looked at me very old-fashioned. "And who mentioned Unions? Do not lecture me about the principles of unionism for I am too old in the tooth. Men working under the lash are not stirred by organisations, boy, but ideals, and the Union is another name for Rabble, a dispute within itself. You shout about negotiation, but you need two for a negotiation and you will not find a master on The Top to sit the other side of a table to bandy words with the Unwashed. So what is left to us—force—force backed by ideals. How else will you win justice when the whip is backed by the bullets of garrisons and the laws of the land are perverted? Aye, Iestyn, blood. Black will be the day of reckoning, with much weeping and the crying of children over the graves of their fathers, and I hope to God I am crumbling when it comes."

His words shocked me.

"Look," said he. "A town tying up its loins for war—see the Hollow of the Scab. See Cwm Crachen!"

I looked down at Nanty. I saw the stunted trees, their blackened arms flaring skyward; the starved grass and bushes —ragged and charred as the lives of men are charred by oppression. And from the tall brick chimneys where the fire-shot smoke poured there came a whisper in a lull of the wind; a whisper that grew into a great noise like the sobbing of a multitude. In hot flushes the sobbing grew, sweeping over the mountain that was trembling to the drop-hammers as to the explosion of cannon. I saw the little stone cottages flatten as the earth heaved and the long lines of coloured washing stripped clean, and women were weeping and begging to men with bright swords in their hands. The fields tore open and mountainous flame and smoke spewed out. Horses reared, wheels revolved into blurs of light, and balls of fire descended into the valley, exploding and maiming. And in my blindness I saw the town of Nantyglo shimmer like the coals of a forge before shattering into nothingness and brilliant light.

And from the heat of the vision came the shape of Tomos beside me. The grip of his hand turned me and his voice echoed from the pit I had created in my dream.

"*Iestyn!*"

I stared at him. Large in the eye he was, and ghostly, and sweat was upon his face. Gasping, I shook away his hand and turned and ran down the mountain with fearful looks at his squat body on the top. For what I had seen was real to me, brought about by the picture he conjured, and I knew the wizardry in him—knowing that all he had related I would see in my generation, when he was safe and dead, leaving me to suffer it.

A drunk I found in Nantyglo, rolling like a barrel on legs, with his cap on the back of his head and a posy in his button-hole big enough to bury him.

"Good God," said he, eyeing me. "Is it Morfydd Mortymer you'll be wanting, man?"

"Aye." I knew him for drunken Irish and was in no mood for humour.

"Is it a politician you are then?" he asked, staggering.

"No odds to that," I said. "Are you telling me or not?"

"No offence meant," and he put his finger up. "I am only asking, see, since this Mortymer woman is a witch for political speeches, and when she is not drawing up Union Charters she is rousing the rabble in Merthyr." He belched and patted his belly. "Old Guy Fawkes is a monk compared with her, man. She would have the Parliament sky-high while he was still mixing gunpowder. . . ."

"For Heaven's sake," I said. "Where does she live?"

"Go you," he gasped, leaning on me. "The last house to Coalbrookvale, she lives, near the chapel, and if deacons are there for the love of God do not mention the name of Barney Kerrigan."

Crowds of men and women thronged the doorways in Nantyglo, whispering and nodding as I passed—puddlers, most of the men, their faces blistered and hands bandaged and heavy in the legs, which is a drying of the joints by heat. Some were nearly blind, and their red eyes blinked away tears for a better look at the stranger. Little ragged children were playing *Diawl bach y ffenest* and screaming with delight, but scores of men were sitting on their hunkers farther down the street, many short of an arm or leg, others on crutches or in splints with grimed bandages. This was the refuse of the Bailey Empire, the price paid in blisters and maiming, when the spit of a cauldron or the fly of a winch brought discharge and starvation. And high above the roof-tops, dulling the sun, rolled the smoke and sulphur of Cwm Crachen, hanging in a pall over the house of Bailey with its round battlements of stone. Beautiful was the garden, a splash of colour in a wilderness, facing square to the hovels of the labourers and the thunder of the works.

At the door of the last house, I knocked.

The door opened and I smiled for Morfydd, but Mari Dirion stood there, and I do not know who was most surprised.

"Good God," she said. "Iestyn Mortymer, is it?"

"Aye. Is Morfydd here?"

"Eh dear, no!" she whispered. "Two days ago Morfydd and Richard Bennet went to Merthyr, and not back yet," and had she said China I would not have raised an eye, for the barrier of shyness was between us, built by absence.

I stood on the doorstep screwing my cap. The room behind her was small but tidy, with a smell of candles and warmth and people about it, and the cloth laid for tea was white.

"Come you in," she said. "Half the windows in town are open and the neighbours cracking their necks."

"It is not decent," I said. "Nobody but you in by there, and the deacons will have us."

"And Morfydd will have the deacons," said she, "and their children down to the fourth generation. This is her house now the widow woman is dead. A cup of tea for you and welcome?"

In with me quick before she changed her mind.

She was beautiful indeed, smiling at me now with something like tears as she closed the door and leaned against it. There was no sound but the hiss of the kettle and the distant thunder of the hammers.

"I did not expect you here," I said. "Tomos Traherne said he had got you with Solly Widdle Jew, and no mention of Morfydd."

"Sit you down," she whispered, and we sat down looking, but mostly at the floor. Pretty little things were hanging near the fire and she got up and snatched them down as if they were burning.

Tall and straight was this new Mari Dirion, narrow in the waist and pointed in the chest, and with a dignity I had not noticed down at the river.

"Are you still with Solly Widdle?" I asked.

"No. Down at Blaina scrubbing," said she. "Start at six in the Agent's office, then to his house to help his wife, but I am home here by evening to cook for Morfydd and Richard before the night meetings."

"Tomos brought you straight here, then?"

"Aye," said she with a giggle. "To make it decent, for the word was round that Morfydd and Richard were living in sin. So three in the bed now, it is, with me in the middle."

"The truth?" I said, frowning.

"Good Heavens, they are backward in your town! O, Iestyn! Can you imagine Morfydd sharing her man with anyone? *Diawl!* But you have to give something to the neighbours."

She laughed and hooked the kettle from the hob and the pot hissed and sighed. It was like home sitting there with the rustle of her dress about me; like a marriage, it was, with the cups tinkling and the firelight flickering on the drawn curtains which kept out the neighbours. A devil of a place for gossip was Nanty, Mari said. Faces six deep over the window-sill very often, she explained, with the one in the middle shouting what was happening to the crowd at the back, and cheers every time he took another piece of cherry cake or she poured another cup of tea—and the whole town knew if the lamp blew out.

Better than a man for telling a tale, she was; her face lighting up and her hands waving.

"Have you given a thought to me, Mari?"

This brought the light from her face.

"Tell me," I said like a man.

She smiled again. "There is nothing wrong with the old feet now," she said, "nor the stomach, come to that. Could I forget the one who fed and bandaged me and took me home?"

"You remember me because of those things?"

"Because of other things, too," she said, wistful. "When walking on the bank of the Afon-Llwyd and watching the colliers bring out the trout, or standing on the Llangattock tram road and hearing the rumbling and jingle of the harness, as I heard in your town."

"Only by those things?"

"It is enough for a start," she said, dimpling.

"Then we will do it again," I cried. "We will leave this dirty old place next Sunday and I will sleep by the river again and you will bathe, then I will catch a fine trout for you and roast him on a spit, be damn!"

"Never tasted the like since," said she, laughing. "Next Sunday, then, and teach me how to bring them out with my fingers, is it?"

"O, Mari!" I said, for she was upon her feet for the kettle and close enough to catch her waist. And before she knew it she was in my arms and hard against me, leaning back with the force of my lips on her mouth.

"Upon my soul," said she, gasping and pushing.

"Are you angry?" I asked.

She stood there with her fingers twisting together and her dark eyes rising and lowering, spreading the lashes wide over her cheeks.

"Mari, I love you," I said. "From the first moment . . . down at Llanelen, my precious."

Smiling, she caught my hand and pressed it against her breast. "Iestyn, not here, boy. Not in Morfydd's house. Next Sunday would be better. Down at Llanelen, I will meet you there to bathe. O, Iestyn, do you love me truly?"

"I love you," I said. "Mari Dirion, I do love you, my sweet."

"Then I shall be yours next Sunday," she answered, whispering, "for I love you, too, and would take a spoon and be your girl. But not here, Iestyn. Not in Morfydd's house."

A quick courtship even by Welsh standards, this one. I went over the Coity late that night before Richard and Morfydd got back from Merthyr, and the moon was a grinning pumpkin sitting on the mountain; grinning at me, perhaps, stepping so light in hobnails that I did not touch the heather.

But I was uneasy in my mind as I took my first tram down the Govilon Incline three days from then. The dawn had been up two hours. The Valley of the Usk lay misted and golden under the rising sun and the air was as crisp as frosted wine. Away to the west the pasture lands rolled to the Brecon Beacons, their peaks mist-shrouded and purple with threats, and below me as I rounded the breast of the mountain the thatched roofs of the Abergavenny wool weavers flashed like sovereigns in the happiness of the morning.

But Idris Foreman was not happy. I reined Elot to a halt, for he was sitting on the tramway with a straw between his teeth, staring into the valley. I spragged my tram and went round to him.

"Sit you down," said he. "Your father is coming for a bit of a conference," and he nodded to a tram coming down fast. Owen Howells bolted up and my father jumped down from the tram with Griff after him.

"You sent for us, Idris?" My father had little time for the foreman of Garndyrus, because of his politics.

Idris Foreman got up. "I have just heard from Merthyr," he said. "Richard Bennet, your daughter's man, has been killed in a riot."

A strange emotion is fear. The arrows of words plunge deep. Rooted, you stand as a furnace bolt screwed tight by men with shoulders, and voices are unheeded sounds that beat on the ears in stupid repetition.

"Two balls in his chest," said Idris. "Tonight his Union

brothers are bringing him home for a decent burial, as he requested."

"And Morfydd?" asked my father, his eyes closed.

"According to Gwallter's brother-in-law who brought the news, she is safe in Nantyglo. She left Merthyr last night after a meeting. The disturbances began after she left and the Redcoats were called out again. Bennet was captured and held for shouting the mob to violence. He was shot trying to escape this morning."

"You sent him," I said. "A set of bloody fanatics, the lot of you, except that some sit at home and others go out to fight."

"Aye," replied Idris smoothly. "The brains for the planning and brawn for violence. One Bennet more or less does not matter, remember it. And I got my position by distinctive service, so remember that, too. Ask them in London who disarmed the Swansea cavalry during the Merthyr riots and sent Major Penrice back to his depot on foot. We have all taken our risks for the likes of the Mortymers who sit and watch which way the wind blows before they act, so do not talk to me of sitting at home."

"What do you want with us?" asked my father, cold.

"Five men," replied Idris. "You four and me, to give a man a decent burial. Gwallter will be waiting in Llanfoist tunnel at midnight. Redcoats are all over the mountains between here and Merthyr and visiting towns in search of arms. Be up here by midnight, all of us, with picks and shovels to meet the tram bringing him up."

"What about the coffin?" asked Dada.

"A shroud is handier, mind," put in Owen Howells. "Griff and I have been sharing a penny a week for Ifor Sheddick our father-in-law, but the way he is chirping. . . ."

"Bring it," said Idris.

"A bit short it will be," whispered Griff. "Old Ifor never topped five feet, see, and no disrespect, Mr Mortymer, but your daughter's chap is damned near a foot taller, though we could tie it like a collar, eh, Owen?"

"A shroud is a shroud—never mind a tailor's fitting," said Idris. "The Mortymers will bring picks and the rest of us shovels, and up here by midnight. Back to work now before the Agent becomes suspicious."

"Eh, dear!" said my father beside me.

The early heat was rising in mists and he narrowed his eyes and looked towards Crickhowell, where the shadows of the trees were shortening and blackening as the sun came flaring red and hot with him over the ridges.

"Eh dear," he said again in a voice of tears. "Empty, empty my girl will be without him."

"Iestyn!" whispered my father.

My dream was peaceful when his hand tightened upon my shoulder; a dream of burial parties and Redcoats and musket volleys. I struggled up.

"Eleven o'clock," said my father. "Out to the back with you and fetch the picks."

The night was black with him and there was frost in the wind as I went into the hen-house near Dai Two's sty at the bottom of the garden.

Queer old things are hens on the roost when they are disturbed; grumbling balls of feather, knocking each other about and complaining to the rooster and making enough noise to raise the neighbourhood. A good rooster we had, too, with a chest on him like the prow of a battleship, tail feathers like a prize peacock and a crow that sent hens broody for miles. And now he was on the haft of the pick, making swipes at me to protect his furnishings.

"Get you over, you swine," I said, but he raved and got me twice on the knuckles, so I clenched my fist and got him with a right that knocked him flat. One pick out. I was reaching for the other when he came at me like a mad thing and no wonder they put spurs on the devils.

"What are you doing in there, laying eggs?" asked my father, frowning in with a lighted match.

"It is this bloody old cockerel," I said.

"For God's sake," said he. "Making enough noise to wake St Peter, the pair of you." And he pushed me aside, brought

130

his fist in and hit the thing out for a week. "Get the pick and let us get on with it. It is a secret burial we are attending, not Newport Fair poultry."

With the pick heads wrapped for clanks, we took the mountain road to The Top, with me growing colder every step at the thought of approaching death. It was a cold black witch of a night with the moon watching us from a tear in the clouds and crooked shadows and little things screaming, for stoats were hunting—right music for a burial party. Up Turnpike, past the Garndyrus Inn and down to the Llanfoist Cable-House we went, and the men waiting there were ghosts of silence with mist for breath, their eyes shining from their corpse faces, the undertakers.

"All quiet up by here?" asked Idris Foreman, coming up.

"Like the grave," said Owen. "But Redcoats are guarding the road by the Puddler's Arms and searching people for weapons."

"And is it clear at Llanfoist?"

"Not a soul at the Wharf, thank God, except Gwallter, who is waiting for the hearse," and he chuckled deep.

"Treat it with respect," said Idris. "You may lie beside Bennet before the night is out."

"Aye aye," said Owen, his face turned up, "but this do strike me as damned stupid, Idris. *Diawch!* Six of us risking a roasting for a bit of dead meat that prefers a hole on a mountain to one in a valley, it do not make sense."

"Leave the sense of it to your betters," said Idris, "and put your ear to that cableway for the tram will be up any minute."

The mountain was shuddering to the forge-hammers of Garndyrus, and faintly on the wind came the plaintive singing of the Irish haulers. Llanfoist farms were sleeping in the pit-blackness below, their blind windows winking at the stars, and Abergavenny was a town of dead, strangled by the ribbon of the Usk that gleamed and flashed in the scudding moonlight. All that afternoon the Redcoats had been in town, questioning and looking for arms by order of the Lord Lieutenant of the county, my father said in whispers. The ironmasters were forming their volunteer units from loyal employees, new Red-coats had arrived at Brecon Garrison. Trouble was coming, God help us, said Griff. He did not know which was quicker, being hung by the rabble or shot by the Military, and what with Unions and Scotch Cattle and Charters it might be safer to vote for George the Fourth or whoever was sitting on the throne of England now. Had we heard of the Spanish arms that were coming in carts from Newport? asked Owen. Down in town the rumours were the same, said Idris, the Red-coats questioning at doors and searching. The Irish, with shot under their floorboards, were as dumb as usual, he said; arms folded on their shovels, watching every move, spitting on the doorsteps when the gold was shown. Dic Shon Ffyrnig, who would blab his soul to the devil in drink, had been refused drink at every beer-house in town. And poor Mrs Jeremiah Jones, the mad woman, had been carried to the cottage of Griff Howells, which was more an arsenal than a cottage these days, said Owen. With a pillow under her vest and a midwife either side of her saying her time was nigh, her screams shifted the Lieutenant sharper than a monkey, said Griff, and all credit to his wife for thinking of it.

"Hisht, you!" whispered Idris. "A tram is coming."

"Midnight," said my father. "He is a better timekeeper dead than alive, if it is Bennet."

In the horror of the mountain stillness I listened to the dead coming up from the valley. Strange that a thing alive is acceptable and when dead horrible. I knew the terror of the singing cable ropes, the pinched faces of the watchers, the loaded tram going down, the mist of the tram making shape, the arm that dangled over the side, the dead fist that thumped the iron, in death defiant; a white arm, clad in silk still bright with Morfydd's washing, thumping its dull blows as the tram lurched and swivelled to the cable stop. My father was in-stantly upon the tram, spragging it to a halt, and from its black inside the head and shoulders of Mr Gwallter rose up like a bear feasting.

"Is it quiet down at Llanfoist?" asked Idris.

"Like a tomb," replied Gwallter, climbing out. "Those

English brothers are loyal. They brought him up from the church, dodging Redcoats every yard. We could do with a few of their kind in town, by God," and he shivered. "A cold ride, Idris, with his dead eyes watching me all the way. Come on, boys, give a hand."

Gwallter, still weak from his flogging, grunted and pulled, and my father leaped to help him. "Come," he said to me. "There is nothing in death, man. Only sleeping and cold with the blanket slipped off."

I nodded, shivering.

"A light, for pity's sake," whispered Owen. "It is black as a pit by here and I do not know if I have an arm or a leg."

I had an arm.

Cold.

Cold as ice; an arm frozen; helpless in its stupid twisting and slapping as my father turned him. I heaved, lifting nothing.

"Up your end, Iestyn; the boy is head down. Put the arm around your neck, man; the dead do not strangle. Up!"

In Richard's embrace I stumbled forward, sweating.

We carried him up to the tram road. No sound but the sighing wind and the grunting men and my own heart thumping. We took him through the heather, in darkness one moment, in moonlight the next, and I saw his face and throat spotted with blood from the smack of the ball and his bared chest starched with blood under his torn, silken shirt. Under the crest of the mountain we laid him, this thing Morfydd had loved.

"Down by here," gasped Idris, wiping sweat. "We will rest for a bit, then dig deep. Young Mortymer—away with you to the tram road and watch for soldiers. Give us half an hour and we will have him down, but any sign of lanterns hurry and tell us or we will finish in Monmouth. Who has the shroud?"

"By here," whispered Owen, "and tidy, for our mam has stitched on the extra foot."

"Right, then," said Idris, grasping a pick. "You and I will take first dig, Owen," and as I left them the picks struck.

Down on the tram road I watched the toll-gate.

Vain things are tears. I fought mine down, listening to the sounds of the diggers. It was like a harmony of voices; the chinking of the picks, the deep thrusts of the shovels were like the piping of a woman and a man's grumbling responses, with a bit of a child butting in between.

And then the light at the toll-gate went out and a new, brighter light came swinging down the tram road from Garndyrus. Scrambling up, I ran back to the burial party.

"Out of it!" I cried. "The light is out at the Puddler's and another is coming down the tram road."

"Away," said Idris, collecting shovels. "Listen, young Mortymer. We are going over the crest. If the lamp passes, then up to the ridge to fetch us, is it?"

"Go," I said.

As the last of their footsteps thumped the heather I bent, turned out their dim lantern and knelt, watching for the light. Over the crest it came; nearer, nearer, straight, as if guided, for the shallow grave where Richard was lying, his face and shoulders in sharp outline against the sky. My heart was hitting away against my shirt as the light came on. Rabbits scampered from the feet of the wanderer, partridge clattered in terror from the waving circle of light, and the moon, findnig a rent, lit the mountain with blueness before pulling down her skirts and covering him with darkness.

Tall and straight was the woman carrying the lantern, and her skirt was billowing and her hair waving behind her as she held it high. Her face was white, her eyes wild as she drew nearer. And seeing Bennet in the grave she knelt and lowered the lantern. For seconds she stared at him, and then she made claws of her fingers and put them in her hair and turned her face to the sky and screamed. Three times she screamed, her breast going up, her eyes shut tight, her mouth gaping, but no sound came forth. Not a sound, not a whisper she made with those screams. And she flung herself down over the body of Bennet and gripped it, sobbing.

"Morfydd," I said, touching her.

She drew from him like a tiger from prey.

134

"Dead, is he?" she said at nothing.

"Aye, Morfydd. Aye. They told you in Nanty?"

The wind hit between us, sighing.

"No," she said, "I did not know. Tonight he was coming from Hereford. Cyfarthfa first, you understand, then Hereford to speak with Lovett, and was lifting back home along the limestone tram road. When he goes to Hereford I meet him at the cable house, but tonight I saw a lantern and came by here."

There was just the two of us in the world then.

I clenched my hands and shut my eyes, my head bowed. When I opened my eyes Morfydd was staring.

"Away," she said. "What is it now, then—peeping?"

The tone of her drove me back. I went into the deeper heather, for there was a strangeness about her that was fearful.

"O my love, my precious," she said. "Late you are to-night, but still time for loving before we go back. Kiss me now, for nobody is watching. Why, there is cold you are, boy, and no wonder with no coat. Take me quick, for I am warm, Richard. Still as brazen as the hussies in London, is it? But you are in love with me, your pretty little Welsh. Wicked enough for three I am, for you," and she kissed his lips in wildness and passion, her hands caressing his face.

I could bear it no longer. Leaping up, I dashed upon her, seized her shoulders and dragged her away. Her bodice tore in my hands. Crying out, I snatched at her waist, locked my fingers and flung myself backwards, but she rolled on top and clawed my face to the mouth. She was screaming now. Her face was with madness and her hair flying across it while she spat and bit like a cat. Sobbing, I fought her off, gasping and pleading, but she was blind in her lust to be back to Bennet. Kicking, scratching, she rolled from my arms and flung herself over the grave. Her hair was down, her breast bare and her skirt ripped to the waist. Like a guardian dog, on all fours, she faced me.

"Back home," she whispered, panting. "*Away!* Touch a hair of his head again and I will have you in bits and swinging from hooks."

I got to my feet.

"Morfydd, for the love of God leave him!"

"Eh dear!" she said, and laughed, her voice shrill. "If it's not parents it's brothers—nobody like the Welsh for busy-bodies, mind. To hell, Iestyn, you should know better! Keep to your own business and leave me to mine. Eh, dear! There is a life, Richard! Back to Nanty, is it? Mari is waiting with supper. Come now."

I saw the kick of her legs as she twisted her shoulders under his chest. She heaved, grunting, and crawled, dragging him after her.

"Morfydd," I whispered, and she looked from under the load with his arms swinging before her.

Kneeling, I brought up my fist.

The blow would have angered a man. Morfydd sighed and dropped flat. I hauled Bennet from her, straightened her clothes, and, sobbing, ran to the ridge for my father.

CHAPTER ELEVEN

For weeks after we put Bennet down our house was like a tomb, everybody talking in whispers. Night after night it was the same; into the bath, out of it, empty it, up to supper, and face my father across the table after shift. Edwina did her embroidery, Mam her spinning, and the old black clock ticked our lives away with nothing but the clatter of plates or the whirring wheel to break the silence.

And up in the best bedroom sits Morfydd. No trouble bringing her back from Nanty, for we carried her; too big a sickness for Mari Dirion, who had gone to work full time for the Agent, Mr Hart.

"Have you finished, boy?" asked my mother.

"Aye."

The wheel spun from light to shape, her hands came down from the shuttle. Opening the oven door my mother put the plate of oatmeal on the table and looked at my father.

"Two mouthfuls a night, Hywel. She is starving to death."

"Only the soul can starve to death with food about," said he. "She will come to it. Take it up, Iestyn."

Up the stairs with it now, open the bedroom door. Jethro is asleep in the bed, Morfydd sits beside it. Still as a cat she sits, watching the window; watching the sun dip behind the mountain where her man lies buried. For three weeks she has sat like this dressed in her Sunday best, dead but breathing, waiting for Richard's knock. Beautiful, she looks, more lovely than when running in the wind with her cheeks bitten scarlet with frost and her hair tangled; lovelier than in summer and dressed in bright colours, swinging her hips through the heather with one or another. Now, in the silence of this grief, her beauty would tempt a saint. The brow is high and pale, the hair brushed back into plaits upon her head, streaked with white at the temples. Her cheeks are stretched tight and with deep shadows, her eyes in repose, sick of weeping. A new Morfydd. No challenge left, no fight. As if the flood had quenched the fierce heat of her, with her hands in her lap, she sits.

"Have you seen Richard today, Iestyn?"

"Never mind about courting, girl—eat this oatmeal."

"What did he say?"

I took a deep breath. "Get some of this down and I will tell you."

"Now," said she, swallowing a spoonful as if swallowing chaff.

"Tonight Richard is going to Coalbrookvale," I said.

"To Zephaniah Williams at the Royal Oak?"

"To a meeting there, more fool him," I said sharp.

"The Charter it will be at the finish, mind," she said quick. "You can say what you like about Benefits and Unions, but the pair of them can be bought for pints. It is ideals the people will follow, the Charter. God, but my boy is climbing!"

"In the wrong direction, if you ask me," I said, for she eats better during an argument. "A pig is this Zephaniah man, and a drunken atheist into the bargain."

"No proof of atheism, mind," she said sharp, "only gutter talk." She had the spoon full in the pan and I helped it up to her mouth and pushed it in. "Educated, is Zephaniah," she spluttered, "even the young Bailey says that. These are the men we want for leaders, not gutter rats and watchmakers, and then we will get the Four Points of the Union's new Charter from Parliament with the help of God or not."

"Four Points, Four Points!" I said. "If it is double-dutch to me, how the devil can the masses understand it?" I got the spoon in again.

"Listen, stupid," said she. "William Lovett, who has formed the London Union of Workers, has drawn up a demand from Parliament which asks four things—the right of every man to vote; a secret vote; a new Parliament every year; and Members of our choice whether they own land or not. And when the people get this there will be no need of Unions. Put the king in a mansion, says Richard, and away with his palaces. Away with dukes and knighthoods, earls and viscounts! This is the new generation pledged to break the grip of the aristocracy who rule our lives. This is the rise of the common people to new heights of liberty when the tyranny of Crown and Church shall be brought to ashes and goodness and equality exist among all men. . . ."

"Morfydd, hush," I said.

"O, God!" she whispered.

I held her hard against me.

"O, God!" she cried. "There's empty I am without my boy, Iestyn. Empty . . .!"

Downstairs with the plate now.

"Heaven be praised," said my mother.

"Clean as a bone," said my father.

"Funny she will eat for Iestyn," said Edwina; "she will not take a bite for me."

Through the madness of the make-believe Morfydd lived, dead inside.

And on the third month after Richard's death she came large in the waist with her and with sickness every morning, being in child.

A terrible thing is the scandal.

Those who live among filth are the first to throw it.

Like Mrs Pantrych and Mrs Ffyrnig and a few more I could mention.

Hands deep in my pockets I whistled my way home after shift at Garndyrus; as important as the accident trolley to Mrs Pantrych and Mrs Ffyrnig. Gabble gabble, gobble gobble. Their hair hangs low, darkness is in their faces. They lean on their gates with their breasts shoved up and split deep; soiled women, dirty in the mind and mouth; a pair of turkeys with noises to match.

"Hisht, Mrs Pantrych! Here is her brother."

"Do not hisht me, Mrs Ffyrnig. If a thing is indecent I be not afraid to say so—let him take it back to the family."

"Ten to one it is Iolo Milk. Twice I saw her up on the Coity with her skirt past her middle."

"Aye, woman, but not lately. Bennet is the second name, take it from me."

"Eh, hush you! Here is Iestyn."

"And he is not much better, mind. Mad for it are the Mortymers."

Whistle louder, go to walk past.

"Good evening, Iestyn Mortimer." The pair of them in chorus and with bows. Gentry now, their lips slobbering as tap-bar spittoons.

"Good evening, Mrs Pantrych. How are all the children?"

"Fine, fine, boy. How is your mam?"

"Happy as a skylark. How is Dic Shon, Mrs Ffyrnig? Still as round in the belly with the funds of the Benefit?"

This sets them looking.

And once they are running you kick their backsides.

"How is your husband, Mrs Pantrych? Well, I hope?" Eight she has now and expectations of ten by the stretch of her apron, and not a father between them.

I gave them scandal at first, but I was running in the end.

"You can always find somebody worse off than yourself, mind," said Morfydd. "Mrs Gwallter and Willie, for instance."

I was with Gwallter when he took the iron. Like Will Tafarn he took it, only worse.

Number Two Furnace was ready for tapping when the Agent brought three visitors round. English, by the look of them, up for the shooting, being August; dandies by the cut of them, proved as dandies later.

Everything was wrong for Gwallter when the Agent called for a tap of Number Two so the visitors could watch the molten iron coming out. Afel Hughes, who kept the furnace, was down in town with the Owner. Idris Foreman was lining a tram road over the Tumble, and Will Blaenavon, who knew Number Two like his hand, was down in Abergavenny for tools.

"Come on, come on!" said the Agent.

A bitch was Number Two. She made good iron but she boiled high and was always losing her bung, so Afel held her with a stone in the clay to keep her tight. But only Afel knew.

"Tell him to go to hell," whispered my father. "I would not touch that furnace with a hundred-foot rod unless I knew her."

But Gwallter, being Gwallter, only grinned and took the firing-iron and stooped and knocked out the stone and the liquid iron spat under blast in a shaft of white fire that took him in the face, and he screamed and fell and it sprayed him over the chest and set it on fire. He bit off the tips of his fingers when they pulled him clear, and died. Four bodies they laid out on the tumps, the other three being the dandies. And when they sprinkled water over their faces to bring them round, they sprinkled some on Gwallter, who had no face, which put the Irish into stitches.

"Thank God he went easy," said Morfydd now.

We sat quiet, thinking about the Gwallters.

"Are you telling Dada soon?" I asked her.

"About the baby? It would kill him."

"He will have to know some time," I said. "If Mam or the neighbours do not tell him he will see for himself."

She stood by the window looking at the mountain. "Do not worry," she said, "I am going from here soon."

"To where?"

"To London, perhaps."

"They are starving to death there according to Lovett, without you adding to it."

"One more will make no difference, then," said she. "If you think I am staying here as fun for deacons you are mistaken. This is Richard's boy and as Richard's boy I will raise him. I will sell myself to raise him, for in him lies the greatness that was his father's, the greatness that will sway his generation as Richard has swayed ours." She put her hands over her face.

"All right, all right," I said. "London it is, then—anywhere you like, but let's have an end to it."

I was half way down the stairs when knocking came on the back.

"Well, here's a surprise!" I heard my mother say. "Dafydd Phillips come to visit. Morfydd, Morfydd!"

From the bottom of the stairs, looking through the kitchen, I saw him. Very smart, looked Dafydd, very prosperous, with his nose back to brown and dressed to kill with buttonholes either side.

"Just come to give my respects to Morfydd, Mrs Mortymer," said he. "A sad time for her this, no mistake, and she will need her friends about her."

Aye, I thought, but you are a little late, and I was right.

Not a whisper had come from Morfydd about her trouble, not a word from me since she confessed it, but a town of neighbours is excellent at guessing. And strange it is, how often a town is right.

A gale of words swept through the rowdies now. Slander flew around corners, expelled in belches, bubbled through beer, undressing the man, raping the woman, but always keeping clear of the family. And from the moment of Dafydd's visit the slander grew.

"It is a wonder Tomos Traherne puts up with it after the way he ran Dathyl Jenkins and Gwen Lewis up the mountain."

And not one of them with proof that Morfydd was in child.

"Ought to have his head examined, did Dafydd—played second fiddle to that Englishman for years!"

Then the Irish got hold of it and said it was time Morfydd had one out. Mervyn Jones Counter put it round the Company Shop, smiling his rhubarb smile and giving short weight in the commotion.

Dafydd Phillips called again and again. He and Morfydd walked out together, unaware of the stares, and if Tomos Traherne knew of it he made no mention. I could bear it no longer. Edwina was down at Abergavenny with Snell, Jethro, my mother and father out for a Reading. Morfydd was dressing for Chapel, Dafydd was due.

"Morfydd," I said, in without knocking. "What is happening?"

"He knows," said she, tying her bows.

"Dafydd knows—you have told him about the baby?"

"He wants to wed me," she said.

"Is he in his right mind?"

Morfydd turned, lowering her hands. "Listen," she said. "I do not care. I am carrying Richard's child and I want a name for it. I have been wife to Richard a hundred times and more—he knows that, too, and still he wants me. Marrying Dafydd Phillips is better for my child, better for Dada."

"You will regret it," I said.

"No doubt," she replied, "but I am not thinking of myself."

"Nor are you thinking of Dafydd," I replied sharp. "No good will come of it, mark me, Morfydd. A marriage like this can be hell."

"Dafydd is willing; it is all that matters," she said. "It takes two to make a hell of marriage, and in return I will treat him decent, clean and cook, and be a wife."

"And loving Bennet every minute."

Morfydd sighed. "Too much store is put on this business of loving," she said. "If I was a man looking for a wife I would marry a girl full if it suited me. But I would kill her if one had his way with her after."

"That is one view," I replied. "Think hard and you will find another to suit you better. One month, two, might be all right. But after that Dafydd will grind you for what you have done to him and hate the sight of you and your child."

"Right, you," she said. "You have had your say. Out."

Things happened quickly after that.

First Harry Ostler, all fifteen stone of him, was found with his jaw smashed, propped against the walls of Ostler Row.

Big in the mouth was Harry and handy with a quart.

"Harry Ostler has been found with his jaw smashed and eyes he will not see from for weeks," I told my father.

We were in the shed, making a new trough for Dai Two.

"There's a pity," said he, staring at his hammer.

"And nobody can think who has done it."

"Really now."

"No," I said. "People are saying that three got him in the dark."

Very interesting was that hammer, it appeared.

"Show me your hands, Iestyn," said he, raising his eyes to mine. I did so, and he turned them over and hit the knuckles. "Shame on you that they are not cut to pieces," said he. "Do you know that grown men are writing things on walls?"

"Yes," I said, looking down.

"About one of your sisters?"

I nodded.

"Then cut your hands and quick," said he, "for men like Harry Ostler are a waste of time to me and should be yours," and he went from me to the door of the shed and put his hands to his face. He said, broken:

"You are close to Morfydd, Iestyn. Tell me, boy, and cut no words about it. Are these things true?"

I stood in silence.

He swung round, his face white, the fury in him striking me a blow. "The truth, Iestyn, or by God I will cripple you. Me, the father, and I am the last to know!"

"She is full, if that is what you want!" I cried. "By Bennet, and no amount of deacon palaver will alter it, and she will still be full though you cast her from Chapel and send her from home."

He stood as still as an image, eyes closed, hands clenched by his sides.

"She loved him," I said.

"Go from me, Iestyn."

I went past him to the door. "Dada," I said, "their love was great and beautiful. You could search the world over...."

"Go," he said.

And I went from him into the kitchen, and there, by the sink, I listened to him sobbing.

It was different up with Morfydd.

Straight to her room I went to tell her, for there was a madness in my father that had made me afraid.

She was kneeling in her stays, pawing the bedroom floor like a mare with a load on, the strings tied to the bed-rail.

Pretty enough to take the breath, this one, with her long, slim legs and her breast white and high-curved above the petticoats she had rolled to her waist.

"For God's sake," said she. "Two inches less and not a soul in the congregation will be the wiser."

"What are you up to?" I asked, gaping.

"Getting into my wedding dress. Now you are here you can help, man. Against the bed with you and your foot in my back and we will pull together, is it?"

"You will have it on the altar steps the way you are going," I said.

"Do not be vulgar, Iestyn."

"It is you who is vulgar for treating it so lightly!"

"It is done," she said, spreading her hands. "Nothing will undo it. Face facts, boy. Like a preacher you are, Church of England at that. Come now, another two inches, for the dress is going at the seams."

Blindly, I helped her. She kissed me as if I was the groom, danced to the middle of the floor and whirled out the measuring tape. "Twenty inches," she said with pride. "How is that for the family honour? Throw me the dress, boy."

I said, facing her:

"Morfydd, it is out. Dada knows."

Her expression changed from happiness to horror and she clapped her hands to her mouth.

"Aye," I said. "He knows. Perhaps for a day or two he has known."

"O God!" she said, and sank down by the bed with the dress crushed to her face and her fist thumping the blankets. "O God!"

To lose myself I went out.

But I did not lose myself, and when I came back down the mountain Snell's trap was outside our house, which meant that Mother, Edwina and Jethro had returned from Abergavenny. I went in my usual way, vaulting the gate. But when I got to the back door it was open and Tomos Traherne was standing there in black and fury, facing my family, who had their eyes cast down. Morfydd, in her wedding dress, pale and proud, had her face up.

"And so," went on Tomos, deep and fine, "as a fit punishment for the sin of fornication you will appear before the deacons tonight and be cast out. For never, as long as I am alive, will you be granted the sanctity of marriage in Chapel."

He had said this before, of course, and there had been weeping and pleading and God help me and God let me die.

Morfydd said, her eyes flashing, "Amen. A man of God you call yourself? The likes of you, Tomos Traherne, and the rest of your deacons will fry on the grids of hell at the Judgment for cruelty to the unborn. Now get from here sharp, you psalm-singing swine, before I take my nails to your face and act like the bitch you make me."

Very fast went Tomos, but bitter were the tears he left behind him.

CHAPTER TWELVE

NEW TINTS were on the trees when Morfydd married Dafydd Phillips in Coalbrookvale, within sneezing distance of the Royal Oak Inn, the Chartist meeting-house, which was a sign of things to come, said Will Blaenavon.

All our family went to the wedding, which was a relief, said my mother, and it was well attended by people from our town, which was to be expected, said Morfydd, for it is unusual to have a bride in child. Dando looked Dafydd in his best suit and his white buttonhole of mock carnations, boots to shave in, a collar high enough to cut his throat and enough airs about him to grace a pack of gentry. Beautiful was Morfydd with her long, defiant stare around the congregation; looking for trouble, said my father, even at the moment of betrothal. But she need not have bothered, for she was loved and respected in Nanty and the people were there in force with bugles going and guns sounding and enough ropes tied across the chapel entrance to hold a troop of cavalry. My father was in a holy quiet all through the service but the demonstration of the people of Nanty impressed him, I think. My mother and Edwina were in tears, of course, which is the custom for the women, and Mari and I sat together with Jethro, waiting for our chance to get on the mountain. Big Rhys Jenkins and Mo were there, Afel Hughes and the Roberts family, with Sara all ribbons and lace and looking daggers at Mari. Mr and Mrs Twm-y-Beddau came in Snell's trap and Idris Foreman and the Howells boys, who brought half the revolutionaries in Monmouthshire. People I had never seen before were present, all friends of Morfydd, I heard; gentlemen, some of them, with good cuts to their suits and dignity about them. And when we got to Market Road the neighbours were waiting with their tables loaded and the children coming and going with their arms full of late summer flowers.

Very impressed with Nantyglo, I told Mari, although I could not get away from the reception and up the mountain quick enough. The sun was shining brilliantly as we walked into the shadows of trees and lay down there, hand in hand, each tense with the magic of the loneliness.

On my elbow, I looked at Mari. Her hair was tied in a black ribbon behind her head and her arms were bare to the shoulders. She looked golden, steeped in sun, the patterned shadows of the branches giving a rich, dark texture to her skin.

There was no need for words lying there. Below us lay the Cwm, about us was the mountain with his changing colours of sun. The stillness of the day brought tranquillity, a drowsiness that seemed part of loving. She was in my arms now. I caught a fleeting glimpse of her eyes, large and startled, as I kissed her. She was as grown from the summer, lithe, soft, resisting; part of the mountain moving beneath me as I kissed her again, and there were no sounds for us but the breathing of the wind and the rustling of the branches that sheltered us. The hammers of Coalbrookvale and the mills of Nanty were silent in that lovemaking, obliterated by the quickening surge of our blood as we lay together lips against lips. There is a searing of the blood when the breathing quickens, a heat and a madness, with the mouth crushing and the hands seeking soft places.

"No," whispered Mari.

And the sound of her brought me back to life, to the trees above us, to the mountain beneath us.

"Eh dear!" I said. "Yes for a change, is it?"

"Not in daylight," she said with business.

"In darkness, then?" I held her, kissing her throat.

"You are wicked to hell," said she, struggling up. "I am from here sharp before I am in trouble." Laughing, I pulled her to her feet and kissed her again, the length of her against me.

"O, Mari!" I said.

"No bathing with you down at Llanelen," she cried, "for you are grown up. Last one down to Cwm Crachen is brainless," and she lifted high her dress and ran like the wind with me after her and shrieking to her to stop. Morfydd and Dafydd we found there, standing in the kitchen of their Number Five, hand in hand, with all the guests gone.

"Five o'clock," said Morfydd. "Mam waited for as long as she could but the men had to get back for the killing."

It was then that I remembered. Murder was being committed that evening, murder by men of one of their fellows. The crime was to have been carried out before the wedding so Morfydd and Dafydd could have had a ham to cut at, but Billy Handy, the murderer, was drunk, so my father would not let him near Dai Two.

In the shock of remembering what was to happen I took my leave of Mari in a dream, bowed to Dafydd and Morfydd and left, leaving the three of them staring.

And back I went up the mountain.

A pig, I think, should die in darkness, so a man cannot see the shame of his neighbour's face. For what kind of man is it who can take the blood of his fellow over his hands with a smile? A pig is a very intelligent animal. There is much of a man in a pig and more of a swine in a man, and who are we to pass sentence over one who eats from soil while we have teeth and nails to tear with? Hypocrites, all of us, especially people like Billy Handy, professional stickers.

The sun was going down as I crested the Coity and I stood there on the top, seeking a movement in the scarred valley, listening for a scream. And then I sat in the heather remembering that I had been making love while poor little Dai was being penned for execution. For an hour I sat there, watching the sun go down, thinking of many clocks striking and cockerels three times crowing and Dai Two looking for me in his terror.

And at six o'clock, Judas, believing the betrayal complete, rose, and went down into the valley.

Mr Snell's trap and mare were outside our house when I got there, with Edwina sitting up in front, waiting. Hearing me coming she turned, up with her skirts and down into the road.

"O, Iestyn! Go from here!" she cried in panic.

"Why?" I asked.

"Because the killing is starting when Billy Handy gets here."

"But the killing is over," I said in wonder.

"No. Not started, see? Billy Handy was drunk again and Dada sent him back home to get sober," and her eyes, like saucers, threatened to drop from her face.

"Good God," I said, empty.

"So away with you, quick," said she, sweeping me up with her skirts.

There was a smell of death in the house, with people bustling about in new bonnets and trews after the wedding, and Mam, peeping round the doorpost to see if Billy Handy was coming, stared straight into my face.

"Good God," said she. "You are in Nanty."

"Do not tell me you have come," said Dada.

I groaned.

"To help in this crime?" He levelled his pipe at me and lowered his voice. "Now listen," said he, "no trouble, remember. There will be enough palaver sticking the thing without Billy Handy losing gallons of blood as well. Look now, Snell is taking Jethro and the women for a trot, so why not slip along?"

"Come with your old mam," said my mother, very damp. "I am nearly in tears myself and the sight of your old pig dying will affect you for weeks, Iestyn."

"Let him go and I will stay," said Jethro, coming up jaunty. "A good pig-sticker I am, says Billy Handy, for I have helped him tie sacks round their snouts to save worrying neighbours."

"Get the little savage from here," said my father.

"A fine future he has," I said. "Foreman at the Panty knacker yard," and I left them all and went down the garden path to make my peace with the criminal. Henry Snell was coming from the shed at the bottom, doing up his flies, something that should be done inside.

"Good evening, Iestyn," said he, pleasant. "A fine evening to be sure."

"Away to hell," I said, "and take that saintly lot with you before I cut a throat or two myself."

I had no time for Snell. Simpering hypocrisy, false religion were in his mouth, the Bible in one hand, the begging box in the other, and to this day I do not know why my father allowed him in the house. Dai Two was cleaner, and I stood by his sty scratching his shoulder until the hooves of Snell's mare faded down the road to Varteg, then I went back to the kitchen.

"I have no stomach for this," said my father, changing into old trews.

"No stomach? I would rather cut the throat of Edwina. For years I have had this pig as a pet and I think more of him than a dog."

"Do not make it harder, Iestyn," he replied. "Do you think I have no heart? And not my old pig either, mind. But big as a house he is getting and eating enough for a regiment of guards—even the pig could see the sense of it."

Tap, tap, tap on the window. The face of Twm-y-Beddau was on the glass.

"For God's sake what does he want?" said my father.

"For God's sake what do you want?" I said, shooting it up.

"It is this old pig, see?" said Twm, jerking his thumb.

"What of him?" asked Dada, lacing boots.

Pale around the mouth was Twm, and sweating. Twenty years he and his woman lived next door to us and not a word of complaint right or left. "Well," said Twm, "it is not so much the pig as my woman, see. Big in the stomach she is, as Mrs Mortymer knows, and most considerate, thank God, but the squealing of a pig could easily bring her on three days from her time. Will he die quiet?"

"If I have a hand in it," said Dada. "So back to your wife with you and tell her there are pigs dying all over the county."

"Thank you, Mr Mortymer, and do not mind my asking?"

"I do not," said Dada. "Now go to hell from here."

Down with the window. Bang bang on the back. "Good grief," said my father, "I am in rags. That will be Billy Handy and the Jenkins—let them in, Iestyn."

"Good afternoon, gentlemen," said Billy Handy, bowing low. "Does a little pig called Dai Two live by here?"

"If you are sober," replied my father, severe.

"Sober as a judge, Mr Mortymer, for I never kill intoxicated for fear of cutting the wrong throat. Tea, is it?" said he, sniffing sad.

"A cup for you, boy?" said my father to Big Rhys coming in.

"Something a little stronger, Hywel," replied Rhys, "for the presence of this man Handy is fair turning my stomach."

"But stomach enough for a slice of decent ham," said Billy, sharpening knives with a leer. "And there is tasty is a cut from the belly after a thick night at the Benefit, Rhys Jenkins. A mug of that very fine beer for me, too, please, Mr Mortymer." He drank deep and gasped. "Well, if it is hating live pigs that makes me a criminal, then you are right. But I am the same as the rest of you when it comes to eating, mind. It is the head of a home-fed pig I do like—slit down the nose and boiled with spice and onions, and the head belongs to the killer, Mr Mortymer, do not forget it. Another mug of this very fine beer again, if you please, and I will have my shilling before we begin, is it?"

"Here," said my father, dropping the silver. "And mind you take it gently with this pig for he is practically a member of the family."

"God help me," said Billy. "Another related pig. Lead the way, gentlemen," and led by my father we all went down the garden. Dai Two came grinning to the bars, happy at this sudden attention from humans.

"Good evening, Dai Two," said Billy, dangling a loop. "Get your snout into this and it will be easier for all of us," and he whipped the loop in and pulled the rope tight.

Captive.

The indecision was in Dai's little red eyes. Then he set his buttocks square and squealed as Billy heaved. The sty door came open, Big Rhys and Mo got on the rope. And as messages from his executed ancestors flashed into his brain, Dai screamed and screamed fit to be heard in Nanty.

Hot and cold, me.

"A very vocal pig this, Mr Mortymer," said Billy, pulling. "A good tenor for the Oratorio, think you? Fetch me a bloody sack, somebody, for I cannot kill during a commotion."

"Never mind sacks, he must die clean!" shouted my father. "This pig will not be tortured, so get him to the board, Billy Handy, and quick."

Up the garden path with us, Billy and Big Rhys heaving on the rope and Mo putting his knees into Dai's backside, and the noise of him was like a thousand babies under torture.

"For God's sake shut that pig!" shouted Twm-y-Beddau, his face over the garden wall.

"Come over that wall and I'll bloody shut you," cried Billy.

"With my woman near dropping her second, it is indecent," yelled Twm, very hot with him.

"If she makes as much noise with her second as she did with her first you will not hear this pig," said Billy, and brought his boot around Dai Two's rear to help him on a yard.

"Easy, easy with the boots!" cried my father between yells.

"It is trying to move him I am," gasped Billy. "And better employed you would be booting than criticising, man."

"Devil take me!" exclaimed Dada. "If you are a pig-sticker, then I am the bishop. Away out of it," and he stooped and hooked his arm under Dai's belly and carried him to the board like a baby.

"A set of cruel swines you are!" shouted Twm above the bedlam. "For years you have been stroking that animal and it would serve you right if he stuck in your throats."

"Hold him steady!" cried Billy. "By heaven, I will settle this palaver," and he reached for his knife and measured the distance to the gullet.

"Never in my life will I touch bacon again," wailed Twm-y-Beddau. "God forgive you, Billy Handy, but you will roast on white-hot grids in hell for what you are doing to that poor defenceless animal!"

"Satan take me!" breathed Billy, resting on the knife and sweating. "How the hell can a man draw blood with people making remarks like that?"

"And my woman in here praying for it to stop," cried Twm. "It is enough to cripple the child having to put up with it."

"Silence!" roared Billy. "Or I will be in there and cut the throats of the three of you!" He groaned then. "Never have I heard the like of this, Mr Mortymer. What with the four of you in tears and half the neighbours in childbirth, it is enough to break the heart of a Carmarthen slaughterer. Do you want this bloody pig slit or not?"

"If there was a law in this town I would have it on you!" yelled Twm, up on the garden wall now and weeping. "A hard man I am in all conscience, Mortymer, but I have grown fond of little Dai and I will pay you double price to save my woman a child with two heads, and hark to her wailing."

And even Dai Two stopped his squealing to listen, I think.

Going very high was Mrs Twm-y-Beddau, howling to raise the churchyard. Easy births and strong in the vocal chords was her trouble, said Mam.

My father took a deep breath now. "Put that knife away and help this pig down, Billy Handy," said he, very firm. "I am decided against it."

"Well!" whispered Billy, gaping. "I will go to my death."

"You are no pig-sticker, see," I said sharp, "or you would have had him from hooks instead of arguing the toss, and now we have changed our minds, eh, Mo?"

"Right," said Mo, cutting his knuckles. "After this show of pig-sticking I would not employ Billy Handy skinning rabbits."

"God help me," said Billy, sitting on the killing board and fanning, and Dai Two took the chance to dive from the board and down the garden path like a hare coursing and nobody saw him for days.

"See what has happened?" said Rhys, looking ugly. "The

pig has left us. Ashamed of yourself you should be, Billy Handy, ashamed, that is the word."

Billy got up. Very pale he looked. "Goodbye," he said. "I have had enough of the Mortymers for one day and their pig in particular, so with all your permissions I am away back to Garndyrus and knock out a bung and lay me under a barrel."

"And welcome," I cried.

"God bless you!" shouted Twm, and ran back to the labour.

CHAPTER THIRTEEN

Two MONTHS Morfydd was married before Mam talked my
father into visiting them. Very firm upon this point of
visiting was he, saying that young married ones should be left
to themselves, which was only an excuse, we knew. Quiet he
went when Morfydd's name was mentioned, filling his pipe as
if to change the subject, and a narrowing of the eyes. Strong
for his Chapel, was Dada, with fornication a long way down
the list, said Tomos. And this business of Morfydd on heather
instead of a mattress had played hell with him, said Big Rhys
Jenkins.

But on the eve of Morfydd's twenty-sixth birthday, being
a Saturday, my mother got him in the bedroom and rolled up
her sleeves and gave it out sharp. And next morning my father
shaved extra close, put on his Sunday best and shouted for
Snell's trap and for Jethro and me to make ready. Here was
a commotion, for I was only just back from furnace shift and
Jethro was as black as a cotton slave, but no matter. Everything happened at once when my father made up his mind.
Edwina went flying down the Abergavenny road for Snell, I
went into the bath and dragged Jethro in after me, and Mam
flapped about in silk and finery giving everybody hell. Out
with my best suit and fit up the creases, borrow one of Dada's
best Chapel collars and away to the mirror for a clean, white
parting.

Off to Nanty to visit the lovers, said Jethro.

A word about Jethro while on the subject.

Dark handsome, he was, and knew it; broad in the
shoulders and thick in the arms and hair on his belly at the
age of ten. He was like my father in his every move and action,
with the same feline grace that is born in the man handy with
fists. Quiet was Jethro, speaking with his eyes, which were
large and dark and filled with shadow. His teeth were

square and white above the thick set of his chin. Hanging on the girls' pigtails to the age of eight, flicking up their skirts to hear them scream, and anything male from ten to fifteen was frightened to death of him.

"Men will be the end of me," said Mam, breathless. "Look at it—three in long trews now."

"Am I tidy?" asked Jethro, coming in.

Eh, tidy he looked, to bring a sigh to Satan, for there is something of sadness when the bony knees of a brother disappear and long trews come in their place. He stood there with his fists on his hips, a miniature Hywel Mortymer. Grief, I thought—with looks like that you will have every girl in town in a bother when you are six years older.

"You would pass in a crowd," I said. "What is that in your buttonhole?"

"Old man's beard," said he. "Morfydd's favourite."

"Visit Nanty with buttonholes and they will down your trews and check you for inches," I said. "Take it off. Flowers are for women, not men."

"Snell wears buttonholes," grumbled Jethro.

"Snell is not a man," I said. "Being dressed like a man does not make you one, either."

"Agreed," said my father, coming in, "there are a few in town who ought to be in skirts, but no names mentioned, mind. If that Dic Shon Ffyrnig calls on me again for contributions to Benefits or Unions, I am losing my temper and hitting him flat."

"Like I am doing to Snell if he calls for Readings," said Jethro, "for I am sick of him. Bloody flat I shall hit him."

"Who is hitting who flat?" asked Mam, coming in with ostrich feathers; "I will not stand for bad language in the house, remember it."

"Not a foul word from any of us yet," said Dada, "but if I start I will take the shine from cassocks."

"What about this old hitting, then?" She looked at us all very severe.

"Our business," said Dada. "And I am in a mood to begin on the nearest, so mind, woman."

157

"Listen you," said my mother, her finger up. "Listen all three of you—you too, long trews. One threat to poor Dafydd, let alone a hit at him, and I will have you out in the street, do you hear me?"

"Yes," said my father. "Eh dear! Hark at her!"

"Aye, hark," said she. "This is a peaceful visit after a kind invitation and I will make it warm for bruisers who are out to make bedlam."

"And who wants to hit out poor old Dafydd?" asked Dada, innocent.

"Never you mind," replied Mam. "We will have no more of it. Mr Snell's mare is clopping outside and it is time we were moving."

"Snell!" sniffed my father, winking. "No need to travel to Nanty to hit out a son-in-law—there is one I fancy clean on the doorstep."

"One son-in-law at a time," said Mam. "Nanty."

I had forgotten that Nantyglo was on strike again, although Coalbrookvale was going full blast by the sound of her. Down in the valley the furnaces were deserted and the chimneys stood red and derelict against the green. Men sat on their hunkers or were sprawled on the tips. Little groups of children played quietly around the Company Shop where the women were standing with their babies in shawl cradles.

Morfydd's neighbours were squatting around their back doors, but they got up very respectable and dropped a knee or knocked a cap as we went up the garden. Morfydd came to my father's rap. Pretty she looked standing there in the doorway with her hair over her shoulders, except for the eye.

Some good ones I have seen from bare-knuckle stuff, but never an eye like this. Shut tight, it was, and black; swollen like an egg, with cuts top and bottom and blood.

"Good God, girl," whispered Mam. "Whatever have you been doing?"

"A long story," said Morfydd with a laugh. "Come in and hear it and do not stand there gaping, the four of you."

It was a tiny room, with not much in the way of furniture

except boxes; but pretty with late autumn flowers she had picked especially for the occasion. No fire in the grate, no kettle singing; a floor of earth, no spinning-wheel. And cold as a Spanish prison.

"It is not much to ask you to," said Morfydd.

"But better than when we first started, eh, Hywel?" said Mam.

"Heavens, girl, do not expect too much when you are beginning. Silver plate she will be wanting next, like Crawshay Bailey," but I knew she was speaking with her tongue and not her heart. Her face was pale. The mess of Morfydd's eye held her like the rest of us.

"A little palace, girl," Mam went on, after the happy birthdays. "Good grief, what are you asking so soon? Better than seventeen to a room as in town. Find me a little house furnished like this one and I would move tomorrow, Hywel boy."

"And Jethro in long trews, is it?" Morfydd threw up her arms and pulled him against her. "Growing, too. After the women now is he, Iestyn?"

"A terror," I said.

"You have no cause to pass judgment from what I hear dropped occasionally," said Mam, severe. "He is over here most of his spare time, Morfydd, and not to visit his sister, I vow."

"Never you mind, Iestyn," whispered Morfydd, winking her good eye. "A pretty little thing is Mari Dirion. She is working full time down with Hart the Agent, so I do not see much of her now. How is Edwina?"

"Where is Dafydd?" said Dada. It was the way he said it that put an end to the stupid makeweight of a conversation.

"Over at the Lodge but back any minute," answered Morfydd. "Wait a bit while I get this old kettle hot. There is a regulation against gathering coal from the tips, so neighbours are sharing the boiling. It is the dirty old strike, see?"

"How long this time?" asked Mam, empty.

"Two weeks, but it will break us. It is the food he puts in the windows of the Shop that does it."

159

"What are you after?" asked my father.

"A rise of a shilling in the pound for everyone to bring us in line with Dowlais. Dafydd a pit overman drawing nineteen shillings for working the Balance, but there are women underground at the Garn drawing eight shillings and less. Six and seven children to keep." Morfydd's voice rose. "What the hell can a woman do with eight shillings and six children, tell me, Dada?"

"It is scandalous," said he quietly.

"It is criminal!" This was the old Morfydd. Her fist hit the nearest box. "The strike goes on. Children are starving to death, and the clerk can pass a three-foot coffin on his way to the office without a lift of his hat. Aye, Dafydd is strong for the strike and I am strong for Dafydd for once."

"That is how it should be," said my father.

"Wait now while I get this boiled," said she, "and I will be back," and she went through the door with the black kettle.

The four of us sitting in a circle now and finding the floor very interesting.

"Where is the furniture?" asked Jethro.

"*Hisht, you!* Bad boy!" hissed Mam, while we all looked daggers at him.

In silence we waited for Morfydd to come back.

"Come with me upstairs, Mam," she cried, running in. "It is pretty upstairs and every stick made by Dafydd."

"Wonderful to have a handy man," said my mother, rising. "Lucky to be wed to a craftsman while I am left with bruisers," and with her black skirt held like a tent she swept upstairs, chattering. Their feet were heavy overhead. My father sat like black stone, his eyes moving around the room.

"Is Dafydd strong for the Union?" I asked softly. "His mam was dead against it, remember?"

"There are no blacklegs in Nanty," he replied. "This town has suffered."

"Then their furniture has gone to feed them?"

"Either that or over the bar of The Bush."

"This is not like Dafydd," I said. "With Morfydd by him he would not go back to drinking?"

"Then did she grow that bruise on her face?" He rose, doubling his hands. "By God, Iestyn, if a fist has shut that eye I will make her a widow before I leave tonight."

"*Jawch!*" I scolded. "What an old fighting-cock you are. Dear me! Hit it on the door she has and not given a thought to mention it."

"O aye?" piped Jethro. "Mrs Tafarn got one like it last pay night and that was put with boots."

"Shut it!" I said. "Nobody is talking to you." I turned to my father. "Now keep your temper under your shirt until Morfydd tells you to lose it."

He obeyed, but it was anguish to him. In came my mother behind one of her best smiles. "A sweet little house, to be sure, Hywel," said she. "The upstairs is just like Evan ap Bethell next door but one in Cyfarthfa, remember?"

"Aye, a grand upstairs, that," said Dada.

"Just needs a bit of furnishing down by here," said Morfydd.

Tap tap on the back and a ghost of hunger aged ninety is there with the boiling kettle. Morfydd took it and paid the halfpenny as if it was solid gold.

"Now then, a cup of tea, is it? Dying of thirst you are," and she flung cups and saucers about just as at home. "How is Mrs Pantrych, Mam—still delivering?"

"Ninth coming, she is safer than a calendar."

"And Mrs Gwallter?"

"Sad with her man gone, but Tomos is good to her and Willie is starting at Garndyrus this week. Both the Edwards boys are courting, I hear. . . ."

They had denied it, but anything would do. Pitiful, it is, when loved ones meet behind the armour of pride, when nothing they say is true or with meaning; a conversation of strangers, unimportant, unloved. I sensed the mounting tension, knowing that soon the words would steam dry into silence. In desperation, I said:

"There is a fine old eye you have collected, girl—better than the one I had from Mo Jenkins, remember?"

Morfydd threw back her head and laughed like the old one.

161

"There now!" said she. "I had forgotten it. Is it that poorly, *bach*. Down at the Shop yesterday I met Mrs Eli Cohen, the Jew girl from London. 'Morfydd Mortymer!' said she. 'Is that Dafydd already knocking you about? For shame, I will take my fists to him, say.'" Morfydd leaned on the table, adding secretly, "And nothing more true, so I could not deny it, and that Cohen girl a terror with the tongue. Dafydd and me chopping sticks, see? A piece flew up from his axe and caught me by here," and she fingered the spot tenderly.

"What was he chopping—trees?" asked my father.

"It is easily done, mind," said Mam like lightning. "Back home a good bit of steak would have brought down the swelling, but no matter, Morfydd *fach*, it will soon be better. Now fill this old cup again, girl, for I am thirstier than a desert."

"How is Dafydd?" I asked, aware that until now he had not been considered much.

"As happy as a man on strike can be," said Morfydd, "but time is heavy. We were doing nicely until he came out. Now he is on Bailey's black list. Strong for the Union is Dafydd, a leader of a lodge, see, and the Agent found out. God knows what will become of us for we are straight from here the moment we cannot find the rent." She raised her head, her hand flying to her mouth.

Dafydd, shadow silent, was standing in the doorway.

Easy to tell when a man has been drinking quarts.

There is the first stage of one or two when the eyes dance; the second stage of three or four when the colour is high. The third is a blueness of the face, eyes half closed, and the manner dangerous. I flashed a look at Morfydd. She was frozen, her hands rigid in her lap.

"Well, well," said Dafydd, and grinned.

"Dafydd," said Morfydd like something wounded. "Mam and Dad have come to visit. . . ."

"Indeed?" he said, lumbering in. "Have I no eyes? Now tell the four of them to go to hell before I bloody shift them, is it?"

"Dafydd!" The shame was such in her face that I could have wept.

"Eh dear! Gentry, now? Not so long ago the Mortymers told me and my mam to go to hell, remember? But a very different story now, eh? What is a little going to hell between relations matter, anyway . . .?"

"Dafydd, my father is here, so mind."

"Aye, I see him. He is too big to miss. How are you, Mr Mortymer? Is it well with you?"

"It will be when you clean your mouth," said Dada.

"Will you please tell us why we are not welcome here?" asked Mam.

"Because you are nosey devils at the best of times, and only because of the old strike you have come, isn't it? Dafydd is drinking again, they told you, eh? It is enough to send any man on the drink to have a vixen of a wife and Four Points of a Workers' Charter for breakfast, dinner and tea."

"It is the meetings," said Morfydd wearily. "He is for the Union like me, but he does not agree with the Charter."

"And I should think not," said Mam sharp.

"O, to hell!" said Dafydd. "It is not only meetings and politics. It is the neighbours waving and pointing and bloody old whispering that does it."

"You knew Morfydd was in child," said my father. "I told you, Tomos told you. It was you who were strong for this marriage, not me."

"Aye," said Dafydd with a belch. "Begged for it, I did, and now I have got it."

"You would be better off without the beer, too," said my father. "A man who drinks in strike-time and blames his wife is not worth visiting."

"Drinking is the trouble, is it?" said Dafydd. "Wait you, I am not standing here to be insulted, Hywel Mortymer. Father-in-law or not, you will go straight through the window before I take orders from you, mind," and he roamed around the room like a dog hackled for fighting, thumping his fist into his palm.

"O, sit you down, Dafydd boy!" said Morfydd, dragging at him.

"And money it is now, I suppose," said he, glaring. "How do I get my money for drinking, is it? Well, that is my business too, Hywel Mortymer, so do not forget it."

"But how you use my daughter is mine," said Dada. He rose. "Drink The Bush dry, boy—join every Union from here to Cyfarthfa, sell every stick of furniture. Send her home if you do not want her, but put your hands on her again and I will be up by here to see you sharp."

"Hywel," whispered Mam, broken.

But Dafydd wheeled quick, ducked, came up and brought over a hook, good for a drunk. Dada slipped it, stepped in and hit up short. Off balance, Dafydd took it in the face, and dropped.

All in a flash; a good family quarrel one moment, fighting the next. Here is a palaver. Women up and rushing with skirts flying, bowls and bandages, and is he all right now, and half the neighbourhood looking through the windows, jawing left and right as to how he deserved it for laying into Morfydd or cursing flashes at interfering in-laws.

"Shame, shame on you!" cried Mam, stamping her foot at Dada, and him not giving a damn, but sitting there frowning and stroking his knuckles. Flat on his back was Dafydd with the egg over the same eye as Morfydd's getting bigger every minute, and breathing for a man embalmed. My father got up, cleared away the women with one arm, bent, and threw water into Dafydd's face. Dafydd groaned and opened his eyes, staring.

"Listen," said my father. "I am going now, but I will be back soon to look for hidings. Everything you give you get, man, but double. Do you understand?"

"Get out!" whispered Dafydd.

"Aye," said my father. "Double."

Not a very successful visit to a bride and groom, that.

I lay in the back of the trap listening to Snell's mare clip-clopping down the Brynmawr Road and my mother giving it to Dada proper. Not a word he said, but I knew what he was thinking. No man could have done more to stop this wedding than him. He sat with his big shoulders hunched and the reins loose in his fingers, and listened, and did not speak.

The autumn nights were drawing in and dusk and bats were dropping around us. Behind us was the red glow, before us the hills shone and sparked, with men working like demons against the glare, and as we came nearer town the night-shift going up Turnpike was whispering in the wind.

Good to be home and away from poor Nanty all weary with strike and fists in the faces of people you love.

Snell and Edwina were in the house together, sitting by the fire too far apart for innocence. They were not supposed to be in the rooms unattended, and I saw my father give Snell a queer old look and a sigh. But a silly view that, I had always thought. If they wanted to be under skirts there was plenty of room in the heather; no need to risk neighbours steaming through keyholes.

"Thank heaven that is over," said Mam, taking off her bonnet. "A decent cup of tea for God's sake."

"How did you find her, Mam?" asked Edwina.

"Happy as a fiddler," said my mother.

"Is Dafydd treating her well?"

"Wonderful."

"A good man is Dafydd Phillips," said Snell, beaming.

"The best," said Dada, "if a woman does not mind a little knocking about."

"Hywel!" said Mam. "Our business, please," and she began to lay the tea.

Snell got up. "I will go now," said he. "At a time like this the family should be alone, not with strangers."

Good for him that he did.

We all went to bed early that night.

Lying there with Jethro asleep beside me I thought of the days when Morfydd and I were children and Jethro a baby and the house full of our gay wickedness. I would have given my soul just then to have such times back. It was black outside and the wind was getting up to tricks, howling in secret places, sighing like cats and hitting gates to bring them from hinges. At times he came to an unholy quiet, as if tired of playing and getting serious. Growing into shape, Tomos once called it.

I like the wind when he is blustering along the cobbles and blowing up the women's skirts, taking the washing from lines and generally playing hell. But in the mood of shape he is different; an animal in shadows crouching to spring, and with claws. And the country he has been thrashing to death all day lies quiet and shivering, awaiting the blow.

That is the wind-silence of fear.

Terrible is this silence, this threat. It comes through cracks and sits by the fire with you, haggard and fearful, snatching at unuttered words, pressing cold fingers around hearts. You cannot see it, but it is there in the lull of the wind; a scent of danger caught on forest air after the world was ice. The stink of the festering claws of the tiger that flies to the nostrils of the trapped hunter.

Jethro stirred in the bed beside me.

"What was that?"

"Lie still," I whispered. "I am going down."

Down the stairs I went like a wraith of silence. The wind was buffeting again, the roof creaking. Landing in the kitchen I crept to the back door. I listened. A footstep scraped the flags outside. Bracing myself, I flung the door wide. And I saw, in a flash of the driving moon, the face of a man terrified, his eyes wide and shining. Something clattered as I struck blindly. Leaping at him I hit a bucket, tripped and fell, cursing. Lying, I listened to the thump of his retreating footsteps, heard the crash of the gate as he flung it back and his hobnails sparking down the cobbled hill.

By the time I had got to my feet my father was in the doorway swinging the lantern.

"Look," I said, and he held the lantern high.

The Mark of the Scab, the Sign of the Blackleg, was painted in red on the door, the bull's head of the Scotch Cattle.

CHAPTER FOURTEEN

GOING ON shift next day was more like a military parade, and the three of us were on early morning at that, which meant half the town was risen at first light.

"Dear me," said Mam, cutting sandwiches. "If ever a man was begging for a hammering it is mine. Hywel, have sense! With the three of you on the books at Nantyglo the Cattle will be here by dark if you spend an hour on shift."

"And plenty of workers here to throw them back where they came from," said my father, easing into his boots.

"Is there going to be trouble?" begged Edwina, her eyes going big.

"If there is you will not be in it," said Jethro. "We will give him Dai Probert Scotch Cattle, mind, and you can tell them that in Nanty."

My father grinned as he sat at table. Jethro was his image, fearless, years before his time for manhood.

Courage was all right, but often, when women are about, there is not enough to go round. The case to me was clear. We were men employed by Crawshay Bailey. We were on the books of Nantyglo, paid by the Nantyglo paymasters but lent to Garndyrus. If Nantyglo was on strike then we should be on strike, according to the Union. The Scotch Cattle, born and bred in Nanty, were getting bolder. Even Crawshay Bailey had doubled the strength of his 'Workmen Volunteers' and strengthened the walls of his defence roundhouses. For the crime of scab or blackleg men were being dragged out for floggings, furniture was being burned. Legs were being broken in Blackwood for the sin of working when the Union said stop. And Dai Probert, the giant Bull of the Nantyglo Scotch Cattle, was a pig when it came to forcing the Union. Nantyglo had been out two weeks—she had been out for shorter times before and my father and I had worked on at Garndyrus. But now the warning had been given.

And the town rose early to see if we had the courage.

"Dai Probert will take some stopping, Dada," I said at table.

"It is time he was stopped," said he, chewing.

"By who—the three of us?"

"Not in front of your mother, if you please, Iestyn."

"Eh? And why not, may I ask?" said she.

"Ears like bats, but sharper. Get on with the bread, woman, and leave men's business to men." He sighed.

"Aye aye?" she replied, the knife a point at him. "But I am in this, too, mind, if there is trouble, and Edwina. Dai Probert do not come all the way from Nanty to paint doors unless they are special ones." She flung down the knife. "The Mortymers—it is always the Mortymers to set the examples and do the spouting, and when it comes to the end of it less notice is taken than if we were Twm-y-Beddau or the Ffyrnigs."

The walk to Garndyrus was worth seeing that morning.

Every light in The Square was on; people very busy hanging out washing when it was too dark to see pegs. Men who should have been abed were smoking in doorways, and the coming and going up and down garden paths was enough for Fair Day. All up North Street it was the same. Two windows out of the whole of the Row were in darkness. Even Polly Morgan was standing outside the door of the Drum and Monkey, and people were clustered in the yards of Shop Row, talking fifteen to the dozen.

Jethro walked between my father and me. He was working in the Garndyrus Forge with Roberts—I was glad he was not out on the tramways, where an attack could be made to look an accident. I was not worried about my mother or Edwina. Probert had not flogged a woman yet, with or without a Union card.

"If they come it will be tonight," said my father, voicing my thoughts.

"Aye," I said.

"And I will see to it my way, Iestyn, do you understand?"

"By hitting the first one flat? That is the way they tried it in Blackwood. One good leg between four of them they had after Probert was finished." I trudged on, my eyes closed to the pale light of the morning stars.

"And how would you handle Probert?" There was a smile in his words.

"By the three of us buying Union Cards and signing off midday," I replied. "I am good for a fight if there is a chance, but the Cattle are roving in sixties."

"The town will stand by us," said he.

"Aye?" It was Jethro this time, his face upturned. "Twm-y-Beddau next door said to hell with the Mortymers when it comes to Scotch Cattle, and straight over the mountain with him at the first sight of Dai Probert."

"Twm-y-Beddau does not represent the people of this town, thank God," said my father. "The town will stand by us."

"And why should it?" I asked sharp. "We are paid by Crawshay Bailey."

"Look you, stupid," he replied, getting short. "We are paid here in the end. It is only a money transaction in the books, see; only an entry, man. It is this owner we work for."

"God help us," I said. "When Dai Probert hits down the door tonight you can explain the money part of it to him for he cannot count up to five."

"Let him come!" shouted Jethro, fists up, striking at nothing. "Over into Twm-y-Beddau's garden I will hit him and bury him in the Baptist churchyard."

"You cannot see or you will not see," said my father, his eyes on me, his face taut.

"I see all right," I said, "but will Probert? It is him handing out the floggings."

"God help him when I am done with him, mind," said Jethro, still sparring.

"I wonder where your sense is, too," I said, eyeing him.

"And I am wondering which son I would rather have," said

my father. "Ten years back you would have been sparring for a fight, like Jethro. Now you are whining about striking and Union cards. What the devil is wrong with this generation?"

I did not reply. I dare not. The injustice was burning me. His obstinacy against the Union was a stupidity that involved not only us but our women. He despised my generation for its refusal to grovel to authority as he had grovelled and his father before him. Theirs was the blind loyalty that had brought about the need for Unions when, if the profits were shared, there was plenty for everybody. I saw my father in a new light that morning: a man of clay; one ready to tug the forelock as the squire went by. He was set against any form of resistance to the masters who were bleeding us; against the Union, which demanded the right to put a standard upon its labour; against the Benefit Clubs, which existed to feed the starving; and against the coming Charter, which was the new standard of decency forged by men of learning and courage, men like Lovett and O'Connor, the heroes of my generation.

We walked on into the gathering light of the morning. There might have been other blacklegs—men who would pay for their courage—but it seemed to me as we walked down the tram road to the Garndyrus furnaces that we were the only scabs in the county.

The shift was changing and the iron was coming out, and I saw hate in the faces of the men around us. Idris Foreman was standing at Number Two, hitching at his belt.

"You are asking for trouble this time," said he. "More sense you should have, Mortymer, with Probert loose and two women at home."

The puddlers were tapping and the iron was streaming and firing in the sand moulds. Eyes on the Mortymers from all directions; the Mortymers who were on the books of Nantyglo and breaking the Nantyglo strike.

My father did not answer.

"For God's sake!" whispered Will Blaenavon to me. "What the hell are you up to, man? And you with a Union card, too!"

"I do what my father does," I said.

"But it is madness. Have sense! Tomorrow or the day after Garndyrus might be out, too."

They were coming in from the mountain: the mule drovers, the miners, the limestone cutters, the sprag-men, to end the old shift. And while we waited in the heat of the furnaces for the manager to check us in, they eyed us. Leaning on shovels or ladles, with their backs against their trams or lying on the slag, they eyed us. Owen Howells came up with Griff, hands in the waist of his trews, his grin wide.

"Look where you like, deacon," he said, "you will never find such stupidity in the Book, and you have told me to look there once or twice. Probert will take the pair of you and draw bones from your back."

All that day not another man spoke to us, not even to Jethro.

So much for neighbours, I said to my father, and nobody can blame them.

We went back home in daylight, watched the same as on the way out. Dusk came, then darkness. We ate our tea in silence. My mother's face was calm, but her eyes strained. Fear was in Edwina's face, in her trembling hands. Earlier there had been talk of sending her down to Snell at Abergavenny, but my father decided against it. When the family runs the house dies, he said. So we cleared away the things and sat round the fire, Mam spinning, as usual, Edwina well into the Old Testament but not reading a word, and the rest of us listening to the wind. At nine o'clock I went down the garden path to look at the night. The town was dead under the bright stars and the roofs shone black and silver in the frosty air. Not a sound the town made. It crouched in its shadows, holding its breath, amazed at the stupidity of the Mortymers, who had broken the Nantyglo strike and told Dai Probert to go to hell.

And then I heard it.

Faintly on the wind came the lowing of the Cattle, and the sound grew in fury. Like a madness, it was, this faint bellowing. Grown men dressed in the skins of beasts, bellowing in grief for the ones to be flogged. They were coming from the

Coity. Sparks from their torches sailed up against the clouds. All up North Street keys were being turned, bolts thrust over, windows pegged down. The lowing of the Cattle grew nearer. Light shot over the garden as my father opened the door of the back.

"Iestyn."

I went to him.

"Listen," he said. "This is the end of Probert, not us. Do not fight. I will do the talking, you will stay with Mam. When I go with Probert send Jethro to bring Rhys Jenkins and Mo. You run for Mr Traherne and fetch as many men as you can to guard the house and save a burning. There is a military troop waiting for Probert and his Cattle on the road to Nantyglo, waiting to catch him with a prisoner. This was arranged weeks back by the owners. You have your Union card?"

And me thinking he did not know . . .

"Yes," I said, ashamed.

"Show it when they ask—they will not touch Jethro. Probert takes me out for a flogging and lands in the arms of the military. It is time his scum was cleared from the mountains—a good thing for the Union, the workers and the owners, all in one, eh?"

"Yes, Dada," I said.

"For what a man believes in he must fight for, remember. In to the women now, Edwina is taking it hard."

They came in minutes, bellowing, but they went silent when they reached our gate and clustered together, grumbling deep, like cattle nosing an empty manger. Edwina was whimpering in my mother's arms. Our door was unlocked, to save them the trouble of breaking it down. Whispers now as they came over the gate. Silence as they huddled together by the window. My father flung open the door. Six deep they stood, their blackened faces streaming sweat from the running and bellowing. Some were in skins, others in rags, with naked chests and shoulders scarred with the weals of old burns. The light from our kitchen flung the shadows into their eyes, and their sunken, starved faces stared into the room.

Silence, but for their breathing, Edwina's sighing, and the ticking of the clock.

"Well?" said my father. "You come with enough noise. Is there nobody with a tongue?" He stood with his fists on his hips like a giant before them.

"Dai Probert will do the talking," said one in a soft Irish accent.

"Then fetch your bull, for at least he is Welsh. I am not talking to Irish."

"Dai Probert coming now," said another, a gnome of a man with a bandaged face. "And take it from me, Mortymer, you will not know Welsh from Irish before we have finished."

He came with a whip, swinging his comrades aside with his wide shoulders. He was dressed as all Scotch Cattle bulls, in ragged skins that left his chest bare. His face was blackened for night beating but his cheeks were criss-crossed with the vicious ridges of a furnace blow-back, and the wounds were white. The red horns of a cow were strapped to his head with a bandage. He was filthy, and the stink of him crept about us. Inches taller than my father, he outweighed him by stones.

"Hywel Mortymer?" he asked in Welsh.

My father nodded.

"And your son—both on the books of Nantyglo?"

"We work for Hill of Garndyrus."

"To hell with where you work, man—you are paid by Bailey?"

"On behalf of Mr Hill," said my father.

"Aye," and he looked very old fashioned at his Irish. "Nantyglo or Garndyrus, let us see your Union cards or the colour of your money. Your names are on the books of Bailey, and no swine of a blackleg starves our children."

"I have no card," replied my father. "And I do not join anything under the threat of a whip, so away, before I kick you and your Irish back to Nanty."

"Dear me, listen to it!" said Probert. "There is too much talk here for my liking. Moc, boy!" he called. "Have this

173

bastard out into the street for a flogging. Pitch out the women, take the food next door and leave me to the furniture."

A brutal-faced man in skins moved through the crowd at the door. Probert turned to me. "Where is your card?"

"Here," and I offered it, but my father snatched it and flung it away.

"Be clear about this, Probert," he said. "One in a family is a member to you but a scab to me, and he has just resigned." Seeing Probert's changed expression, I looked down. My father held a flintlock pistol. "Now out!" he cried. "Or I will blow your stomach into the legs of the man behind you. Fetch me for a flogging now, man, do not run. To hell with you and your Union that is backed by the whips of bastard Welshmen," and he drove forward into them, the pistol in one hand, hitting out with the other. They flooded before him, tripping over the smashed gate, crying warnings to their comrades on the road.

"Rush him!" roared Probert.

"Aye, rush," cried my father, "for I am tired of playing bloody fancy with scum. Scotch Cattle you call yourselves? Unionists, are you? God forbid that I ever drop a penny a week to the likes of you. Rush and be damned to you," and he walked through them, striking them down, working closer to Probert, who was afraid of the gun. I could not see Dada for the crowd now, but I heard his voice from the road:

"Iestyn! Back in with the women while I drive this rabble back to Nanty where they belong!"

And those were the last words I heard as the Cattle rose about him and struck him down. Baying, lowing, they dragged him to the Brynmawr Road. I watched them take him, sick with despair. And the thing shining in the gutter was a little flintlock pistol. With this he had shifted fifty Scotch Cattle.

I went back to the kitchen. Jethro was there with his arm about my mother. Edwina was crying alone.

"He has moved them from the house, Mam," I said. "He is taking them to the military, who are waiting for Probert."

"God help him," she said at nothing.

"He is working it for the owners, understand?" I shook her. "He is the bait through which the military will catch Probert. It is all arranged. No harm will come to him."

My mother rose. Little and old she looked then, as if ten years had come with the mob and touched her. "Believe that and you are a larger fool than I took you for," she said. "He is too big a man to be a bait for the English against the Welsh—even Scotch Cattle Welsh. He has told you that to keep you safe." Bending, she picked up my Union card and tore it to pieces. "Jethro," she said, "Run down to Mr Rhys Jenkins' house and tell him to come with all the men he can collect. Iestyn," and she turned to me, "go and fetch Tomos Traherne, then away to your father and share what he is having. We will watch the house so you have a roof to come back to, and nothing on your conscience."

In a panic at the thought of dishonour, I ran.

Over the tumps to River Row I went, and screamed it at Tomos, then on to the mountain, sick inside that I had let Dada go without lifting a finger. It began to rain and the night was coming down black and with a nip of winter frost in the wind, and the Coity was blue and misted against a sodden moon. The rain came harder, blinding me in the open country and driving in waves over the heather. A madness seized me then and drove me on down the slope of the mountain. For half an hour I searched before I saw three torches smoking in the rain and another four taking a path to distant Nantyglo, waved in the hands of men. Three more blazed steadily, in a triangle, and I knew that the mob had delivered its justice. The undergrowth thickened in the valley and I tore a path through thorn and bramble towards the three points of light. The scent of burning wood was in the air, changing to the tang of melted tar as I drew nearer. I crashed on, flinging aside the branches towards a far clearing that I saw reflected in red light. Sobbing for breath, I stumbled to the edge of the clearing and a man's shape rose up clearly outlined. I saw the curve of his jaw and the swing of his shoulders as he leaped to face me. With my last strength I hooked a blow at the jaw and felt the jarring pain in my elbow as my fist caught him square. He fell, tumbling sideways against me, and I held him off with one hand and smashed him to the ground with the other. He lay down with a sigh, and I tripped over his body into the clearing.

They were cutting my father free. Rhys Jenkins and the Howells boys were kneeling beside him, and blood was on their hands. Nearby lay Mo Jenkins, his chin upturned against the light and his chest heaving like a dying man. I knelt by my father.

"Better late than never, man," said Big Rhys with bile in his voice. "Will your friends always have to do your fighting?"

My father was lying as the Cattle had left him, face down, arms and legs outstretched, but cut free of the pegs. He was bare to the waist and his shirt had been flogged into bloody shreds over his trews. His back, from the bulge of his biceps to his hips, was stripped of skin, and the weals of the whips were as proud as fingers on his flesh.

"Dada," I said.

Not my father, this one. Slits for eyes, this one, with cuts running across each other and the mouth split top and bottom; suffused with blood, this face, from the booting of the mob.

I wept.

Big Rhys stirred his feet in the soaked grass beside me.

"Do not bother him," he said. "And do not mind his face —it is not so bad as it looks. I have had worse in my time from hobnails, but his back is down to the bone."

"Not whips, see," said Owen Howells. "Willow sticks, the swines. Two of them at him, and Probert dancing mad because he would not give a groan."

"And he still has not signed for the Union," said Griff. He peered at me. "Where the hell did you get to, boyo?"

I told them about the Military.

"Where is your sense?" Rhys asked him. "A man has to save his furniture, and why should two wage-earners take a

176

flogging and miss shifts when one will do? Even Probert would see the sense of that." He grinned at me. "Your flogging will come with the Union card. That will be a pretty one to answer."

"He knew," I said. "He knew all the time I was in the Union." I stood up. "What is wrong with Mo by there?"

"Just a stone on the nut, nothing to bother," said Rhys. "We were coming out of the Lamb Row public when we heard the palaver, see? So me and Mo followed the Cattle to here. Owen and Griff waded in minutes before, but the Cattle pinned them down to watch the flogging. But Mo put Probert on his back and took a stone on the nut from behind. Very handy are these hooligans with hitting from behind."

"Mo is breathing now," said Owen, kneeling.

"Good," said Rhys beside my father. "Rattle him under the chops—no need for him to make a meal of it."

My father spoke then. Bloody froth was on his lips.

"Iestyn?"

"Yes, Dada."

"Away with this old coat and let the rain on my back. I am not going home in this state." He clutched the grass and buried his face in it.

I lifted my coat from his back and watched the rain wash him clean.

"There is cool," he said. "God, there is cool!"

"Look you, Hywel—are you there, boy?" called Rhys from the darkness.

"Aye, here, Rhys," said my father.

"Do not disturb yourself, mind, but hearken to me. This son of mine by here. There is a good old stone he took on the nut. Only a relation of the great Dai Benyon Champion could expose his brains and live to see them."

"That is the first brains I have heard of in the Jenkins family," said my father, tearing at grass. "Tell him not to overdo it—he will get worse from Knocker Daniels at Carmarthen a week next Friday."

"Ready, is it, Hywel?"

"Aye, ready, man," said my father.

"Up then!" said Rhys. "Home with the invalids. Come on, Mo, step lively!", and he rattled poor Mo under the chin to straighten him. "Home quick, or the women will have chest troubles to deal with as well as split heads and backs. And me to rub salad oil into my hands, for they are stiff to hell with hitting out hooligans."

"Is it all right with Mam and Edwina, Iestyn?" asked Dada.

"Aye," I said.

"The furniture is safe?"

"Yes, Dada."

"Good, my son." He turned on his side. "Rise me now, and easy with you on my poor old back, eh?"

"Look, Dada, I will run for old Snell's trap and we will do it in style. . . ."

"To the devil with Snell's trap," said Rhys, coming up. "You cannot drive a man home from a flogging. He will fit snug across my back."

"Nor is he frogmarched," said my father. "He walks. Iestyn, rise me."

Owen came on the other side and we lifted him while Big Rhys snorted in disgust.

"Now leave me," said my father, and Owen and I stood aside, leaving him bowed and swaying. And if my mother had come in search of him she would have passed him by, not knowing.

"Mo is ready," called Griff. "And what is more he remembers the one who stoned him, so his brains are undamaged. It was Moc Evans, a spare time Scotch Cattle, one who did the flogging."

"Then he can write his will," said Rhys. "I got the other flogger, mind. I had him with my boot when he had finished and put him down in the heather by here, but the swine crawled off."

"And I put him down again coming in by that path," I said.

"God be praised," exclaimed Owen. "The devil may still be with us," and he ran to the edge of the clearing and kicked aside the heather.

178

He was there.

We ringed him as he climbed to his feet. With Griff holding a torch high we pulled him out and blood was on his hands and the willow stick with which he had flogged my father was near him. Down he went again now, grovelling, pleading, reaching for our boots.

It was Dafydd Phillips.

"Aye," said Rhys to me. "There's a surprise. Very friendly are the relations in your family by the look of it." He bent and handed me the willow stick. "Peg him, flog him fifty and kick him back to his criminals in Nanty. Owen, you will help Iestyn. Griff, you will help me get the invalids back to town. We will go slow, Iestyn, and meet you on the Brynmawr Corner."

I saw Dafydd's face as he raised it to the light, streaked with rain and sweat, one eye still shut tight. He opened his mouth to shout for my father but Big Rhys shut it with the toe of his boot.

"Give it him," he said, "before I start it myself."

It was the law.

Owen and I waited until Big Rhys and Griff had got my father clear, then we pegged him and I tore back his shirt and flogged him fifty with the same stick he had taken to my father.

And when I had finished and his howls were over, we booted him across the grass to the Brynmawr Road, and left him.

Big Rhys and Griff were resting Mo and my father on the Brynmawr Corner. There we formed up and went into town. Down North Street we went, past the people huddled on the doorsteps of the Row, and I knew in an instant something was wrong, for the women were wringing their hands and weeping. The crowd parted as we reached it, and my father, soaked with blood and rain, walked through it to our front door. Twm-y-Beddau was there beside my mother. Edwina and Jethro stood nearby. There was a smell of burning in the air and ashes were hot under the feet.

"They came back, Hywel," said Twm-y-Beddau. "They flogged you first to be sure of it, they said. My woman has your food. Dai Pig is alive, although they looked at him twice, mind."

This was the law of the Scotch Cattle. Every stick of furniture was burned, every possession except the clothes we stood in, Edwina's Bible, food and money.

CHAPTER FIFTEEN

FOR TEN days my father lay on straw with bandages over his face and back, groaning at times, but mostly playing hell because I had left the house unguarded.

But heroes overnight, the Mortymers.

"Mind," said Tomos Traherne on one of his visits to us, "you are popular for handing back a flogging, for that is a rare thing to happen to Scotch Cattle. But it is not forgotten that you were scabs, either here or in Nanty."

That was right, too, as we found out later.

The whispering grew into thunder when Mr Hart, the Nantyglo agent, came to visit us. Neighbours were hanging on the garden walls like beans when his pony and trap came up to The Square all burnished and jingling.

Very toothy, this Mr Hart, handy from the waist down, I heard, every inch of him bowing and scraping on the threshold, for he knew how the Welsh loved an ironmaster's agent. Six feet of skin and bone, this one, with an onion for a head sitting in the bowl of his high starched collar; wringing his hands and blessing us for our courage and wishing to God there was more like us.

My mother wished him to hell privately. A visit from an Agent often meant one from the ironmaster, she said, and not even the Mortymers deserved that.

Ten shillings he brought as a gift towards the furniture we had lost, but better were the gifts that came from neighbours.

A scrubbing brush and broom from Mrs Roberts, Sara's mam. Mrs Tossach up at Cae White sent us two blankets, and Willie Gwallter brought down three pictures of country scenes and a ram dying in snow. The Howells boys made up a chair and Rhys and Mo trundled down a settle. The Stafford men landed us with pots and pans, the Garndyrus Irish came loaded with two tables and a chest of drawers. By the time everybody was finished we were only short of beds, and that went round like fire. But nothing could replace the things we had lost, not even the kindness of neighbours.

But there are neighbours and neighbours, and there were some who hated us. Mrs Dic Shon Ffyrnig, for instance.

I was knocking in nails, making a bed for my father when Mrs Ffyrnig called with something to go under it; a two gallon china one by the size of it. Mrs Pantrych, full again by the look of her, was there beside her, grinning on the door-step.

"Good morning, Mrs Mortymer," they said in tune.

Here to bring the Mortymers down a peg. Sin and mischief was in their faces.

"Good morning," said my mother, enough to freeze.

"Just called with the good wishes of the Benefit, Elianor," said Mrs Ffyrnig. "And Dic Shon do say what a terrible thing it is mixing labour with politics."

"I have been telling your husband that for years," said Mam.

"Aye, but the Benefit might have saved him, girl. All your good things burned, and some were good quality, too, as I was telling Mrs Pantrych when Mr Moc Evans brought them out."

"Especially in the bedding line, if I might say," said Mrs Pantrych. "How is your poor man now?"

"Healthier than before he was flogged," said Mam, "and life is easier for the family."

"Eh no! Fighting for his life, they told us."

"Ten days from now it will be Dai Probert Scotch Cattle fighting for his," replied my mother. "He will give them Scotch Cattle and Probert in particular, or I was not born in Cyfarthfa. Thankful I am for seeing you, good morning to you, now."

"On behalf of the Benefit, please accept this token of our respect," said Mrs Ffyrnig. "A special collection was made last night and this brought from Pontypool," and from behind her she brought out the china, not even wrapped. "Something to go under the bed when you get it, girl," and they threw back their heads and cackled like hens.

Very fast down that path went Mrs Ffyrnig and Mrs Pantrych with the special collection after them, and Mam slammed the door to warm its hinges.

"There is a pair of old bitches," she said.

"Do not mind them, Mam," I replied, starting my sawing.

"They came to laugh and gloat, not in charity like the others." Twisting her fingers now and walking about. "Special collection, indeed. I would not have their old china if it was silver-plated, but it is all you can expect from people not Chapel."

"Easy," I said. "It was a gift, Mam, though it was stupid of them to giggle. Church or Chapel makes no difference, dear."

Suddenly, without warning, she began to cry in gasps, her fingers forming a cage over her mouth, stifling the indignity.

"Hush you," I said. "Dada has not given a sigh."

"O, my poor Hywel, sad I am! Sad for you and my home, and all my pretty little things from Cyfarthfa. Not a bed between us, and all because of politics like the old bitch said."

"Dada flogged for a principle, not politics."

"Principle or politics, it is all the same," said she, sniffing and wiping. "There is a mess for you. His back torn to shreds and his face booted in. And it is not finished yet, mark me. I know that one upstairs."

"It is finished, we have won," I said, my arms around her. "The town is with us to the end, now. Next time Probert shows his nose will be the last. Every worker from here to Garndyrus will be after him since Dada made his stand. And as for furniture, you will have a houseful when I get this old saw going smooth."

"God bless you, Iestyn," she whispered. "But it is a bed I am after first, see? This old cot you are making can come later, boy. It is a bed I need to raise my man from straw."

"One coming tonight," I said, and went on sawing.

"Have sense," said she, drying up. "Where from, may I ask?"

"Never mind where from," I said. "A good strong iron bed with a mattress is due this evening, and do not say it is any the worse for belonging to Iolo Milk."

Up on her feet now and blazing. "Do I hear right?" she cried. "Iolo Milk, is it? And his bed at that? Listen, you! Unconscious I will be when I place my body on a bed belonging to that one, and do you hear me? We are poor in all truth, but I would rather sleep with the devil than on a bed of fornication." Pale and shocked she looked. "An old hair mattress too, I suppose."

"Feather," I replied. "But what does it matter if you will not have it?"

"Indeed not. I am not having the couch of the Devil in the house and it was shameful of you to suggest it."

I sighed, and went on sawing.

"Do you hear me? Shameful!"

"Yes, Mother."

"Then do you mind me," and she went round the room looking daggers and twisting at her fingers.

"I hope I have made myself clear," said she after a bit.

I was hitting in nails now. "Clear on what?" I asked, the hammer up.

"This old bed. Over my dead body it comes through that door, you understand?"

"All right, all right. *Dammo di!* I will tell Iolo Milk to kick it to China and back so long as we have some peace."

"Double, is it?" she asked then.

I put down the hammer. "Listen," I said. "The thing will sleep four in comfort, not that you are interested. It is solid iron with brass balls, a spring under a feather mattress and rollers on its feet, and Iolo Milk said he can bounce his backside six feet high and it doesn't give a groan, which is more than can be said for the ones Probert burned."

"No need to be vulgar," she replied sharp. "Anyway, we would never get it through the door."

"It comes to bits," I said, "but I am sorry I mentioned it."

"Well then, I will give it some thought," she answered. "Kick it to China and back, indeed! There is good in everybody and I am not having Iolo Milk insulted. So you get this bed up to Dada the moment it comes or you will never hear the end of it."

"Good God," I said.

With her mouth a little red button and her nose up, she left me.

As long as I live I will remember the coming of Iolo's iron bed.

Jethro saw it first and came in whooping like an Indian and pointing. Up the hill laboured Enid Donkey with the bed over her back and steadied either side by Iolo's Irish friends. And up to the door came Iolo, dressed in his Sunday best with the mock carnation he wore especially for women-killing and his white teeth flashing.

"Good afternoon, Mrs Mortymer," said he. "Here is a good strong bed fit to hold a fighter for the community," and he swept off his cap into the gutter with a nobility and grace that would have brought joy to the Young Queen.

"God bless you, Iolo," said Mam, all blushes.

"And the same to you, girl," he replied. "I am having a better welcome this time than last, remember? Flat down by here your man hit me, and I came with the same honourable intentions as now, mind."

"But he was not himself that day, boy. Eh dear! There is a strong iron bed," said she, patting it.

"Very comfortable the pair of you will be, Mrs Mortymer, for I have spent enjoyable hours on this feather mattress. And with a woman of your proportions a man would be a fool not to follow my example, no offence intended."

"O, Iolo!" giggled Mam.

"In with it," I said to him, "no need for details," for the neighbours were gathering and whispering. Giggles, too, for everybody knew that Iolo used his beds for anything but sleeping in.

"How now?" asked Iolo, when it was set up for examination.

"Wonderful," said Mam, and everybody nodded, for the window was up and the door open and half the neighbours were in or coming.

"Then up with a broom to scatter the crowd," shouted

Iolo, "for we need a bit of privacy. There is a history to this four-poster, Mrs Mortymer, and I am just in the mood to tell it."

"Hush, you!" I said, elbowing him while the neighbours roared and my mother went scarlet.

"*Diawl!*" he cried. "Here is an example of false modesty. With little Iestyn scarcely out of his woollens it is understandable, woman, but for the likes of you and me, girl, we could teach this old bed a thing or two, look you. *Dammo!* Do not look so grieved, Elianor. A very fine friend is a bed, with blankets over it in cold and nothing at all in hot, and every other page of the Good Book talking about courtings, deaths, and births between four posts. And look you how soft!" Up with him then and down on it and bounced three feet. "Now settle yourself here with me, Elianor, and we will christen the thing, for to lie full length with a milkman in the sight of neighbours is going half way to a fortune."

"O, Iolo!" giggled Mam. "Hell and damnation on you for such a suggestion, and me married!" And she peeped and wriggled like a maid. "True, is it?"

"*Mam!*" I said.

"Whoo, there!" cried Iolo, getting ferocious. "Here is sixpence to clear the neighbours while I tell your mam the story of this very fine bed, Iestyn."

"Good afternoon," I said. "We have had enough of you."

"Enough? And with your little mam here just coming girlish? I would harm her, you think? In the same house as her man who has taken a flogging? Cleanse your mind, my boy. When the great call comes I will be there in the Upper Palace under the hand of St Peter while you brew tea in the coals of hell. Eh dear, Mrs Mortymer, forgive the rising generation who do turn a little harmless fun into an improper suggestion."

"Do not heed him, Iolo," she replied, keen now. "What about the history of this bed?"

"It is a pleasant history in truth," said Iolo, sighing. "Megan and me were two years married and childless when this bed came to us—through the family, you understand, after knowing nothing but happy lovers and easy births. My grandfather from Carmarthen bought it in London from a travelling tinker who was in tears at parting with it, for his three wives had rested their fair limbs in it, cleaving in joy before dying in peace on it. Fifteen children had that tinker, all on this bed, mind, and two wives had my grandfather and each brought forth six. And since we are four now and Megan waiting for the fifth you cannot but respect an article that bore half the population of Carmarthen before coming to Monmouthshire to start all over again."

"Wonderful!" everybody cried.

"Aye," said Iolo, "so you can have it with my blessing, for with Megan full again I would rather she slept on heather than this old mattress. Out with the old thing, Megan said, and take it down to Hywel Mortymer, who has less chance of being caught turning than me."

Which put everybody double, of course.

"And proper, too," said my mother, crimson again "for some beds are suspicious things indeed, but my man will sleep soft upon it. A cup of tea before you go, Iolo?"

"Something stronger, woman," said he. "I am away to the Drum and Monkey to fortify my soul, for I was hoping to find you alone. I am a wicked man indeed, but I know I am beaten when faced with such virtue and a six-foot son within kicking distance."

"O, go on with you!" said Mam, very pretty with her.

And he took her hand and kissed it, bowing low, which put the neighbours on tiptoe and screaming with laughter.

"This way out," I said, showing him the door, but Edwina came flying through it with her basket waving and her white hair blowing over her face.

"I will have that cup of tea now, Mrs Mortymer," said Iolo at once, eyeing Edwina. "Two of a kind are always more enjoyable than one."

"Indeed you will not!" cried Edwina. "You will away outside and clear that Enid Donkey from the gate for there is a visitor with a coach and pair prancing outside and postillions grinding their teeth with rage."

187

"Who is it?" I asked, for the neighbours were vanishing.

"A man in a cape," she gasped, "and blue in the face with him and get to hell out of it with that damned old donkey."

"O, hisht, Edwina," breathed Mam.

"A coach and pair, you say. What like was he?"

"Thick and black, with a riding crop and boots."

"And postillions, you say?" whispered Iolo.

"Two, and two white mares," said Edwina.

"Coming in here? God help us!" said Iolo. "Crawshay Bailey!" and he was straight through the door and over Twm-y-Beddau's hedge without touching a leaf while the rest of the neighbours scattered.

"Crawshay Bailey!" whispered my mother, going white.

"Aye, and what of it!" I asked, but she swung from me. "Edwina," she said, "upstairs to the children's bedroom quick, and not a sound from you till I say come out."

"But why, Mam?"

"Away!" And she drove Edwina before her with her apron, locked the bedroom door, and dropped its key down the neck of her bodice, all in seconds. Trembling, she came back to me, her hands to her face.

"Easy with you," I said. "He has two legs, two arms and one head, and he is not the King of England."

"But damned near it," she said. "Crawshay Bailey coming and that old Enid Donkey and Iolo Milk dropping the tone of the place," and she went around the bare room demented with a duster.

No time for more. He was in.

No knocking from this one who owned a town, its people and his iron empire. He stood on the threshold with his cape thrown back, showing the fine cut of his black frock coat. Lace was at his wrists and throat. This was the iron master who looked like a country squire, the man notorious in commerce, hated equally by workers and unions; disdaining aristocratic gestures, this one, brother to Joseph, the tramping boy, who took a donkey to Cyfarthfa and borrowed a thousand pounds to crucify Nantyglo. Feet astride he bent his riding crop over his belly and peered at us.

"Mistress Mortymer?"

Mam bobbed a curtsey, speechless, her hands shaking her skirt.

"And you?" His florid, baby face swung to me.

"Iestyn, the son," I said.

"The son of the man who was flogged."

"Aye, sir."

He walked in, owning the place, and the authority crept out of him and owned us, too.

"My sympathy on the loss of your furniture, ma'am," he said. "But it is happening every week between here and Blackwood, the Welsh breaking the limbs of their fellows and destroying the homes of the Welsh. We are doing all we can to stop it."

"Thank you, sir," said my mother.

"Irish workers, mostly," I said, "and from Nanty."

His eyes flicked to me. "Is Probert Irish?"

"For every Probert there are fifty Irish."

"Interesting," said he. "I will note it. What trade are you?"

"Spragger," I said.

"What do I pay you?"

"Six shilling a week."

"Remember it. Speak when I bid you or you will find yourself on the blacklist." He turned to my mother. "You were here when the furniture was burned, woman?"

"Aye, sir," she said faintly.

"Then you recognised the man Probert?"

"Yes, sir."

"Could you identify others if called upon?"

"Only Probert, sir. . . ."

"God," said he, and groaned, turning.

"It was night," whispered my mother. "Both my men had gone when the Cattle came back and drove me out and pulled out the furniture. Their faces were blackened. . . ."

"And where were you?" he turned to me.

"One for the flogging, one to earn, or the family starves," I said. "My father ordered me to stay here when they took him."

His expression changed and he nodded at the sense of it.

"But I flogged one back," I said. "I flogged him fifty to mark him."

"You knew this man?"

"No."

"But you would recognise him?"

"It was dark," I said. "I did not see his face."

There was no sound but the steady tap of his crop against his high leather boots, then he said, "And that is the end of it. There is no law, no recognition of authority. One is flogged, his son flogs back. At a time when the transportation hulks are filling their holds with hooligans you flog a man with a whip, a nameless man." Walking to the window he stared out. "I pay taxes for military protection, but not a single worker can pick Scotch Cattle from the identity parades." He lowered his voice. "Your memory appears better than your son's, Mrs Mortymer. If Probert is caught I will depend upon you to identify him, remember it."

"She will not," I said quickly. "My father would never allow it. It is asking for death to name one of the Cattle."

"Name a few, hang a few, and we will soon be rid of them," he replied.

Blindly, I went on, in dread of the blacklist but forced to answer him. "Hanging a few will not sweep them from the mountains," I said. "The Cattle are with us because of the blacklist, and the blacklist is with us because of the Irish you import as ballast to undercut the wages of the Welsh. You will never sweep away Scotch Cattle. As the Union grows stronger they will multiply to force the hand of the workers against the wages and conditions of labour."

He fixed me with his eyes.

"You are trying to help but doing it backwards," I said. "You bring the Irish in barrels, put them in the bridge arches and pay them in iron coins, with fat old prices in your Company Shops and cheap beer for them in The Bush. You expect us to be the same but we will never be, because we are Welsh."

"O, Iestyn!" whimpered my mother, eyes wide.

"Shut it, woman," I said. "He can starve us but he cannot hang us, so to hell with him and anything to do with iron."

"Well said," replied Bailey. "Pray continue."

"Aye, and welcome," I said, desperately. "My father belongs to no Benefit or Union. He has taught me that it is loyalty to the master that counts, but I am changing my mind, for it is a stink to work on the books of a man who treats his workers like trash, drives them to the mountains as outlaws and expects their countrymen to betray them."

"Are you finished?" he asked, calm.

"Just about," I said. "Get rid of the Irish, negotiate with the Union, close the Tommy Shops and raise wages all round. That will get rid of the Cattle. Leave the rest to the workers and you will send more iron to Newport than Dowlais and Merthyr put together."

The room tinkled with silence. From his waistcoat pocket he drew out a little book and pencil.

"Name?" he said.

"I have told you. Iestyn Mortymer."

"Good," said he, and wrote it down. He snapped the book shut and put it back into his pocket. "Raise your voice to me again and I will bring this family to its sense, but flog a few more Cattle and I will raise your pay." He turned to my mother. "Pack what you have left, Mrs Mortymer, for you are coming to live in Nantyglo, but keep a guard on this boy's tongue for he is too young to know the length of it. Now take me to your husband. I can do with men like yours to speak with honesty and break strikes and flog Scotch Cattle."

Not much wrong with Crawshay on the day he came to town.

CHAPTER SIXTEEN

AND SO, on a cold day in mid-October, we cleared from home and set off for Nanty, and it was sad.

Good people are neighbours in time of trouble, and anyone moving to Nantyglo at a time like this was in for plenty, said Tomos Traherne behind my mother's back. For news from Nantyglo was bad. Special arrangements were being made to receive us, it was said, with bands of strikers waiting on the roadside to welcome the blacklegs and give them hell.

But worst of all, Dafydd Phillips had left Morfydd and taken to the mountains with Dai Probert Scotch Cattle, which meant transportation if he was caught, or worse, said my father.

"The Redcoats are after arrests and convictions," said Owen Howells, "but the Volunteer squads will shoot on sight with a set of cow horns for proof."

It was more like a wake than a moving out, for the Irish came up from the valley and packed ten deep on the road outside to sing their songs of home to the Welsh. The children brought leaves and winter flowers to decorate the rooms, and everybody was dressed in best Sunday black to mourn the parting neighbours.

Straight inside for the last sweep up, me, as the Irish began their songs to the Welsh, which is enough to start a fight any Benefit night. For the terrible thing about Irish is that they think they can sing. But how can voices that bear a grudge give joy? All the Irish can sing about is how wicked it is in Ireland under the English and how cruel the rest of the world is to the Irish, but we will straighten our backs and put up with it all for the sake of Killarney.

No offence to the Irish, says my father, but he would rather listen to the Welsh.

On that morning of parting no instruments made sweeter

sounds than the voices of our neighbours in full harmony. I stood at the top of the stairs and leaned on the broom and listened to the pure altos, the soaring tenors and the sweet sopranos sitting on a foundation of rough bass. From the window I saw the people packed in the square. Big Rhys and Mo Jenkins were there shoulder to shoulder with the Howells boys, Will Blaenavon, Afel Hughes and Mr Roberts, all the men of Garndyrus. Mrs Gwallter was leading the sopranos; Mrs Pantrych and Mrs Ffyrnig, respectable for once, were letting it fly, Dathyl Jenkins and Gwen Lewis were singing to the sky, and round them were ringed the neighbours of the Rows, and people come from as far afield as Cae White.

And there in front was Tomos Traherne, double bass, beating time.

Give me a hymn to a good Welsh tune to bring out pride of race and love of country. The key is minor and the very breath of Wales. I thought of the mountains and valleys; of the great names of the north filled with magic; of Plynlymon, Snowdon and Cader Idris, the mountain chair of the clouds, and the great flat tracts where the Roman legions formed; of ancient Brecon that still echoes the clash of alien swords; of Senny, and the Little England beyond Wales. I saw a vision of ancients long dead whose bones have kindled the fire of greatness; of Howell Harris and William Williams, great with the Word. I thought of my river, the Afon-Lwydd, that my father had fished in youth, with rod and line for the leaping salmon under the drooping alders. The alders, he said, that fringed the banks ten deep, planted by the wind of the mountains. But no salmon leap in the river now, for it is black with furnace washings and slag, and the great silver fish have been beaten back to the sea or gasped out their lives on sands of coal. No alders stand now for they have been chopped as fuel for the cold blast. Even the mountains are shells, groaning in their hollows of emptiness, trembling to the arrows of the pit-props in their sides, bellowing down the old workings that collapse in unseen dust five hundred feet below.

Plundered is my country, violated, *raped*.

On goes the hymn. The wind was playing tricks with hair

and bonnet streamers, sniffing at the dewdrop on Willie Gwallter's nose, picking up the hem of Polly Morgan's skirt, bringing Owen's eyes down. From the window I saw it all, and could have wept.

I knew then that I loved my town, my people, my country.

The room faced me, the room where Mam delivered Jethro.

What is there in a house that lodges so deeply in the heart? Here is the little square window that faces the mountain, always red with furnace glare, here is the board with the knot shaped like a little brown mouse, here is the stair that creaks, the banister for sliding down, the big black ball at the end that was dangerous to boys, Mam said.

"Iestyn!"

"Aye," I called back. "Coming."

"For God's sake," said my father. "We are off directly."

I knew, then, how the miner feels when he strikes the Farewell Rock. The hymn had finished. Snell's mare was clattering on the cobbles. Everybody was embracing and back-slapping and kissing, with the women letting it go into their handkerchiefs. What little we possessed was loaded on the cart of Shant-y-Brain the undertaker and the back of Enid Donkey. Up we went to the Brynmawr Corner. Over my shoulder I saw Mr and Mrs Roberts and Sara moving in without enough furniture to fill a sty. I was glad the house had gone to Sara. Driving Dai Two before me I followed Snell's trap carrying the rest of the family, and behind me came Shant-y-Brain's cart and Enid Donkey.

And I would have given my soul to turn and run back to the house in the Square.

Nantyglo was still a dead town with the blacklist strikers sitting on their heels, their starved faces pinched in the weak sun of the cold October morning. Redcoats marched in pairs from Brynmawr to Coalbrookvale to keep the peace, and I was thankful to see them for once, although there was no signs of a reception committee. Morfydd was waiting for us at the end of Chapel Road, strong and healthy by the look of her, carrying enough milk to satisfy six, by the size of her. Snell's mare nearly went up when she stepped on the back of the trap, but I got her in somehow, and away we went past Cwm Crachen to Market Road and the house Crawshay had laid for us. Up went the windows and out came the heads and doors came open and washing went aside to size up the new tenants. Solly Widdle Jew was outside the door of Number Six bargaining with the tenant for the furniture he was moving out.

"What is happening here?" asked my mother.

"Shanco Mathews and his family turning out," said Morfydd. "He is up to his neck in debt at The Bush and the Company Shop and last week he was in a row with the Agent for taking part in a demonstration. Crawshay listed him, so now he is out."

"To make room for us, by the look of it," said my father.

"Aye, but it is chiefly the demonstration."

"No home at all now, then?" said Mam, her eyes on Mrs Mathews and three children sitting on the furniture where Shanco and Solly Widdle were bargaining.

"They are going to the old ironworks," said Morfydd. "Their friends are up there now bricking a space. It is the demonstration, see—none of us agree with them. It is branding us all as hooligans for a few, and people in Nanty are respectable." Very happy she looked standing there, waiting for us to move in next door to her; and beautiful, too, as most women are when carrying, with her hair over her shoulders, bright in the eyes and rosy in the cheeks.

I got in front of my father as Shanco Mathews came up from the bargaining. He was middle-aged, quite as tall as me but great in the shoulders and with the look of a mountain fighter. His nose was flattened, both ears screwed to balls. Loose-limbed and free he came over the slag towards us and stood there, hands on hips.

"How are you?" said he, and his voice was as light as a girl's through too many throat punches.

I nodded, sizing his chin for a right.

"Morfydd's relations, is it?" he asked. "The strike-breakers, they tell me."

"Now, now!" said Mam, sharp. "Who are you?"

"Blackbird Shanco Mathews," said he, "and do not say now now to me, ma'am, or I will hit your two men flat. A little stiff I am in the head from fighting men two stone larger, but I am still good for boys, so do not get free with them."

"We have had enough fighting to last us a lifetime," said my father. "Speak your business and go, man."

"Goodness me," said Shanco. "There is a large mistake. And they told me I would have trouble from the Mortymers. Caradoc Owen Foreman told me to get free with them, but I am addled in the brain from head punching or I would have had Solly Widdle Jew flat down here before now, the bastard."

"Why?" I asked.

"Four pounds he is offering for my furniture, and me and my woman paid nine for it not twelve months back in the city of Carmarthen."

"Do not mind us," said my father. "Flat on his back he should be for making profit out of misfortune, but please mind your language in front of my women."

"Forgive me, ma'am," said Shanco, and he bowed and swept his cap in the slag at my mother's feet, "but it makes life hard when one is surrounded by ironmasters, Irish and Israelites."

"Five it is worth from this distance," said Dada. "Take us closer and we may offer you more, for we have Scotch Cattle furniture."

"Dear me," replied Mathews. "You are sent by the grace of God," and he elbowed me aside. "Shift you over, boy. Do not stand on guard or I will be damned fretful with you. Me and your dad are full of years. Away!"

And from then I heard no more. High on the tram road Mari was waving, and she ran down into the hollow, calling me. Without being seen I got away to meet her, and we ran into the shadows of the furnaces. There, I twisted her into my arms and kissed her lips.

"You are here!" she cried.

"But God knows for how long," I replied. "I can smell trouble—we got in too easy. It will be harder getting out."

"Caradoc Owen is the enemy," she said. "He will leave you alone unless you try to break the strike, so Hart says. The owner is waiting to see what happens when you and your father go in with tools."

"One thing at a time," I said. "At last I am here with you, in the same town."

"In the same house for today," Mari whispered. "I have the day free from Mr Hart to help with the scrubbing, for with Morfydd full and Edwina lazy it will all fall on your mother."

"Come, and I will find you a bucket," I said.

My father bought Shanco's furniture and we got it in and lost ourselves in labour, with Mam giving it to everybody about the state of the house. With Dafydd gone from next door Morfydd moved in with us. By darkness the rooms were clean and furnished after a fashion. Mari and Edwina were upstairs making beds when I met Morfydd out in the garden. She came down the path to me while I was building a roof for Dai Two. There was talk from the neighbours that furnace ashes sprayed white-hot from the chimneys, and I did not want him blistered. Morfydd came quietly and leaned against the shed and gave me a wink.

"Aye aye?" she said. "At it again, eh?"

"At what?" I said, hammering.

"Poor Mari. She do not dream what is coming to her."

"Do not be evil," I said.

"Manna from heaven," said she. "*Duw!* No wonder he wanted to come to Nanty. Hell support us. If I were her dada I would not sleep a wink with a mad Mortymer after her, poor girl."

"She is English," I said. "She will not get a second look," for it was asking for a life of hell to tell Morfydd your business.

"Half English, perhaps, but a dear little girl. High in the breast and narrow in the waist, she is, and the English things under her dress are just as pretty as Welsh, for I have seen them, dear me!"

"Away back to your scrubbing; it is all you are fit for," I said.

"Treat me civil," she answered, "or you will regret it. Do

you think she would be interested to hear the scandal of Polly-Without-Trews?"

"Go to hell," I said, grinning.

"Do not love her more than me, then," said she, "for I am jealous," and she kissed me on the cheek.

"Away," I said. "I am trying to get this roof up."

It was twilight now and I saw her profile against the rising moon, still beautiful, young, and her eyes were happy.

I said, "Morfydd, where is Dafydd?"

"Lord!" she exclaimed. "My business now, is it?"

"Gone, has he?"

She laughed. "Out on his neck," she said. "Do you expect me to lie with a man who flogs my father?"

"You know, then?"

"Not much misses me," she answered. "He came in crying for bandages and breathing fire over the Mortymers for the flogging you gave him. I called for the Chartists and they threw him out. Now he has taken to the mountains with Probert, they tell me."

"He is dangerous," I said. "I am glad you are living with us."

"Perhaps you would be safer without me," she replied.

My father called us and we went in together and sat down at table. It was as if the years had rolled back and made us one again, but with the joyful difference of Mari's eyes, rising and lowering above her plate opposite, where Morfydd used to be.

We were seven in family now, my mother said, counting Mari Dirion who worked down the road at Coalbrookvale.

Report to Furnace Five, said the Agent next morning, and my father and I went out and worked it, lighting it from cold while the Nantyglo puddlers stood at the entrance and watched. We lit it and brought it to blast and coaled it and tipped in ore, and by night we had tapped it and filled the sand moulds with iron. Alone we did this, watched by half the strikers of Nanty. They made no move to stop us, they spoke not a word. On the second day we did the same, and by midday eight men had joined us despite the warnings pinned up overnight by the Scotch Cattle. We tapped earlier that day, and when nineteen men had returned to work we decided on a night shift and ran it to two tons of iron. By the fourth day the strike was broken. Ninety men were back and more flooding in every hour.

And with them came Caradoc Owen.

Here was a sample of a man; a trouble maker famed for striking, a foreman Bailey could not do without. What Owen could not drive with his tongue he drove with his fist or the nearest thing handy. Men feared him, women despised him, children ran from him. He had his wife down in Shant-y-Brain's shippon carting dung when she was full, and one Christmas he had lit a furnace with a Roman Catholic crucifix.

"So the strike-breakers are here, I see," said he, coming into Furnace Five. My father was stoking when Caradoc Owen tapped him. Coming in with the nose-bag Morfydd had cut for us I saw my father turn and face the foreman. Dada was full six inches taller but Owen was a foot the wider, deep-chested, hairy. Other workers crowded in, Owen's men, silent, threatening.

"Aye," said my father, throwing down the irons. "When the children begin to die the strike has been on long enough, or don't you see the sense of it?"

"Marked by the Cattle, too, God be praised," said Owen, touching Dada's back where the stripes were still raised and red. "Some people never learn, it seems. Not enough scabs in Nanty so Bailey brings his pets from Garndyrus, eh?"

I pushed my way through the men and tossed the bundle and my father caught it. "Nose-bag," I said, "and tell him to go to hell before we shift him," and I picked up irons and carried on stoking.

"Blacklegs and bruisers, is it?" said Owen, cool as ice. "Out, Mortymer, and take this cheeky swine with you. I am in charge here."

"Good grief," said Dada to me. "What is the use of signing the pledge?" He turned to Owen. "We stay. If you want to shift us, take your pick—the Agent, or make a ring and the best man is in?"

Owen spat, grinning. His men murmured. I saw their faces in the glare of the firebox. Many had the scars of fighting over their eyes, their faces streaked with sweat and lined deep with hunger. Half of them in touch with Scotch Cattle by the look of them, standing very quiet for men with hobnails, but all were with honour when it came to a ring.

I had never seen my father fight; only heard of him from men like Big Rhys, who said he was a terror, more afraid of his woman than any man on the mountains. But he was still weak from the flogging, and his back was still crusted and split deep. Already the workers were out, making a circle in front of the Company Shop in full view of the office, and from all directions the townspeople came running, as they always did for a fight. The news spread like a furnace blow-back, and before a blow had been struck the tap-rooms had emptied and the cinder-pit in front of the furnaces was solid with people. I watched my father as he pulled off his coat. The old casual air had come upon him that I had seen before in time of trouble, but his face was pale as he drew on to his fingers the thin leather gloves he wore for stoking. He squinted into the sun and looked towards our house. I knew he was thankful that my mother was down at Abergavenny for market.

Caradoc Owen, ten years the younger, rose from his haunches at the edge of the crowd.

"Ready?" he called.

My father nodded. Left hand out, he circled, frowning over his clenched fist, and Owen followed round, giving time for the laying of bets, as was the custom. A Hercules, this one; broad as an ox across the shoulders through years of breaking pig at Dowlais. The muscles bulged and swelled along his thick arms, his movements were ponderous, drunk with strength. He moved flat-footed, swaying from the waist, his black-maned head thrust forward, inviting a blow. Round, round the circle they went, Owen bunched and tense, my father lithe, the long slim muscles of his fine body shining with furnace sweat, and I heard women gasp at his bright red weals.

"Bets laid!" cried a man, and Owen grunted, spat over his

shoulder and rushed, hooking. Dada stepped aside. Owen went sprawling into the crowd and rose, kicking them away for room. Steadier now, he walked in, chin upon his jutting chest, his thick arms working in widening swings, but he took a left like a whiplash that stopped him dead and a dig to the midriff that doubled him. Opening his fingers, Owen clutched and ran, seeking a hold, and the blow that felled him hooked between his arms flush to the point of his chin. His head snapped back, his shoulders followed, his heels lifted and he landed with a crash on the slag. Dust rose. The crowd gasped. There was no sound but the wind and the simmer of Furnace Five. And Caradoc Owen, who had never been on a knee before, turned upon his side and rested, shaking his great head. Blood and froth bubbled from his mouth and ran down his hairy chest. I glanced at my father. He was looking at the mountain, deep in thought, it seemed, eyes narrowed. Owen got on all fours and rose. Swaying, his legs wide, he walked in again, hitting with tremendous blows that swept the air as they were neatly parried or guarded. There was no expression upon my father's face as he retreated. Swaying easily from the waist, swerving, riding the chopping fists, he paused only to smash single, vicious blows into the face of the man before him; blows launched on the twist that cut and blinded the bull-like Owen. Grunting, cursing, Owen lumbered to his doom, his senses numbed by the first terrible blow that had felled him; lumbered into a poetry of hooks and smashes that brought the blood pouring over his chest from a dozen facial cuts. And he reeled and moaned under the precision of the hands that lashed him, cried aloud when the cutting lefts stopped his forward plunge, doubled and gasped at the uppercuts that sank deep into his body. His breathing came in sobs as he flung out his arms for holds that missed by yards. Battered, peering through his puffed slits of eyes, he walked into the avalanche, taking everything, succeeding in nothing. And when, bewildered and in agony, he cried aloud in rage and dropped his hands, my father took his first step forward. With the brutal Owen staggering on bowed legs before him, he began to cut him to pieces. The crowd gaped, held its breath as the artist steadied himself. The last blow came. Owen's head snapped back and he took the following crude swing full in the throat. He fell, face down, full length at my father's feet, his big white body shuddering to the gasping intakes of his breath.

Not a soul moved except my father. He flung his shirt up and waved his arms into it, took a breath and tucked the flaps under his belt. With his coat trailing, he walked back to the entrance of Furnace Five, raised his face and looked for me among the crowd. Thrusting men and women aside I ran to him.

Sad he looked, standing there, his head low.

"Well done, Dada," I said. "That is the last of Caradoc Owen for one."

"Poor man, but it was the only way, God forgive me," he said.

"Look who is coming, Mr Mortymer," said a man nearby.

The crowd was shuffling and swaying near the road by the Company Shop. My mother walked through the press of men and into the narrowing ring. Her face was white and pinched with anger. The wind took her hair and flung it about as she knelt beside Caradoc Owen. With her hand upon his naked shoulder she looked up at my father. In Welsh, she said:

"This is the last time, Hywel, do you understand? The last time, or by God I will leave you."

A man called, "A fair fight, mind. Clean as a nut."

"Bloody old Caradoc do ask for it, woman!" shouted another.

My mother rose and faced them. "A fair fight, you call it? Look at him!" She pointed down. "You have set this one up for slaughter, not a fight." Her voice rose to a shout. "Not any ten men here could pull my man down, and if you doubt me then go to Carmarthen and ask what happened to Dai Benyon Pugilist in his prime. Champion of Wales, is he not? Aye, the champion, until he quarrelled with my man for easy money and went home over the back of a pony. And any man alive would have the same as this one if he tried booting my

Hywel from his furnace. Who began this fight? Ask it fair, now. Not the Mortymers, I am bound, but Nanty. For the few days we have been here we have been ignored and insulted because we choose to work instead of strike. You call us scabs and blacklegs. You string my husband up and flog him raw because he has no Union card; did you see his poor back just now? You shout about Benefits, but you have no benefits for the funds are drunk away by the organisers. You shout about the Union but you have no Union. All you have got is a disorganised rabble that is better at beer than seeking fair negotiation of complaints. Do you expect me to starve my children for that kind of Union?" She was striding among them now, shouting into their faces. "Do you? Starve if you like, the little ones, too, but mine will still be eating, for my family will work where they like and on masters' terms, for better or worse until it gets decent representation. It was that in Garndyrus, it will be the same here in Nanty, mark me. Aye, and I can fight too, so try me, any woman here, and my boys are handy with them, so watch out. And for every flogging and insult we will give twenty back for we are here to stay in Nantyglo whether you like us or not. Iestyn!"

I went to her through the men.

"Lift this man and take him home for repair," said she. "Edwina! Down to Mr Owen's house with you and bring his woman here sharp before he dies on us."

Edwina, frail and trembling, hurried away.

Ten minutes to thrash Caradoc Owen, two minutes to thrash a town. The eyes of everyone was on her as she led the way home for the bandaging. Hooking Owen's arm around my neck I dragged him after her. Like the Queen of Sheba she went, her dress held as a tent before her, her nose high, back to her kitchen.

It was pleasant living in Nantyglo for a while after that, with the men knocking up their caps to my mother and some of the women even dropping a knee, for it soon got round that the Mortymers had broken the strike four days after landing. Special invitations came from the chapels and women dropped in for cups of tea and chats, for women hate strikes whatever they say to their men. Little else happened that first Christmas, except that Morfydd had her baby.

Trust Morfydd to be inconvenient, starting her pains with the house empty for one reason or another, and having it on the floor of the bedroom like a Kentucky labourer. Eleven pounds after two hours, said my mother, and not so much as a whisper from Morfydd according to the next-door neighbours. And when my father and I came in at the end of day shift Morfydd had him on the breast.

Richard, she called him. A miniature Richard, too, lusty, and as hungry after Morfydd as Jethro had been for Mam.

Eight of us now, with Mari practically living in the place; two rooms up, one down. The men slept in one bedroom, the women and Richard in the other, but nobody got much sleep with the baby screaming.

On the first night of full working I laid on my back beside Jethro and watched the room change from moonlight to red as Furnace One grew into blast. By midnight it was shrieking and the house trembled to the thudding drop-hammers and the new rolling mill whined like something from the pit of Hell. Plaster flaked and drifted down from the ceiling, light ran in red tongues over the window as the thunder grew and the night caught alight. Jethro and my father were on their backs, sleeping through it. Throwing aside the blanket I went to the window and looked out. The side of the mountain had dissolved into a single fire; a maze of individual furnaces that blended their flames into an orbit, and along the flaming rim of the cauldron the stone cottages of the workers withered and shrank into strange shapes. This was the Bailey empire where the iron bubbles into a thousand moulds. Sweat pours here, beer is taken by the gallon, men die in mutilation, children are old at ten. Eyes are put out here, sleeves are tied with string. The turrets of the ironmaster's house were stark black against the glow, the windows glinting, his defence towers threatening any challenge. From Cwm Crachen to Coalbrookvale was a river of fire. Ash drifted past the window, settling like snow. As the night went on the clamour grew and the sky flashed red as the bungs were tapped and cauldrons stirred. And next door, beyond the thin partition, Richard cried on Morfydd's breast; the new generation to be charred by Bailey's son.

I longed for my town on that first night of full blast in Nantyglo. I longed for it more on a night of early spring when my mother came to my father for comfort, and I was a witness.

It was a Sunday, after chapel, with the darkness of many a winter's night between me and Garndyrus. The hoar frost had gone from the hedges and the early buds were green and the Coity thinking of changing colour. Those were the nights when the moon was full and rolling along the Coity and the nightingales left alive were calling to lovers.

On such a night, when the furnaces were simmering, my mother came.

"Hywel!" she whispered from the door.

Pretty she looked in the moonlight with her knitted white shawl over her shoulders and her nightdress beneath; like a young girl, I thought, ready for her lover. The door of our bedroom rasped as she opened it wider and she came, her hand out as if in sleep, and called again:

"Hywel!"

I heard my father rise in the bed by the window.

"Elianor," he whispered back.

Over the boards she went on tiptoe, the shawl brushing my hand. Her face, in the moonlight, was shadowed. He opened his arms to her and gathered her to him, his lips against her mouth. They were lovers, and I the watcher. Trapped, I laid there.

"Elianor, not here, my sweet," he said. "Tomorrow, girl. I will meet you up on the mountain, not here. . . ."

"The boys are sleeping, Hywel," she said back. "Is there nothing for us then except eating and sleeping? And work? O, Hywel, take me; the boys will not hear."

Fathers slept with daughters, mothers with sons, brothers with sisters in the hovels of Nanty. Sixteen to a room in Coalbrookvale, four to a bed.

Now I heard the springs go down as she got in beside him.

I heard the quickening heat of their breathing change to low sobbing. Anger and sickness I knew, and pity.

The night went on, the pattern of moonlight crossed the floor, and I saw by the curve of the blanket that covered them that they were one; lost, unmindful of sounds.

They did not stir as I went from the room, down to the kitchen and through the door to the mountain. There, I watched the dawn come up, a flaring streak of red out of the blackness. And with the dawn the mystery vanished, the sickness in me passed. The beauty of it came and brought me peace as the stars paled and faded from sight. There was no sound from the cwm; nothing but the song of the mountain streams as I sat there praying that Jethro would not wake, until their loving was finished.

CHAPTER SEVENTEEN

I CUT a spoon for Mari in springtime.

It was still cold and there was a stillness over the land as if the sap was breathless with waiting. And it was dark on the night of our meeting. We met most nights, of course, but this was special; necessary, too, for very strict about herself was Mari, wriggling and slapping, and not a decent kiss she would part with unless things were done properly, she said.

Which meant a spoon, of course, although I could hardly expect her to ask for one. So I cut a spoon for her, being full of ambition to lie with her, and so far getting nowhere.

Out in the yard I looked up at the mountain. Away over the dim jag of the Coity Pleiades, brilliant in silver, ran before the wind, Orion was flashing gold and green and Venus was making her sign of the Cross, the old ones say. Up to meet her, me—straight up the long green slope, and I sat in the crisp heather with the blaze of Nanty below me. There, with fingers of ice, I fashioned the little spoon.

I had planned a small one; something Mari could wear on a trinket chain in the divide of her breast. From cedar I cut it, out of a piece I chopped down at Llanelen last summer.

There are spoons and spoons, of course. Morfydd had quite a few in her workbasket, some as trinkets, others for wearing, and one from a Carmarthen farm boy big enough to fork manure. The one from Dafydd Phillips had *Cariad anwyl* carved upon the handle, for trust Dafydd not to think of anything unusual. She had no spoon from Bennet, he being English. But the biggest spoon I have ever heard of was the one Will Tafarn carved for Martha, his wife. It stood on the hillside between Nanty and Varteg, and was ten feet high from the roots with 'Those whom God hast joined together let no man put asunder' cut on its trunk in six-inch letters. But it has sprouted branches and leaves, they tell me, as if God has done what He can to hide it, for Will beats Martha every pay night now.

So with this in mind I did a little spoon for Mari, whittling it free of wanes and shakes. It was slender and curved in the handle and holed for the trinket chain, and due to be finished by half past eight. I had just fixed the chain when I saw Mari coming up the slope, so I got it away and hid out of the moonlight behind a rock.

"Oi!" said she, peering. "Iestyn, are you there?"

"Scotch Cattle, God help you!" I said, and caught her by the waist and swung her down among the leaves. Panting, she put her hand between our lips.

"Is it finished?" she asked, breathless.

"Aye, but still doubtful if you will get it. Six weeks I have been carving the thing and there is nothing on the end of it."

"Do not be too sure," said she. "It depends if it is a good one."

"One kiss for a start?" But she shook her head, sending her hair flying, and wriggled off. I was after her, drawing her against me, and her body was warm under my coat. I tried to kiss her but she nipped me and turned her face away, smiling, her teeth white and her cheeks patterned by the moonlight through leaves.

"Not until I get the spoon," she said with business.

A dog fox barked from the valley and the vixen answered away to the east, and the sounds were like wine on the still, cold air. All the beauty of the night was about us, the rushing of streams, the low chord of the wind in dark places, buffeting the heather, shivering round our clothes, sighing down the mountain to the black roofs of Nanty that glistened with frost under the lanterned sky.

"No," whispered Mari.

Down on the Brynmawr Road the lights of a trap winked in blackness and the clatter of hooves came crystal clear, bringing to us a deeper remoteness, a warmer nearness.

"No," whispered Mari. slapping.

"Eh dear," I said. "There's a woman for no's. Yes for a change, is it?"

"Give me the spoon," she said against my throat.

I fumbled with fingers of ice, found it, and held it clear.

"Answer truly, then, or descend to the grids of hell with Satan. Who do you love, Mari Dirion?"

"A boy from Garndyrus," said she.

"Tell his name, then."

"Iestyn Mortymer."

"Do you swear to that love?"

"On the Bible black," she said. "Three times I swear."

And I kissed her once on the lips, longer than the rules allowed, which was only a peck. Gasping, we laid close, our breath steaming in the frost.

"Who do you love, Iestyn Mortymer, and answer truly or descend to the grids of hell."

"A girl from Carmarthen," I said.

"Tell her name, then."

"Mari Dirion."

"Will you swear to that love, boy?"

"On the black Bible," I replied, "three times. Will you take my spoon and be my love, Mari Dirion?"

"Aye," she answered, and she kissed me on the mouth.

So I took the thing out and fastened the trinket chain around her neck and opened the top of her dress and dropped it down, but it stuck half way because we were lying.

Beautiful she looked then, her face turned away and the redness flying into her cheeks.

"The old thing will not go down," I said. "Sit you up and give it a shake, girl."

But she did not move. I felt her trembling, though, and her trembling crept into me and flew to my thighs, and I was ashamed.

White and smooth was her throat. Soft was her breast under fingers that were brittle with cold, and the shock of my hand took her breath. I had never before touched a woman's breast. There was wonder in it, and longing, and a desire to press secret places. There was no winter with us then. The cold vanished and warmth came with our kisses, and there was no sound in the world but our sobbing as we lay together.

"Am I sinful?" she asked in a whisper.

"Sinful enough to bring deacons from pews," I said, "but I do not care. O, Mari!"

She smiled, her teeth white against the dark curves of her lips as she whispered, "The deacons are on furnace shift or loving their wives in bed," and she kissed me with a new fierceness. "Iestyn, boy, take me up to The Top?"

I knew what she meant by instinct, for there was a wildness about her that caught me up, making me a part of her passion that was mysterious and strange after her coldness of past months. It was as a chord singing between us, growing in increasing beauty and power, strident and clear as a clarion call; a chord that took a swing at the senses, forging us into one as the red iron is forged, in heat and shape, together.

The moon had gone now and the sky was alight with silver clouds and owls were hooting east of the Coity. Other sounds echoed; the wind-sigh of the heather, the clattering panic of a disturbed bird as we rose to our feet. All Nature seemed to call us with relentless strength. The flood-gates of longing had been opened by a single touch. I kissed her again and again, lost in the magic, all reason obliterated by the rushing urge to possess her.

"Do you know what will happen if we go up there?" I asked.

"Yes," said Mari. "And I do not care. We are one now, in honour. I have wanted you long enough, Iestyn. Take me."

"Come," I said, and I led her to a path.

Beautiful is the woman a man is to mate with, in moonlight.

We walked up through the heather in silence, hand in hand. The night was strangely quiet now, for the wind had dropped and the air was warmer with a threat of rain. Up in the blackness thunder boomed faintly and lightning flashed over Coldbrook. We had reached the crest of the Coity with the glow of Garndyrus in sight when the first rain pattered on the heather.

"Dammo!" said Mari. "The pair of us will catch our deaths."

"Can you run?" I asked her, dragging at her hand.

"Aye, but not back to Nanty!"

"Down to Shant-y-Brain's," I cried. "Over the tumps and into his barn. It will be warm in the hay—look, the light down by there, see it?"

"Satan fry the one behind," said she, and she was away and leaping over the boulders with her dress up round her thighs and her bare legs twinkling. After her I went like something demented, shouting to her to stop. Down, down we went as the storm broke about us, cracking over the sky and brushing sweeps of water over the dark country. Lightning split the clouds in blue flashes, the rain sheeted down in an explosion after the calm. Catching Mari, I caught her hand and dragged her on. Her shawl was gone, her hair was wet and flying. Laughing, breathless, we staggered and slipped down the slope to Shant-y-Brain's shippon, scrambled over his gate and ran to the barn where last year's harvest was streaking out in the wind. Scrambling up the ladder we flung ourselves down in the hay with the roof bible-black a foot from our faces. Our hearts were beating wildly, but not with running, as I turned in the bed and heaved over into the warmth of her.

"Quiet now, mind," I whispered, "or Shant-y-Brain will have us out with pitchforks. No giggling, no shouting for help, or he will put it over the county. Is it wet with you?"

"Soaked, man. I will chatter to bring him out if I stay in this wet old dress; the only dry thing on me is the spoon."

"Do not mind me," I said. "I have seen you wearing less."

"Heaven bless me," she giggled, "there's a big mistake if you think I am stripping for you in March. That was nearer June."

"Lie quiet, then, and let the hay dry you out."

The storm blew like a mad thing over the moontain, hammering everything in thunder and wind and away as quick as he came. The night was bright again with moonlight, the stars were washed clean.

"There's a handy old storm," I said, "getting you in this barn with me and no chance of you getting out."

Quiet, she was, her breathing steady.

"Mari," I whispered, up on an elbow.

"Hush you, go to sleep," she said.

"Sleep? Be human. Do you think I am risking Shant-y-Brain for sleep? I can do that in bed back home."

"Sleep," said she, "for I have changed my mind. Put a finger on me and I will howl like ten thousand cats and rise every deacon for miles."

"Too late," I answered, finding her lips. "The deacons are on furnace shift or loving their wives in bed, as I am loving you."

And her arms went about me as I kissed her, pulling me down.

Strange and wonderful is the first loving.

The blood runs hot with the kiss, hammering on the heart with quickening beats, forging muscles to steel in a riot of manhood as yet undiscovered. Trembling are the fingers that twist and seek, searching warm places blindly in darkness, and, finding, grip to hurt. There is no pity for the captive then. The pain is deep under a rush of breathing as the lancing steel is poised. Pennants fly, forests rise and swords go reaping in satanic joy. The back is bent in the bowman's hands and the arrows fly, plunging to wound, rending, as befits a conqueror. The tongue is noble then, the breathing is a sigh.

All in hours, all in seconds.

"Iestyn," she said.

Her hair was wet in my hands, lying in thick strands over her breasts, and hay was upon her shoulders. We lay together, listening to the sounds of the night growing out of the wildness and silence: the cattle lowing from the farm, the swish of the rain over the heather, the distant thuds of Garndyrus making iron. I looked at Mari. Her eyes were wide and moving over my face, large and glittering in the faint, blue light.

"Eh dear," she whispered. "You loved me, Iestyn."

"Aye," I said.

She giggled then, which was shameful, but wonderful.

"O," said she, "there's wicked I am, and you for doing it. This time next year I will be walking twins round town."

"They will beat you up the mountain with Bibles and sticks months before that," I said, kissing her.

"Well," said she, "I will be caught for two as happily as one. Love me again, my precious," and she reached up and pulled my face down, kissing.

So I loved her again.

"You will catch your death in this soaked dress," I said, and raised her and pulled it over her shoulders.

"Whee!" she whispered. "Now I must strip to please it, eh? Here I lie as a hoyden, naked in a barn with Iestyn Mortymer. There is a handy old storm for the boys of Garndyrus."

I did not answer, being a man.

Warm were her lips, and her trembling was not with cold.

CHAPTER EIGHTEEN

ALL THAT spring the Chartists gathered and workers from towns as far apart as Hirwaun and Blaenafon flooded up the mountain to the torchlight meetings. The movement grew. As the Benefit Clubs were the springboards of the workers' Union, so the Union was the backbone of the new Charter. Speakers for Chartism were travelling from London and Birmingham: men like Henry Vincent, who could sway a thousand men with a phrase and change the politics of women with a song. Pamphlets were being distributed at the furnaces and pinned on the lodge gates of the owners, and sermons of sedition were preached against the young Queen. Chartism was the promise of freedom, and the workers seized at it. The Chartists met openly in defiance of the Military, and the Benefit Clubs and Unions flocked to the meetings and sent their invitation to attend to the owners. Even the men of Garndyrus came over the mountain. Just as Big Rhys and Mo and the old crowd did on the night I first heard the words of Zephaniah Williams of Coalbrookvale.

"A pig of a man if ever there was one," said my mother at table, and she smoothed Richard's black hair. "If the likes of little ones such as these are dependent upon him, then God help them, I say."

"Have you met him, then?" asked Morfydd, innocent. Richard was at her breast, her voice was gentle, but her eyes burned with the old fire.

"No," retorted Mam, "and not likely to. Hearing about him is enough."

"From the gossip in town?" asked Morfydd.

"From what I read in *The Merlin*."

"If you want the truth you must read the pamphlets, Mam. But there are none so stupid as those who will not try to understand. Have you heard about William Lovett's new Six Point Charter for the workers, even?"

"Leave it, Morfydd," said my father, glancing up.

"Stupid, is it?" flashed my mother. "Is it stupid to know the truth now? Charters, indeed!"

"It is stupid to reject it," replied Morfydd, shifting the baby on to the other.

Very pretty were Morfydd's breasts when she was feeding Richard, and although she was my sister I could not help a peep when her eyes were turned away. Mari's breasts were round and firm, pink-tipped, each small enough to be cupped in my hand, but Morfydd's were melon-shaped, standing straight out from her shoulders, and Richard's tiny fingers were red against them as he buried his face in their smoothness, his slobbering rosebud of a mouth running with milk.

"Get on with your dinner," said Dada.

"Yes," I said.

"And an atheist into the bargain," said my mother. "If this landlord of the Royal Oak Inn is a sample of a Chartist, then thank God the military are in Brecon Garrison and the Volunteers on a five minute tap."

"Do you think we could have a little less of the politics?" asked my father, polite. "We have it from morning to night now, which would not be so bad if either of you knew what you were talking about."

"He keeps a picture of Our Lord in his room," said Edwina bitterly, "with the words underneath, 'This is the man who stole the ass'. It is blasphemy that, not politics."

"Well said," answered Mam. "None shall stand who deride Him, and neither will Zephaniah Williams, mark me, for God will take revenge, and hell hath enlarged herself and opened her mouth without measure, and men like Williams will ascend into it with all his pomp and glory."

"Descend," said my father, reading now.

"Ascend," said my mother.

"Look," said Dada. "How the devil can anyone ascend into hell, woman?"

"Ascend or descend, it is all the same to me so long as he finishes up there," said Mam, "which he surely will."

"Where does his glory come in?" asked Edwina. "There is not much glory in an atheist, mind."

"And not much pomp in an unpaid Chartist," said Morfydd.

"Good God," said Mam, fanning. "You open your mouth in this house and six are down it, and all of you together have less sense than me."

"Then use it," said Dada. "Isaiah Five, verse fourteen. Look it up, for I cannot stick a wrong quotation. Or pamphlets or *Merlins*, come to that. The newspapers roar at us like lions, telling us what they would have us believe," and he got up and took Richard in his arms, and cooed and bounced to make him chuckle while Morfydd, eyes lowered, tucked away her beautiful, full breasts.

Not much interest in Chartists, my father.

I had just finished helping Edwina wash the dishes when the kitchen door came open to a boot and several faces peered around it, grinning, which brought my father to his feet in joy.

"In with you all!" he cried, giving Richard to Morfydd, and he pulled them in—Big Rhys and Mo, Afel Hughes and Mr Roberts, and the Howells boys and Will Blaenavon pushing up behind until the room was full and Mam tipped on the end of her chair and cursing flashes. Pretty full, too, by the look of them, and noisy enough for rowdies, with Mo sporting head bandages from cuts he had taken prize fighting on the Blorenge. Hard and strong was Mo these days, a grown man, with fifty guineas of a gentry's purse to back him against the best in Wales.

"Look you, boys, what we have here!" he roared, kissing my mother and ducking her slap. "The best cook in Garndyrus and the prettiest mother in Nanty," and he bowed low to Morfydd, who closed a fist and threatened to straighten him. Very pretty she looked then, smiling and sparring.

"Clear in the eyes she is and strong, see?" said Owen Howells. "And they talk of the Carmarthen girls. Firm in the legs and good in the milk by the size of her, look you!"

and he feinted and pinched but took a swing from Morfydd that sent him staggering.

"Out of it, all of you!" shouted Mam, giggling. "With all these decent chapel people in town, Hywel, you have to fill the house with indecent bruisers from Garndyrus. Out, out!" and she flapped at them with her apron, delighted, while Will behind her was on his knees handing out her cakes from the oven with oh's and ah's from the invaders as they bit them steaming hot. Good it was to have them and all their commotion and cheek.

"Let us have some sense in this," pleaded Dada. "What is the reason for the visit?"

"The meeting at Coalbrookvale tonight," spluttered Rhys, wiping his mouth. "Do not say you are not going, man!"

"Have you never heard of Zephaniah Williams, then?" asked Mo.

"*Duw!* Not again," said Dada, suffering. "Stuffed and cooked he is, and we have him for breakfast, dinner and supper in here."

"Then you will come with us to hear him?" asked Owen.

"Not if he is talking Charters, Benefits or Unions, for you know my views upon them, and so will he if I am fool enough to go."

"Charters it is tonight, man, and it will be lively, for Henry Vincent is coming over from Pontypool, they say."

"Zephaniah is explaining the new Six Points in Welsh and Vincent is driving it in English, see?"

"Where to?" asked Mam.

"Good God," said Big Rhys, while Morfydd giggled. "It is rules and regulations, do you understand—six points that the workers are driving into the gentry to get a fair deal from Parliament."

"Parliament now, is it?" said she. "There is a funny old place to drive anything to, least of all six rules and regulations. You would be handier employed getting better conditions and lower prices in the Shops."

"I am getting from here," laughed Rhys, "for one is bewitched and the other noodled. Iestyn?"

"Aye, I am coming," I said.

"Morfydd?"

"The Devil take me!" cried Morfydd. "Coming, indeed? And I helped organise it. Away, before I take boots to you all."

"Where is Jethro?"

"On shift," I said. "We do not want him with us, Mam. Keep him here when he comes off."

Down to Coalbrookvale we went, all eight of us, with Afel Hughes giving Nanty the trumpet to let it know who was in town, and more than once we ducked slops from a window. The Royal Oak Inn was crowded to the door, and with Mo leading we pushed a path to the bar and hammered it for beer while men whispered behind their hands at the sight of Mo and God help Dai Benyon Champion when this big boy got his hooks on him, for Mo's fame with his fists was spreading like a fire. Zephaniah Williams was out speaking, they told us, so we polished our quarts and went out to the tumps.

It was a strident, witch-ridden night, with the full moon throwing the shadows of the stricken trees like hunchbacks on the grass, and the rocks of the mountain were squat and evil in the light where torches flared. Hundreds were standing there in the wind: men from the valleys of Gwent, their faces still black from shift; women, shawled and shivering, with babies on their backs, and little barefooted children crying on the tips.

For the first time I saw the Chartist, Zephaniah Williams; the man of destiny standing high on a rock, wonderful in oratory, ominous in silence. So will I remember him all the days of my life, then, in the greatness of his power, not chained in the working gang under a pitiless sun and with an overseer's lash to drive him. Fine he looked on that rock with his arms outstretched.

"Look," whispered Mo. "There is Henry Vincent, and William Jones Watchmaker beside him," and he pointed.

"To the sword, then!" Williams cried in Welsh. "To powder and shot, then, if it is forced upon us, for how else can we negotiate if they will not come to table? And even if we got them to table can mere words sway the likes of Guest of Dowlais and Crawshay of Cyfarthfa, these dogs of masters? Has Parliament any interest in petition when it is run by these aristocrats of wealth who rule our lives? What kind of freedom is it when we are driven to the polls to vote for Whig or Tory under threat of the blacklist? Where is a recognised anti-Truck Bill or a Bill for stabilised prices? You have none, and you will never have one, for Parliament is run by men who own the Shops and fix the prices that starve us—not by the will of the people, mark me, but by the law of birth and wealth, and so it will be until we dislodge them!"

The crowd howled at this and showed their fists.

"We are men of peace and threaten nobody!" shouted Zephaniah. "But if it is blood they are after they shall have it, for the time is past when they can ride roughshod and break up meetings with crops. So if Crawshay Bailey has ideas about breaking this one let him come with his Volunteers and try it, for we will meet him with muskets."

"Damned near sedition," whispered Afel Hughes to me. "Soon he will be baiting Victoria."

"Aye!" roared Zephaniah, as if he had heard. "The Gentle-men Cavalry, booted and spurred, straight from the hunt to flog the Unwashed. Do you want the truth of them—these men of idleness who sit in their Company Parks and make profit from your misery and watch your children die—pro-tected by the laws they alter to suit their pockets, hiding under the skirt of the Queen they use as a puppet, God bless her," and he winked while the crowd yelled. "To hell with them and to hell with Parliament, and God help our Virgin Queen, I say, for if words cannot shift the iniquitous laws of England that bind her hands, then the cannon of the people must, and blow into oblivion her enemies, the parasites of her crown and the wanglers of the Pension List!"

Bedlam.

"Sedition now," cried Afel. "To the devil with Zephaniah Williams, boy—give me Lovett, for I would rather have a sea trip to Botany Bay than hang my head on a spike in London and the rest of me in strips."

"That is because there is no stomach to you, Afel," cried Rhys. "I am all for Zephaniah; it is all or nothing now, man."

The crowd was thick about us, swaying, with lanterns on sticks and flares flaming madly. "A bit of room by here!" shouted Mo, widening his shoulders and shoving, and fists went up as a mad stampede nearly overturned us. For another figure mounted the rock as Zephaniah leaped down, and stood there, serene and smiling.

"Henry Vincent, is it?" bawled Rhys. "Dock me in the stomach and tie me in skirts. Soon they will be sending us women for agitators. Do you sing, too, lad?"

"Not so loud," said Will. "In Carmarthen they are fair bandy over him, so give him a hearing, for I heard him speak by Picton's Column on the night Mo here flattened Knocker Daniels."

Fine and handsome Henry Vincent looked, the English Chartist who was reckless in his criticism of the aristocracy, Church and Throne. "Do not heed him," he cried, jerking his thumb at Zephaniah Williams. "Even the truth is sickening if you hear it too often. Let us take another course for a lark. Who is with me for a visit to Mr Crawshay Bailey?"

Roars of laughter greeted this and hoots of delight.

"A little walk to Nantyglo with a bottle of brandy to entice him out, eh? And call the place to strike if he cannot show a Union card?"

"A tidy old boy, this Vincent," said Mo, nudging me, "but I am wondering where he will land us all."

"On a gibbet," replied Big Rhys, "or picking oakum in a poorhouse, but I am following the lad for courage, tenor or not."

So we worked our way to the head of the column with Mo and Big Rhys pitching out the rowdies right and left. Hundreds strong now and growing every minute, we took the track back to Chapel Road, singing and shouting with the torches a fiery stream right down to Blaina. Windows went up, doors came open, and women and children were dancing in the street as we roared our way towards the home of Bailey. But then, above the tumult, I heard Mari's voice and saw her running beside the column with men pushing her off when she tried to break through to me. In seconds I was beside her.

"For God's sake!" she cried. "Home quick, Iestyn. Jethro has been splashed!"

My mother and father were with Jethro.

He lay on the floor where the accident men had put him down, his eyes clenched tight, his jaw set. His right sleeve was rolled up, and I saw the cuff charred and the knuckles of his hand, wrist and forearm burned to the bone in a bright red weal where the molten splash had laid its finger. But the iron was cool now, tucked down and rigid, and the swollen skin was heaped high above it where the blood had boiled.

"Up with his head, Iestyn," whispered Dada, and we got the whisky flask between his teeth. He took a full mug before his eyes opened and rolled at us, and he screamed once and went out again, which is usual for a bad burn, the old puddlers say.

My mother was sobbing, her hands over her face.

"O God!" she whispered.

"Away upstairs if you cannot stomach it," said Dada. "Iestyn, fetch me a knife."

I did so, and gave it to him and gripped Jethro's good hand and bowed my head, and hatred, deeper and stronger than I had ever known it, ran riot in me. Mari was standing by the window, shivering in her shawl, and beyond her I saw the torches smoking at the gates of Bailey's house. The murmur of the mob entered the room, gushing into sound as the door came open, snapping to a whisper as it slammed shut. Morfydd stood there, her face white, her eyes large.

"Jethro," I said to her. "Caught by a splash."

"I know," said she. "Barney Kerrigan it was, and he is ladling drunk on Caradoc Owen's shift at Number Five."

I looked at my father. He was levering with the knife and

the iron came clear, long and jagged as it dropped on the boards. Jethro tensed and sighed.

"I will bandage him," said Morfydd, and took the roll and ointment, kissing him first.

"Somebody will pay for this," she said through her teeth.

"Who ordered him into the furnace shed?" asked Dada, cold.

"Bailey's agent, they say. Most of the men had thrown their tools to go to the Coalbrookvale meeting. Furnace Five had just been tapped," she said. "Jethro was coming in from Llangattock, and the Agent saw him and sent him with Kerrigan to ladle."

"Was Owen there?" he asked, frowning.

"Aye, I have just left him."

"Dada," I said, rising, "leave it now. The harm is done. See to Jethro now and leave trouble till morning."

"Aye," he said.

The women got the bed ready and we carried him up and covered him, deep in the sleep of whisky. Mari, Morfydd and I came down, leaving the others with him, and thank God Edwina was out with Snell that night, said Morfydd.

"A child, and he is splashed by iron," said Mari, walking about, pressing her hands.

"Know them by their children who labour in dark places, to be burned and maimed," said Morfydd. She went to the window and flung it open. The mob was chanting for Bailey at the lower lodge, and waving its torches. "Thank God for men like Vincent," she added. "With him and Frost and the Charter we will change it all."

"I am changing it now," said Dada, coming in. "I am having the skin from every man in Furnace Five and the bloody Agent when I land on him." And he reached for his coat, pulling Morfydd from the door.

I was quick and turned the lock. "For God's sake," I said. "If you start trouble at a time like this Bailey will blame you for violence with the mob."

"Out of my way," he said. "Nobody splashes my son with iron."

"Kerrigan is nearly blind with furnace glare," I said, "and find me the Irishman who ladles sober," and I pushed him back.

"Do not blame the drunken Irish," said Morfydd. "And remember this. Lay a finger on that precious Agent at a time like this, and Bailey will blacklist the house."

"So be it," said he. Reaching out he flung me headlong, unbolted the door and ran into the cwm.

CHAPTER NINETEEN

ACCORDING TO Shanco Mathews, who was grubbing for coal on the night Jethro was splashed, he had never seen the like of it. A swinging boot blew the near-blind Kerrigan out of harm's way, a right uppercut dropped Caradoc Owen for dead, Mr Hart, the Agent, had every tooth rattled loose and his face smacked black and blue, and two puddlers from Furnace Two who came running with ladles had never been heard of since.

Very businesslike was the Agent, very just. Dada was suspended for a month for unprovoked violence, Jethro with him for being implicated, and me for two weeks for being a relation.

The only breadwinner left was Mari, and Mrs Hart saw to her.

"Now perhaps you are satisfied," said Mam.

"I am," said my father. "The owners have seen the last of my loyalty."

"Thank God," said Mam, cutting him. "Now we will eat. Can you tell me how I manage with nothing coming in and two pounds left of our savings?"

"The Lord will provide," whispered Edwina.

"Amen," said Mam, "but there are people already starving in Nanty and He will see to them first. Can anyone tell me what happens in the meantime?"

"We share," said my father.

"God help me," said Mam. "I was born in a manse on black cloth, and ever since I can remember I have been mixing with bruisers who cannot keep their hands to themselves. The two pounds will keep us for a month, but before you begin hitting Agents about again, remember we will starve."

"Do not worry," said Dada, and got up.

"And where are you going now, pray, with the supper on the boil?"

"To Coalbrookvale," said he.

"And what for, may I ask?"

"To a meeting of the Chartists, with Idris Foreman, Garndyrus," said he, "and never get mixed with politics for views can change overnight, I find."

"Good God!" breathed Morfydd, putting down her sewing.

"Upon my soul," whispered Mam. "Suspended now, we will all be hung or transported next. O, Hywel, do not drive me mad. Are you from your senses?"

"I have never been saner," said he. "At Garndyrus there was little need for a Charter. Under Bailey, in this town, it is a necessity for he shows no justice."

"Amazing what an iron-splash can do," said Morfydd. "One moment cursing Chartists, the next moment joining them, and me hitting the principle of the thing for the last ten years. Next he will be standing for Mayor."

Dada did not answer, except for his look, but he did not slam the door behind him.

"*Dammo di!*" said my mother. "What a life it is! Charters and Unions, torchlight processions, Benefit Clubs and secret meetings. Down to Abergavenny with me, I think, and join the Quakers or wear sackcloth and ashes, and to hell with the damned old cooking."

"Very beautiful you would look in sackcloth and ashes, too," said Mari, kissing her. "Do not worry, Mam, he will take care."

The month of my father's suspension pulled us down, and with three weeks of it gone Crawshay Bailey cut wages by a seventh and put up his Tommy Shop prices an eighth, thinking that it was cheaper for the workers to live during summer.

And cheaper for masters, too, said the workers, so the town came out. Every man and boy from rollers to Irish labourers, greasers, furnace men, and ballers came out, taking the women and children. The cauldron began to boil at last. Pikes were under beds, powder and shot were being stored in the mountains, muskets stolen from sentries, swords and pistols from the gentry's private collections. Government spies came from London and some never went back. The pamphlets, bolder every week, screamed the cause of Chartism at the workers and openly criticised the aristocracy as puppets of the Crown. The gentry struck back. Harry Vincent, the first to see the strength of the masters, was thrown into Monmouth Gaol. John Frost, at the head of the snowball, was open in his contempt of Church and Throne. Twelve grooms of the bedchamber had the young Queen, said he, and each one of them drawing a thousand pounds a year while the workers starved. And what the poor girl was doing with twelve grooms was beyond his understanding, he said. For if he had a groom he would give him a horse to polish, and his pay would be ten pounds a year, not a thousand. So would somebody please tell him what the Queen was doing with twelve at a cost of twelve thousand?

"Very dangerous, all this," said my father.

"It is about time it was told," flashed Morfydd.

"She is like any other girl," said Mam. "She does as she is told. Twelve grooms in a bedchamber, indeed, I do not believe it. And if one of them smelled like those in Cyfarthfa stables she has my sympathy."

It was a joy having my mother in the house when things went political, but it was not as bad as the old days with my father and Morfydd at each other's throats, one waving the Union Jack, the other giving lectures on Feargy O'Connor. My father had changed since his loyalty was destroyed by the master who could have strengthened it, but he was not an extremist. It was justice he was after, not blood; negotiation, not violence.

I was with him on this. I wanted Lovett's new Six Points of the Workers' Charter as much as any man on the mountains, but I was against the torchlight meetings, the inflamed speeches, the mouthings and cruelties of men who would bawl anything for a laugh from the mob. And I was sorry for the Queen. She was about my own age then, alone, unaided.

Over the length and breadth of the country her crown was being used by men in authority to increase their personal fortunes. A pretty little thing was Victoria; one bound by the chains of the community, said Tomos Traherne; educated since her birth to put her signature where grasping ministers put their thumbs. So Frost went a bit small to me when he criticised her, and smaller still when he was taxed with it and denied it, saying he was misquoted. Not misquoted at all. I was in Blackwood that night and heard him.

"Twelve grooms or one," said Morfydd now, "we cannot afford her. And whether she agrees with her ministers or not, whether she has a tongue of her own or not, she is head of the State and responsible to the people."

"She is a child, a child," said my father, sick of it.

"I do not care if she is in arms," answered Morfydd. "She is put there by the people who expect something back. Give her a groom if you like, give her a palace, but not twenty, for the God she prays to never owned a palace in His life. No grooms for Him Who had nothing but a rag around His middle. No bishops and convocations and three-cornered hats and mitres and five thousand a year pension in the name of God. For the ministers of her church are better than the politicians for squeezing pennies out of the poor every Lady Day and Michaelmas."

"We were discussing Victoria," said Dada wearily. "How the hell we have got to three-cornered hats and Michaelmas I do not know."

"One and the same," said Morfydd. "When we tip her we will tip her gently, but there will be a clatter when the gentry and clergy come down with her, with their silver plate, decorations and money bags."

"Do you tip her with boots?" I asked.

Morfydd sniffed.

"With tumbrils and guillotines, then?"

"Jethro," said my mother, "into the bath and quick."

"Not in front of Mari," said he, for she sat in a corner, her eyes down, as she always did during the politics.

"Into the bath," said my father, pointing.

227

Morfydd said earnestly, "It matters little how we do it, but it must be done, by force if necessary. We plead for negotiation, and where does it lead us—deeper in iron, deeper into the pits. Unwashed, they call us, but if they blind themselves to our power they will regret it."

"Aye," said Mam. "Unwashed is the word, and if Jethro is not down in that bath in under five seconds I will hit him sideways, iron-splashes and all."

"What is for supper?" asked my father, changing the subject.

"Nothing," said Mam, "the same as last night, unless somebody can spare a shilling for the Shop?"

"What is the debt there?" I asked.

"Thirty-two shillings, and likely to go higher now the strike is on again. Upon my soul, what a state for a country! I pray for little Victoria, but I am hungry enough to eat her."

"Do not waste your breath," said Morfydd. "The bishops pray better, and there is nothing in the Convocation of Canterbury to stop you going hungry."

"What is this old Convocation thing now?" asked Mam. "There are new words cropping up every minute."

"The laws of the Church," replied Morfydd, "and God bless the Queen every two minutes. I could write them a Convocation that would leave them breathless and take the robes from every bishop between here and Glasgow."

"No doubt," said Dada.

"Charters for the last two years, now Convocations," said Mam, pulling down Jethro's trews while he hopped and covered his front with his good hand. "*Diawl!*" she said. "A tail back or front is much the same, and Mari is not interested. God help us. Soon it will be John Frost in Nantyglo House and Crawshay puddling iron," and she belted Jethro to steady him.

"One devil in exchange for another," said Mari, tossing over a towel.

This sent eyebrows up—the first time Mari had wasted a word on politics. My father smiled. "Some views at last, eh? These spots are catching. Air them, girl."

Mari shrugged. "A still tongue is wiser, Mr Mortymer. The house is split from top to bottom already, but I say this— a little more love of God, and the world would be happier, for it is greed you are discussing, not politics. And until greed is taken from the hearts of men you will always have masters and poor, and which way round it is matters little. I am much more interested in my wedding."

"Well spoken," said my mother, swabbing at Jethro's back. "Births and deaths, too, if you like—anything but the politics." Sweating, she brushed stray hairs from her eyes. "Chapel is it?"

"Church of England," I said. "You have known it since a week last Sunday, for I told you."

The expression on her face was enough to freeze us, but she knew I was acting to rules. Mari was Church for three genera-tions, she said, but she left it to me nevertheless. My mother stood up, hooking Jethro out with her arm and he stood there dripping and shivering.

"With respect to Mari," she said, "we have been Chapel since the start of time, never mind about three generations and rules to suit people who cannot agree to something reasonable. Not much to ask, is it?"

There was no sound but Jethro chattering.

"Eh dear!" said she.

"Mam, it is not important," said Morfydd.

"Not important, you say? Only the difference between the Upper Palace and Damnation. *Diawl!* I do not know what the modern generation is coming to." She pointed at Dada. "And it is your fault for encouraging them, mind!"

"Upon my soul," said he, removing his pipe. "I have not breathed a word."

"Then it is high time you did," said she, getting it up her apron. "If you had taught the children the difference between pagan rites and Christian behaviour we would never have been within a mile of a Church of England." Stamping about now, looks to kill, flapping the cloth and throwing cups at the table. "God forgive me if ever I stand before a gilded altar."

"No need for an altar, come to that," said Morfydd. "Just

an old man in black spouting to make it legal and two and sixpence please and out with you quick to make room for the next. A waste of good money is weddings and burials. Like Owen ap Bethell's daughter, for instance. The Bishop himself wedded her; in white lace, she was, with train-bearers and bugles and half the gentry in the county, but where did she land them? Found in bed three nights after with a red-headed preacher from Ponty and cast out by her dada by the end of the week, and they talk about the working classes."

"Found in bed with red-headed preachers is nothing to do with Church or Chapel," said Mam, "and kindly mind your words before Jethro."

"Taken in adultery, nevertheless," said Morfydd, "and that was Church of England. If you want some examples of Chapel marriages I will start now and we will stay up late."

"What is adultery, Mam?" asked Jethro, scratching.

"See now?" said my mother. "Ashamed you should be, Morfydd! A wicked thing it is, Jethro, and terrible to have a loose-mouthed sister in the house."

"Loose-mouthed when it comes to the clergy," said Morfydd. "When the Devil opens his gates the men in black will be first in and the gentry pushing up their shoulderblades."

"Politics again," sighed my father. "Give it a rest, girl." He turned to me. "Church or Chapel, no odds, boy. Please yourself, for I have been trying to please your mother for the last twenty years and I haven't managed it yet," and he took his handkerchief from his pocket and pressed it against his eyes. It was Furnace Five, they told me; she was a bitch for glare. Thank God for the suspension, in one way, said my mother. At least it gave his old eyes a rest.

He rested all right, so did everyone else in town. The only people working were the women in childbirth. The spring went on. The pits were idle, the furnaces cold and the people starved, the children dying first, with the old ones hard on their heels in the long black columns going to the chapels. For the first time since I could remember it was hungry in our house, for there was eight to feed and not a penny coming in, and Morfydd had gone very pale and stately while Mari's waist was so slender that I could nearly span it with my hands.

The mountain was bright in the sun as Mari and I came down hand in hand on the last day of the striking. The valley below us was misted, the dusty air rising in billows as the carts went by. Over the road to Brynmawr had passed cattle for slaughter at Shant-y-Brain's, and the white dust was criss-crossed with saliva trickles from their mouths. Later we saw them, froth on their necks as white as snow, standing together in the furnace heat, bellowing for water. And above us the Coity, great and golden, reared into the sun, her rocks reflecting strickening light, not caring whether anybody lived or not.

But for all the desolation of that afternoon the strike was broken, and out of it came hope of life. Back on workers' terms, too, the first victory.

And before spring was out Mari and I had planned our marriage.

To celebrate the coming event, said my father, we will take Dai Two Pig down to Shant-y-Brain's for mating.

"Wait, I am coming!" cried Jethro.

"Back here, you," said Mam. "You are staying for cutting down."

A devil of a palaver this cutting down, with Jethro up on the table near to tears and Mam, Edwina and Mari pushing and shoving him, the trews going on and coming off him like lightning, and are they too tight or too slack, with the baby crying and everybody shouting directions.

It was always the same for Jethro when Dada or me moved out on a pair, for money was short.

"Let us go," said my father. "The boy will be amputated the way they are going," for scissors were cheeping right and left and pins were going in and coming out.

"Aye," I said, "there are enough here to stop the bleeding."

I will always remember Jethro standing there on the table with tears in his eyes surrounded by women with needles and knives. Mari looked longingly at me, but I did not spare her a look extra. The mating of an animal is a very delicate thing and not for the eyes of women.

Out in the yard came Dai Two, very happy and snorting to get going for his wedding, and along Market Road went the three of us with my father raising his cap to the women and Dai Two grunting his pleasure.

"You are sure of the time, now?" asked my father.

"Aye. Seven sharp," said I.

"Is the boar tame? I am not having a maniac, mind, and I know that Mo Jenkins."

"Big Rhys has seen the thing, Dada. A Hereford boar, it is, sawn in the tusks and short in the privates, he said, and like a cat for eating from a human hand."

"Heaven help the pair of them if it is wild," said Dada. "A family pig like Dai Two is not likely to take to a bruiser and a virgin pig is always tight, mind."

Very fond of Dai Two was my father since the day we saved him from Billy Handy, years back, it seemed. But he saw the sense of my argument squarely. An easy life had Dai Two up to date, rooting the years away, eating his head off. Work days, strike days, they were all the same to Dai, while every other pig on the mountains had a heart attack when the men came out. It was past time he did something with his life, said Mam, so I arranged a date with Mo's new Hereford boar for a furrowing.

Down the mountain to Shant-y-Brain's we went now, the three of us, which was a convenient place for the mating.

All was quiet when we reached the shippon, but people were about, for the manure had just been stacked for spreading and it steamed like a volcano in the fenced yard.

"Ho, there!" I shouted. "Anybody home?" and out of the farm came Mo and Big Rhys, roaring and sparring up at the sight of us.

"Well, man?" began Rhys. "Very happy the three of you are looking for people half starved in Nanty. How are the rest at home?"

"Healthy enough," said my father, eyeing them, for Mo was doing a giggle and there was a bit of boot tapping and

O, aye's and dear me's between the pair of them that was unnatural.

"And your good neighbours? Well with them, is it?" asked Mo.

"Never mind our neighbours," I said sharp. "We are here for a furrowing."

"And a quick one," said Dada, "so I can get back home to supper. Where is the boar?"

"Eh dear!" whispered Mo, "have patience, please. Just like you Mortymers to bring a pig and loose her to the boar. Have you any experience with pig mating?"

"No," we said, feeling small.

"Well, then, leave it to your betters," said Rhys. "If you think it is in with him and out with him and pick up your pig and back home in five minutes you are mistaken, eh, Mo?"

"Indeed," said Mo, grinning.

"For a very romantic business it is, and done tidy, so do not flurry us into speed or the boar will get his temper up and be into the three of you, for standing by here I see little to choose between you and the pig."

"No offence intended, mind," said Mo.

My father rubbed his chin, grinning. "Eh, now!" said he. "I can smell trouble. May I remind you that we are here for a furrowing? And if anything goes wrong with the deal somebody will be bedridden for weeks. Out with your boar now, and get it over and done with."

"The two shillings first, then," said Mo, his hand out.

"One and sixpence!" I cried, indignant. "It was agreed."

"Two shillings now. True Hereford blood is this boar, and he charges sixpence for walking from Garndyrus," and he spat.

"Take it or leave it," said Rhys.

"Damned highway robbery it is," said Dada.

"Put it on the price of the litter," replied Mo. "Sixpence extra is little enough to pay for an aristocrat, and the pig he is serving is nothing but an insult—all ears and backside she is."

"An ordinary boar would not give her a second look," said Rhys. "Two and sixpence would be fairer, Mo."

"Pay him quick, Dada," I said.

"That is better," said Mo, spitting on the silver, and they walked off, grinning.

"I do not trust them," said my father. "Something is afoot or I am not Hywel Mortymer."

With Dai Two standing between us we watched them walk back to the farm, nudging each other and giggling like Sunday school girls instead of grown pugilists. At the door of the outhouse Big Rhys turned and cupped his hands to his mouth. "There is nothing in the contract against an audience, mind. A few of your old friends have come as witnesses all the way from Garndyrus, Hywel, so treat them tidy," and he hooted and yelled like an Indian.

Out they came—Owen and Griff Howells, Afel Hughes, Iolo Milk, Twm-y-Beddau, Will Blaenavon and half a dozen others, blowing on hunting horns and bugles and enough drum beating to send any boar raving mad. Dai Two cocked an ear, took one look and was off with his nose cord flying. Round the manure heap he went like a whippet, while I cursed his ancestors and flung handfuls of manure at him to head him back to the rails.

"Look out!" yelled Dada, but his warning was wasted. I was over the fence and out of the yard like lightning. For through the gate came Mo's boar, roaring and furious; a full twenty stones of him, grizzled and hackled, driving everything before him with tusks like a rhino. Little Dai skidded to a stop, looked, screamed, and cleared the manure by a foot.

"Good God," said Dada.

Round and round the heap went Dai with the bruiser after him, while the Garndyrus criminals whooped with unholy joy. Into the manure now, to come out streaming, with the old boar looking for short cuts to head him off, and the grunting and screaming could be heard in Nanty. Will Blaenavon was helpless on the ground, clutching his stomach and choking with laughter, Big Rhys was hanging on the rails, fisting the air and roaring, and the rest of them were shrieking like women. Mo was rolling his backside along the gate, sagging at the knees, his eyes streaming, shouting encouragement to his boar between breaths. Poor little Dai was tiring, but I dare not go to his aid. It was a mad boar now, his red eyes gleaming above his whiskered snout, and galloping scarcely a yard behind poor Dai, who was bellowing his last as he leaped high and laid there shivering. On top of the manure the bruiser had him. I could bear it no longer and covered my eyes. And when I looked again little Dai was disappearing into the muck with nothing but the boar's backside to tell which way he was going. No pity in Mo, as if his triumph was incomplete, for he lined up the Garndyrus buglers for unison blasts as the boar's tail came up and drum beats and rolls every time it went down.

"Somebody will pay for this," said my father.

"Aye!" whimpered Mo, agonised. "Two shillings, is it?" and he rolled away, his ribs shaking.

Not much of a palaver about boars when they are down to business. This one was off in half a minute and rooting and grunting like a spring lamb, but no sign of little Dai, and my father and I were two feet into the muck, throwing out armfuls of kale before we came across him. It took an hour to get him clean, and we were still at it with the pump long after the Garndyrus hooligans had whooped and blasted their way down the mountains to home.

"One we owe them," said my father, severe.

"Two," I said, "if this pig is not in litter."

And then he chuckled and began to laugh, and my father's laugh would drown the basso profundos of the Italian opera. Just the pair of us there in the middle of Shant-y-Brain's shippon, opposite the barn where I had made love to Mari. I will always remember it, the way we laughed, him and I, while Dai Two winked and snorted at the stupid humans.

Very happy was Dai Two, we noticed; most contented, and with good reason.

Later, my mother sat with him by lamplight, and he brought forth twelve, two for each week of strike, they said in Nanty.

CHAPTER TWENTY

APRIL WAS the month of my wedding to Mari.

I awoke early, went to the window and looked beyond the ash tips to where the mountains met the sky, wondering at the changing colours of the heather as the sun took charge of the day. The night shift was coming off, whooping and quarrelling in the valley, nearly drowning the clatter from the bedroom next door where Morfydd and my mother, clucking like layers, were stitching the white dress around Mari. A great business it had been for weeks now, this dress on borrowed money: special material bought from Abergavenny, full of frills and laces and ribbons of colour. Take it in here, let it out there, down to her ankles, up to her knees, and for God's sake keep if off the ground at sevenpence a yard. Glory to marriage, I thought, to its frills, lace, pins and fittings; glory to all that is written in the Old Book about the joining of one to the other in body and spirit. I can see Mari now as I opened the door in mistake. Beautiful she looked in her white petticoat, her shoulders naked, her long slim arms held high as the women measured. Aye, glory to love and desire! For while the mountain is vast and full of secret places, there can surely be no sweetness like possessing the one you want within the warmth and quiet of walls, away from chance eyes. With Jethro still snoring I was first down the stairs and into the tub outside. The dew was sparkling upon every leaf as I splashed into the icy water and rubbed myself for a glow.

"Hurry!" called my father, coming down. "Mam wants us out of the house before eight, remember."

"What the devil is happening?" she cried then from the landing. "The pair of you due at Shant-y-Brain's at a quarter past and you are creeping for a funeral. Move!"

"What is all the hurry?" I asked. "The wedding is not until two o'clock. Am I going to sleep on the mountain?"

"To hell out of it," said Morfydd half through the window, "or do you want me to come down with boots?"

Claps and cheers from the window now as Dada and I moved off. The women were at the doors, chattering and happy at the prospect of a new bride, and they shouted good wishes as we went by. Very fine I felt walking up Market Road that morning; dressed in my Sunday black, brushed up and pulled in and polished in the boots to shave in and my starched collar killing me. My father, as usual, was perfectly turned out, and still a fine figure despite the slight swell of his stomach. His collar was snow white and his black satin stock beneath it arched proudly under the square cut of his chin. Only his eyes saddened him. The glare had taken them proper now, and they were red and slow to move, as if dying in his face. Dada knew, we all knew, what was coming, for nine puddlers in ten were half blind, but we never spoke of it. Side by side we went up the mountain now, and over the crest down to Shant-y-Brain's for the trap, and the ferns were a dazzling green as we turned our faces to the valley.

"It is a long time since we walked like this together, boy," he said after a silence. "Do you remember how I once talked of women and marriage?"

I laughed. "Aye, but it was so long ago that I have forgotten. Is it something you are doubtful about now?"

"No sniggers," he said, "or I will have you flat, big as you are."

"Yes, I remember," I said. "I remember, too, how I wished you to the devil and back."

"Wait now," said he, sitting on a hillock. "Down here beside me, my son, for I would speak to you again. Come, Iestyn, it is important to Mari."

Until that moment I had not realised the limit to his sight. For weeks now he had not read the pamphlets, and I had seen the failure of his eyes in small things—the outstretched hands, the fixed stare of the pupils, unblinking to the white-hot swing of the firebox. Now, in bright sunlight, I saw them clearly; their light blue strangely opaque and filmed, and his left hand went up to me as I flung myself down to his right.

"What the hell," I said, swallowing my grief. "Is she marrying a bruiser, then?"

He said into the sun, "You will treat this girl with tenderness, Iestyn. Times are hard and likely to get harder, especially for women who bear the children and work to make the money spin. A man in his full strength can torture. The woman beneath him is as clay to be honoured or crushed as he wills, and by the way he treats her she will remember him. Go gently."

"Yes, Dada," I said.

"Save your strength for the men, where you will need it. Do not pour your goodness into the bed. A woman is not an animal to be filled every night out of habit, remember, nor did God ordain that she is loaded with child every year to be kept in milk. She is your wife, mother, your sister if you like. Do you heed me?"

"Yes, Dada."

He went on, his face turned down, "Do not rebel too much. A rebel is all right in his place—there is a place for all kinds of men, but do not defy every law and authority, Iestyn, or you will suffer. Do not hate—not even your masters. Ironmasters may seem born of the devil, but they are not without character, nor are they short of their troubles. They represent the class and system we hate, but they dominate us, and they will not be easily brought down. They suffer as we suffer, remember, so be charitable to them, and be loyal to your Queen."

"Yes," I said.

"But I did not intend to mouth politics, boy. I wanted to speak of the holy bond of marriage, the gift of God. Keep it holy always. Its sanctity is above any system and government, so do not defile it whatever else you see go down, or you will defile the law of the Maker."

He went quiet, so I chanced a look at him. A sudden weariness seemed upon him, a premature age. He had been working in iron for over twenty years now, only three years less than Barney Kerrigan, the blind puddler. Many good men had given their sight to the firebox and gone into the Quakers' Home, those blessed people who were giving back to my country what the ironmasters were taking out of it. Others, like Grandfer Shams-y-Coed who could not see his nose now, had taken to the farms again, which was their birthright. I looked again at my father and saw his face suddenly lined where the sun searched it, the heaviness of the jowls that sagged over his stiff collar. It was a shock to know that he could age; that the muscles of his neck and throat could wither and his great shoulders sag. He had not been the same since Probert had flogged him, and the torchlight meetings of the Chartists, their heat and plans for power through force, seemed to have sapped him of strength. In a morning he was old, for the sun was pitiless.

"Now away," he said, twisting up. "Are we sitting here all day?"

When we reached Shant-y-Brain's farm the wedding trap and mare were ready, together with my old mare Elot, whom Griff Howells had brought over from Garndyrus the previous night. The trap gleamed in the sun and the lively little mare flashed her burnished brass and danced along merrily under the reins while I rode Elot behind. A good judge of nature was Shant-y-Brain, with his wedding trap jaunty and gay and shining red and white and the wheels a golden yellow. Like a bride herself was that little black mare, too, so polished and willing and laden with flowers. But his funeral carts were bible-black, and to get good squeaks he never greased the wheels; pulled by the oldest nags he could find, with soot well rubbed into their hides to add a little more misery, and special flower beds he kept behind his shippon for lilies of the valley. Aye, when it came to business Shant-y-Brain was a mile in front of Evans the Death, who used the same cart for every occasion. And there should be a difference between a funeral and a wedding, although Morfydd says there is nothing to choose between the two. Like the time when Twm-y-Beddau our next-door neighbour married. Evans did the business then, and Twm and his bride went to Chapel sitting on the coffin of Butcher Harris, who burst. Killing two birds with one stone, said Evans, and a cut rate it would be at the settlement. But not much of a wedding with the bride fainting away when Twm lifted the seat, for there was Butcher Harris with flowers in his hand and not even screwed. Refused to pay, did Twm, and the parson backed him, but Evans carved a twin coffin on the wedding night and put Twm's name on one lid and *Jane, Beloved Wife*, on the other, and carted it up to the bedroom window, and Twm paid full price to have the inscription removed.

Not undertaking that, but plain deceit, and people took note of it. No, not a patch on Shant-y-Brain was Evans when it came to business, and the way Shant-y-Brain was going—with the Mortymers, for instance —he would soon be burying gentry.

"Right, you," said Dada now. "Away out of it anywhere you like. At one o'clock sharp we will leave Nantyglo, and if you get to Church late you will never hear the end of it," and he waved his whip above his head and was off in the trap back to Nanty.

A beautiful day for marriage to a bride like Mari. The mountain swelled up either side of us as Elot trotted. The stillness of the trees, the blue loveliness of the sky brought me to tranquillity. Mari Dirion! How lovely was her name! I said it aloud again and again, delighting in its beauty, saying it to the sky, to the rhythm of Elot's hoofbeats on the mountain turf. Spurring her, we made a gallop, entering a line of firs standing bright green and misted in the growing heat, then we swung across the mountain to the Whistle Inn.

A pint to settle the dust, a pail of spring water for Elot and a sleep beneath a tree. It was past one o'clock when the landlord woke me, pointing. And there, on the Brynmawr road was the long line of the Nantyglo guests, the women on the right, the men on the left, following the trap that carried Mari, Mam and Morfydd, and Snell's trap with Jethro, Edwina and Dada coming up behind.

Bread and cheese then and another pint for courage, and I was away. Short of the Corner I dismounted, tethered the mare and lay in the grass by the roadside watching the larks nicking and diving against a sky of unbroken blue, then I re-mounted and took the short cut down into town, and was waiting at the lych gate as the wedding traps came up.

I saw Mari first, of course, radiant in her long white dress with frills and laces and her face flushed and beautiful under her big summer hat.

"All right," said Tomos. "Take her and God bless the pair of you, church wedding or not."

"God bless you, too," said my mother, tearful, a sure sign she was enjoying things.

The bells were ringing joyfully, the sun blazed down. It was a happy, golden wedding day.

The church was crowded, even the balcony was filled, and the tall hats of the women came round as we walked in and up the long, red carpet to the altar while Mrs Gwallter played 'And He Shall Feed his Flock' on the organ, and trust Gwallter to make a damned mess of things for the Mortymers, said Mam. The altar was beautiful, heavy with flowers, and the sun shafted through the stained glass in golden pools of light in which the dust of well-hung clothes hung suspended and glittering. Together we knelt, Mari and I. Behind us the congregation was tuning up for the singing, shuffling and coughing until the minister appeared. I looked at Mari. Her face was pale and her eyes cast down. And I wondered, with the black shine of the Book between us, if she was thinking of home, being in loneliness because there was nobody to give her away. But she said her vows with a smile, her head up-lifted. Yes, glory to marriage, I thought then, to a home, a woman and her children. Then, with the ring on, came the prayers and the flapping of the pages as the congregation got ready; a clearing of throats and an elbowing for room, and when Mrs Gwallter gave the note for the chanting every soul in the place let fly. I heard my mother's deep contralto, my father's bass above the heavy swell of sound, the sweet soaring of the tenors, and the church timbers trembled as they reached for the high ones. Even Mo was singing, mostly out of tune, with Big Rhys making faces and nudging him. Fine and strong looked Mo then with his chest up and his coat seams giving to the great width of his shoulders. I watched Mari's profile under her straw hat; her teeth were even and white, her lips red and faintly smiling as she sang, the voice of youth and beauty. She is far away now, my Mari, but as I saw her that day I will remember her, my wife.

Out into the sun after the signing, and if every soul in town was there I am not mistaken, for the rattle they made with their muskets and whistles has never been heard since, said Tomos afterwards. Good, it was, to own a woman like Mari, to eat and walk with, to take to bed in love. These things I thought with her hand in mine and the wedding ring clutched tight, loving her amid all the commotion.

"Into the trap and away!" shouted my father, so I handed Mari up and got in beside her while Morfydd and the others scrambled for seats, with everybody laughing and shouting and taking deep breaths for room. Like herrings in a barrel now, and Morfydd took the chance to slip her hand up Mari's leg and screamed with joy when I caught one and was told to behave since the pastor was watching. The crowd pressed around the trap, hooting and whistling as we moved off and guns were popping to set the mare into a trot. Other traps followed for the return trip to Nanty, fifty yards long, said Jethro after, and everybody in town hanging from the windows shouting good luck and congratulations to the mad Mortymers. The clamour died as we reached the Brynmawr Corner and the mare took into a run along the rutted road. The sun blazed down, slanting in reflected brilliance off the green slope of the mountain. The swaying of the trap, the clopping of the hooves were a drug to the senses, and Mari was against me, whispering love one moment, pulling at Morfydd's bonnet streamers, chattering and laughing and giving herself to me with secret glances. At Garn-yrirw cottages the neighbours were out in force, waving and cheering, and the top of Market Road was lined with people welcoming us back. The little mare was sweating and frothing as we ran down into the hollow, and whoops of joy went up at the sight that met us, for the women had got their chairs and tables out and made a collection of food; enough to feed Brecon Redcoats, said Mam, and to run them all short for the month. Even Billy Handy had sent a two-gallon cask as a present from the Garndyrus Benefit, and Mo was carrying it above his head to our doorstep. Out came the mugs and the beer was soon flowing, and when all the traps got in from the mountain the whole street was thronged with people.

"Look you!" shouted Owen Howells, running up to us. "It is not a wedding this but a political meeting," and he pointed.

"It is Zephaniah," said Morfydd, breathless.

"Talking to the parson, too," whispered Edwina.

"And about time, from what I hear," said Mam.

"Plenty of room for them," cried Griff, "especially Chartists, but if I had my way I would kick the little one out. It is more pigs and less parsons we are needing, for I am sick to death of collars back to front bowing and scraping over hungry children."

"Steady, Griff," I said, seeing him flushed with drink already.

"Oh dear," whispered Mari. "It is politics already? Can't they forget the old Charter for a minute?" Turning, she ran through the crowd into the house. Following, I caught her in my arms, kissing her lips.

"Tantrums already, is it?" I cried.

"O, I am sick, sick to death of the politics!" she gasped.

"Easy!" I said. "Why pick on it now, of all times?"

"Because it is even at my wedding," said she. "Will we never get peace and quiet from it? Even now, at this time, do you see? Do you understand, Iestyn?"

"Only that I love you," I said.

"And I love you, my precious," and she clung to me, her body shaking. "But promise me this is the end of it, Unions, Charters, meetings and the Six Points being driven to God knows where—promise me you are finished with it, boy?"

"All this because Zephaniah Williams arrives and talks to a parson, Mari? There is much more to it than that."

"Promise, Iestyn! No more demonstrations or mountain meetings or threats of fighting?"

"Aye," I said, kissing her, "we will talk about it later."

"We will talk about it now," said she, cool. "Promise."

Strange are women. No man knows their secrets. Within an hour of her wedding she stood before me, face pale, hands clenched, chaining me to a decision.

I said, smiling, "Enough I do's in the church to fill a coal-tram less than an hour back, Mari. But the kind of promise you are asking for now is best got before the ring, not after. You keep the house. I will take care of the politics."

She turned to the window and stood there watching the people dancing. Mo Jenkins was going it very gay with Mrs Twm-y-Beddau, who was lifting her skirts in the ring and showing her black stockings and stamping to raise dust. Dathyl Jenkins and Gwen Lewis were there, and other people from Garndyrus whom I had not seen for months. My father was filling the mugs and Jethro was carrying them round and Snell and Edwina handing out food. Harps were down on the cobbles and Irish fiddles were going and skirts rising and falling and coloured scarves waving in a medley of movement and joy. I looked at Mari. Her eyes were bright, her hands trembling.

"I am afraid, Iestyn," she said.

"For God's sake!" I said sharp. "Do you have to choose a time like this for it?"

Open came the door then and Morfydd was there, her hair tangled, her face flushed with happiness. "*Duw mawr!*" said she. "Everybody is shouting for the bride and groom and the pair of them at it before dark? What is happening?"

"It is Griff Howells has upset her," I said, "talking politics about more pigs and less parsons, she says."

"I did not," said Mari.

"And why not?" asked Morfydd. "Griff Howells is a moral force Chartist, I am physical force, so listen. Cut the throat of every parson in the country, I say, and put all the pigs in collars and pulpits and the nation would be saved overnight. Is that upsetting, girl?" She pulled me aside and brought the flat of her hand across Mari's rump. "Outside into the dancing the pair of you, while I get the beds made up."

Taking Mari's hand I pulled her into the crowd. As simple as a child she was then, laughing, gay in a moment as the young men crowded up to kiss her and whirl her away.

Until dusk the celebrations went on. One by one the chairs and tables were collected by the neighbours and the hollow began to empty. It was getting dark, but Zephaniah Williams was still talking to my father with the friends he had brought down from Coalbrookvale Royal Oak. The traps moved off. The hollow was nearly silent as Mari and I went hand in hand together up the mountain.

"To give them time to get settled and abed," I told her.

"And time to be sound asleep," said Mari, giggling.

And I shivered in the moonlight as I kissed her, knowing what she meant.

Her body was trembling. A moonlight to remember, that, standing with my wife, knowing her longing was as great as my own.

"Together, at last," I whispered.

"Not a stitch between us," she said, and giggled again.

"Do not be vulgar," I whispered. "Down into the bed with you and we will see what you are made of, for you are a devil of a girl for promises."

"Promises?" she said, and kissed me with a fierceness that sent my blood racing. "You will see," she added through her teeth, "and be lucky if you are alive in the morning."

There is only one place for a woman who talks like that, so I seized her hand and we ran down the mountain to the hollow, down to the house whose windows were glinting in the moonlight, and the moon, who had seen it all before, was as round as a pumpkin, rolling on the ridge of the roof.

For a day before the wedding the furnaces had been cold for cleaning, but now the wood was crackling in the Aames as the fireman got going on them all, making ready for the dawn shift. The house was dark and dead as we crept up the stairs hand in hand to the room set aside for us. A little spray of primroses my mother had pinned on the door, and I have them still, pressed in the leaves of a book. The room was in darkness save for a chink of moonlight through the drawn curtains, and the tassled blanket Mam had brought from Cyfarthfa was cut by a sword of light.

There is much to be said for mountain lovemaking when two meet in a room with the same thing in mind. All Nature is in love on a mountain; the kiss of water is in the wind, birds give their song, leaves and branches their movement. There is no embarrassment in nakedness then, no shock in new learning, no hiding of faces. There is a laughter in mountain loving that cannot enter a room which has a place in the middle to lie on and another for laying the heads, and you stand here and undress while I do it there.

It is one thing dreaming of love between walls, but now we had come to it I longed for the mountain places.

Outside in the blue the firer was singing to himself as we undressed, Mari on one side, me on the other, both disappointed, both on the hot side after our run, and I, for one, was dying to giggle. Taking my time over my boots I watched her. No shame in Mari ever since Llanelen; just secret smiles as she took the things off. Down on the bed for the high-buttoned boots, put them tidy; up with the dress, shake the hair free, start on the stockings. Off with two petticoats, the last one flannel, and she is there in her stays. Down with the stockings, roll them for shape, down with the lace-trimmed drawers, off with the stays and she stands in her vest.

"Good God," I said. "How much more?"

"Pull that old curtain," said she, "for now I am shy."

Very strange are women, I thought then. They are lovely with everything on and provoking with everything off. But when they stand before you half on and half off they are maddening, as Mari was that wedding night, in shadows with the dim white bed beyond her.

"Iestyn!" she said, gasping to breathe.

I was with her at the start of time, kissing her in love and fierceness, losing her lips and finding them as she twisted away for breath, fighting her strength, defeating her, clasping her to the hoarse strains of the firer's song. No sound but that song, not a whisper.

"For God's sake," she said. "Would you eat me? Bread and cheese now, is it?"

"I am sorry," I said.

"Not me," said she. "I enjoyed it. Into bed I am now. O, I am a hoyden and you are one worse! To hell with the pair of us," and threw back her head and shrieked with laughter.

"*Hisht!*" I whispered. "You will have Morfydd in."

"Three in here now! *Whee!* There is an ocean of a bed—have you ever seen the like? One finger on me and I am round it and you will not see me all night."

Glory to marriage when the moon rides high and the world is sleeping and lovers are awake. We stood like statues in that beam of moonlight, kissing, naked, unashamed.

"Cold for April," said she. "Away to go I am before I catch my death," and she was out of my arms and dived full length. She bounced once, did Mari, and rolled over and sat, her jaw dropping, her eyes transfixed as the old thing crashed and shrieked and twanged with enough bell-ringing to wake Nanty.

"Good God," I said, going cold.

"*Jawch!*" whispered Mari. "Harps are tied to it," and she rolled over for a look underneath, bringing it to fresh peals.

"Keep still!" I whispered, and she lay like a dead thing while I ran my hands over the big brass balls above her head.

"Just as I thought," I said. "That Morfydd is a damned bitch, mind. This is Iolo Milk's bed changed with Mam's especially to ruin the first night."

This set Mari off again and she hugged herself and rolled up and over the thing, giggling, and the springs clanged louder and brought me out in a sweat.

"Lie still!" I commanded. "It is fine fun now but different at breakfast with the family knowing we have been up to capers."

Nothing funny in that as far as I could see, but it set her off double, holding her stomach and blue in the face with her, while the tears streamed down, and spluttering.

Five spring bells I got from that bed, bells like the gentry have in kitchens, wired on solid, while Mari lay like a mouse above me, her face buried in the pillow and pressing in her sides to stop her explosions.

"Wait for the morning," I said, working under it. "I am stripping that damned Morfydd and hang for murder."

No sleep for either of us now; not in the mood for love-making, for I was never one to turn it on and off like a tap, as I explained. Back into my nightshirt, me; back into her vest and drawers went Mari, and both pretty civil about it, too. We were getting the Cyfarthfa blanket straight when Mari went to the door.

"Damme, how did that get there?" she asked, pulling down a note. "From Morfydd, it is," she said, taking it to the light.

"We missed it coming in," I said. "Read it loud," and she read, saying, "Have the house to yourselves for once and make the old bed happy, for the family are staying at Garndyrus."

And Mari smiled and kissed me. "Back into bed with me now, is it?"

So I kissed her, forgetting my sulking, and we put the blankets back and the sheets tidy, and crept in. And had Lucifer been under us with fiddles and gongs, we would not have heard him. For sounds vanish with lovemaking when there is no fear of a listener. A man is great then, with the petal smoothness of a woman's body under his hands and the rushing sweetness of her breathing in his ears. Tired, we watched the moon lifting her skirts over the Coity, flooding the earth and paling the stars with her brilliance. The fade of the moon meant sleeping, each awakening a dawn of new loving, until the clouds dropped their curtains and brought us to darkness, and the furnaces quickened and shrieked into blast.

Honour to woman and her secret haven where the lancing steel goes deep, wounding in love and fierceness.

Honour to Mari now the first heat is past.

Honour to all things that breathe; to this land that powders the bones of its conquerors, honour to my father's strength, to Jethro in youth, to Morfydd's sad beauty and Edwina's new faith. And to the people of the earth, rich or poor, give the joy of this dividing, O God, until the darkness fades and reality breaks and the lights come flaring over the mountain. Glory to St Peter and the One Who united us, to the ring of gold that binds us, to the rivers, the stars above us. Glory to Wales and the men who will lead us—*Gogoniant i fywyd, i gariad , i wreigiaeth, i Mari, gyda mi'n Un!*

CHAPTER TWENTY-ONE

.AND SO passed the summer, in loving. Autumn came in cold and brown, and Mari and I got the house that Morfydd had next door, being on the list, at one and threepence a week, enough to break us. But it was best to be on our own, said my mother, for two women in a kitchen can be hell and four were in ours.

It was the Sunday that Tomos Traherne called that will stay for ever in my mind.

The early darkness was upon us, a sadness of twilight between summer and winter, and The Top was wreathed in perpetual mist, a blanket to the drilling of the Chartists and the torchlight meetings of the Union. Music, brittle and high, came from the stripped hedgerows, and the corn scythed from the old farms stood in long stooks of shadow when my father, Jethro and I came off shift. The moon and stars held a new brilliance, blue on the blackberry cobwebs in the frosty mornings as I went into the outside tub, and the road to Blaenafon stood out sharp and cold against the dull country.

It was such an evening that brought Tomos over from Garndyrus; wheezing after his five-mile walk and the weight of his Book, the old fool, which was enough to cripple a donkey. My mother was spinning, as usual, Morfydd sewing and Mari making pretty little things and giving me secret looks across the table. Dada, dozing by the fire, was snoring and waking in fumbles.

It was the first time Tomos had visited since the birth of Richard and it took Morfydd all her time to give him a glance. But it was so much like the old days when Tomos came for a Reading; ducking his head under the sill, arms out to my mother and kissed her, his hand, the size of a ham, out to me and Dada. Here is a commotion! Back with the chairs, poke up the fire, everybody chattering and congratulations on the new baby, which put Morfydd very dull, and they pulled the little thing from his cot and Tomos kissed and blessed him, which set Richard howling. One moment peace, the next bedlam; a very different tune this to the one Tomos sang when he threatened to have the pair of them for casting out; illegitimate and sinful then, heartiest congratulations now. The one thing the Lord left from His Bible was a Commandment on the ways of His preachers, said Morfydd. She was cool now, and little wonder.

"Excuse me, please," she said, and took Richard up to bed again and did not come down.

"Where is Edwina?" asked Tomos, taking her place by the fire.

"Over with Mr Snell in Abergavenny," said my mother, flapping on the tablecloth.

"Is that business still strong?" he guffawed.

"It is," said my father, cool on purpose.

"Another marriage into the Church, I suppose? What with Iestyn's wedding and Edwina's crucifix you will soon have enough converts to open a theological school, Hywel. Is it true you are taking the cloth, too?"

"See now," said my mother. "I am not alone when I uphold Chapel, it appears," and she looked most satisfied and waved things about.

"I wonder I did not meet her on the Brynmawr road," said Tomos, changing the subject.

"She went across the mountain," I said.

"Eh now! In darkness? Alone?"

"It was light when she went," said Mari. "Mr Snell is bringing her home by trap from the service at St Mary's."

"Is that safe with Probert and his Cattle loose on the tracks?" Tomos turned his head to the stairs and lowered his voice. "Wise, is it, with men as mad as Dafydd Phillips running riot over The Top? Seen in Blackwood last week, they tell me, breaking legs."

"No!" whispered Mam fearfully. "Whee, hisht you man!" and she turned her eyes upwards.

"Aye," said Tomos. "And fifty pounds upon his head

now, the same as Probert. It is sorry for his mother I am, Hywel, for a good little woman is Mrs Phillips and she do not deserve it."

"Blaming the Mortymers, though, I'll be bound," said Mam. "Everyone do blame the Mortymers, poor souls, and not a word of blame for Dafydd throwing himself at Morfydd's head and blacking her eyes after he was sure of her. Breaking legs now, is it? Let him come down by here and try it."

"Hark at the old fighting cock," said Dada.

"Aye, I can fight when my children are involved, mind."

"Are you for the Chartists or the Union when the time comes?" asked Tomos, winking.

"There is no politics about my fighting, thank you," said Mam. "One side is as bad as the other."

"Maybe," replied Tomos, "but one is more dangerous."

"The aims of the Charter and the aims of the Union are indivisible," I said sharp.

"Well now," replied Tomos, swinging. "The babies are from their long clothes at last. Did you read that in *The Vindicator?*"

"The aims are the same," I said. "Freedom."

"Unionism," said Tomos sedately, "is the bonding together of the workers for the purpose of negotiation of complaints. Chartism is the banner of revolt against Queen and State. They blacklist you for one and hang you for the other, so be warned, for the time is nigh. There will not be enough chains in England to fetter us if men like Frost and Vincent have their way."

"That is the chance we take."

"You see what I have to put up with?" said Mari.

"I see that you are bound for trouble," said Tomos. "What do you think, Hywel? Peaceful negotiation is our only hope, not arms, for one volley from the Military and every Chartist in sight would go flying, leaving the brave to swing."

"I am with Iestyn," said Dada, sitting everybody up except Tomos. "The owners will not negotiate and we have been sitting tight too long. It is war if they insist on it. It has taken me twenty years of loyalty to learn that they make profits out of peace."

"Sense at last," said Tomos, grinning.

"Tomos, you old fox!" I exclaimed.

"And where does God come in on all this?" asked Mam. "You agree with violence and killing, man?"

"Not with killing," replied Tomos, "for the Commandments stand firm in my faith, but with violence, yes—as He showed them in the Temple, the men of greed."

My mother said, coming near, "If this old Charter thing means drunkenness and insulting Bailey on his doorstep, then we are best off without it, so go, Tomos."

"Hush, Elianor," said Dada.

"Hush, indeed!" she cried. "Are the men and a pixilated daughter the only ones to count in the house, then? And now we are getting violence condoned by preachers and deacons. Politics every moment of the day, it sickens. Four Points here, Six Points there—paid members of Parliament when we can get them free. Secret voting, and women are not entitled to a vote, Whig or Tory. Leave us in peace, Tomos Traherne. Working in iron is misery enough for a woman without ending up a widow as well." Close to tears she looked then.

"Listen, Elianor," said Tomos, "you have children—you have grandchildren. This violence is the risk we must take—not for this burned out generation, but for the next. Or are you satisfied with conditions that will make them perpetual slaves, as we are? For the Negro children of the Kentucky plantations do not labour as ours. Freedom has been fought for down the ages, with tooth and sword and fire. Listen, you! To everything there is a season, and a time to every purpose under Heaven. Remember, girl? A time to be born, and a time to die; a time to plant, and a time to pluck up that which is planted; a time to kill, even, and a time to heal; a time to break down, and a time to build up."

"A time to weep, and a time to laugh," whispered Mari by my side, and the shock of her voice turned us all. "A time to mourn, and a time to dance. To love, hate, make war and make peace, Mr Traherne, and to them I could add a hundred of equal virtue, every one telling of love, not hatred, peace, not war," Mari rose to her feet. "How will the men of God stand in this at the Judgment?"

"Thou knowest the Book," replied Tomos, "and the purpose of the Word. By thy obedience to it shalt thou be judged, I also. But there is nothing in the Commandments that instructs men of honour to hide behind a woman's fear while the young and old are starved and maimed for the price of bread. There also lies a duty to the oppressed, a raising up of those cast down. And we will sweep the oppressors from the land, even as Moses sent the tribes to war against the Midianites, Numbers, chapter thirty-one, to slay even as the kings of Midian were slain; namely Evi and Rekem, and Zur, Hur and Reba, and Balaam the son of Beor. So shall we sweep them away, slaying if they oppose us."

"I am off from here," said Mari. "As you found a chapter for casting out Morfydd, so you will find one to suit your every argument. It is wicked when men like Iestyn turn to revenge and killing, but there is no hope for us when men of the chapels come to incite them," and the door went back on its hinges and she was away.

She was half way up the Coity before I caught her, and turned her to my lips. Gasping, leaning upon each other, we laughed a little and then walked on, hand in hand.

"I told him," said she at length. "The damned old God-botherer he is, and not a streak of the Christian in him."

"Oh, he is not so bad," I said.

"No indeed, he is not—he is wicked. A lot of old soaking about the benefits of Chapel over Church and then biblical quotations and a preaching of blood and killing to make the Devil dance. Iestyn, I am afraid."

"Do not heed him," I said.

"I will not," said she. "But will you? All the old ones are the same now, telling the young ones to get set for the battle, but you will not find an old one in sight when the Redcoats come out. O, Iestyn, where will you land us if you follow the Chartists? Keep by me, boy. Leave it to the old ones."

"To hell with the Chartists," I said. "Do not tell me you ran me up here just to talk the politics."

The leaves of past autumns were piled here, a softer bed than any made by man. Her breath was warm and sweet, and beyond the curve of her cheek I saw the mountain sweeping away in blueness down to the red fires of the Garn. The wind breathed about us, twanging the branches like harp strings and hissing softly through the grass. Mari slipped to my feet and the sight of her lying there brought the old dryness and trembling back from the days of courting. Long and slim she looked, a part of the dusk in her loveliness. Kneeling, I kissed her, and she turned away her face as I unbuttoned the high neck of her dress, and her heart throbbed wildly under my hand.

"There is stupid," she whispered, "with a good strong bed back home and sheets."

"But beautiful, Mari. Will you have me here?"

Wildly she kissed me then and her arms went about me hard and strong, and her hands moved over my body, making me the loved and her the lover. The stifled sobbing of her breath against my mouth became a whisper as she held me closer.

The moon, respectful, hid while I loved her, pulling down black dresses over her brightness, covering us with night and a temple of silence. Warm and quick was Mari beneath me, responding in wildness and a murmuring joy as I divided her body, and the lightning of youth flashed between us. And then, spent and near sleeping, we laid together, kissing, while the world of wind and water crept back with all its sounds.

A cry I heard then, a scream like an animal trapped. Far below in the valley it was and the wind took it and whirled it over the peaks into the night.

Mari stiffened. "What was that?"

Again the scream. Not the scream of anything human but that of something unknown, fearsome in its terror.

"For God's sake what was that?" whispered Mari, sitting up. Strange how I can remember the beauty of her naked legs, long and slim against the leaves, and the way her dress, flaring from her waist, stained them like a crescent pool, and the frantic working of her fingers as she pulled it down.

"It is a woman," she said then, and clasped me, and from beauty grew horror for the woman screamed again, long and clear from the valley, and the scream faded into mutterings and guttural cries of suffering, and silence.

"O God, there is terrible," said Mari, trembling. "From the Brynmawr road, is it?"

"Down at the Garn by the sound of it," I replied. "One of the Irish beating his wife, perhaps?"

"She is dying, then. He is beating her to death."

"The neighbours will see to it," I said, sweating. "There are good men down at the Garn, and it is too far away for us to help. Home now, is it? Mari, you are shivering."

Tomos was in the middle of a Reading by the look of things, so we did not go back in for supper. Lying together in the bed next door we listened to the drone of his bass voice, my mother's treble replies, the scrape of my father's chair from the hearth. By midnight I was asleep, but the crying of Richard awakened me, and Morfydd's soothing voice was clear in every word as she comforted him, for the wall between us was thin. And that was the last sound I remember before Snell's mare and trap came down the slope of Market Road, the hoofbeats ringing. Getting out, I went to the window and looked down. The trap was deserted in the moonlight, the flanks of the little mare steaming, and her jaws and bridle were white with froth.

And then came Morfydd's voice, broken with fear, calling my name, and a hammering on our door.

"Edwina left Snell for home at eight o'clock after the service at St Mary's. She is missing somewhere on the mountain," she cried. "Dada has gone to search already."

"Good God!" I whispered.

"The fool to let her come back alone!" Mari whispered behind me.

"We will sort out the fools afterwards," I said, and called, "Where is Snell now?"

"In with Mam crying his eyes out."

"Free the mare from the trap," I said. "Keep Snell here. I will be down in a minute," and I ran upstairs and pulled on my clothes. I was lacing my boots when Mari came in. She said, her eyes wide:

"The screams. Do you remember them? Leaving Snell at eight o'clock it would give her an hour to get to the Garn, on foot."

"Mari, for Heaven's sake!" I said, sweating.

"It was her," she went on, weeping. "O, holy God, we are cursed!"

"Shut it!" I said. "Worse than Snell you are. Pull yourself together and go down and comfort Mam."

"We are cursed," said she, thumping her hands together. "Cursed we are, because of the politics."

"Away out of it," I said. Morfydd held the mare steady and I took her bareback into the night, across the tracks, galloping.

The moon was like a platter on the back of the mountain, and I saw the thorn spiked and black against its light, and the tops of the hedgerows streaked past me all white and smoking as if on fire. She was a good little mare at the best of times, this one, and now she was free of the trap she excelled herself. To the quickening clatter of her hooves we took over the mountain, leaping the boulders, flattening down over streams. Away to my left burned the lamps of Garn-yrirw cottages, and doors were opening, for yellow light was flashing against the mist. I wheeled the mare towards them, struck the road and slackened to a trot, for men with lanterns were gathering outside the rank and spilling over the slope, and I heard shouting and a voice raised in command.

"What is happening?" I cried, reining in.

Lanterns went up, shadowed faces were thrust into the light.

"A search party going out for the Nanty girl," said one, thick and bearded. "Where you from, boy?"

"The girl is my sister," I said. "One of the Mortymers. Has my father been up by here?"

"Now just, with Traherne the preacher," came the cry.

"But he is on the mountain now going up to Waunavon with Garndyrus men, and God help any man loose tonight if she is harmed. Raving is Hywel Mortymer, and Rhys Jenkins with him sweating blood."

"Look you!" shouted another. "There are the torches."

A mile away, on the foothills of the Coity, the torches burned in the mist. Rain began to fall then, and the men about me turned up their collars, blinking the wet from their eyes as they waited for their search leaders. A sickness rose in my throat, stifling my breathing, and an anger greater than anything I had known spewed up in me. I thought of my father's agony, of my mother comforting the useless Snell while her heart was breaking, and the stupidity of the man in allowing Edwina to return home alone with mad Scotch Cattle loose and baying. Reining the mare I turned her, and she brought up her forelegs, neighing, and galloped over the tumps toward the distant torches.

Mo Jenkins I found standing in a hollow of mist, with Will Blaenavon and Phil Benjamin, soaked, all three, and looking murderous.

"Have the others found a trace?" asked Mo.

"None of the men at Garn-yrirw," I said. "What the devil is my father and the others doing so far off the track?"

"Searching the slopes up to Waunavon. We have been over here every inch. The Whistle Inn landlord saw her on the road near the Garn at nine o'clock, but no sign of her since, not even from Betsy Garn-yrirw who was sitting outside waiting for her man. Only the screams Betsy heard."

"Screams?" I said, going colder, remembering.

"You know Betsy ap Fynn," said Phil. "If she heard no screams she would bloody soon invent some. Do not look so ghostly, boy. If this sister is anything like the rest of the Mortymers, she is tucked up safe and sound in a quarry and screaming because he is slow."

"Easy," said Mo, elbowing him. He wiped rain from his face. "Up to Waunavon with you, Iestyn, and tell Rhys we will meet him at the Whistle for a pint going back, is it?"

"Aye," I said.

"And sharp," said Will, smacking the mare's flank. "By the time you get there Edwina will be safely home. You will work yourself into ten murders sitting here doing nothing. Away!"

It was raining sheets now, the water running in icy trickles down my chest and back. The heather was loaded, and each brush of the mare's chest sent the spray high. The track was narrower here, the ground rising sharply to the Coity foothills. Before me, ascending the ridge, was the red line of torches where my father and Big Rhys were searching with the Garndyrus men, and their hoarse shouts came faintly on the wind. To my left burned a single torch, a lonely searcher who was bending into the heather. Wheeling towards him, the mare slipped on flints, nearly unseating me. Dismounting, I led her, picking my way cautiously. I had not gone ten yards before the man held high his torch and whistled shrilly. Throwing aside the mare's bridle, I ran, shouting, but the man's frantic whistling had already turned the torches on the ridge and I saw the sparks flying as the men came down. I dashed on, tearing through undergrowth, leaping high over the flooded streams, shouting to ease the growing panic within me. From all directions the men were coming now, even from the Garn where the night-shift miners were thronging in on their ponies. And only one man was still, the man in the heather, standing upright, his fingers in his teeth, blowing his shrill whistles of terror. I was the first to reach him. Shanco Mathews it was, wild in the face and hair, and his clothes soaked with rain. The smoke of the torch had blackened him as with the smoke of hell itself, and beneath him, half naked, arms and legs flung out, lay Edwina. With my hands pressed to my face I stood there in horror while Shanco blew his whistles beside me. A man joined me, then another, and soon a ring was made with others pressing in closer. In the red light of their uplifted torches I saw their faces, sweating and horrified, and the burning stares of their eyes. I was upon my knees with Edwina's hand in mine when my father burst into the ring and went down and flung his arms around her, calling her name.

"She is dead," I said.

Squatting, he lifted her across his lap and the men sighed and moaned as he kissed her and held her fast against him.

"Hywel, she is dead, man," said Rhys.

Aye, dead.

Her hair was stained red in the torchlight but black where the mud and leaves had caught it, and her face and breast were white, too, except where smeared with blood. All white, she was, except for this; nearly naked, for shreds of her dress had been ripped from her body by the claws of Beast and lay scattered about her on the sodden grass. But my father saw none of these things, it seemed. Like a lover he sat there with his arms about her, kissing her face and whispering. My bowels were shrinking tight, my heart pulsating in the agony. Clenching my fists I lowered my face from the sight.

"Iestyn," said my father.

The torches went up and I saw his face. His eyes were the eyes of a man crucified, brilliant from their shadows of a face stark white and old.

"Find him, Iestyn," he said then.

"Find him we will, Mr Mortymer," said Shanco Mathews. "If it takes all winter we will find him and kill him with red irons."

"Home to Elianor, Hywel," said Big Rhys, kneeling.

"Leave me," said my father.

"For God's sake, man," said Rhys, pulling at his hands. "She is dead, look you, you cannot kiss her back. Come now, she is bare, let us make her decent."

"Her crucifix is gone," said Mo, pulling his coat up to her throat. "O Christ, I will kill, kill! Bloody murder I will do for this!"

"Away," said my father. "Leave us," and his eyes, sightless, looked past us towards the flare of Nanty. But Rhys knelt and gripped Edwina and tore her from his arms and flung him back.

And my father went full length, face down in the place where Beast had raped her, and clutched the grass, and wept.

CHAPTER TWENTY-TWO

CHURCH OF England for everything now, said my mother, weeping.

No need to tell of the grief. No need to tell of the miles we searched. From Cwm Crachen to Ebbw Vale we searched in our hundreds, and the time off was paid by Bailey, to his credit. With pitchforks and cudgels we went, night and day, carrying our food, sleeping in quarries. Even the Irish came, hitting the heather flat with one hand and telling their beads with the other. Strangers were taken and laid out. Down with their trews, up with their shirts for bloodstains. Beards were pulled aside, faces peered at in the light of lanterns. God help the man who cut himself shaving, said Mo. God help the man if we find him, said my father.

But we did not find him.

As one goes out another comes in, said Tomos.

Mari was coming full with her by September. And very pretty she was, red in the cheeks and full in the breast, and Morfydd and my mother pushing and prodding and slitting up the seams of her skirts where the hollows of her stays used to be.

There is beauty in the body of a woman with child, when she carries as primly as Mari. She walked with dignity, lifting the men's caps in every direction and dropping the women in bows. It is strange how some fall to bits when they are caught, like Mrs Twm-y-Beddau and Mrs Pantrych. Very objectionable, says my mother, with their hair tied with string like the poor Irish, and their breasts half bare and skirts pulled up short in front with ropes to carry their stomachs while labouring. And they are loud in their chatter, too, as I heard one night from Mo Jenkins' sister, who ought to have known better. Putting the Shop into fits, was Dathyl, saying how she would never turn her back to her man after a Benefit Night, and always slept with her chastity belt on, for he was a madman and whooping after ten quarts unless she had a stick handy to cool him. Yes, it is amazing how low some women sink when they get into corners, and they are the first to play hell about jokes when the men get hold of it. Thank God women like Mari are above such discussion, as Afron Madoc, the Swansea deacon, and Caradoc Owen discovered.

"Look you," said Mari in bed, balancing the tea cup upon her stomach. "Whee! There is an old kicker you have coming, man; he is worse than a Staffordshire mule."

And she folded her hands behind her head and giggled and shook, balancing the cup to the kicking within her. "Whoops!" she cried as the tea splashed into the saucer. "O, Iestyn, look!"

"A boy it will be, with hobnails," I said, dressing. "If it is a girl then heaven help you," and I kissed her.

It was still dark, five o'clock in the morning, and the early frosts were into us, lying white over the country. My father was on night shift and I was due to follow him at six. Morfydd and Mari were working underground now, pulling trams—Mari due there an hour later because she was pregnant, which was very kind of the Agent, said my mother.

"Aye," said Morfydd. "Special treatment because she worked for him once. Very special treatment I would hand to Agents who work expectant mothers, and they talk of the Spanish Inquisition. Boiling lead is too good for him."

"Why?" asked Jethro, at breakfast now.

I said, "You should know better than to shout in front of children, Morfydd."

"Aye?" she answered. "Then let me say this. Six shillings a week she earns on the trams like an animal, too big round the waist for the towing belt. In less than four months she will drop it in coal dust. It is time she worked here with Mam."

"There is stupid," said my mother. "She is good for weeks."

"She is signing off this morning," I said. "An hour ago the child moved, and she is not delivering underground like the Irish."

"Thank God for sense," said Morfydd.

"Eh dear," sighed Mam. "Times are changing indeed. Half the population of Wales is born underground these days, and they are none the worse for it."

"None the better for it, either," said Morfydd. "A good boy you are, Iestyn, for stopping Mari's shift."

"She is full and the child is kicking to be out, is it?" asked Jethro, chewing.

"Get on with your breakfast," I said.

And Furnace Five split under blast.

With a shudder and a roar it split further, and we sat crouching at the table as fire leaped at the window and iron rattled in drips on the roof. Transfixed, we sat, and Mari's feet drummed on the stairs and the door burst open and she stood there, shocked white and trembling.

"In the name of God what was that?" she whispered.

"A split," I cried, and ran from the house, pulling my coat over my shoulders.

The hollow was a beehive, with men running and others coming in from the tram roads, and crowds were already pressing around Furnace Five where my father was on shift. Women and children were screaming, men shouting commands, and a pump was already manned and buckets of water being passed down the line. Shanco Mathews came face to face with me, his hair smoking.

"Where is my father?" I cried.

"Three men are in the puddling shed," he shouted. "For God's sake fetch the Agent."

"Away out of it!" I pulled him aside, but he tripped me, sending me sprawling. Up then, and I had two others down before I barged headlong through the men.

"Come back, you fool!" shouted Caradoc Owen. "She is split and will topple any minute."

Free of them, I stripped off my coat and wound it around

my head and shoulders and stumbled into the heat of the furnace. It was going like a pillar of fire, burning in quick, noisy flares that licked at the base of the cylinder and puffed up in balls of flames to the lip of the flue. Smoke was exploding in mushrooms from the wrecked puddling-house, weaving around the shattered roof and condensing in shafts of steam. Splintered timbers projected from the ruins where the roof slanted drunkenly, and beneath the roof a man was screaming, his voice as shrill as a child's, in short staccato cries, catching his breath to the torture of the scalding. The sand moulds were overflowing and the molten iron was running in little rivers of flame. The choked furnace was under pressure again, bellowing at the blocked shaft. Leaping past it I jumped the moulds and reached the door of the puddling house. The charred wood, slammed shut by the blast of the split, went down like paper as I charged it, and I fell flat, gasping. It was strangely cool here away from the furnace, but the timber in the walls was coming alight as the glowing fingers of iron moved in. The man was no longer screaming, for the water in the steaming pits had dried, but I heard a low sighing that came from the overturned cauldrons where the metal was cooling on the floor. In darkness I stumbled forward, hands groping. Tripping over fallen beams and scattered ladles I lurched towards the sighing, and my path was lighted by the burning walls as the iron took them into a bonfire.

"Dada!" I cried.

No answer, and the piled wreckage about me made shape in redness.

The centre wall was down and with it the puddling flues, and the cauldrons that tapped from the furnace direct were on their sides or upside down. Ladles and tools were lying as the men had flung them, coats and gloves and eye-shades were scattered about. Looking through the torn roof I saw the stars and racing white clouds sweeping over the moon.

"Dada!" I cried, sobbing. Iron was dull black on the floor and every footstep was agony.

"Three men are in there!" shouted the Agent from the door. "Can you see them?"

"Dada!" I called. "Dada!"

"Are the basins upright, Mortymer?" bawled Mr Hart.

"Where are you, Iestyn?" Shanco Mathews this time.

"Over by here," I called. "Bring a torch, for God's sake, and watch your feet, the basins are over."

In he came. No Agent this, hanging back by the door. With the flaring torch held high he came, hopping to the heat of the floor, and I kicked at a ladle to give him direction. On came Shanco, cursing, and reaching me he raised the torch and I saw his eyes widen.

A man's face I saw then, in profile at my feet, burned black; a face of marble, drawn clean against the sooted walls of the house, and I knelt, touching it. The flesh of the cheekbone was hot on one side. The other side was melted into streams and the tips of my fingers touched jaw and teeth. Dead, this man, by iron scalding, but the ladle was still in his hand, gripped like a shepherd's crook. Dead, with his legs and hips in the puddling cauldron, rigid to the waist where the forty gallons had caught him in its arms of molten iron, and cooling, gripped him.

"Blood of Christ," said Shanco. "Barney Kerrigan," and he turned away his face.

Sickened, I raised myself, wondering what I would find for a father.

The walls were well alight now, and the wind was sucking out the smoke in gusts through the roof.

"Over here," cried Shanco, hopping.

"Iestyn," said my father.

Under the arch of the furnace we found him; one leg and one arm thrusting out from the heaped bricks of the firebox lining, and the rest of him buried but safe from the iron.

"Iestyn," he said, and his voice echoed strong in his tomb.

"Dada!" I cried, and we went to our knees and heaved the beams and bricks aside as men came flooding through the entrance.

"Faster!" I called to Shanco.

"Watch the wall!" cried the Agent, but I saw no wall. Only my father I saw, his buttocks arching as the weight of the wall was raised, and I heard no sounds but his gasping. A dozen men were working now, spitting, coughing, cursing in the smoke. The walls were roaring with flame as we pulled the last beam up and dragged him clear.

"Easy, for Christ's sake!" I whispered, but I knew we were too late.

His face was wealed with furnace burns, and the black iron splashes were rigid in his cheeks and across his chest, and he sighed as a man in death and moved his lips.

"Iestyn," he said.

"Still breathing, though," whispered Shanco. "Down to Abergavenny with him and quick, or bring the doctor here. . . ."

"Leave him," I said, and caught my father's hand and gripped it.

"Stand aside, Mortymer," said a voice.

"Dada," I whispered, and he opened one eye, but he did not see me, though he smiled.

"For God's sake, Mortymer," said Shanco in a panic. "It is Mr Hart ordering you and Crawshay is coming behind him."

"Out of the way, Mortymer," said the Agent then.

"Let him die in peace," I said, swinging a fist at his legs.

"Is that the son?" said another voice. "Out of the way, young man, or you will regret it."

"Dada," I said, weeping.

"Watch for your mam and Jethro, Iestyn. Take them back to the farms. . . ." Clear, every word clear, despite the iron that was taking over his soul.

Whispers behind me, shuffling feet, and men pecking at my coat and plucking at my sleeves. "I give you one last warning, Mortymer," said the Agent, pulling me.

"By God," I said, and gripped a ladle. "Away to hell out of it or I will have you down with this iron, you and Bailey, so bloody leave him!"

"Elianor," said my father.

"Good little man," I said, and kissed him.

"Eh, dear."

I got up then, blinded, pushing them all aside. Steam was

rising and the walls were smoking under the buckets. Through an avenue of men I walked, seeing nothing, until I came to the entrance where the women were waiting. My mother was before me suddenly, with Mari and Morfydd standing either side, and women were sobbing, but no sound came from mine. I raised my face.

"Finished, is he, Iestyn?"

"Aye, Mama," I said.

"In peace now, my boy?" Her fingers screwed at her apron.

I nodded, choking.

The wind whispered between us then, bringing smoke. My mother lowered her face and clenched her hands, and weeping, said:

"O, Hywel, my dearest one, my precious."

I went from them, shivering, cold.

Jethro I met on the doorstep. His hair was ragged, his eyes wild. I saw in his face the face of my father, then; square, strong, unravaged.

"Dada, is it?" he said.

"Aye, man," I replied.

Three times he called to me as I walked towards the mountain.

Cursed, we are.

Cursed, said Mari, cursed by Nanty.

Two in six weeks.

CHAPTER TWENTY-THREE

Two in six weeks, we said; Edwina, Dada.

But you can starve to death grieving, said Morfydd. We must live for the living, if Bailey will let us.

Not even gunpowder will shift me from Nanty, said my mother.

"Mari is coming very big in the stomach still," said Jethro out on the tram road where Hart had sent us.

"Yes," I said.

"Waiting for her sign, is it?" he asked, frowning.

"Yes," I said, jerking at the reins.

"Is it bad, then?" he asked, squinting.

"What now?" I was miles away just then.

"Mari's stomach coming big these days. Bitten by a worm, she is, a boy said."

"She is with child, you know that," I replied, furious.

I looked at him. Beautiful was his face, the features noble and clear, yet strong with a man's strength. A lone boy was Jethro, one removed from the font of knowledge, the whispers of the dark quarries. At thirteen he was more the man than many ten years older, and his virtue must have delighted the saints.

"She is with a baby, Jethro," I said then. "Which is a cleaner way to speak of a girl like Mari."

The morning was cold with early frost on the hedges, and the country of Llanwennarth Citra was mist-covered except for the church tower. We had become closer, Jethro and I, since my father died, and when Hart reduced my rates and kicked me back to the tram road he kicked Jethro too, which suited me.

We took the tram round to Llangattock and the cutters loaded it with limestone. On the way back to Nanty the tram horse was straining and his flanks steaming. Side by side on the limestone we sat now, Jethro and me.

"About Mari again," he said, his dark eyes slanting over the rails. "A boy, is it?"

I was tiring of the stupid conversation, but then I remembered my father and the pains he took with me. Jethro's ignorance was stupidity, but it was like that with some children of the mountains. Too much Chapel was at fault, perhaps, with deacons dancing along the pews and hush this and hush that and pushing everything into corners.

"Look you," I said, taking a breath. "Mari is with child. When we were married I took her to bed and loved her, and now the child is growing within her. Like an apple it grows, see, but takes nine months, which is up next January, and we do not know if it is a boy or girl until it is out."

"Good God," he said.

"Until the women deliver it, do you understand?"

"Aye," said he. "Dada told me a bit."

So sad he looked then that I fisted his chin, bringing him to a smile.

The horse was walking easily between the rails, his harness jingling, and the frosted peaks around the Lonely Shepherd were bright with a sudden warmth that shone through a rent in the clouds and struck us like furnace glow.

"Anyway," said Jethro moodily. "I am pleased that you are the father." Sober serious, he was, not a muscle in his face moving as I glanced his way.

"Not more than I am," I said, trying to be calm.

"Then it is not true that Hart jumped her, eh?"

I closed my eyes. "Where did you hear that?"

Jethro squinted into the weak sunlight. "Whee! If I tell you that you will be as wise as me, boy. But I will hit him, mind, I will hit him to bounce six feet, the swine."

"Who?" I asked, boiling.

"Eh! There is an old long-nose! It is not your business anyway, it is Mari's. Jumped by Hart, indeed—just because she worked for him and the date comes right." He sighed. "But old Hart is the trouble, mind. He always do have the single girls who come in scrubbing, with a register for the single births and another for the twins, like the Bad Old Man of Cyfarthfa."

"Do not believe all you hear," I said. "And do not believe such things of Mari, who is pure, and would not allow the likes of Hart within a yard of her."

"Aye, aye?" said Jethro, and whistled at the sun.

I sat there in growing anger. Rumours were flooding and Jethro was a parrot repeating slander he did not understand. The incline steepened. Foam was on the bridle as I reined in the tram horse for a rest before beginning the climb.

"Good," said Jethro as I pulled up the sprag. He was looking over his shoulder, grinning, the sudden image of my father. "Now we shall see."

"See what?" I asked, turning. Caradoc Owen and his driver were coming up behind.

Caradoc Owen had been begging me for trouble since the day my father died, in hope of revenge, perhaps, for what Dada gave him. And since the fight he had fallen from grace, like me, being sent on the road as mate to Afron Madoc.

A handful was this Afron Madoc, and new to Nanty. Swansea born and Swansea temper, a man quick with his fists and wicked with his tongue. Ambitious at work, too. He was hitting it up for tram-road foreman and tipped his whips with wire and blackthorn for an extra journey a day. Now, jumping down from the load, I spragged my tram, and the horse eased back, snorting for breath. Round the curve behind me came Owen and Madoc, flogging their mare to death. She came at a gallop, drenched with sweat and reared as she saw the line blocked, and Afron cursed her and spragged and up he went to the top of his load.

"What the devil!" he cried. "Half a dozen more like the Mortymers and Bailey would go out of business. Shift that old tram along so busy men can earn their money."

"I am resting the horse," I shouted back.

"Then shift you off the line!" roared Caradoc, getting hot.

"You come and bloody shift us," said Jethro.

"Hush you!" I whispered, slapping his ear.

"What was that?" roared Afron. Black and broad, this

one, though not much taller than Jethro, and hackled for a fight to prove his worth.

"Five minutes rest at the incline is the Agent's rule!" shouted Jethro. "So down on your knees, Afron, and five minutes prayers while you wait, is it?"

"I am coming!" roared Afron, scrambling down.

"Thank God," cried Jethro, "and bring along old Caradoc for my brother. Eh dear!" he sighed. "Manna from heaven. For weeks now I have been waiting for Afron Madoc and for months to see you dust old Caradoc."

"Listen," I said, swinging him round. "This is your fight, for you have made it. I am sick to death of quarrelling. So your fight, mind—Afron Madoc first and Caradoc Owen after —I am not raising a finger to help."

"Good grief," said he, his eyes like saucers. "I can handle Madoc but Caradoc will coffin me, Caradoc is grown."

"I know," I said. "I will pray for you."

Up came Caradoc Owen, off with his coat, up with his sleeves. "Right you, Mortymer," said he, but I ducked his swing and got behind the tram, watching for Jethro, who was taking his first man, Madoc, ten years older. Madoc came raging. Jethro tripped him, sending him skidding on chest and elbows. Up got Madoc, shouting mad, and leaped. But the fist that caught him knocked him spinning, a glorious hook. Up again, and Jethro, cool, stepped in with a cross. Down went Madoc, howling with rage, to rise immediately, fists white, ready for murder. But under his guard went Jethro, flatfooted, ducking, weaving, the image of my father as he squinted up. One in the stomach brought Madoc's head down, up came a knee to bring his head up, for Jethro was never particular, a vicious right-hander sent Madoc staggering and a swinging left put him flat.

"That for my sister-in-law," said Jethro, walking away.

And even Caradoc Owen stared at the speed of things. Afron Madoc pulled himself up.

"A harlot, she is!" he shouted, choking with anger. "Mari Mortymer is a harlot, and I am putting it over the county!"

And Jethro, walking back, put him flat again.

The horror of it struck me dumb. Sick, I stared at Owen. He smiled, his teeth white in his square brown face, and clicked his tongue. "Dear me," he said, "the Mortymers are fighters, indeed to goodness. But out of the mouth of Madoc has come the truth, mind, and before a man is punished he should be judged as to whether he speaks falsely. Surely now, it is two whores we are dealing with, not one. For your sister Morfydd was jumped by an Englishman as well, I hear, and that was years before yours worked for Hart."

I stared.

"When will you Mortymers learn you are not wanted in Nanty?" he asked. "Away sharp, now, before I tip you from the road."

My first blind punch spun him like a top. My next checked him and flattened him against the tram. As his knees went I straightened him, and his cheekbone cracked under my knuckles. With his bloodstained face swaying before me I hooked and swung, hitting to go through him, until Jethro dived at my legs and brought me down.

Missed fourteen shifts, did Caradoc Owen; worse than from Dada.

Afron Madoc missed eight, with teeth.

Suspended for fighting, me. Nobody would believe that Jethro had a hand in it.

"For a month," said the Agent. "You Mortymers are nothing but a pest and I shall be glad to see the back of you. Were it not for the distressing circumstances of this case, I would certainly have put you on the blacklist."

"A fine state of affairs," said my mother. "As if things are not bad enough. *Jawch!* Talk about the bruising Mortymers. Tongues are the trouble in most women's families, fists in this. And a disgusting thing to fight about, too, it seems, without the grace of a word to explain it," and she stared at the ceiling.

We were at the table. Morfydd with Richard asleep in her arms, Jethro reading the pamphlets. Mari's eyes, bright with unshed tears, were lifting at me in sorrow and understanding.

272

"For God's sake," said Morfydd. "You must have had reason?"

I stirred my tea.

"Why did you fight?" asked my mother.

I drank, blowing at the steam.

"Jethro," she said, swinging to him, "I demand to know."

"Leave him alone," I said.

"Oh, dear me!" Her hands were on her hips now. "Head of the house, is it?" She thumped the table. "And since when, may I ask—since suspension and everybody going to rags since Dada died?"

"Iestyn," whispered Mari, her eyes warm.

"Do not appeal to him," said my mother. "All he can think of is hitting holes in Mr Afron Madoc. It is a wonder the poor man is alive, they tell me."

"We know who hit hardest, see," said Morfydd, very sober, "for I have just seen the poor soul, thank God."

"You keep from this, Morfydd," shouted Mam, rounding on her. "A man of peace is Afron Madoc, a deacon with the Word in his mouth, as God is my witness."

"*Dammo di!*" exclaimed Morfydd, "there is ignorance for you! For my part I am happy about you hitting deacons out, too. But why Afron Madoc?"

"He was the biggest and handiest," said Jethro, ducking my mother's swipe, and he was away through the door, leaving the rest of us sulking.

"I will be back before supper," I said, getting up.

"If there is any supper," said my mother.

It was cold in the wind of the mountain, and the cattle were bellowing for milking down at Shant-y-Brain's where the night mist was steaming in the heather. Nanty was roaring in blast like something demented; the new rail consignment for Spain ringing and clanging like bells during loading, and the hoarse commands of the foremen came up to me on the road. Cold as ice I stood there waiting for Mari. She came as I had expected, muffled against the wind.

"Do not heed her, Iestyn. Sick and sad she is for Dada."

"How much have we in the box?"

"Four shillings," said she. "The debt at the Shop is six."

"Pay it," I said, giving her two shillings. "It is better to start square on the starve. Take it quick, here is Morfydd."

"The chinking of money always brings me," said Morfydd. "Count it well, for we will need every penny. Hart came in as you went out. He has been thinking things over, he said, and is going to teach the Mortymers a lesson for life. The month's suspension applies to everybody, which means that Jethro and I are out, too."

"Good God," I said, going colder.

"And any more trouble and we go on the blacklist."

Her face was white and strained against the outline of her shawl.

"It was Dada they wanted, not us," I said.

Morfydd laughed. "Has it taken you so long to work it out? It is the first time a man has been suspended for a sober fight." She put her arm around Mari's waist and led her away.

"Is the credit still good?" I called.

"We are in trouble if it is not," said Morfydd.

When they had gone into the house I went back to the hollow. The light of the Company Shop shone bright despite the glare, and at the end of Market Road I saw Bailey's paymasters and clerks bending over their books. A few Irish women were standing outside as usual with their babies in shawls. I have never met anyone like the Irish for eating through glass, standing with their lips frosting the loaves and cheeses. The Irish were expert in starving in Nanty, especially the women, who gave their share to the children.

"The credit is dead, too," said Shanco Mathews, coming out of the shadows, "so do not lower yourself. Who the hell do you think you are, man, under suspension and expecting credit?"

Cold, cold I felt, with the faces of Mari and Morfydd before me, Jethro, my mother, and Richard, the baby. And soon my own child would come, making seven. If a strike came after the suspension it would be the end of us. Sick, I felt.

"Damned lucky not to be turned out, mind," said Shanco. "Bailey had no truck with me and mine, and all for a ten-minute demonstration—bloody out, it was, over to the old ironworks, remember, boy?"

"Aye," I said, scarcely hearing.

"Away from the light where people can see us," said Shanco. "There is always a friend for a man suspended," and he pulled me away. A man was standing under the wall of the Shop. Tall and broad, he was.

"Iestyn Mortymer?" said he.

"Aye," I said.

"Blacklist or suspension, what is it?" he asked.

"Suspended," I said. "What is it to you?"

"My name is Abraham Thomas of Coalbrookvale. Do you stand for the Union?"

"Aye," I said.

"Show your card, then," whispered Shanco, nudging me. "It is a Union representative."

I did so. The man peered at it and gave it back.

"You will be welcome down at the Royal Oak as your father was before you," said he. "Good, staunch, independent brothers are needed for the Chartist army under Zephaniah Williams. Deacons are needed to take charge of sections. The men of the Six Point Charter are asking for your name."

"It is money I am after, not politics. I have mouths to feed," I said.

"You will have no money while we have such politics," said Thomas. "You will have suspension, blacklist, hangings and transportations all the time we have men like Bailey for masters. The people are rising, one for all, all for one. Give your loyalty to the people and the people will feed you and yours, none shall go hungry."

"Through this suspension?" I asked. "Four weeks?"

"Four months if needs be, though we will have the Charter long before then and none shall go hungry again. Shall I mark you for a Deacon?"

"Down with his name," whispered Shanco. "He will serve."

"You say my father was down at the Royal Oak?" I asked.

"He joined for an iron splash upon his boy," said Thomas.

"Zephaniah himself took your father's name. He attended the torchlight meetings, he drilled, he handled arms, and took the oath of allegiance to fight and bleed for the Charter."

Very educated, this one, for a man working in iron.

"How will you get the Charter?" I asked him.

"For Heaven's sake," whispered Shanco, "leave things like that to your betters, Mortymer."

"If I am going to bleed for it I have a right to know," I said. "For a start I cannot see us shifting the Church without a struggle, and men like Lord John Russell, Melbourne, and the Duke of Wellington will nail the crown to Victoria's head before she loses it."

"Where did you learn such things?" asked Abraham Thomas, peering. "You are better informed than most, by God!"

"Is the mass of the people behind this fight," I said, ignoring his surprise, "or is it a few hotheads like Jones, Frost and Williams?"

"The masses are with us!" cried he, recovering himself. "The executions of Bristol and Nottingham are not forgotten. The Chartists are everywhere. Through the length and breadth of the land the people are waiting to force evil from their midst." His voice rose. "Peaceful negotiation is out of date. Physical force will be met with force. Down with the tyrants who rule us, away with the Crown and its landed estates!"

"Hisht!" I said. "You will get us all hung with your shouting. Thank God we are not all like you, Abraham Thomas. Cool men may win, but Wellington will cut the fanatics to pieces, as he did the French. What would you have me do?"

He straightened. "Sign for shot-making, on Chartist pay. Over at Mynydd Llangynidr you will be paid puddler's rates for a fair day's work."

"And hang in Parliament Square if I am caught, eh?"

"Better than starving on the blacklist," said Shanco.

"Sign my name," I said.

The three of us went to the Royal Oak Inn, through the back entrance to a room set aside from the tap-room where the men were putting it down and singing. A man called Edwards, a black-maned giant with a fist like a ham, took my oath of loyalty to the Charter. "Perish the privileged orders, death to the aristocracy," said he. "These are the words of our beloved Henry Vincent, the Englishman. If these words are uttered by Englishmen they should be good enough for the Welsh, you think?"

"Good enough for me," I replied, and repeated them.

"Do you know the Points of the Charter?" he rumbled.

"By heart," and I said them.

"We are wasting our time with this one," said Edwards. "He should have been enrolled years back. Puddler's rates down at Mynydd Llangynidr at once, and pay him over his suspension. Bring in the next."

I lied to them all except Morfydd.

"There is money on the end of it," I said. "If I do not earn we will starve."

"If you are not careful you will hang up at Mynydd Llangynidr," said she. "Making arms for rebels is a bigger crime than firing them, and if a stray patrol of Redcoats puts its nose into the caves the ones inside are caught like rats, they tell me. There is no back way out."

"It is a chance I must take."

"What are you telling the others?"

"That I am working with a farmer over the suspension."

"With Llewelyn Jones of Llangattock, then. Have a name ready, for God's sake, you know what Mam is, and at least it is in the right direction."

"God bless you, Morfydd," I said.

"God help me," said she. "God help us all in this forsaken country. O, that my Richard were here!"

"It will tide us over," said my mother next day. "At last we are back to the farms. Make good there, Iestyn. Who knows, it may be the end of us in iron. I curse the day we ever came into it."

"You will come and see us often?" begged Mari.

"Every hour I can get away."

"An easy journey, mind," said Jethro. "If it is Llangattock you can lift there and back by tram road."

"Not now Afron Madoc is hitting up for road foreman," I replied, to put him off.

"Get on with your supper," said Morfydd, nudging him.

"To hell," he said, his eyes big. "Leave on the night tram and back on the dawn one, Iestyn. You could sleep at home every night and save the expense of the lodging."

"O, could you?" whispered Mari, her hands clasped.

"Have sense, man," I said to Jethro. "You know what farmers are. Half the value of having a milking drover is having him live in with the cattle."

"How did you find this position?" asked my mother, sewing.

"Through Shanco Mathews," said Morfydd.

My mother frowned up at her and her eyes were old and weak in the light of the lamp. "Has he no tongue to speak for himself, then?"

"It was Shanco Mathews," I said. "When he was suspended for the demonstration he worked for Llewelyn Jones of Llangattock."

"I see," said she, and I sighed with relief when she said, "I remember how Dada used to long for the old days back—the days of the farms. Eh dear! You children did not know our generation. Quiet and full it was, with nothing happening except milking time and meal times and three times to Chapel on Sunday. No ironmasters then to pull us from our beds for killing and maiming, no roaring furnaces, no fighting, no Charters, and it was a different kind of gentry to the Baileys and Crawshays." She smiled at her needle. "Aye," she said, "the days were sweet, with weddings and biddings coming in for miles, and if a finger was slammed in a gate it was known all over the county. Beautiful, it was, until the ironmasters came and destroyed it. No lies, no deceit we had then, with the family one in love and truth." She raised her eyes to mine.

"As with this family," said Mari.

If my mother knew that most men on the blacklist or suspension were earning their money at Llangynidr, she never mentioned it. That night I kissed Mari goodbye and rode with Abraham Thomas on a Chartist horse over the mountains to the wild desolate range of Mynydd Llangynidr. It was midnight when we struck the tram road near Llangattock, and the trams were rumbling under a misty moon, limestone on top, muskets underneath, and one in every six carrying powder and shot. Down the line of trams we went to the cave entrance where a man was standing guard. Big and broad he was in the shadows, with the smoke of his clay curling up in the still air.

"Good grief," I said, reining in.

He peered from beneath his cap. "Heaven preserve us," he whispered, then slapped his thigh and shouted, "Mo! Come out here, man. The Mortymers are with us."

"Not so loud," hushed Abraham Thomas, flapping at him.

"To hell with you," said Big Rhys. "Now that Garndyrus men are running arms you can call out Brecon Garrison." He gripped my hand. "What has happened, boy?"

"Suspension for fighting a deacon," I said. "What brought you and Mo up here?"

"*Diawl!*" exclaimed Mo, running up. "It is like old times, eh? Six of us here from town, Iestyn—Dada and me, Will Blaenavon, Afel Hughes, and the Howells boys, and Idris Foreman and Iolo Milk coming up tomorrow, whatever!"

"Have you struck, then—it is half Garndyrus!"

"It was the Union," explained Big Rhys. "What the devil is the use of a Parliamentary Bill permitting the Union if the owner is going to suspend a man for being a member? Where is the sense of it? asked Idris Foreman, and he took it up official, so here we are working for Chartists."

"Get inside and chatter, do not do it here," said Thomas.

"Shade down the light!" shouted Rhys, and pulled aside an entrance board. I tethered my horse and followed him in. It was a cavern inside, a fissure cut through solid limestone by the rushing waters of a world melting from ice a hundred million years ago; a weird place of grotesque shadows and chilling echoes where the only light was flung by lanterns. Deeper into the mountain we went, through cavern after cavern where

279

men sat at tables pouching shot and filling powder horns. Deeper still, crouching at times, we reached the gunsmiths' rooms where skilled men fitted barrels to stocks of pistols and muskets. On, into the bowels of the mountain of Mynydd Llangynidr, and into the pit of hell itself. Here were the blacksmiths, stripped and sweating, and the air was ringing to the beat of hammers. Here red iron was hammered into steel. Here, in neat rows, were the pikeheads and spears that were to wrest power from the aristocracy and give it to the people. I saw men armed, coming and going with missions of importance. And on the tram road outside the arms were being loaded and transported to all the valleys of Gwent. Men from Risca and Pontypool, Blackwood and Dowlais were working here, said Rhys.

"Blacksmiths from Newport smithies," added Abraham Thomas. "Gunsmiths from London, powder mixers from as far north as Lancashire, Chartists all, men prepared to die if needs be, to force the Six Points."

"Where do I work?" I asked.

"On the tram road for the time being," he replied. "At puddler's rates less food, like all the rest here. Jenkins, see to him."

"Come," said Big Rhys now. "I will show you to a bed."

Two weeks passed, every hour a fever to be back with Mari. I spent the days working at the forges in the ventilated caves with Owen and Griff Howells, stripped to the waist, with the encrusting soot in layers on my sweating body. From daylight to dusk we laboured on casting. And at night, like moles, we crept down to the mist-laden valley and the brooks that sang and splashed their way to Llangattock. There we bathed naked with the Llangynidr mountain sharp and clear against the stars and the owls hooting their heads off in the thickets.

On such a night, when the moon lay white and cold over the country, I walked down the bank of the stream towards Llangattock and saw the lights of the village winking like eyes from the darkness. The track, beaten flat by countless hooves, lay like a grey ribbon through the heather. Above me came the clatter of the Chartist patrols, below me the rushing music of the brook. And before me flared Nanty, making strange shapes of red beauty against the clouds, flashing white now as the iron poured in strickening brilliance, and the air was cool after the incinerating heat of the caves.

I burned for Mari, for the sight and sound of her. I longed for her with a power that caught me up and guided me towards the red glow that shone as a beacon. The patrols passed on the high ground. Llangattock came nearer, and I heard the rumble of the night-shift trams and the cracking of whips as the spraggers urged their horses to the loads. Lamps burned along the face of Llangattock mountain and burnished iron flashed as the cutters filled the trams. Cutting away from the track I went across country, leaping through the heather to the foot of the mountain. The trams were rumbling above me as I climbed, impelled upward by the same strange power that had no reason. Hand over hand I climbed until I reached the tram road. Lying motionless in the heather I waited until a line of trams passed, then ran to the checking point at the end of the line.

Shanco Mathews I found there, as expected, sitting hunched in a cutting, warming his hands over a glowing brazier.

"God alive," he whispered, leaping up.

"Hisht!" I said. "Are you alone, Shanco?"

"Aye," he replied, wiping away sweat, "but it will not be for long with Chartist sentries coming one way and Redcoat patrols coming the other. Have you a pass for this far, man?"

"Never mind the pass," I said. "Have you news of my people?"

"Dear me," and he groaned. "I mind Iowerth Morgan last month when he left Llangynidr without permission. Rags and bloody bones he was by the time his Chartist brothers had done with him—hit his old knee-caps up, they did; crippled his descendants for a century, poor soul. And right and fair, mind. We cannot have damned lankies streaming right and left away from an arsenal."

"For God's sake, Shanco, quiet! How is Mari?"

And Shanco sighed and spat and just looked at me.

"Answer me!" I took him by the coat and shook him to rattle.

"Right you," he said. "In labour, they tell me. Now then."

My hands dropped from him.

"You are lying. She is only seven months gone."

"You should know," said he at the stars. "But three days she has been at it, so my woman tells me last pay night, and that is two days back. And there is nothing like a bellyful of trouble to bring production down, mind, for half the Irish-women are holding their stomachs and having it with her, but God knows, if she is only seven months it is bound to be a little one, but she is making enough fuss for breech-birth twins."

I stared at him.

"Never you mind," said he. "And do not bother with dirty old Shanco, boy. If she loses this one the next will be that much sweeter. And now I had better tell you all. Jethro came. Three nights back he came, for Hart has tipped them into the Old Works."

I closed my eyes, seeing a vision of the disused works where the debtors and the infirm lived, the place where was tipped the human refuse, the diseased, with cholera in the heaped garbage. Leaping to the rock face I climbed up and was away into the darkness high above the road. Reaching the top I buttoned my coat and turned my face towards Garndyrus.

I took the road to Abergavenny and wealth by running, not daring to use the Blorenge Incline for fear of being recognised. The clocks were striking one o'clock as I entered Abergavenny through the Western Gate, going like a ghost up Byfield Lane, soaked to the waist and shivering with wading Llanfoist ford. Redcoats were in the town I had heard; brought in to put down a wage disturbance at a Govilon forge, it was said, but that was only the excuse for bigger things. A pair of them passed the top of Tidder Street as I approached the old gate. Standing in the shadows, I watched them out of sight. Fine and proud they looked, these men of the English counties, their coats purple in the moonlight, their burnished brass flashing—Chartists every one, from what I had heard at Llangynidr—men enduring an oppression from their gentry officers worse than we were getting from ironmasters; men of the working classes like us, it was said, waiting, like us, for the signal to rise.

But we know better now.

It was as black as a witch's gown in Tidder Street, and Nevill Street was cast in shadows, asleep behind its shuttered windows, but beams of light shafted the cobbles under the windows of the gentry. Distantly on the still air came the music of a minuet. I went towards it and found myself opposite a window where ladies and gentlemen were dancing to a spinnet. Beautiful they looked under the flash of the chandeliers, the men with lace at their wrists and throats, the women in satin gowns down to the floor and hawking enough bosom for harlots in gin. All was beautiful in colour and symmetry, all was grace, and the whole glittering chorus of wealth and music and chatter came through the window.

The passage that led to the stables echoed to my boots, but I reached the yard without being seen. The music of the minuet came clearly as I raised myself to the stable roof and reached for the sill of the nearest window. The horses rustled uneasily beneath me, scenting an intruder. The stable yard below me was white in the moonlight, so I waited until it sank again into blackness. The dance below ended. In the surge of applause I elbowed the window. Glass tinkled faintly on to the thick pile of the carpet within. Hooking my arm through the hole I slipped the catch and slid the sash up. Swinging myself into the bedroom I listened, staring at the open door, the scarlet stair carpet of the landing with its rich mahogany handrail, the hanging lamp bowl as lovely as mother-of-pearl. Nothing stirred. The music vibrated gently against my feet. Turning, I began to search. It was a man's room. Loose change in silver and copper lay in a stream across the dressing-table. I gathered it silently, brushing aside jewelled studs and cufflinks, a silver snuff-box. Crossing the room I searched a wardrobe. Almost immediately I found a purse heavy with sovereigns, and another smaller one in the pocket of a frock-coat. I was still behind the door of the wardrobe when I heard footsteps ascending the stairs. Time only to push the door of the wardrobe shut and leap towards the window. I stood behind the heavy velvet curtains of the window and waited, holding my breath. The room tingled with silence, and the sweat started to my forehead and trickled down my face. Somebody had entered, making no sound, and then I heard the faint turn of a lock. A girl's voice then, a whispered protest, a man's soft laugh, a kiss. No more sounds they made in that lovemaking save the swift inrush of their breathing and their endearments. Minutes passed in kisses and faint sobbing from the rustling coverlet of the bed.

"I must go," she whispered.

"I will light the lamp," he said.

"No, please," she answered, and I heard her dressing in the darkness scarcely a yard from where I stood. The lock turned.

"Do not be long," she said. The door clicked shut behind her. The man grunted and sighed and swung himself from the bed. I tensed myself as he approached the window. As he flung the curtains back I struck, seeing a glimpse of the white silk shirt open to the waist and the square set of his chin above a stocky neck. Crying out, he staggered back, hit the dressing-table and overturned it with a crash of splintering wood and glass. Legs waving, jammed between the table and the bed, he screamed like a woman. Through the window, me. Landing on the cobbled yard fifteen feet below I rolled once, scrambled up, flattened an ostler coming from the stables and raced up the narrow passage into the street with cries of pursuit growing every second. At the head of Tidder Street I turned left and ran swiftly to the freedom of the Meadows. Down to the river I went and swam it opposite the Castle, not daring to cross at Llanfoist for fear of Redcoats. Soaked, shivering, I made my way to the foot of the Blorenge and climbed into the safety of its woods. Wading the canal I climbed upward past Keeper's Pond and down Turnpike to the Brynmawr road and the open ground of the Coity. The stars were still bright in the sky as I came down into Nanty. There, as at Garndyrus, the furnaces were flashing to the night shift and the little bloomeries all along the Garn were pinned with lights.

But below me, near the pit of Cwm Crachen, there shone no light. The hollow was wreathed in mist, and the ragged walls and chimneys of the disused works rose up like wounds in the blanket of white. Sitting on a tump I buried the two purses and counted the money; thirty-eight sovereigns and loose change, more than I had seen in my life. Tying it in my muffler I went down the slope, into a stink of garbage. A baby was crying from the broken walls. Dogs drifted like ghosts from the refuse piles, eyes gleamed from corners. The whispers of living beings came through shattered windows, voices crucified by battens. Smoke from makeshift chimneys stood in grey columns in the windless air, and firelight flickered from the makeshift rooms where the aged and ill, the useless and the maimed slept amid the rubble of furnaces they had once worked. Shattered engines, rusted through, stood guardians of the misery; wire ropes coiled fitfully over the littered floors. Like a tomb the relics of the town breathed in the November mist, its breath steaming up in the strange, dejected silence. Here lived the debtors who owed no debt: the old who had built the iron empire and become worked out, the men of strength whose joints were dried, the women whose breasts had vanished in the muscles of underground hauling, the blind, the diseased, the dying. Here lived the blacklist men because of a difference with master or agent; here lived their children, the skeletons of the tumps who spent their lives begging and playing on slag.

I found my mother standing in a doorway, bareheaded, her shawl low over her shoulders, her face pale, her eyes hollows of shadow.

"Iestyn," she said, as one aged.

I went past her to the smashed flagging of the old forge room with its twisted girders rising from the baseplates; grotesque arms that caught the moon and stars of the shattered vents in the grip of an octopus. The candle that flickered in the draught cast shadows among the piled bricks and furnace slag, and in its light I saw them: Jethro clutching at the floor in sleep; Morfydd propped against the sooted walls with Richard snuffling in her arms, awake, her eyes brilliant and strange. Mari I saw then, lying with the blankets heaped on her stomach, her face wet with sweat, her hair tangled. And as I knelt the pain bloomed within her and she clenched her hands and bit at them, whimpering.

My tongue cleaved against my teeth. Her eyes opened and she gripped me.

"Mari!"

"Steady," said Morfydd, rising.

"For God's sake, what is wrong with her?"

"It is a seven month child, and it turned," said Morfydd. "She is coming to her time now, boy. Away out of it if you cannot stomach it, like Dada says."

I left them, seeking oblivion in the yard, away from the noisy intakes of Mari's breathing and her bright explosions of pain. Shivering, I ran to a wall and leaned against it. The mist had risen from the cwm and the moon was high over the Coity, bringing the ruins into deeper shadows. I do not know how long I stood there. My mother came once, I think, for I heard her whispering, but Morfydd drew her away, and there was no sound but Mari's sobbing and a little hammering of the dawn wind.

Footsteps then, and Mrs Shanco Mathews went past with a bowl and flannel; Old Meg, they called her, as fat as Mrs Twym-y-Beddau and as dirty as Mrs Ffyrnig; rolled to the elbows, she was, important in her business.

"Right, you," said she, passing. "Do not look so jaggerty, boy, Old Meg will soon have it out. This is the trouble with the Mortymers, mind—the men putting in twelve-pounders and the women with hips for fairies," and she threw back her head and cackled with laughter.

Number Four over the road went into blast then. With a mushroom of smoke and flame it blew from its simmering for the dawn shift and screamed like a thing demented. Soot and sparks shot up, white ash swirled in the frosty air and red light played on Cwm Crachen, glinting on the windows of the forge room as I gripped the sill, looking in.

And in the hours that brought the dawn in golden light over the Coity, I grew to manhood.

"They have got it!" shouted Jethro, skidding into the icy yard. "Eh, by God, there is a business!" He clattered to the door, and skidded back. "And a boy, mind, the spit and image of Dada, Mam says!"

"Away!" said Morfydd, clipping him. "Inside for your son, Iestyn; I will come, too."

"He goes in alone," said Mrs Shanco Mathews, coming with a shawl. "Out of it, everybody," and she put the baby into my arms, a screaming bundle of life against my chest.

"Steady, man," said Morfydd. "You are squeezing the stomach from him. In to Mari quick now, she is asking for you."

And I went within and knelt on the floor beside my girl.

"Iestyn," she said.

I was with her at the start of time, kneeling there; kissing her in love. I was down at Llanelen, binding her feet. Under the summer moons of the Coity I was with her, in Shant-y-Brain's shippon, or carving her spoon from cedar. Her face was wet against my lips, her eyes bright and dancing in the red light.

"Jonathan, is it?" she said then, but I heard no sound.

I heard no sound but the sudden screech of the mill and the clanging beats of iron bellowing under the hammers as the dawn shifts got going. Whips were cracking as the tram roads came lively, horses stamped, curses and commands filled the bitter air.

I looked around the forge room, at the heaped debris beyond the door, at the shattered place where my son was born; slowly, never to forget it.

"Aye," I said. "Jonathan."

CHAPTER TWENTY-FOUR

"The Lord giveth," said Tomos. "The Lord taketh away. May the Lord shine the light of His countenance upon you, and bring you peace."

And he closed the Book.

His voice, clear and deep, the scene in his little room, will stay for ever in my mind. Big, black and severe was Tomos that early November day when we left the hospitality of his house, after Cwm Crachen. I can see it through the mist of years; my mother in the best black I had bought her, smaller and greyer; Morfydd, beautiful still, and Mari beside her, pale but smiling. And Jethro—how well I remember Jethro—the square cut of him inches past my shoulder, and his eyes so childlike in his man's brown face; Jonathan, my son, was asleep on a chair.

So clearly I can see them, as if it was yesterday.

And with good reason, for it was the day that the men of Blaenau Gwent sickened of the yoke and gathered for the march; the day when every furnace between Hirwaun and Risca, Pontypool and Blaenavon was blown out. The pot that had simmered for fifty years boiled over. Colliers and miners, furnacemen and tram-road labourers were flooding down the valleys to the Chartist rendezvous; men from Dowlais under the Guests, Cyfarthfa under the Crawshays, Nantyglo under Bailey and a thousand forges and bloomeries in the hills; men of the farming Welsh, the Staffordshire specialists and the labouring Irish were taking to arms. The Chartists were rising in the towns and cities of England, too, from every line of the compass, but the Welsh were chosen to spearhead the attack on the old aristocracy and the newer, profit-seeking classes.

Faintly, into the quiet room, came the tramp of their marching.

"Eh dear," said Tomos now, "black it will be. Torches will flare and pulpits tremble, and the very crown of England quake before the onslaught. And there will be no victory, I tell you. To win will be to lose, for government by physical force will be worse than a government of kings, as France has learned, for we are not yet ready to rise." Deeply he sighed while we stood in respectful silence, and turned to face us. "Would you have them back, then? Are those who have gone from us not happier standing in the light of the Father, Elianor, as your man is, and his daughter? Aye! Think on this and bring yourself comfort, or be of greed and wish them back to the spiritual poverty that we in this room will share. Do you hear me?"

"Aye," we said.

"Then do you mind me, for I have little time for grief, which is nothing but self-pity when you boil it down. Let there be no tears when loved ones die in this hell, my people; save your tears for the day they are born."

Faint light from the overcast sky shafted the room, falling on my mother's black gown, and her hands, thin and worn, were as yellow as old parchment. Dust from our new Abergavenny clothes, bought in Flannel Street with the stolen money, danced in the beam of silence.

"God rest you, Elianor," said Tomos to my mother. "You are wise to take Iestyn's advice. Back to the Carmarthen farms with you, and put a lifetime between yourself and iron that will scar you to the third generation of sons. Indeed, I wish to God that I could go, but my place is here with my people."

"You are welcome, mind," whispered my mother. "As in the old days when my Hywel lived, remember? Just as welcome, remember, Monmouthshire or Carmarthen town, we will always find a bed for one like you, Tomos."

"Bless you, Elianor," and he raised his eyes to Morfydd, lowering them to the frowning challenge that greeted him, as usual, and he drew sharp his breath.

"And you, Jethro. What do you plan?"

"To work for Mam," said Jethro, a light in his face. "On the farms, see, with milking and fleecing and crowstarving like old Granfer Shams-y-Coed down Llanelen way, and I will see to it pretty, for I have always wanted for a farmer."

"Iestyn?" Tomos turned to me.

"The coach is here," I said, rising. "She is beating over at River Row by the sound of her. Are you ready, Mari?"

Out with the little travelling-bundles now. Morfydd and Mari gathered the sleeping children, and Tomos went outside with Mam and Jethro to await the coach.

"Wait you," I said to Morfydd at the door.

The wind had frost in him all night from the Coity, but the sun of midday had melted it and the rain came now in spears of light at the window, sweeping in gusts over the dull country, drowning the distant clatter of the marching men.

"I am not coming," I said after Mari had gone.

She looked at me, disbelief in her eyes.

"What is this nonsense?" she said.

"I am not coming," I repeated. "I have work to do here."

She stood looking at me, beautiful still, but with the besetting matron of iron touching at her face for entry. Suddenly older, she was, in the light of the window, the fullness of her lips looking forward to thirty, until she smiled, and then she was Morfydd.

"Take this," I said, and I gave her the rest of the money, twenty sovereigns left over from buying the clothes.

"I had been wondering," she said, her eyes lowered. "Lucky for you that Mam and Mari think well of you. Stolen, is it?"

"Stolen from us in the first place," I replied, "so do not play the virgin. It is eat or be eaten, kill or be killed. Twenty in gold will settle them in Carmarthen for weeks, until I come to you. Take it."

"Mam would die of shame, Iestyn."

"Aye? Then more fool her, for this is a stink of a country. From now I am having the things that are mine."

The coach and pair came streaming in the rain and pulled to a halt outside the window.

"Iestyn, Morfydd!" shouted Jethro.

"Into it and away quick," I said. "I am not saying goodbye.

Tell them I am doing what Dada would have done, I am fighting for the Charter."

"Because of Dada?" she said.

"Because of Jonathan, because men like Frost and Vincent are right, because of Cwm Crachen; to change things, as Richard said, and make them decent. If foreigners like Richard are prepared to die, then the least we can do is to fight. Quick now, or Mari will be back."

"Fight, then, and God bless you," and she kissed me and turned away her face. "Goodbye, my boy," she said.

I did not wait for Tomos. He shouted once as I went into his kitchen, but I did not answer. Through the back I went and down his garden and through the gate, climbing the hill that led to Turnpike. Standing there I listened to Mari calling me, my mother's voice raised in argument and Morfydd's commanding replies. The door of the coach slammed shut, a whip cracked, and the hooves of the horses clattered. Mari called again, her voice breaking. I waited in the teeming rain and saw the coach up Turnpike. I stayed until it was outlined against the sky over Garndyrus; saw it slowly disappear over the crest to Abergavenny.

"Goodbye," I said then, and I turned my face towards the mountain.

"*Mae'r Siartwyr yn dod!*" was the cry. "The Chartists are coming!"

Dic Shon Ffyrnig I saw in the street near Heol ust twi, rolling drunk as usual, and Sunday at that.

"For God's sake, Mortymer," he gibbered. "Have you heard the news? *Mae'r Siartwyr yn dod!* It is the end of us!"

"The end of drunken Benefits," I said. "The end of men like you and Billy Handy who have drunk away the funds of honest men."

"Have pity!" he wailed. "Never in my life have I breathed a word against the Mortymers. Tidy people, all of you, and ready to forgive a few mistakes, for none of us are perfect, mind."

Up he came and running beside me, pulling at my hands.

291

"Oh, for God's sake do you speak for me, Mortymer!"

"Aye," I said, and threw him off, and he went to his knees, the spittle dripping from his chin in threads. "Aye, Dic Shon Ffyrnig, I will speak for you, and Billy Handy, too. Away now and lock yourself in until the Chartists do come for you. Red-hot pokers, it is, for drunken Benefit chairmen who have thieved the funds, and I will be doing the poking."

"Wait!" His terror brought faces to the blind windows, but I pushed him down.

Gibbering, biting at his hands, he went like the wind to the Drum and Monkey, Gwennie Lewis told me, to kill a few more pints.

"Good morning, Iestyn Mortymer," said Gwennie, shooting up her window.

Very pretty and prosperous looks Gwennie, with the room behind her neat and tidy, and not a child in sight.

"Going like the Devil with a saint behind him," said Gwennie. "A terrible thing it must be to have a conscience, and Billy Handy gone to a shadow, too, they tell me. Eh dear! there is a life; one moment up, next moment down like Polly Morgan's petticoats. She is the red woman now, you know, for I am respectable."

"Indeed," I said.

"Married to Iolo Milk; have you not heard?" and she patted her hair and tidied her shawl. "Well, not married exactly, but I have expectations, mind. He has left his old Megan now, and no wonder. There is a slut for you, that Megan, living in filth and cannot boil water, and at least I am clean, says Iolo. So Mrs Pantrych has taken Meg's children, making fourteen, for she lost one of her own last strike."

"And yours?" I asked her.

"Gone with the cholera," she said. "What time is it?"

"Iestyn Mortymer!" cried Gwennie now. "What the hell is wrong?"

In a corner, out of the rain, I cleaned my father's pistol.

"Well! Good grief!" said Willie Gwallter nearby, "if

you did not expect to be kissed you should stay in the light."

I saw him through the glass of Mrs Tossach's shop; tall, straight, fifteen, but gangling—narrow in the face like his hatchet-faced mam, but great in the shoulders like his elephant of a father these years dead.

"O Willie, do not be wicked," came the answer.

"Wicked, is it!" said Willie. "Wait you, Sara Roberts, I have not started yet. I am grown up now, remember."

"Dear me! Listen to it," said Sara, bored.

Stamping and heaving is Willie Gwallter, his eyes on sticks, his breath frosting the glass.

"I will fetch you one in the chops, mind," said Sara. "So stop it this minute, Willie Gwallter."

Strange about Sara Roberts of the Garndyrus cave; always short of a man, said Morfydd once—there for the boys to learn on, and Willie is big for fifteen.

"First thing in the morning, too," said Sara with business. "Like a mad bull and roaring you must be at night. Loose me."

But Willie fights on, losing his battle of growing up. Now he whispers.

"No, indeed!" said she. "Down by here? In the middle of the town? With preachers loose and Mrs Tossach due back any minute, to say nothing of Chartists with swords and muskets? Have sense, boy; I am not Gwennie Lewis."

The wind howls down the mountain, rain is streaming on the glass; darkening the doorway of the Tossach shop, and the drowning cobbles of the town are flying in sheets to the river. Kissing they are now, with Willie subsiding, and about time, too, says Sara. Above them flashes the Tossach sign, groaning in the wind. Above it is the window and the curtains blowing out. Mrs Tossach's hair is flying, too; her eyes are burning in her puddle of a face as she lifts her bucket.

No time to warn them as the bucket goes up, only time for a shriek as the bucket tips. Very handy is Mrs Tossach with a bucket of slops.

"Put that skirt down," said Sara, the last words she spoke as the Tossach slops hit her.

"And pull your trews up, Willie Gwallter," said Mrs Tossach, shaking out the drops. "I will tell your mama. Fornication on a Sunday and on my doorstep at that."

Down by River Row I met Mrs Phillips, Dafydd's mam, God help her. Weak in the head was Mrs Phillips now, said Tomos; pining for Dafydd who had ambitions for the Church, once. Pining to death for him, her only love.

"Good afternoon, Iestyn Mortymer," said she now, standing beside the Avon Lwyd that was roaring in flood.

"Good afternoon, Mrs Phillips," I said.

"Now then, have you seen my Dafydd lately, boy?" she asked, and I saw the madness of her face shine under her black Quaker bonnet.

"Not lately," I answered, wondering if he was caught for leg-breaking with Dai Probert Scotch Caattle.

"And you living in Nanty, they tell me? Where are your eyes, boy, with my Dafydd head deacon of the Ebenezer!"

My mother was strong for the Ebenezer, but she had never mentioned Dafydd.

"My mother has often heard him preach there," I lied.

"Then she is privileged. Aye, strong for the Lord is Dafydd. Taking after his English father, but he was Church, mind. Eh! Hitting the old pulpit about is Dafydd, from Swansea to right up north, and the like of him has not been heard since Howell Harris hit the devil flat at Talgarth, they tell me. Do you hear me, boy?"

"Yes, Mrs Phillips."

"Got on, has my Dafydd. A different tale to the day he wed your bitch of a sister and lent his name to a bastard, eh? Do you hear that, too, Iestyn Mortymer, or are your ears gone loose?"

I did not answer. She came nearer, leaning on her staff, needing only a brush to make her a witch, saying, "A curse is on her. Cursed was your father from the day he laid hands on my son, cursed was Edwina and your wife Mari, and I do know, for I did the cursing," and she laughed with her face to the rain and clutched at her hands.

I looked at her, at the lonely fields about us, the shining roofs of River Row drowning, and I looked at the river beside me.

"Black be your house, Mortymer," she said, coming within reach. "Black be the Mortymers from the youngest to the oldest; from the cradle to the grave down to the third generation do I put my stain. Even on the soul of Richard Bennet and on the body of his living son, black, black!"

The river foamed in torment beside us, crying for her, throwing up its white arms, begging for her.

"And cursed are you, Iestyn Mortymer," she said, "before three days are out."

Blindly, I left her, to save me the sin of murder. And the wind caught up her shrieks and flung them after me along the road that led to Nanty.

CHAPTER TWENTY-FIVE

ON THE track to Pen-y-Carn the mountain was drowning under skies leaden with rain and the brooks were roaring in flood through the heather.

But the wilderness was alive with men I knew; men from the valleys of Blaenau Gwent, deacons, sidesmen, drunkards, fighters, all were flocking to the tumps. Men from Garndyrus and Blaenavon, Coalbrookvale and Abertillery, Brynmawr and Nantyglo; wild men, starving men, soldiers with military bearing were on the march to freedom. I saw them bending into the rain, marching to Pen-y-Garn and Zephaniah Williams, the leader. They came armed, with pitchforks, mandrills, swords and muskets, they came with powder and shot. Every ironworks on The Top from Hirwaun to Blaenafon was on strike, every furnace blown out, and owners who challenged were kicked aside or beaten. In the rain we gathered, lawless, leaderless, seeking Zephaniah Williams. We were the men of the valleys three thousand strong, it was said. Over at Abersychan the men of the Llwyd Valley were marching under William Jones the watchmaker, and they were twice as many, while John Frost himself was gathering an army at the Coach and Horses, Blackwood.

At Pen-y-Garn we found the great Zephaniah, his fists raised and his voice like thunder.

"This is the day of reckoning!" he cried. "This is the day of revolt when Welshmen band together in the name of justice and equality to seek the banners of freedom. Listen, you!"

And we listened, lifting our arms and cheering.

"As our brothers in France have gained victory over tyranny, so we will gain ours. This is the end of the yoke, the end of the insults. To the march! Frost is driving from Blackwood with an army, and William Jones is leading the Eastern Valley. Who knows the password, boys?"

"Beanswell!" roared the men of Nanty.

"Aye, Beanswell. Last verse by Ernest Jones, then, and roar it, lads! 'Then rouse, my boys. . . .'"

"Then rouse my boys, and fight the foe,
  Your weapons are truth and reason,
We will let the Whigs and Tories know,
  That thinking is not treason.
Ye lords oppose us if you can,
  Your own doom you seek after;
With or without you we will stand
  Until we gain the Charter!"

I looked at the mob. Wild men, mad men were there, their faces blackened and streaked with rain, soaked bundles of rags with their arms held high at the leader; unkempt, bearded, as ferocious as the Frenchmen who stormed the Bastille.

"So we will take a turn as far as Newport!" cried Zephaniah. "We have nothing to fear, I pledge it. Even the Redcoats are Chartists waiting for the signal to rise. Even their captains are in sympathy with our cause!"

Cheers to split the heavens at this, with boys on the edge of the crowd turning cartwheels in joy.

"Second verse of the Charter Song!" cried Zephaniah.

"The labourer toils and strives the more
  While tyrants are carousing.
But hark! I hear the lions roar,
  The British youths are rousing.
The rich are liable to pain,
  The poor man feel the smart, sir.
But let us break the despot's chain,
  We soon will have the Charter!"

"Well sung by good Welsh voices!" roared Zephaniah. "Now listen again. Our comrade Henry Vincent, beloved and respected by all men who fight for justice, is languishing in Monmouth gaol. Starved and beaten, he lies there on lying charges, this man, the English martyr. Will we let him die?"

"No!" roared the mob.

"Will we let die the spirit of Dic Penderyn that has brought us this far? Will we let go all that we hold dear—wives, children, homes? For we are committed already, mark me! God help us if we turn back now. And the same can be said of every city in England where the workers are waiting for the Welshmen's lead. We are the spearhead, remember! Upon what we achieve tomorrow depend the liberty and happiness of Britons for countless generations. From London to Newcastle the Chartists are ready for rebellion, from Sunderland to Birmingham our comrades are under arms!"

The rain beat down, the wind swept like a mad thing over Pen-y-Garn, drowning the drunken cheering. They pressed about me, maddened men inflamed by beer and Zephaniah's oratory.

"One question," called a man from the crowd, King Crispian, the Brynmawr shoemaker. "If we are going to release Vincent from Monmouth gaol, why the hell are we going to Newport?"

"Good Heavens!" cried Zephaniah, shocked. "Would you have me splash the plan over the county? But out of the goodness of my heart I will tell you, and take the risk of Government agents among us. We are going to Newport to take the town and seize the schemer Prothero, then on to Monmouth to release Vincent. Are we ready now?"

"Aye!"

"Then forward. We will take the road to Llanhilleth."

Cheering, waving arms, the men of Gwent began the march; gathering strength with every mile; pulling laggards from their houses and kicking them into line, threatening women who protested, pushing aside screaming children. The rain teemed down. The wind lashed the long black columns sweeping down from the mountains. Through Llanhilleth we went, shouting and wailing, putting the gentry under beds and deacons under pulpits. All that day we marched, with food from looted bakeries being handed down the line; like a column of locusts, drinking the beer houses dry, shouting the poems of our defiant Ernest Jones. Into the darkness of the cold November night we marched, shivering, hungry but relentless. Through Newbridge and Abercarne we roared; and on the tram road leading to Risca, we rested under the stormy moon of midnight. Huddled against the downpour I walked the tram road in search of the men of Nanty.

Deacons and Captains were arguing nearby and sending scouts in search of Zephaniah Williams, who had not been seen since we left Llanhilleth. There, in the darkness, I heard the voice of Abraham Thomas shouting commands, so I sat by the roadside and watched the mob rise and march past me. A man was lying near, too drunk to stand, and singing and groaning in sickness. He was old and wasted and lying in a brook with the water foaming over his bearded face. I pulled him clear and dragged him to a tump. I was wiping rain from his face when he opened his eyes, and I saw in the light of the torches that he was blind; a puddler, this one; near to death by the look of him, and as sober as me.

"You feel young," said he. "O Christ, to be young at a time like this! Are you Cyfarthfa?"

"No, old man. I am Garndyrus," I said.

"Do they make good iron there, boy?"

"Better than at Cyfarthfa," I said, to humour him, but it only angered him.

"Have you seen the iron of Cyfarthfa, then?" he asked, struggling up. "Have you even heard of Merthyr that is dying under Crawshay? Have you heard of Crawshay, even?"

"Yes," I said.

"Yes, indeed! You cheeky hobbledehoy! And Bacon the Pig before the Crawshays? God alive, we thought him bad enough. What right have you to march for freedom, Garndyrus, if you have not worked the firebox under Bacon and Crawshay? Tell me, have you seen Cyfarthfa by night even?"

"From the belly of my mother," I said, talking the old language to please him. "She was born in Cyfarthfa before Bacon puddled a furnace."

"Well!" said he.

"Can you walk?" I asked him.

"I have walked from Merthyr hand in hand with Saint Tydfil," he said. "I have been splashed eight times and blinded, but the saint led me across The Top to the great Zephaniah Williams, for I put no trust in our mad Dr Price. I put my trust in no man but Williams, whom I once saw spit at the feet of Robert Crawshay, who starved us."

The column was thinning, the marching song of the Chartists growing weaker.

"He will starve you no more," I said. "Can you stand, old man?"

But he was still. Quite still he lay in the fading light of the torches, and his hands were frozen to the musket he held.

Through the night we marched, down to the Welsh Oak and Ty'n-y-Cwm Farm, and in the first faint flushes of a watery dawn I saw an army of men resting along the tram road. These were the men of Blackwood, Caerphilly and Pengam; the men of the Western Valley under John Frost, the leader, who had preceded us from Newbridge according to plan. I saw him for the second time in my life, short, square and dominant; wearing a heavy greatcoat and a red neckscarf, dwarfed by his bodyguard of gigantic Blackwood colliers. I saw him again in daylight, sitting at a table in Ty'n-y-Cwm Farm shippon while two men of Pontypool, Brough the Brewer and Watkins the Currier, were brought as prisoners from Croes-y-Ceiliog. And I saw him set them free, in anger, demanding that William Jones the watchmaker, the leader of the Eastern men, be brought instead, for lingering.

And among the men who brought the prisoners in were Mo Jenkins and his father Rhys.

"Great God!" whispered Mo, peering. "Is it Iestyn Mortymer?"

"It is," said Rhys, gripping my hand. "Where is your Mam, Mari, and the children?"

I told them.

"And safest, too, for this business stinks," whispered Mo. "If there are two thousand here I am surprised, and they promised us twenty. Out of his mind is Frost for trusting the Eastern Valley to the blabbering watchmaker—going like a snail, he is."

"Where is he now?" I asked.

"At Llantarnam Abbey when we left him," replied Rhys, "and playing the devil with the Member of Parliament there. Too much shouting and too little marching is William Jones's trouble, and enough Eastern Valley men with him to eat Newport, if he ever gets there. Will Blaenavon is kicking his feet off to get forward, and Caradoc Owen and Dafydd Phillips are saying they will be lucky to get as far as Cwrt-y-Bela."

"Those two are together, eh?" I sniffed. "With Scotch Cattle floggers among them Jones will be lucky if he gets to Allt-yr-Yn. There are Redcoats in Newport, have you heard?"

"Aye," said Mo. "With my little pistol here and my right knuckles sound I am good for two hundred."

"Perhaps," I said, "but look at the rest of us. Half of us drowned and the rest of us drunk. The Redcoats have got discipline, we are a rabble."

"A rabble that outnumbers them fifty to one, though," said Big Rhys. "And it will take a day to gallop artillery from Brecon. Frost is no fool."

"And the Redcoats are Chartists, anyway," added Mo.

"I hope to God that is right," said Rhys. "Scores of muskets they handed out from the Bristol Beerhouse at Ponty, but the powder was liquid in the pouches and the ball rusted. Can you imagine that happening under Wellington? Aye, it is discipline we need, as you say, Iestyn. Taking Newport and releasing Vincent from Monmouth is one thing, but resisting the Royal Army is another, and I will not believe the army is Chartist until I see the white flag over Brecon Barracks."

"That is a fine musket you have got," said Mo, taking it. "Have you ball and powder for it?"

"Aye," I said, and told how I took it from the dying puddler of Cyfarthfa.

"But it looks too big on you to be comfortable," said he.

301

"Will you change it with this good little pistol made at Llangynidr by a craftsman?"

"Change your arms and you change your luck," said Rhys, chuckling. "Here I am with two sound fists and good enough for anyone, including Tom Phillips the Mayor and his friend Mr Prothero."

"Protheros I cannot hit holes through I will blow holes through," said Mo, handling the musket, "and this will blow a bigger hole than a pistol."

"Change, then," I said, "you bloodthirsty swine, but do not blame me if you swing over Parliament Square for carrying it. Have you heard they are having us for treason already?"

"On what grounds?" asked Rhys.

"For carrying arms in defiance of the Queen."

"When I go duck-shooting every Sunday over the mountain?"

"Be fair, Rhys," said Jack Lovell, coming up. "You are not marching down Stow Hill looking forducks."

A good-looking man was Jack Lovell, one of the captains, square and strong, with the face of a soldier and breeding in his voice. I will remember Lovell as I saw him then, matching Big Rhys for size and strength, not as I saw him three hours later, shrieking on the corner of Skinner Street, spilling his blood on the cobbles.

"Aye, then," answered Rhys, "treason it is, but I will swing in pretty good company. When do we move, Jack?"

"When William Jones arrives, which is not until he has drunk Y Ty Gwyrdd dry at Llantarnum, from what I hear. Are you three armed?"

"Aye," said Mo.

"Forward with me in the vanguard, then. Firearms will be carried in front, pikes next and mandrills in the rear. Move, boys."

Zephaniah Williams came then, striding through the crowd into Ty'n-y-Cwm Farm. Weary and sick he looked, drenched to the skin and cursing as he swung the men aside. I was near when he met Frost later.

"There is no sign of Jones, I understand," he cried. "And him playing the trooper captain on horseback. Riding, if you please, while I have marched every inch of the way."

Which is a lie, said Big Rhys quietly, for I have seen you dozing in a tram down the valley.

"He will come," said Frost.

"He had better," shouted Zephaniah. "I am in no mood for traitors." He turned his face to the sky, to the black clouds tinging red with dawn. The rain poured down, splashing over his breast, running in streams from the brim of his broad felt hat. Great and powerful looked Zephaniah standing there; a god among Chartists, a man of war who was bringing to the masses the freedom others had promised; the man of destiny for whom we had prayed. Thus will I remember Zephaniah Williams. Not as the man of clay, who ran before the wind in search of his freedom, leaving captivity to his comrades and his cowardice to his relations.

We moved down the tram road from the Welsh Oak at break of day with John Frost leading and the Deacons urging us to follow. Jack Lovell marched behind Frost with his lieutenants, about a score all told. And behind them came Big Rhys, Mo and me, and William Griffiths, the man from Merthyr who died, was on my right. The gale that had raged all night fiercened with daylight, rising into a frenzy of howling, and the bitter rain cut our faces. For hours the icy water had been chilling my body. My boots were ragged with marching, my limbs heavy. Up and down the line of thousands of soaked, dispirited men came sounds of anger, at the forced march. Muskets were fired to test the dryness of powder, for at Llanhilleth I had seen powder flasks filled with rain and shot-firing packets soaked to destruction, while at New Inn Croes-y-Ceiliog, said Big Rhys, desperate men had dried powder in a housewife's oven. No Charter Song echoed now. There was nothing but the wind-silence that foretold the horror to come. I looked at Mo Jenkins. His face was stained red in the torchlight, split with the white grin of determination he had worn since a boy, and his eyes were shining with hope of a fight. No weariness in this one, my friend since childhood, since the night of the swinging lamp over the Keeper's Pond signpost when I ducked the swing of his right boot and ran into the left. Good it was, to have Mo beside me at a time like this, marching to take a town; marching for the good of women like Mari, men like my father, and the ghost of Richard Bennet. These things I thought as we went down to Pye Corner and forward the two miles to Cwrt-y-Bela, where we rested for the last time before Newport.

"Why are you fighting?" said a man to me at Cwrt-y-Bela.

"It is a funny thing to ask," I replied. "Why are you?"

"For my children," said he, "to get them out of iron."

"Where you from?" I asked, and he smiled.

"From Nanty," said he, "same place as you, for everyone in Nanty, Welsh or foreign, knows the Mortymers. But nobody is likely to notice Isaac Thomas at five-feet-two, the limestone cutter on Afron Madoc's shift, Llangattock." He grinned through the rain, and spat. "You did him pretty well, old Afron—remember?"

"Aye," I said.

"Two of his teeth my mate Joseph picked up and wore them on his watch-chain, threaded, thank God. A pig is Afron Madoc, and Caradoc Owen is one worse."

"Aye, but Owen is here today, they tell me—back with Jones the watchmaker, give him credit, though you will never find Afron Madoc."

"Never again," said Isaac Thomas, "for he is down six feet, and I put him. I put him before I left, you understand? An eye for an eye, says the Book, and I had him for killing my girl. Ten years old, she was, and pretty, until he took her underground at the Garn—working at the face—at ten—on Afron's recommendation, filling trams, and the roof came down and took her legs to the thigh."

I pitied him.

"But I had all of Madoc."

"Do not talk too loud," I said, glancing around.

"Do not worry yourself, man," said Isaac. "I am not that

stupid. I had him legitimate, under ten tons at Llangattock quarry, but he died too quick for decency."

"And now?" I asked.

"Now I am fighting for the others, for my wife bore me nine. Three of them are working under the Coity as colliers and four of the others are in Crawshay Bailey's iron. It is a stink and it must stop, says my wife, with a four-pound debt at the Shop in the bargain. It is dying, this, says my wife, not living, and we are decent Chapel people, mind."

The wind wailed about us and we shivered as the rain flooded into us with a new fury.

"Why are you fighting, then?" asked Isaac Thomas.

"For my son and against Cwm Crachen," I told him. "Do not ask more, leave it at that."

Through the head they got Isaac Thomas. He was the first to die, they say, when the shutters of the Westgate Inn went back and showed us muskets. For the Redcoats took us low with their first volley, and Isaac was five-feet-two.

CHAPTER TWENTY-SIX

It was broad daylight when Frost and Rees the Fifer got us moving again, and David Jones the Tinker and men like Lovell took the word to arm right down the line. The rain had stopped as we left the tram road and climbed the hill past the Friars and St Woolos Church to the crest of Stow Hill. With Frost at the head we waved and cheered at the Redcoats crowding in the entrance of the workhouse.

"You see!" cried Lovell near me. "Chartists to a man. Not a musket raised to stop us."

"Aye?" replied Big Rhys above the din of cheering and the clatter of shots. "Very funny that they did not wave back, then."

Down Stow Hill we went, calling to the people staring in terror from their windows. Down to the high footway where the townsfolk were clustered, waving and firing into the air we went, our hopes soaring with every step, drunk with power, top dogs at last, as Lovell said. But God knows where we were going, said Mo marching beside me, and God knows what we do when we get there, said Big Rhys.

"To the Westgate!" shouted Frost then, throwing up his arms.

At the bottom of Stow Hill little groups of watchers were pressed against the buildings, frightened faces peeped from shop windows, children peered from behind half closed doors and shutters. Singing the songs of Ernest Jones, shouting at the top of our lungs, we swept to the entrance of the Westgate yard, following Lovell's command, but the gateway was chained and locked.

"Show yourselves at the front, then!" shouted Frost. "Chartist prisoners have been taken. Demand their release or let them take the consequences!"

We left Frost at the stable-yard gateway. With Jack Lovell

leading, the column wheeled right in front of the Westgate Inn.

"Look you!" roared Rees the Fifer, pointing up. "The old swine himself is up at a window!" and he pointed his musket high just as Mayor Phillips ducked down.

A sudden silence came over the men about me. With Lovell leading, a column of men pressed up the Westgate steps towards the open doorway. And in that silence my mind flew back across the years to my last visit to Newport; to the hiring fair where I first laid eyes on Mari; to the hand of John Frost who raised me from the cobbles, to the sixpence he gave me that I still carried in my pocket, and these same steps that later he had climbed with mayoral dignity. I looked for Frost now, but the mob was thick as it packed down from the Hill, and sticks and mandrills were raised like a forest.

"Surrender your prisoners!" shouted Lovell in the doorway.

"Never!" cried a constable.

Muskets and pikes went up, voices were raised in protest, a shot rang out and the inn door slammed shut. The mob about me swayed and roared. I saw Lovell fight himself free of the press of men; saw his fist shake at the door.

"In, my men!" he yelled, and I forced myself forward with Mo and Rhys either side of me as the hatchets went into the big door. The men about me were screaming to get forward, many roaring the Charter Song, others discharging pistols and muskets at the high windows of the Westgate. Before me, between the swaying heads, I saw the hatchets rising and falling and the polished wood splintering white as the panels went down.

"In, in!" It was Lovell's voice again, pulling the men against him with his fire. Muskets were crashing, the air filled with the bitter smell of powder. Glass tinkled from the windows as the shots went home. Mo was using his fists now, and heads disappeared as he chopped them down. Driving onward, he tripped on the bottom steps of the inn and fell with me on top of him. Cursing, we staggered upright. A hatchet-shaft hissed past my head. Ducking, I caught at Mo and dragged him forward, and the door went down and Lovell was in with fifteen or more falling headlong after him on to the polished floor. I was on my back now, levelled by the mad rush of the men behind me, and Mo was beside me, pinned by the tramping feet. We were kicked down as we tried to rise, an army passing over us, forced on by the maddened rush from the square where thousands were heaving hundreds forward. As the rush subsided and we clambered up, we were forced out of the entrance and headlong down the steps by men retreating. Explosions were shattering the hall. Men were screaming in pain, their voices falsetto. Lying on the steps, enduring the hammering boots that crashed against my head and shoulders, I struggled for consciousness. Blood streamed into my eyes from a cut on my forehead and I dashed it away with my arm, rolling down the steps in an effort to escape the entangling forest of legs, the boots that trampled me, thudding into my face, crushing my hands on the cobbles. I rolled sideways to escape a fresh rush of the mob. I saw them coming, yelling their battle cries, shoulder to shoulder, their mandrills and pitchforks swinging before them, their pistols and muskets exploding in shafts of fire. This was the second mad charge, and I escaped it by rolling to the wall, under the very windows of the ground floor as their shutters went back with a crash, exposing Redcoats. The mob swept straight to the windows, firing wildly, flinging stones. Staves came showering against the windows as men streamed from the hall; staggering, crawling some of them, most of them clutching at wounds. And then the Redcoats fired. Flame and white smoke burst from the public-room windows in a volley of death. I saw the mob shudder as the balls went home into the packed ranks. They dropped like wheat to the scythe, these men, in long fingers through the mob, and to my death bed will I remember their cries. Yet above the bedlam, the explosions, the shrieks of wounded and dying, I heard Jack Lovell's voice from the hall, and turned. Wiping the blood from my eyes I crawled up the steps.

The Westgate entrance was a shambles of blood and arms, with dead and wounded entangled in grotesque attitudes over the floor. Commands from soldiers and Chartists cut across the cries of the wounded. Muskets were detonating in the confined space, and the air swirling with smoke and fumes.

"Charge down the door, my hearties!" yelled Lovell. "Down with the door and we gain the day!" and I followed his cry, leaping over sprawling bodies. The passage turned here and I collided with a wall of men. This led to the public room that housed the Redcoats. Once inside and our numbers would tell. I saw the hatchets going up again, the splinters flying.

"In, in!" screamed Lovell, but his voice was lost in the bedlam of battle cries. I heaved at the back. Other men from the square joined me and we set our shoulders and thrust our weight at the backs of the men before us. But the door held. And then I saw Mo Jenkins with Big Rhys behind him. Mo had a hatchet and was going at the door, driving its head deep into the solid oak, tearing aside the panels that sheltered the Redcoats.

"Give him room!" shouted Lovell, and flung himself back. Again the hatchet went deep with all Mo's brute strength behind it. He was wrenching the steel clear and preparing for a swing when the door flew back, opened from within. Five Redcoats were kneeling, others standing above them, muskets levelled, bayonets fixed. They fired, and the volley raked us. Hit in the shoulder, I spun, and I saw my blood spray high on the gilded walls as I fell. Mo was down, the hatchet twisted under him, Big Rhys on all fours, his arms thrown over his son. Lovell was down, but crawling, blood gushing from his mouth. I writhed. The pain in my arm was excruciating, but I lay still. Above and behind me men were cursing and groping in the smoke-wreathed graveyard of a passage, blinded instantly by the flash of the volley. The door of the public room slammed shut. The lock grated. Another concussion shook the building as the soldiers sent a fusillade through the windows into the packed mob outside.

"Iestyn! For God's sake!" cried Rhys like a child.

Throwing aside the weight of a body, I dragged myself up and fell on my knees beside him.

"Mo, my son!" cried Rhys, weeping. "O holy Christ, do you save him, my son!"

"Quick," I whispered with a glance at the door. "Quick with us and we will get him out of this hell. Are you hurt, man?"

"If that door comes open again they will bloody carve you," gasped Mo. "I am dying, can you see straight? Leave me."

"Here, catch hold," I whispered, panting with fear, and I hooked my good arm under his. "Up, Rhys, for God's sake, before they swing the door."

The passage was empty except for the dead, and one named Shell. He stood in an alcove, his pike held tight against him, his young face white, his lips trembling.

"To hell out of it, boy!" I whispered as we dragged Mo past him into the hall. And even as we reached the entrance I had to heave Mo aside, for the mob was coming again for another attack and pouring through the hall into the passage, whooping and cheering to its death. Back went the public-room door again and the vicious volleys of the Redcoats raked them, cutting them down, knocking flat the ones who sought to rise. I caught a glimpse of George Shell running, on tiptoe, leaping lightly over the packed bodies; I saw his pike go up and the startled cry of Phillips the mayor pierced the commotion. But a musket flashed and Shell staggered, to spin and fall flat, the pike shattering beneath him. The door slammed shut.

It was the end. I saw it at the entrance steps. Caught in the open by trained men under cover, the Chartists were breaking. The square was emptying, littered with writhing men, and arms; groans and cries rose from the smoke. Big Rhys and me, with the dying Mo held between us, crouched in the doorway of the Westgate, the only three in the world, it seemed. Under the portico of the mayor's house at the bottom of Stow Hill a man was dying—Abraham Thomas, men said later, Abraham who had sent me to Llangynidr. And he called for the Charter now, his voice vibrant, a contrast to Jack Lovell. Lovell died in screams, as a woman being mutilated, writhing on the corner of Skinner Street, beating his hands against the cobbles. Before me in the road lay Isaac Five-feet-two of Afron Madoc's shift; hit in the face by the look of him, because he was short, but he went in peace, not like his girl. Like a tomb it was, crouching there; hell itself said Big Rhys later. Behind us the Chartists were dead or wounded, before us they lay under the scorching fire of the Redcoats. Only one fired back now, a man with one leg, the last broken hero of the Chartist cause.

Idris Foreman died, they told me; in a field near Pye Corner, in the arms of the Howells twins. Always handy with shovels, Owen and Griff had him three feet down still warm while the special constables and troops from Newport Workhouse were beating the hedges nearby. Will Blaenavon, too, according to reports, and Dathyl Jenkins, his unwedded wife, put laurels on the Chartist graves in St Woolas Yard on the Palm Sunday following, though they never found his body. Some say he took the chance to die and puddled for ten years over at Risca, just to lose Dathyl, but I never had the proof of it. Dai Probert Scotch Cattle died, they said, deep in the mountains near Waunavon, with a ball in his chest, among his men; and so did Caradoc Owen—of drink to drown his cowardice, at the bar of the Drum and Monkey. Many died that were not recorded, in fields, under the hedges and in barns and ditches from Malpas to Pontypool, Newbridge to Blackwood. Some died in days, some years after, in foreign lands or the starving prisons under foreign gaolers. Most died with friends about them, in the hall of the Westgate or its bloodstained yard.

But Mo died alone.

"Get up," said the constable, and swung his boot to hasten me.

"My friend is dying," I said, kneeling. "Let me stay."

"Get up!" and he brought out his bayonet.

I rose, but Rhys was quicker, and stretched him flat with a right to the throat. They were round us then like locusts, Redcoats mostly, kicking us away, levelling their muskets.

"My boy is dying," said Rhys. "Let me to him."

"Aye?" said one. "You should have thought of that before."

"Take him gently, Dada," said Mo, grinning, as they backed us away to a wall.

Ten Redcoats came through from the public room; fine men, good soldiers, give them credit. They brought out the mayor next, short of an arm by the way it was bleeding, and another wound in the thigh, playing hell with Welshmen from Newport to Cyfarthfa. A lieutenant followed him, swarthy and confident, this one, and get these damned ruffians out of here quick.

"Officer," said Big Rhys, begging with his hands. "My son is over by there and dying. For God's sake let me to him."

"Take him out with the rest," said the officer. "Let nobody near him. Keep the people away from the wounded, let the dead lie where they have fallen. Nobody near them, do you understand? By God, we will teach these bloody Welsh a lesson."

"O, fy mab," said Rhys, "fy machgen, fy macghen bach dewr!"

They took Mo down and spread him on the cobbles, and he moved but once to wipe sweat from his face. And Big Rhys, with a Redcoat bayonet against his stomach, watched him die.

They took us to the stable yard, the first prisoners of the Westgate, and they herded the rest in after us. Hour after hour they were brought in from tram roads as far as Pye Corner; broken, dejected men and boys, soaked and weary, many of them wounded; silent, unprotesting under the musket butts of the Redcoats. I saw in their grey faces of defeat the tragedy of my generation. They came from the iron towns of Beaufort and Tredegar, Merthyr and Dowlais, from the employ of men like Robert Thomas Crawshay who ruled them from the hated battlements of his Cyfarthfa Castle; or the Baileys who used starvation wages to beat them into submission. Was there no end to the persecution? Or was this misery a birthright handed down through generations of men oppressed by men of power?

"Where is Frost?" was the whisper.

"Going like a rabbit for Tredegar Park," came an answer. "Dodging the keepers and playing touch-me-not. Thank God for such a leader. No wonder he is English."

"English? Do not blame the bloody nationality, man, or is Zephaniah Williams not Welsh? Watch your tongue. We are big enough fools as it is."

"And what of William Jones Watchmaker and his five thousand terrors from Ponty, look you! Aye, terrors indeed, for the swines never got nearer than Cefn, while we were out with the hatchets."

Another spat. "Every Redcoat a Chartist, eh? Every man ready for the march on London, is it? God help us now, our wives and our little ones. Starving and beating Vincent to death in Monmouth, are they? Vincent is lucky. They will give us bloody Chartists, with burning too good for us."

"And Dr Price of Merthyr, eh? Where the hell did he get to with his thousands starving under Crawshay? There is a hot one for a Welsh nationalist—racing round Merthyr with his bardic sword and goat cart. What with this one and that one I am ashamed of being bloody Welsh."

They pushed, they quarrelled, they cursed; comrades one moment, enemies the next.

"Iestyn," said Rhys. "Little Mo is dead. Dead, do you hear me?"

They fought one another, bitterly. Some wept, some prayed. They fought the Westgate over again, taking it in the rear this time, pulling cannon down Commercial Street, flinging firebrands through its windows.

"The organisation was wrong, see? Men like Frost and Zephaniah could not lead a pack of women, let alone men. Leaders, you call them? They have not the sense to be good politicians. By God, if I get my hands on William Jones Watchmaker!"

"What the hell is wrong with you, Boxer?" said one, passing. In a corner of the yard Big Rhys was weeping.

"What is wrong with him?" they asked me, nudging.

"His son is dead," I told them.

"Eh, dear! It is too late for snivelling now, bach."

"O, God," sighed Rhys, biting at his knuckles.

"Steady," I said.

"Dear me," shouted one in passing. "What will my old woman say when they string me? She hit me black and blue about coming on this caper with Frost."

"Thank God the debt is still good at the Shop, man. If Lord John Russell transports me, Crawshay will have to sing for it!"

"Does Bailey pay pensions to widows, you say?"

They joked, they bantered, they laid wagers on their lot, and some wept.

"Mo Jenkins was your boy, eh, man?" one asked Rhys. "Eh, now! The boy who was chasing Dai Benyon Champion? Good grief! Call him lucky, and weep for the living, do not weep for the dead. For they will burn us alive now, these English, with burning too good for us. They will bring back the stake to tame us and put other rebellions down. They will hit the country so hard that she will not stand straight for a hundred years, mark me."

"My son is dead," said Rhys to me, not listening. "O, Christ, pity me."

And he beat his fists together, weeping.

Is my friend dead? Is Mo Jenkins gone, the boy of the Garndyrus cave, of the fight up on Turnpike. He who sang when I was wedded to Mari, great in his strength, fearless before the might of the terrible Dai Benyon; is he gone for eternity on the rush of his father's tears?

Is Idris Foreman gone, and Afel Hughes to his burned wife and his girl Ceinie? Is Richard Bennet in the Great Palace, entering in his youth the portals of the dead when all his life he had fought for a heaven of the living? He whom Morfydd loved, is he with us this day of defeat, this tumult of a day that has beaten down all he strove for?

Is Edwina gone, the sister I never understood? Does she sleep under the yew trees in St Mary's, her frail, white beauty going to dust? Is my father gone, he so great in strength? Is my country dead, this beloved land that has powdered the bones of other conquerors and trampled their pennants into dust? O, this Land of the Ancients that has echoed to the feet of Rome and known the laurels of victory; who has snatched her soul from the fire of her persecutors and held high her honour in the face of shame! I can see from here the black outline of The Top. I see the white streams tumbling from the Afon Lwydd through the heather of Waunavon. I see the mountains green again in the lazy heat of summer, and cold and black under the frozen moons of winter. Is the hay still flying from the barn down at Shant-y-Brain's? Is the canal still swimming through the alders from Brecon to Ponty?

The Redcoats came to search us, clearing a path with musket butts, knocking up our elbows, slapping at our pockets.

"You swines! There are enough arms among this lot to fit out Brecon Garrison."

"You—your name?"

"Iestyn Mortymer."

"A Chartist, eh? We will give you Chartist. You will dance for eighteen bloody months when we get you to Monmouth."

Aye, I thought, *if* you get me to Monmouth.

"You are wounded," said a sergeant.

"This man's arm is broken. Hey, you! Drop that musket and break me a pike for splints."

His hands were rough, but he served me well. He spoke Lancashire while he bandaged, but I did not heed him.

For I was up at Garndyrus watching the iron coming out.

I was away down the Garn hunting for Edwina. I was walking with my father over Llangynidr Mountain, and kissing Mari in the heather after Chapel on Easter Sunday.

"Right! Into the carts!"

They kicked us out of the stable yard and into carts for Monmouth, standing too tight to fall out. The Redcoats marched beside us, muskets primed, bayonets fixed, and we went like the tumbrils of France.

"By God," said a man beside me, "they are doing us fine, eh? We are going like the aristocracy. Take it proudly, Welshmen; and last verse of the old Charter Song to guide the way for others," and we sang:

"For ages deep wrongs have been hopelessly borne;
Despair shall no longer our spirits dismay,
Nor wither the arm when upraised for the fray;
The conflict for freedom is gathering nigh.
We live to secure it, or gloriously die!"

Alexander Cordell (George Alexander Graber) was born on 9th September, 1914 in Columbia, Ceylon. His father was a professional soldier and Alex followed in his footsteps by joining the Royal Engineers in 1932. He served in the ranks until 1936 and was then commissioned, attaining the rank of Major during the Second World War.

Seriously injured during the British Expeditionary Force's retreat from Boulogne in 1940, he spent his convalescence in Wales and developed a love and fascination for the country and its people. As a result, after being demobilised in 1950, he went to live in Llanelen, near Abergavenny in Monmouthshire.

In his spare time he began to write short stories and his first novel, *A Thought of Honour* was published in 1954. Unfortunately, it was not very successful, but his second novel, *Rape of the Fair Country* became an international best-seller, being published in no less than seventeen languages. Cordell in later years commented: 'I wrote the book at white heat, scarcely altering a chapter; in between spells of writing I studied at the University of Wales, Aberystwyth and befriended every available librarian; more, I suddenly discovered that hand in hand with the tale of the mountain town of Blaenavon, went the last bloody revolution, in Britain, the Chartist Rebellion.'

This novel was the first of a successful trilogy set in 19th century industrial Wales, being quickly followed by *The Hosts of Rebecca* and *Song of the Earth*. A second Welsh trilogy was later to follow.

Now established as a successful novelist, Cordell took early retirement in 1968, and became a full time writer. In total he wrote thirty books, which were set in a variety of locations, but his most popular novels describe the turbulent times of 19th century industrial Wales, for that undoubtedly was his favourite subject.

In 1985, the well known Gwent author, Chris Barber published *Cordell Country* as a tribute to Alexander Cordell and it resulted in the area where *Rape of the Fair Country* is set, becoming established as a tourist destination. Visitors now come to walk in the footsteps of the Mortymers, visit the old iron town of Blaenavon and enjoy the wide sweeping views from the slopes of the Blorenge mountain.

Torfaen and Blaenau Gwent County Borough Councils have also published a leaflet describing a car trail around Cordell Country. It is 25 miles in length and takes in some of the locations which feature in *Rape of the Fair Country* and Cordell's later novel *This Proud and Savage Land*.

Rape of the Fair Country has been performed as a play on the stage by the Chrysalis Theatre Company, Swansea Grand Theatre and Theatr Clwyd. The latter company will also be producing the *The Hosts of Rebecca* and *Song of the Earth* during 1998/99. The BBC have broadcast a radio play based on the book and musical versions have been performed by the Monmouth Arts Project and more recently by the New Venture Players at the Dolman Theatre, Newport. For over thirty years there has been talk of a film of the book being made and it was always a disappointment to Alexander Cordell that this did not happen during his lifetime. To most people who have read the book it is very surprising that the film has not been made for it would undoubtedly prove very popular.

Alexander Cordell died of a heart attack near Llangollen, North Wales in July 1997. His final novel *Send Her Victorious* was published during the following month. He is survived by his daughter, Georgina, who is married and lives in Finland.

OTHER TITLES PUBLISHED
BY BLORENGE BOOKS

Walks in Cordell Country
by Chris Barber (ISBN 1 872730 116 – £6)

The Seven Hills of Abergavenny
by Chris Barber (ISBN 1 872730 02 7 – £5.25)

Classic Walks in the Brecon Beacons National Park)
by Chris Barber (ISBN 87230 08 6 – £8.95)

Arthurian Caerleon
by Chris Barber (ISBN 1 87 2730 10 8 – £3.99)

The Ancient Stones of Wales
by Chris Barber and John Williams
(ISBN 0 9510444 7 8 – £7.95)

Portraits of the Past
by Chris Barber and Michael Blackmore
(ISBN 1 872730 05 1 – £19.95)

In Search of Owain Glyndwr
by Chris Barber (ISBN 1 872730 07 8 - £11.95)

Stone and Steam in the Black Mountains
by David Tipper (ISBN 0 9510444 1 9 – £5.75)

We Shall Sing Again
by Marguerite Shaw (ISBN 1 872730 00 0 – £6)

Shall We Meet Again?
by Marguerite Shaw (ISBN 1 872730 0 9 – £4.75)

Valley of Shadows
by Charles Hawkins (ISBN 1 872730 14 0 – £4.95)